CW00552348

THE WORKHOUSE LASS

CHRISSIE WALSH

Boldwood

First published in Great Britain in 2024 by Boldwood Books Ltd.

Cover Design by Colin Thomas

Cover Images: Colin Thomas

A CIP catalogue record for this book is available from the British Library.

Paperback ISBN 978-1-80280-971-8

Large Print ISBN 978-1-80280-970-1

Hardback ISBN 978-1-80280-969-5

Ebook ISBN 978-1-80280-972-5

Kindle ISBN 978-1-80280-973-2

Audio CD ISBN 978-1-80280-964-0

MP3 CD ISBN 978-1-80280-965-7

Digital audio download ISBN 978-1-80280-967-1

This book is printed on certified sustainable paper. Boldwood Books is dedicated to putting sustainability at the heart of our business. For more information please visit https://www.boldwoodbooks.com/about-us/sustainability/

Boldwood Books Ltd, 23 Bowerdean Street, London, SW6 3TN

www.boldwoodbooks.com

In memory of my mother, Dolly Manion, 1914–1989

Let your hopes not your hurts shape your future.

— ROBERT H. SCHULLER

1

DERBYSHIRE 1903

'Why do you do this to me, Dora?'

Lissie's father's impassioned cry floated through the open door of the little cottage like the wail of a man whose sorrows were beyond bearing.

Across the yard, Lissie cowered deeper into the bole of the old oak tree that was always her refuge at times like this, and biting down on her bottom lip, she tried to block out the angry words she knew would spout from her mother's mouth.

'Why?' Dora's harsh response was followed by a derisive cackle. 'I do it to take away the misery of living with a penniless excuse for a man like you. You're no good, Tom Fairweather, and you never will be.'

'But to let the child see you behaving like a slattern.' Tom's horrified reply let Lissie know her father was close to tears.

'And whose fault was that?' her mother taunted. 'If you'd gone by the road, she'd be none the wiser. But you, fool that you are, had to take her on one of your blasted nature treks.' She gave an ugly laugh. 'You should have seen the look on your stupid face. You're the most—'

Lissie pressed her hands to her ears. She didn't want to hear the cruel words that her mother so often used when she was berating her lovely, kind dad. It was always the same; her mam screaming and shouting whenever she had done something nasty and her dad pleading as he tried to understand why.

Just lately, her mam's rages were much wilder and far too frequent, and with each fight Lissie's fears were exacerbated. Being only seven years old, she struggled to understand why her mam behaved in the way she did.

An almighty crash from inside the cottage made Lissie drop her hands from her ears and sit bolt upright. Her mother had most likely upended the table. She often did that, as well as flinging plates and pans and anything else that came to hand. They'd barely enough crockery left to eat off.

'No, Dora! Not my tools!' Lissie heard her father yell as a resounding metallic crash rang out: that was most likely the workbench he used when mending shoes or carving wood.

'Your tools,' Dora jeered. 'They're as much use as you are, you yellow-bellied turd! You couldn't satisfy a hen in the yard. Is it any wonder I seek it elsewhere?'

Lissie puzzled over her mother's ugly, grating words. Did her dad have a yellow belly? What was that about the hen? And what was it her mam was looking for? As the unanswerable questions tumbled inside her head, she felt a twinge in her belly. Her bladder was full, but rather than leave the safe haven of the tree and go to the privy, she pulled up her knees, and sinking her teeth into her forearm she rocked back and forth making little moaning noises as she waited for the fighting to stop. She needed to pee, badly.

Less than an hour ago she had been happily walking the streets in Thorne village, her hand snug inside her dad's roughened palm as they delivered the shoes he had mended: a tall, handsome man with kind, grey eyes in a finely chiselled face under a head of curly black hair, and a diminutive little girl whose angelic features, sparkling blue eyes and lustrous black tresses caused people to stop and admire her. Tom Fairweather and his daughter, Lissie, were well liked in Thorne.

Lissie had been pleased when her mother had stormed out of the house earlier that morning. Otherwise, Dora might have vented her spite by refusing to let Lissie accompany her dad. Even at her tender age, she was well aware that her mother used her as a weapon with which to dominate her husband, her threats to leave him and take Lissie with her terrifying to him. There were nights when she couldn't sleep, thinking how dreadful her life would be if she was separated from her dad. She loved him, and she knew with all her heart that he loved her. Of her mother's love she was less certain, and once again her mother was taking the joy out of what had been a lovely day.

They'd made one delivery after another, and when the last pair of shoes had been handed over and paid for, her dad had squeezed her hand and his grey eyes twinkled as he'd said, 'Now it's time for a treat.'

Lissie's insides had thrilled. She'd known exactly what he meant, and long before they'd stepped inside old Mr Brooks' shop in Church Street, she had anticipated the sweet, pungent smell of tobacco and mint humbugs.

'Good day, Mr Fairweather,' the elderly shopkeeper had said, smiling at her dad. Lissie had smiled too; everyone respected her dad. He mended their boots and shoes, fixed their cupboards and made tables and chairs, never charging too much for those who had little to spare. 'I see you have your pretty little helper with you today.' Mr Brooks had nodded and smiled at Lissie and she'd blushed, pleased that she had put on a clean smock over her grey pinafore dress and that she'd brushed her tangle of curls for their trip into the village; she hadn't wanted to let her dad down by looking scruffy. As she had gazed at the tidy shelves filled with colourful packets, tins and large glass jars, her dad had bought ten Woodbines and two ounces of aniseed balls, Lissie's favourite.

Now, crouched in the bole of the oak tree listening to her parents fighting, she licked her lips, searching for traces of the spicy tang and wishing she had saved some so she could suck away her misery. Her happiness was like aniseed balls. It never lasted long enough.

On their way back home her dad had said, 'Let's go by way of the wood. The bluebells are at their best.'

Leaving the streets of Thorne behind, they had ambled into the wood. The sun was high in the sky, its bright rays lancing through the canopy of ash, oak and beech, and on either side of the path the ground was carpeted with bluebells.

'It's like the sea,' Lissie had said as a gentle breeze riffled the flowers.

'Aye, only the sea goes on for ever and ever, whereas the bluebells will be gone before we know it. We must enjoy them whilst we can,' her dad had said with a far-away gleam in his eyes. 'Let's pretend we're on a ship, Lissie, sailing the seven seas to our own secret island.'

He'd raised his hand to his forehead, peering ahead like a sailor on lookout. Lissie had done likewise, and as they ploughed their imaginary sea her dad named the trees and birds, and pointed out a badger's lair. Walks with her dad were always magical.

They had reached the middle of the wood when they heard the panting yelps and grunts, and looking in the direction from where they came, Lissie had gasped and gripped her dad's hand all the tighter. She'd felt her eyes stretching wider and a hot flurry of blood staining her cheeks.

Her dad had pulled her sharply to a halt.

Her mam had been pressed up against a tree, her skirt round

her middle and her bloomers round her ankles. The man pushed up against her had his trousers down round his knees and he was pumping up and down as her mam clung to him, her head tilted back and rapturous moans springing from her throat.

Her dad had given a hoarse cry. Then, like a man possessed, he had set off running back the way they had come, trailing Lissie by the hand, dashing through the trees and trampling the bluebells underfoot.

'Go back! Go back,' she had panted when they reached the road and he slowed his pace. 'That man was hurting Mam. We have to help her.'

'Forget what you saw, Lissie. You saw nothing,' he'd snarled, tugging on her hand and almost dragging her along the road.

Lissie had blinked, shocked by her dad's tone. He never spoke to her unkindly. She'd glanced up into his face. It was creased as though he had a bellyache. His lips were clamped and she could tell he was angry. As she'd hurried to match her steps to his, she'd tried to make sense of what had happened. How could you forget what you had seen with your own eyes? And why hadn't he wanted to rescue her mam? She just didn't know.

Now, still hiding, what she did know was that if she didn't get up and go to the privy, she was going to wet her knickers. She crawled out and stood on legs that were shaking. Could she make it to the privy that was attached to one end of the cottage without them seeing her? She didn't want to be dragged into the fight.

She tottered across the yard and was just about to creep past the open cottage door when her mam spied her. Before she could say lickety-split she was whisked off her feet, her mam's sharp finger-nails biting into Lissie's arm as she yanked her into the cottage and pushed her towards her father.

'Go on, you spineless dolt. Tell your precious little darling what her slut of a mother was doing in the wood. And don't forget to tell her why I—'

Hot pee gushed into Lissie's knickers and down her legs.

'Stop, Dora! Don't involve the child,' Tom Fairweather pleaded, his eyes glancing wildly from his wife to his daughter who was now standing in a pool of shame. Two quick paces took him to where Lissie stood, head down to hide her tears and her little body visibly shaking. Gently, he pulled her close against his leg, his arm wrapped protectively round her. Lissie's tears flowed over.

Dora's lips curled as she spitefully eyed her husband and daughter.

'Look at the pair of you. Snivelling and crying like babies,' she said scornfully. 'One of you like a beaten dog, and the other standing in a puddle of her own piss.'

Then, as though her venomous rage had reached boiling point, she cast about her for something with which to vent her spleen. Her eyes flashed maniacally as she surveyed the wreckage in the little room, the upturned table, the broken plates and Tom's over-turned workbench and his shoe mending tools. Spittle dripping from her mouth, she stooped and grabbed the iron shoe last.

'No, Dora! No-o-o!' Tom's frantic cry hit the rafters. Giving Lissie a hefty shove that sent her sprawling across the floor, he reeled backwards as the heavy metal object thudded into his right shoulder. His knees buckled and as he toppled, his head cracked like gunshot against the stone sink behind him.

Lissie screamed and screamed.

Staggering to her feet, she stared at her father's huddled body and the pool of blood seeping from his head. The yellow flagstones turned red. Gathering her wits, she flung herself down beside him, her tears falling on his ashen face as she cried, 'Dad! Dad!'

She glanced round for a cloth to staunch the blood pouring from his head, and spying the dishcloth hanging over the edge of the sink, she pulled it down then pressed it against the gaping wound. His eyes were closed, and his cheeks stark white where the blood hadn't reached. 'Wake up, Dad, wake up,' she cried.

Stunned, Dora stood fearfully taking in the gruesome scene. *My God. She'd gone too far this time.* Her skin turned clammy. She'd be gaoled for this – nay, not gaoled – she'd hang for it. A violent shudder mobilised her into action.

'Stop that wailing. Come away from him,' she shrieked, and darting forward, she grabbed Lissie by the arm and yanked her to her feet.

Lissie struggled to break free, crying, 'No! No! My dad's hurt! You've got to get the doctor.' She turned beseeching eyes on her mother, desperate for her help. Seeing no pity there, she kicked at Dora's shins then sank her teeth into the back of her hand.

Whack! The blow that Dora delivered to Lissie's head sent her spinning across the room. She landed on her knees, her vision blurring as she tried to stand. Her mother towered over her.

A swift kick on her rump had Lissie struggling to her feet. Dora barged into the bedroom. Flinging open the cupboard, she began stuffing clothes into a canvas bag. 'Get your coat on, Lissie. We're leaving.'

Leaving! Lissie stared round-eyed.

'But... but we can't leave Dad...' She hurtled into the bedroom, and tugging at Dora's skirt, she screamed, 'Get the doctor! Help my dad.'

A swift, hard slap across her cheek silenced her and she backed out of the room in a daze, her tear-filled eyes drifting from her mother frantically packing two bags and her dad lying still and bleeding on the floor.

Dora dashed back into the kitchen and dropped the bags with a thud by the outside door. Grabbing her own dark green coat from the nail behind the door, she thrust her arms into it then tossed Lissie's grey coat at her.

'Put it on,' she ordered. 'Cover that...' She pointed at the dark red smear on the hem of Lissie's smock.

So used was she to obeying her mother, Lissie threaded her arms into her coat sleeves without thinking.

Dora dropped to her knees beside Tom.

Lissie's heart lurched.

At last! Her mam was going to help her dad. They'd fetch the doctor and he would make him better.

But Dora was rifling through Tom's pockets.

Lissie watched, horrified, as Dora clinked the coins from his trouser pockets into a pile on the floor. She seemed oblivious to her husband's pitiful state, and at that moment Lissie hated her with every fibre of her being. Bile gushed into her throat. She retched. Spew splattered down on her boots.

'You dirty little bitch!' Dora threw Lissie a disgusted glare. Then, when the last penny had been extricated from Tom's pockets she snapped, 'Pass me my purse. It's on the mantelshelf.'

Lissie didn't move, couldn't move. Hatred and anger had glued her to the floor even though her limbs were shaking uncontrollably.

'Do you hear me, you mardy brat?'

When Lissie still made no move, Dora got to her feet and fetched the purse. In three swift movements she scooped the coins into it, stepped over her husband's sprawled legs then swiped the purse hard against the side of Lissie's head. Coins clinked. Lissie wobbled, lights flashing before her eyes as she struggled to maintain her balance.

'That'll teach you to ignore me. Now, lift that bag and come on.' She pointed to the smaller of the two bags.

Her head still ringing and her eyes fixed on her father's lifeless body, Lissie stood her ground, only moving when a violent shove propelled her out of the door into the yard. Hearing the door slam, she turned, desperate to go back to her dad. Dora barred the way, her eyes gleaming malevolently as she looped the long handles of the smaller bag over Lissie's head. 'There, that'll do.'

Then, lifting the larger bag, Dora grabbed hold of Lissie's hand. 'Now don't dawdle,' she commanded, setting off at a brisk pace, her grip tightening and hurting Lissie's fingers as she trailed her across the yard and onto the lane leading to the road into the village.

Lissie's feet felt like lead, and deliberately dragging them and twisting her hand to free it from Dora's grasp, she stumbled alongside her mother, stubbornly making no attempt to speed the journey. She had to go back to her poor dad. She wouldn't leave him.

Cursing under her breath, Dora persisted until they reached the road. Then letting out a frustrated scream, she abruptly halted. Caught unawares, Lissie skidded to her knees at her mother's feet. Dora threw aside the bag, and using both fists she pummelled Lissie from her head to her toes. 'Keep up or else you'll get more of this,' she gasped, her fists flailing.

Dazed and broken, Lissie allowed her mother to pull her along the road to the village, the bag bumping uncomfortably against her aching chest and her wet knickers chafing the tender skin on the insides of her thighs. Every now and then she risked glancing back. Who would help her lovely dad now?

2

The streets in Thorne village were quiet at this time of day, most people at home eating their midday meal. Those that passed by the rather dishevelled but pretty young woman and her crying child paid them no heed.

'Wait here,' Dora ordered when they arrived outside the Boar's Head, the public house where Lissie's dad sometimes dropped in for a pint.

She dumped the bag at Lissie's feet and ducked inside the pub. Lissie leaned against the wall. Should she run away, back to her dad, or should she find someone to tell? She glanced up and down the street but it was empty, and her exhausted little body refused to move. Before she could summon enough energy and pluck up her courage to run, her mother came out of the pub accompanied by a big, beefy man with long whiskers sprouting from his florid face. He was wearing a thick waterproof coat, the sort favoured by carters.

'Me wagon's round t'back,' he muttered, lumbering to the rear of the pub.

Dora picked up the bag, and twisting her free hand into Lissie's long, black curls, she chivvied her to follow him. Lissie's scalp tingled with each stumbling step.

'Say nothing,' Dora hissed. 'Mention a word and we'll both end up in gaol.'

Lissie knew exactly what it was that she hadn't to mention but she couldn't fathom why she would go to gaol if she told someone. *She* hadn't done anything wrong. If she were to tell the man, maybe he would go and help her dad. No sooner had that thought entered her head than a flood of other nasty thoughts swiftly followed it.

It was my mam who did the bad thing, but I did nothing to stop her.

I hid in the oak tree when the fight started.

I should have run and fetched the doctor.

I shouldn't have left my dad lying in a pool of blood with no one to care for him.

I should have fought harder. Will they send me to prison?

I'm just as much to blame.

Lissie's blood turned to ice as these thoughts took root. She gave an almighty shudder and would have fallen to the ground had her mother not been clinging to her hair. Great, gulping sobs leapt from her throat as she stumbled over the cobbles in the inn yard.

Two large Shire horses whickered impatiently and shuffled feet as big as dinner plates as they waited between the shafts of a large cart filled with hay and a few bulging sacks. Their ears pricked at their master's approach and they turned their huge heads, two pairs of big, soft brown eyes alighting on him and then Lissie. She liked horses. So did her dad, she thought forlornly as she breathed in their warm, friendly smell.

'You can sit up front wi' me,' the man said to Dora. 'The little 'un can sit in the back.' He unhitched the horses and climbed into the driver's seat, taking the reins in his rough, meaty paws.

Dora heaved the large bag into the back of the cart then half-lifting Lissie, she shoved her in after it. Lissie sprawled in the hay. It scratched her cheeks and tickled her nose, and the straps of the small bag still looped round her neck were threatening to choke her. She crawled further in until she was wedged between two lumpy sacks. Turnips poked out of the top of them.

Dora walked to the front of the cart, and one hand sweeping her long, green skirt up out of the muck in the yard and the other gripping the arm of the seat, she swung lithely up beside the driver. He flicked his reins and made a clucking noise. The horses strained in the shafts and the cart trundled over the cobbles and out of the yard.

'It's ever so good of you to give us a lift,' Lissie heard her mother say in the same treacly voice she used when the butcher had given her an extra rasher of ham, or the milkman allowed her to miss paying him until the following week. 'The sooner I get to my poor, sick mother, the better.'

Lissie pricked up her ears, frowning.

'I just hope we get there in time,' her mother continued in a sad, little voice. 'Let her see the little 'un mebbe for the last time.' She faked a little sob then a deep sigh. 'Lissie loves her granny.'

Lissie sat up straighter. *Do I?* she asked herself.

As far as she knew she didn't have any grandparents, unlike her school friend, Jenny, who had two grannies and two granddads. When she had asked her dad why this was, he had told her they were dead, but now her mam was talking about a granny who was poorly and needed her mam's help.

'We only got word late this morning after the bus to Castleton had gone. I was in despair wondering how we would get there. My husband is in the navy, you see, so I'm left on my own to manage things. That's when I thought surely some kind carter might be going that way. And I was right. It's lucky for me I asked in the inn and the landlord pointed you out.'

All this was said in a voice brimming with self-pity and some gratitude. The carter, clearly a man of few words, mumbled something in reply.

Lissie was dumbfounded. Her mam was telling lies. Her dad wasn't in the navy. He was lying in a pool of blood in their cottage. She shuddered as she pictured the iron shoe last flying from her mother's hand, and inside her aching head she heard the thud as it landed on her dad's shoulder, and the sharp crack as his head hit the sink. She wondered if he'd woken up yet. She began to sob noisily, but neither her mother nor the hairy man seemed to notice.

The cart wound its way through the village past the houses where she and her dad had delivered shoes, and Mr Brooks' lovely little shop where such a short time before she had felt so happy. As they left behind one familiar house, shop or street after another Lissie's fears mounted. She was being taken away from her dad, and there was nothing she could do to prevent it. If only... if only... As her jangled thoughts played inside her head her eyes drooped, and exhausted by the terrible and confusing events of the day she fell into a fitful sleep.

* * *

Lissie wakened to a darkening sky, streaks of purple and grey clouds above the fiery glow of the setting sun. She was surprised to find herself lodged between two sacks and her feet buried in a pile of hay. Then she remembered. An icy shiver ran down her spine as she pictured her dad lying in a pool of blood.

Blinking the sleep from her eyes, she glanced from one side of the road to the other. There was nothing much to see, just a wide expanse of moorland and hills in the distance. *At least I know now where I'm going,* she thought, recalling that her mam had told the driver they had missed the last bus to Castleton.

One day, not long ago, her dad had said he'd take her to

Castleton to see the Blue John Mines now that she was old enough. He'd told her they were like fairy grottos, that the walls of the caverns deep underground were crusted with purple and yellow and creamy white ore that glittered and sparkled like stars.

'I'll buy you a crystal to keep on your bedside table,' he'd said. The memory brought tears to her eyes.

The cart rumbled on. Strangely enough, Lissie found the steady clop of the Shires' massive hooves and the rocking motion soothing, for at least her mam wasn't screaming and shouting and dragging her from pillar to post.

She looked down at her sore left wrist. It still bore the imprint of her mother's fingers and she rubbed it with her right hand. That's when she noticed that her fingers were dark red and felt sticky. She stopped rubbing, and opening her hands palms upward, she stared at them. A wave of nausea curled her tummy. Her hands were stained with her dad's blood. Her chest heaved. Shuddering and shaking, she cried for her father.

When her grief was spent, she raised her wretched little face and looked around through eyes that were red and swollen. She had expected to see the moors and the hills, but now the cart was rumbling down a busy street with houses and shops on either side. She sat upright to get a better look. This must be Castleton.

The pavements thronged with people taking advantage of the fine April evening, and the unusually warm weather. Ladies in hats bedecked with ribbons or posies, and men in Homburgs or cloth caps were gazing into shop windows or strolling along the street. Everywhere there was motion and noise, much of it coming from the stalls that were selling hot pies and peas and baked potatoes, the vendors shouting out the attributes of their wares. The savoury smells made Lissie's nose twitch and her empty belly rumble.

The cart slowed to a halt. 'This do you?' she heard the carter ask.

'Perfectly,' Dora replied. 'My mother lives just along there by the river.' She jumped down, singing out her thanks as she hurried to the rear of the cart. 'Get down,' she ordered, lifting the big bag and giving a Lissie a stern glare.

Lissie slowly lowered herself to the pavement, her legs stiff and unsteady. The cart pulled away, and Dora began brushing bits of hay from Lissie's hair and coat.

'Just look at the state of you, you dirty little bitch. Wipe that snot off your face and try to look presentable.'

Lissie raised her bloodstained hands to her cheeks and cleaned the snot from her face with her tears. Her cheeks turned pink.

'That'll do,' Dora snapped. 'You're not fit to bring anywhere.'

She looped the small bag over Lissie's shoulders, and lifting the other, she grasped Lissie's wrist with her free hand. 'Walk properly, and stop wailing. You're making a show of me.' She set off at a brisk pace, threading her way through the crowds and pulling her daughter along with her.

Outside a long, stone building Dora halted. Lissie looked up at the sign swinging above the door. A bull with a ring in its nose looked down at her and she read the words, The Bull's Head.

'Wait here,' said Dora. She went into the inn.

Lissie waited for a moment then retraced her steps to the shop she had caught a glimpse of just before they reached the pub. Her heart swelled as she gazed in the window. There they were: the glittering crystals her dad had told her about. She fastened her eyes on a large, rugged piece edged in deepest purple that faded into snaky yellow swirls around a creamy white centre. It was just as he had said. As she gazed at it, Lissie made a silent promise. *One day, Dad, I'll come back and buy it to remember you by.* Not that I'll ever forget him, she told herself as she hurried back to stand outside the door of The Bull's Head.

3

The small room on the upper floor of The Bull's Head was warm and cosy. Dora fetched soup and crusty bread from the kitchen downstairs. Lissie cleaned her bowl in no time, and feeling somewhat revived and rather brave she asked. 'Will my dad have wakened up yet?'

The spoon in Dora's hand stopped halfway to her mouth. Her lip curled. 'Forget about him,' she snapped. She began slurping soup again.

'Is he dead?'

'No, he just got a knock on the head.'

'Will he come looking for us?'

'Stop talking about him.'

The soup in Lissie's tummy curdled. She couldn't forget what had happened to her dad even if her mother could. How could her mam be so cruel?

'You hurt him.'

'It was your fault. Tell anybody what happened and you'll be in big trouble.'

'But... but I... It was you...'

Dora gritted her teeth. 'I told you to forget about him. He didn't want us.'

Another lie. Lissie knew in her heart that her dad wanted her. He loved her.

'He did. My dad lov—'

Smack! The back of Dora's hand swiped across Lissie's mouth.

'One more word about him and you'll be sorry. Now get undressed and get into bed.'

Lissie slid off her chair, ready to do as she was told. Dora always dealt with provocation by lashing out, and Lissie had grown so used to her slaps that she had learned to expect and accept them without crying.

'Will I get washed first?' Lissie's lips were stinging and her hands felt sticky.

'Don't bother. You can do it in the morning.'

'I feel mucky. Can I just wash my hands?'

'For Christ's sake, stop mithering.' Dora's shriek was warning enough. Lissie's arms and legs were still sore from the beating she'd received on their way into the village, and the skin on her wrist was still burning. Admitting defeat, she undressed, used the chamber pot, and wearing only her vest and knickers, she climbed into the big bed with its brass and iron ends.

'Will we go back home tomorrow?'

Dora loomed over the bed with her hand raised. Lissie slid further under the quilt. 'Go to sleep,' Dora said. 'I've business to attend to.'

She opened the bags, pulling out what she needed, and within the next few minutes she had changed her dress, brushed her long blonde hair and made up her face. Pouting at her reflection in the cheval mirror and appearing to be satisfied, she left the room.

Lissie huddled under the thick quilt. She had never slept in any bed but her own in the cottage in Thorne. This should have been an exciting adventure, she thought sadly, and it would have been if her dad had been there.

She turned over onto her back and gazed up at the ceiling. Its gnarled oak beams were full of knots like ugly little eyes staring down at her. She couldn't sleep even though she ached with weariness. There were too many uncertainties rolling round inside her head. Where were they going? And what was to become of her now that she no longer had her dad to protect her from her mam's terrible tempers and flailing hands? She let her thoughts linger on the feel of her dad's strong arms as he'd swung her up and run from the house to escape her mam's wrath. Who would do that now?

The thought playing in her head, she fell asleep only to waken what seemed minutes later. She was coated in sweat and she knew that the screams she had heard were her own. She had been in the cottage, blood everywhere, and as she lifted her dad's head to stem the blood it had come away from his neck, his lovely grey eyes staring into her own. He had grinned hideously, and she had tossed his head aside and run. She had kept on running, trampling bluebells under her feet until she felt herself falling. Down, down, down she went past craggy walls gleaming with purple and yellow and creamy white slime that slithered under her hands as she fought to break her fall. Screaming, she woke up, alone, in a strange room. Her heart thudded inside her chest so hard that she thought it might bounce out.

The sound of laughter, noisy chatter and the clinking of pint pots penetrated the floorboards. As her heartbeat steadied, tears seeped from the corners of her eyes. They trickled into her ears and dampened the pillow. In an attempt to dispel the nightmare, she recalled all the lovely things she had shared with her dad. How he had taken her on his knee and read to her from his poetry and storybooks. How they had walked in the woods and fields, Dad naming the birds and the flowers and telling her magical tales about the lore of the countryside. Her mam hated that sort of thing and had scorned him for wasting his time, but her dad hadn't let that deter him.

Lissie turned over onto her side, and drawing up her knees, she let her mind play with all the beautiful things her dad had said and done, the memories so comforting that, as her breathing slowed and her eyes closed, a spurt of hope burned in her chest. Mam had said he'd just knocked his head, that he wasn't dead. If that was true, he'd come and find her.

* * *

Downstairs, sitting in the snug next to the taproom with a glass of gin in her hand, Dora was feeling rather pleased with the progress she had made. So far, she had covered her tracks. Sipping thoughtfully, letting the gin's sharp sweet taste linger on her tongue, she wondered if she really had killed Tom. It had certainly looked like it.

Yet again, he might have regained consciousness, and if he had he would come looking for her – she was sure of that. Perhaps he had already called the police. He might not want her but he would want his precious daughter.

She didn't want her, but Lissie had witnessed what had happened. Her word, and Tom's, might be enough to land Dora with a gaol sentence. She didn't want that, so – if he'd survived – it was better to have the kid under her control.

On the other hand, he might have bled to death.

Dora scowled, irritated by the thought. She hadn't meant to kill him, but whichever way she looked at it there was all the more reason to put a good distance between herself and Thorne. If the police were looking for her, they'd most likely make enquiries at the train or bus station. They'd not expect her to be travelling by cart.

Smiling at her inventiveness, she raised her glass in celebration and took a long swig of gin.

The carter who had brought her to Castleton hadn't asked for payment. Now she intended to find another soft touch with a vehicle to take her on the next stage of her journey where she'd start her new life away from Thorne and Tom Fairweather. She lifted her empty glass and sashayed into the taproom.

4

'Lissie! Wake up! We've got to get moving.'

Lissie was skipping through a vast forest of bluebells that swept down to the sea where her dad waited for her in a shiny white boat with a red sail. She had almost reached it when she wakened with a start. The bluebells, the boat and her dad suddenly faded, only to be replaced by her mother's flushed, angry face.

'Get up, Lissie!' Her mam shook her roughly by the shoulder. 'Out of bed, this minute.' Dora began flinging things from the bags onto the bed.

Lissie rolled over, sleepily trying to recapture her dream. An iron hand yanked her from under the covers and onto her feet. She swayed groggily.

'Get washed,' Dora snapped, pushing Lissie towards the nightstand.

Colourful flowers and birds in flight shimmered under the water in the pretty China bowl on the nightstand. Wishing she could fly away, Lissie dabbled her sticky hands. The water turned the faintest shade of pink and Lissie shuddered.

'Brush your hair,' Dora barked, waving the hairbrush then smacking it bristle side down on Lissie's bare arm. Lissie flinched. Dora shoved the hairbrush into her hand.

When they were both dressed, Lissie in her grey dress and a clean smock and Dora in her best blue skirt and blouse, she repacked the bags. Then putting on their coats, they hurried downstairs. Out on the street they ran to the rear of The Bull's Head, Dora breathing a sigh of relief when she saw the red lorry that the driver had told her to look out for was still there. 'Look nice and smile when the driver comes,' she urged.

Dora reckoned that the lorry driver had only offered to take her to Bradford because he'd felt sorry for the child. Lissie was proving useful after all.

Last night in the taproom, as she'd ordered another gin, Dora had overheard the lorry driver telling the landlord that he was leaving for Bradford first thing and was looking forward to getting home to his wife and daughters. Snatching her opportunity, she had piped, 'I'm for Bradford meself.'

The man had turned warm brown eyes on her and Dora had sighed and given him a sad smile. 'Though how I'll manage all the buses and trains, not to mention the expense, I just don't know. Travelling with a small child who's very nervous isn't easy.'

He'd immediately taken pity on her, and after she'd finished spinning him the same sad story about her sick mother, he'd offered to give her and her little daughter a lift. Now, Dora looked impatiently round the inn yard waiting for him to keep his promise.

'Where are we going?' Lissie demanded.

'Wait and see.'

'I want to go to back to my dad.' Lissie stamped her foot and jutted her lip.

'Well, you can't! And don't say a word about what happened,'

Dora snarled, the warning slap she was about to deliver suddenly turning into a hug when she saw the lorry driver approaching.

Bemused, Lissie allowed Dora to hold her close.

'You're in good time,' he said cheerfully, 'an' this must be your little lass.' He gave Lissie a kind smile. 'She's a beauty. She puts me in mind of my Sarah.'

'She's a darling,' Dora gushed, ruffling Lissie's curls before letting go of her. 'And she's such a good little thing. I don't know what I'd do without her.'

Lissie thought her ears must be playing tricks on her.

The man opened the lorry's passenger door. 'You can sit between me an' your mam,' he said, swinging Lissie up in his arms and setting her on the long seat. 'Slide over into t'middle an mek room for your mam.' He handed Dora up then went round to the other side of the cab. Lissie watched as he took an iron bar bent into a funny shape from the floor of the cab. Standing in front of the lorry, he did something with the iron bar and the engine roared into life. It made Lissie jump. Laughing, the driver hopped in behind the wheel.

Another adventure, thought Lissie, excited for her first ride in a motorised vehicle and temporarily forgetting her sadness. Squashed in between her mother and the driver, she looked in amazement at the clocks on the panel behind the steering wheel, and felt the man's hand brush against her leg as he gripped the stick next to it. He pushed it forward, the engine juddered, and they were off.

The lorry travelled much faster than the cart of the day before, and Lissie turned her head this way and that as they whizzed by shops and houses, out of Castleton and onto the open road. Here the traffic was lighter and the driver, no longer having to negotiate narrow streets, pedestrians and other vehicles, began to talk to Dora over Lissie's head.

'As we're travelling together, we might as well be on first name terms. Mine's Sam, an' I know she's Lissie,' he patted her knee, 'so what's yours?'

'Dora,' she said, immediately regretting giving him her real name.

'Well, Dora, it's lucky for you I had to make an overnight stop. The job I was doing kept me late, and it's a fair distance between here an' Bradford. I was removing a houseful of furniture for a customer.'

'My dad makes furniture and mends sh—' A sharp dig from Dora's elbow silenced Lissie.

'Does he now?' He glanced at Dora. 'I thought you said he was a farmer.'

'He is. Like I said last night, that's why he couldn't come with us. He can't leave the animals what with them needing to be fed and milked.'

'Aye, you can't leave 'em to fend for theirselves.'

'That's true,' said Dora, 'and usually I'd be helping him. But what with my mother breaking both her legs, she needs me more than he does.'

Lies! Lies! All lies. Lissie wondered how many more her mam was going to tell.

'What part of Bradford are you for?' Sam asked.

Dora hesitated. She had never been to Bradford. 'The centre, you know... er, hmm...' She made a wild guess. 'Near the railway station.'

That seemed to satisfy the man and he began talking about his work and his children. Dora pretended to be interested and said things like 'Nice' or 'Fancy that' every now and then.

Lissie gazed through the windshield into the distance. Moorland and craggy rocks flashed by. Here and there farms and cottages dotted the hillsides, and every now and then they drove through small villages with clusters of houses, a church, and a school. *I should be getting ready to go to school*, Lissie thought, *but instead I'm sitting in a lorry going to a place I've never heard of before.*

Sam slowed the lorry at a crossroads, and Lissie saw a signpost: Yorkshire. She knew she lived in Derbyshire, in the Peak District her dad called it. Sam revved the engine and the lorry surged onwards, Lissie thinking, *It's taking me further and further away from my dad.*

'That's Sheffield over there.' Sam pointed to a huge grey sprawl of buildings.

Up above them high clouds moved on the wind. She watched them, searching for a shaft of light or a sign that might help her make sense of what was happening.

* * *

It was late in the afternoon when Sam brought the lorry to a halt outside Bradford Exchange. Lissie wakened to the sound of a train chugging out of the station. They had stopped for something to eat in a place Sam called Barnsley, and after that she had slept; it was easier to sink into oblivion than worry about her dad, and wherever it was her mam was taking her.

'Will this do you?' Sam asked.

'Yes,' Dora mumbled. She was feeling confused for she had also been dozing up until a few minutes ago. 'My mother lives just back there.' She flapped her hand.

'Right then, let's get you on your way.' He jumped down from the cab then rounded the bonnet to help Dora and Lissie out. They stood, dazed by the prospect of what lay ahead. Sam set their bags at their feet. 'Well, nice meeting you,' he said, 'I'm glad I could be of help. I hope your mother gets better soon.'

'Thanks. Thanks very much,' Dora said, still at a loss for what to do next.

Sam drove away, and Lissie and Dora stared after the lorry like drowning men might when robbed of a life-line in a stormy sea.

Dora picked up the bags. 'Come on. We've got to find somewhere to stay.'

5

'Who's that?'

Lissie's horrified cry pierced the ceiling of the shabby room in the cheap boarding house where they had spent the night. She had just wakened after a restless night to find a half-dressed man pissing in the chamber pot. Curly black hairs matted his chest and a black, bristly moustache covered his upper lip.

'He's a friend, and keep your voice down, you mardy brat.' Dora was sitting on the edge of the double bed wearing just her petticoat, her blonde hair in tatters around her blotched face. The man finished what he was doing then loped over to the nightstand.

Lissie, still lying in the uncomfortable truckle bed, watched as he sluiced his head and arms, the water splashing all round him. He didn't look anything like her dad. Her dad was tall and slender and his skin smooth and golden whereas this man had dark, swarthy skin, thick knotty arms and legs and a chest like a barrel. She didn't like the look of him.

Dora was pulling on the clothes she had worn the day before. 'Get up and get dressed,' she ordered, glaring at Lissie.

Mesmerised, Lissie didn't move.

The man put on his shirt and trousers and a leather jerkin, and taking a comb from his jerkin pocket, he went to the mirror and slicked his greasy wet hair back from his forehead. Black as a crow's wing, it reminded Lissie of the underside of a giant fungus she and her dad had once found in the wood. She thought of her dad's soft, black curls. When the man glanced over and met her gaze, his eyes glistened like two shards of coal. She thought of the kind grey eyes that used to smile into her own. Tears trickled down her cheeks and she wiped them away with the edge of the blanket.

'I told you to get up.' Dora pulled the blanket from the truckle bed.

Lissie climbed out, the soles of her feet tingling on the rough, cold floorboards. She wanted to pee, but she didn't want to do it in front of the man. Neither did she want him to see her in just her vest and knickers. She dithered, wailing when Dora's sharp smacks across the backs of her bare legs forced her into action. She began to get dressed.

'You didn't mention owt about her when you brought me up here last night,' the man growled. His gravelly voice grated in Lissie's ears. She liked him even less. 'I hadn't reckoned on tekkin on a kid when I said you could stay at my place. She'd best not be any bother.'

'She won't be,' Dora said. 'I'll make sure of that.'

To Lissie's amazement and disgust, her mam went and put her arms round the man and kissed him. He clasped her backside in his meaty paws. They stayed like that for what to Lissie seemed ages and she hid her face in her hands and clenched her thighs. She really did need to pee.

'We'd best make a move,' he said, letting go of Dora then putting on his trilby.

Dora stuffed their things into their bags then covered her tatty hair with her cloche hat and put on her coat. 'Hurry up!' she barked as Lissie fumbled with the buttons on her boots. Trembling, she put on her coat. Panic swelled in her throat. Where were they going now? Were they just going to keep moving from one strange place to somewhere even stranger with someone they didn't know? A little dribble of urine seeped into her knickers, and clenching her buttocks, she tottered out of the room behind her mother and the horrible man.

They walked down the busy street, the man carrying Dora's big bag and Dora linking his free arm with one hand and toting the small bag in the other. Lissie struggled to keep up with them, dodging in and out of the crowds on the pavement. She didn't want to be with them, but neither did she want to get lost in this big city. Huge soot-stained buildings towered on either side of the street and carts and lorries and motorcars clogged the road.

In her entire life the furthest Lissie had ever been from Thorne was Sparrowpit, the village next door. Up until yesterday her life had revolved round the cottage on the edge of the wood, and the school and shops in the village. Now they were going to some mysterious place called Great Horton, so the man said.

When her mam and the horrible man stopped part way down the street and joined the end of a queue of people, Lissie caught up with them and stood beside them. They seemed to have forgotten all about her. Across the road she could see the huge iron and glass roof of the railway station outside which Sam, the lorry driver, had left them the night before. She wondered where he was now. He had been a nice man.

Then, amidst all the noise and bustle, a huge red and white monster came clanking down the thoroughfare, sparks flying from the metal rails on which it travelled and its wheels grinding to a stop level with where they were standing. Lissie stared in amaze-ment as people spilled onto the pavement from the inside of the leviathan. Through its many windows she could see the heads of more people and was reminded of the goldfish her dad had won at Sparrowpit fair and put in a glass bowl when they got home. She'd never seen a tram before.

Dora caught her by the arm and pulled her closer. The queue shuffled forward and as Lissie admired the tram's gleaming paint-work, her legs trembled with anticipation. Another new experience; one she might have enjoyed had circumstances been different.

When it was their turn to climb on board, her excitement made her bold.

'Can we go up there?' Lissie pointed to the narrow spiral stairway leading to the upper deck.

Her mother and the man ignored her, and she reluctantly followed them to seats on the lower deck. Dora sat next to the man and Lissie sat behind.

As the tram lumbered past large and small buildings, shops and houses, Lissie was fascinated by the colourful signs on some of the walls: Colman's Mustard, Reckitt's Blue, Bird's Custard and Fry's cocoa. She read them all, and when the tram stopped outside a building with an ornate front and a sign above it that said it was a music hall, she stood up from her seat to get a better look at the placards on either side of the doors. Painted ladies in frilly dresses were kicking up their legs high enough to show their fancy garters. Lissie thought they looked rude but even so, she wished her dad were with her so that he too could see this big city with all the new and amazing things. There was so much to see that she almost forgot to feel sad.

The nasty man stood up. 'We get off here,' he said, nudging Dora to her feet.

She stumbled from her seat then grabbed Lissie by the arm and bundled her down the aisle and off the tram. Lissie's knickers felt damp.

They walked down a busy street lined with shops and houses, then leaving them behind, they entered a warren of narrow streets and alleyways. The houses were small and shabby and the cobbles littered with horse dung. Lissie skipped round it to avoid dirtying her boots. Her dad had made them for her only two weeks before. A few short paces more and the man said, 'Down here.' He jostled them into a dark, dank passage between the houses. It smelled of tomcats.

On the tram ride Lissie had been so engrossed in all the sights that she had forgotten that her bladder was full, but now she felt that it would burst. As they came to the end of the passage and into a cobbled yard she began jigging from one foot to the other as she cried, 'I need a pee! I can't wait!'

'Privy's over there.' The man pointed to a row of four small outbuildings across the enclosed yard. 'Ours is the end one.' He turned and mounted the steps of the house next to the passage.

Lissie dashed to where he pointed, and pushed open the privy door. Pulling down her damp knickers, she climbed onto the lavatory. She sat for a while taking in the whitewashed walls and the cobwebs in the corners. She watched a spider dangling from an invisible thread. Down it plunged, then just as speedily it ascended. She recalled a story that her dad had told her about a king and a spider: if at first you don't succeed, try again.

She climbed off the pot, and as she pulled up her knickers, she thought that that was what she should do. She should keep on trying to get back to her dad.

* * *

The house in Hart Lane wasn't what Dora had expected. Last night, over several glasses of gin, Jed Fletcher had told her that he had his fingers in all sorts of pies, and that he did a tidy bit of business in buying and selling, but there were no obvious signs of wealth in the poky run-down terrace house.

When Jed had told her that he could use a pretty assistant like her, Dora had reckoned on making an easy living, one with the excitement that she'd missed when living with her husband who, in her opinion, was nothing but a dreamer with his head full of poetic nonsense. She'd jumped at the chance when Jed had offered to let her stay with him at his house in Great Horton, and she'd brought him back to the room in the boarding house to show him her appreciation; that and the fact that she'd fallen for his rough, flashy persona. Now, as she breathed in the fetid smell of the cluttered, shabbily furnished room, her euphoria dissipated.

Damp brown patches stained the walls that had long ago been distempered a drab shade of green. The hearth was filled with dead ashes, and the sink held a pile of greasy dishes. Still, Dora thought dismally, it was somewhere to stay for the time being. She'd wait and see how the business he had promised to put her way turned out.

'It could do with a bit of tidying,' she remarked.

'You can soon see to that,' Jed replied. 'I don't have time for housekeeping.'

Neither do I, thought Dora, but she kept her opinion to herself. 'Will I make a pot of tea?' They'd had nothing to eat or drink before leaving the inn, and now she resigned herself to playing the housewife.

Outside, Lissie emerged from the privy into the yard, its cobbles slimy with mud and not a tree or a patch of grass in sight. Six scruffy houses formed a small court, their walls high enough to shut out the pale, watery rays of April sunshine.

At the far end of the yard a gaggle of children were taking turns swinging on a rope tied to a clothes post. The swinger held the rope taut then pushed off with both feet against the post, whirling outwards as the rope coiled round and round. It looked like fun, and Lissie wondered if she would be staying in this place long enough to have a turn on the swing.

On feet that didn't feel as though they belonged to her, she crossed the yard and mounted the steps of the house that the man and her mam had entered. She lingered in the doorway.

'Come in. Don't stand gawping,' Dora said when she saw her daughter.

Lissie was staring in dismay into the gloomy, untidy room. *It's not at all like our cottage.* There the walls were a pretty shade of blue, and the furniture her dad had made was clean and shiny. He'd pegged brightly coloured rugs to cover the flagged floor and her mam had hung flowered curtains at the windows where the sun streamed in. She stepped into the smelly room feeling very small and very frightened. She didn't want to live here with the nasty man – or her mam for that matter. She felt like crying.

'We're going to live here now with Jed,' said Dora as she put the blackened kettle on a gas stove thick with grease.

Oh, so that's what they call him, thought Lissie, deciding it was a horrible name for a horrible man. Jed sprawled in a battered armchair, a cigarette dangling between his thick fingers. He glanced at Lissie. 'She doesn't say much, does she?' he said sarcastically.

'No, she's always been a quiet little thing.' Dora gave Lissie a warning glance that said, *And keep quiet from now on or else...*

Scowling, Lissie leaned against the doorframe. Dora emptied the sink of dirty dishes, looking for teacups. Finding three, she then scanned the room, her eyes alighting on a low stool. She carried it over to the now empty sink, and then poured hot water from the kettle into the bowl. 'Stand on that stool and wash up,' she said to Lissie then turned to Jed. 'We could do with the fire lighting.'

'There's coal an' sticks under t'stairs,' he said, jerking his thumb at the dark space under a sloping ceiling. Dora gritted her teeth.

Lissie climbed onto the stool and turned on the tap to cool the water, then rubbing her fingers inside the cups, she removed the brown tea stains, and using her fingernails, she scraped dried on food from the plates and dishes. The greasy scum on the water made her feel sick.

Dora cleared the ashes and lit the fire and by the time the kettle had boiled again, Lissie had washed the dishes and stacked them on the slimy draining board. She climbed off the stool and Dora handed her a grubby tea towel. 'Dry up while I mash a pot of tea.'

Lissie could tell by her mam's sharp tone and the scowl on her face that she was angry. She wondered if she would start throwing things and calling Jed nasty names like she did when she was mad with Dad.

She knew what had raised her mam's temper. Dora never cleaned out and lit the fire at home; Dad always did it, and if her mam didn't feel like washing up or cleaning the house, he did that too. Lissie helped him and they made a game out of it, seeing who could be first to finish their task.

Lissie sat on the stool to drink her tea. She felt miserable and tired even though it wasn't yet midday. 'Are we having something to eat?' she whispered, thinking that something inside her belly might make her feel less shivery.

Dora looked at Jed. 'Have you anything in the house?'

He flicked his thumb at a cupboard with a mesh door. 'There's bread an' cheese in there. You can make do with that, an' when we've had it you an' me'll go out an' do a bit of business. I'll show you the ropes an' see if you're as wily as you say you are.'

'I'll soon show you how crafty I can be,' Dora boasted, giving him a naughty wink and wiggling her hips.

Jed laughed; a dirty sound that made Lissie ashamed of her mam who, excited by the prospect of working along with Jed and earning money, was making sandwiches as happily as though they were a family about to go on a picnic.

The bread was stale and the cheese hard. Lissie choked it down.

6

Lissie was alone in the house in Hart Lane. Her mam and Jed had left soon after the makeshift meal had been eaten, Dora's parting words, 'Do a bit of tidying before we get back, and don't go wandering off.'

Wander off to where? Lissie had silently asked. *I'm so far from home I don't know where I am.*

The fire was burning low so she lifted lumps of coal from the bucket and tossed them into the grate. Her mam would be angry if she let the fire go out after she'd had the bother of lighting it. As Lissie washed her hands in the sink then the cups they had used, she puzzled over the possibility of running away. But to do that she would need the tram fare; a man with a lorry or a cart would hardly give a lift to a little girl travelling on her own. Abandoning the idea, she folded Jed's clothes into an untidy pile on a kitchen chair then wiped the cracked oilcloth on the table. At a loss as to what she could do next, she sat down on the stool by the fire and cried her heart out.

When she could cry no more, she got to her feet and went and stood in the doorway. The air was fresher there than in the smelly room. She could hear the children laughing and shouting. With her heart in her mouth, she descended the steps into the yard then slowly walked down to where they were playing.

A girl of about her own age was chasing after four younger children. Catching hold of a little boy with thick fair curls, she whirled him round and round, her own long flaxen plaits spinning out like golden ropes. When she saw Lissie she frowned, and letting go of the boy, she stared at her.

'Who are you?'

Lissie swallowed a lump that felt like a stone in her throat.

'What you doing here?'

Lissie had no answer to that so she looked down at her boots.

A plump woman in a flowery crossover apron came to the door of the house nearest the clothes pole. Her rosy cheeks were wreathed in smiles. 'Who have we got here then, Emmy?' she asked, looking from the girl to Lissie.

'Dunno Mam. She din't say,' Emmy replied. The woman came down the steps into the yard.

'Are you lost, lovey? Are you lookin' for somebody?'

Lissie shook her head, first of all up and down for yes, and then to the left and right for no. The woman's friendly smile and kind voice made tears spring to her eyes. She blinked them away.

'Eeh, lovey, don't get upset. There's nowt to cry about.'

Yes, there is, thought Lissie, but feeling rather foolish in front of Emmy who was chewing on the end of one of her plaits and looking at her oddly. Lissie took a deep breath. 'Me and my mam have come to live here with Jed Fletcher,' she said, her voice wobbling as she pointed towards his house. 'They've gone out.'

'Oh, I see,' Emmy's mother said in a voice that seemed to say a lot more. 'Well, I'm Nelly Jackson and this is my daughter, Emily. What's your name?'

'Lissie Fairweather,' she croaked.

'That's a pretty name, an' you're a pretty girl,' Nelly said. 'Now, why don't you play with our Emmy while I get on wi' me house-work.' She waddled back indoors calling over her shoulder, 'Mek her feel at home, our Emmy.'

The two girls stared at one another then Emmy grinned and Lissie managed a wan smile. By now the younger children had gathered round, sizing Lissie up. A boy of about ten came out of one of the privies doing up his trousers. His head was shaven, revealing a ring of red sores.

'Who's she?' he asked Emmy.

'Beggar off, Freddy! Me mam says we haven't to play with you.'

Freddy scowled and sloped off into the house in the corner of the yard. 'He's got ringworm,' Emmy informed, 'so keep away from him.' Dismissing him with a glare, she asked Lissie, 'What school are you going to? I go to the National.'

'I go to Thorne Infants.'

'Where's that?'

'A long way from here,' Lissie said forlornly, looking around her as if she might suddenly see the way back to Thorne. Emmy looked bemused.

'I'm off school today 'cos I got nits from Shirley Higginbottom. Me mam got rid of 'em with vinegar an' coal tar but she says I can stay off the rest of the week.'

Lissie's hand automatically buried itself in her long black hair and she scratched unnecessarily as she recalled the time when she'd had head lice. 'I caught them in school as well,' she said. 'My dad combed them out of my hair and killed them.' Her throat filled up as she spoke and she began to cry.

'There nowt to cry about. Everybody gets 'em,' Emmy said loftily.

'I'm not crying because I had nits. I'm crying because my dad's not here.'

'Where is he?' Emmy's sharp blue eyes were bright with curiosity.

'In Thorne.' Best not mention that she and her mam had had run away and left her dad bleeding on the floor.

'My dad's at work. He's a tuner at Lane Close Mill.'

'My dad mends shoes and makes furniture,' Lissie volunteered. It felt nice talking about her dad. Maybe he was just a few miles away looking to find her and take her home.

Nelly Jackson appeared in the doorway again. 'Come in, Emmy, an' bring our David an' your new friend with you.'

Emmy grabbed the hand of the small boy with thick fair curls then turned to Lissie. 'Me mam says you can come to our house if you want.'

Lissie followed Emmy and David into the house. The pleasant homely smell of stewed meat and pastry tickled her nose.

'Ah, here comes Dandy Davy an' Nitty Nancy,' a grey-haired old man sitting by the hearth cried as they entered. 'An' who's this you've got wi' you?'

'She's called Lissie Fairweather, an' shurrup about me nits, Granddad, 'cos I han't got 'em any more.'

The old man laughed, and sticking his pipe between his lips, he puffed out a cloud of smoke and sparks.

Nelly put cups of milk and a plate of biscuits on the table. 'Get this into you. It'll tide you over till teatime.'

'Are we havin' meat an' tater pie?' Emmy asked. Nelly nodded.

Lissie sipped her milk and crunched on a custard cream as she gazed round the Jacksons' house. It wasn't grand or as pretty as the cottage but it was a palace compared with Jed Fletcher's. She dreaded having to go back there.

'So... you an' your mam has come to live with Mr Fletcher,' Nelly said.

Her mouth full of biscuit, Lissie nodded.

Nelly gave an imperceptible shake of her head and exchanged a knowing glance with her father. They both knew what the women Jed kept company with were like, and this new one seemed no different. Going off and leaving a small child on her own in a strange house, a house not fit to keep a dog in, said it all.

'Well, you're welcome to come to our house any time you like, lovey. In't that right, Dad?' said Nelly. The old man winked at Lissie and flourished his pipe. 'Now, finish up an' off you go an' play,' Nelly continued. 'Give us a shout, Emmy, when your dad comes into the yard.' She gave a deprecating little smile to Lissie. 'I like to have his dinner on the table ready for him to sit down as soon as he comes in,' she confided.

That made Lissie smile sadly. Her mam didn't like cooking, and she rarely ever had Dad's dinner waiting for him. Dad did most of the cooking like he did everything else.

Nelly saw the sadness in the little girl's smile, and as Lissie slipped off her chair Nelly gave her a big hug. 'Off you go, an' don't forget to come again, lovey.'

I mustn't start crying again, Lissie told herself as she bit down on her lip to stem the tide, but it seemed so long since anyone had spoken to her kindly or hugged her that she had to struggle to hold back the tears.

'Can you play hopscotch?' Emmy asked when they were out in the yard.

Lissie said she could, and whilst they were tossing the stone on the numbered squares the boy with the shaven head walked by them.

'You've got nits, Emmy Jackson, mucky nitty nits. You gave 'em to everybody in your class.'

Emmy stopped mid-hop and flung the stone. It hit his leg.

'Liar, liar, your pants are on fire,' she yelled. The boy walked off, laughing.

Lissie gasped. The fire! She'd forgotten to mend the fire.

'I have to go,' she blurted, racing up the yard to Jed's house.

Emmy ran after her. 'Pooh! It stinks in here. It's mucky, in't it?' She looked round the room with a disparaging gaze. 'I've not been in here before. Me mam says to keep away from men like Jed Fletcher.'

Lissie gazed in fear and dismay at the dead ashes in the grate. She was about to ask Emmy if she knew how to light a fire when they heard a man's deep voice and a woman's high-pitched giggle outside the door.

'I'm off!' Emmy scooted to the door, almost colliding with Jed and Dora.

'What's going on here?' Jed's roar bounced off the ceiling.

'You've let the fire go out,' Dora shrieked, dumping a parcel wrapped in newspaper on the table. She darted over to Lissie and gave her a resounding slap. Lissie started to wail and Jed continued to shout.

'You told me she'd be no bloody trouble, an' here she is lettin' blasted kids into my house.' He towered over Lissie, his black eyes glinting slits in his meaty face. 'You bring anybody else in here again an' you'll feel the weight of my hand,' he bawled. He swung round, shouting at Dora, 'Get them chips an' fish unwrapped whilst they're still hot an' make a pot o' tea.'

Dora glared at Lissie. 'This is all your fault,' she hissed, banging the kettle on the gas stove then dividing soggy portions of fish and chips onto three plates. They ate in silence and Lissie thought about the Jackson's cosy kitchen and the meat and potato pie. It had smelled lovely.

Jed shovelled his food into his mouth, bits of fish clinging to his bristly moustache. Dora had made tea, and by the time she handed him his pint pot he seemed to have forgotten his rage. As Dora sat at the table to eat her own, now cold, fish and chips he reached across and fondled her arm.

'By, but you're even craftier than I took you for,' he said, his voice thick with praise and a mouthful of fish. 'You played him for a right fool. You nearly had him in tears wi' your sob story.' Dora flushed prettily and giggled.

'It was dead easy,' she said, fluttering her eyelashes and smiling smugly.

Then, shrinking in her chair and adopting a pathetic little voice, she re-enacted the charade she had performed earlier that afternoon in the Fleece Inn when she had persuaded an elderly businessman to buy the stolen necklace Jed was fencing for one of his accomplices. Like a poor man's Sarah Bernhardt, she clutched at her breast and sobbed, 'I'm just a poor, broken-hearted widow selling my last piece of precious jewellery that my dear, departed husband gave me on our wedding day so that I can feed my four darling little children.'

She cackled noisily. 'I never knew making money could be such fun.'

'Well now you do. An' there's plenty more to be made if you do your stuff. I've all sorts o' things planned for you.' Jed stretched across the table and gave Dora a greasy kiss. Dora threw her arms round his neck and kissed him back.

The food in Lissie's belly curdled. She jumped off her chair and raced out to the privy. Leaning over the smelly pot, she was violently sick, and when the retching subsided, she sank down on the cold stone flags. She felt hot all over. Leaning back against the wall, she drew up her knees and buried her face in her hands. She had never felt more desolate.

She stayed for some time in the sanctuary of the whitewashed walls, and as her thoughts tumbled, the heat left her body and was replaced by icy rage. How could her mam kiss that horrible, slobbery man and giggle over the things she had been doing with him? Lissie hadn't really understood what had passed between them, but she was smart enough to know that they had been up to no good. And her mam had been telling lies again.

She got to her feet and marched out of the privy, her back rigid with cold and fury. The shadows had lengthened in the yard and the sun had disappeared. Stamping up the steps, she burst into the house shouting, 'I'm not stopping here. I want to go home. Take me back to my dad.'

'Oh, for Christ's sake,' Jed roared. He was sitting in the armchair, Dora on his knee. He shoved her off. 'Get that bloody bairn out of my sight afore I kill her.'

Dora grabbed Lissie and shook her till her teeth rattled. 'Don't you start that carry on with me,' she yelled. 'You'll do as you're told.' She turned to Jed. 'I'll put her to bed. Where's she sleeping?'

'She can have t'smallest room. Me an' you are in t'other.'

Dora bundled Lissie up the narrow flight of stairs and into the smaller of the two bedrooms. 'Get undressed, get into bed and go to sleep,' she said.

Lissie looked at the unmade bed. The sheets were wrinkled and grubby. 'I'm not sleeping there,' she sobbed.

'You damned well are,' said Dora, smacking Lissie's wet cheek. 'Now, not another word out of you or I'll give you the best hiding you've ever had.' She flounced to the door. 'Don't you dare go spoiling things for me, you mardy brat.'

Lissie looked at her as if she was mad. *Spoiling things! Everything is already spoiled. You've hurt my dad and brought me to this nasty place to live with a man who says he'll kill me. Things can't get any worse.*

Dora went back downstairs and Lissie went and stood at the small window overlooking the yard. A cat was slinking past the privies. Suddenly its ears pricked and its back arched. In a flurry of black and white, its jaws open and its front legs clawing, it pounced.

Lissie heard the faint squeaking as the rat struggled to free itself. She shuddered. *Please, Dad, come and take me home.*

The room was perishing cold. She pressed her face to the windowpane, raising her gaze up to the darkening sky, looking for the stars. Her dad had told her all about the stars. She knew how to pick out Orion's belt and the Plough and the Pole Star but it was still too light for them to make an appearance. If you wish on a star, your wish comes true, Dad had said. Closing her eyes she pretended she could see the Pole Star.

Lissie made her wish.

Then, knowing there was nothing else for it, she undressed and crawled into the messy bed. It smelled sweaty. Pulling the covers over her head, she let the tears flow, sobbing wretchedly until finally in bewilderment, fear and exhaustion she fell asleep.

Lissie was on her knees picking bluebells, breaking their tender stems and horrified to see that her fingers were stained not with their milky white sap but with dark, sticky blood. She scrabbled among the trampled flowers and found her dad's broken, bleeding head. Her heart pumped and her breath was trapped in her throat. She gulped and screamed at the top of her lungs. Then, with the hideous nightmare still playing inside her head, she came fully awake to find Dora's hand clamped over her mouth.

'Stop that bawling, you're annoying Jed,' Dora hissed, slapping Lissie's cheek with the flat of her hand before darting back downstairs.

Lissie slid further under the covers, afraid to go to sleep in case the nightmare came back to haunt her.

7

Lissie had lost count of the days since she had been dragged from the cottage in Thorne, leaving behind her dad and everything she loved. It had in fact been but three miserable days and nights, but it seemed like a lifetime.

The morning after she'd arrived in Hart Street and made friends with Emmy Jackson, Emmy had waited until she saw Jed and Dora leave the house before calling for Lissie. 'Seein' as it's Sat'day we can go an' spend us Sat'day penny,' she'd said. 'Are you comin'?'

Lissie didn't have a Saturday penny but she went anyway. Anything was better than staying alone in the dirty house. On their way to the shops in High Street, Emmy pointed out familiar landmarks: the dye works in Crag Lane, the spire of St John's church, the Fleece Inn and the Four Ashes pub, the Co-op and the Wesleyan chapel. 'Just so's you get to know your way round,' she said.

Everything Lissie saw seemed to be much bigger and greyer than in Thorne.

The narrow, cobbled streets were busier with people and traffic and everywhere she looked she saw huge buildings with towering chimneys. She pictured the little cottage and the trees and fields at home then asked, 'Is there a bluebell wood near here?'

Emmy looked askance. 'Nah,' she said dismissively then rather proudly, 'That's Lane Cross Mill where me dad works.' Lissie felt a stab of jealousy at the mention of Emmy's dad and thought of her own dad's workbench in the cottage as she gazed across the distance at a massive arched gateway and the rows of windows in one of the biggest buildings she'd ever seen. Whatever did the workers make in such big places? Curious, she asked Emmy.

'They weave worsted cloth. Me dad says Bradford's famous for it.'

Lissie was none the wiser, but not willing to show her ignorance as to what worsted was, she left it at that. Compared to Emmy she thought she must seem very babyish and it made her feel small and insignificant.

Emmy bought sweets in the Co-op. Lissie gazed longingly at glistening boiled sweets, soft jelly babies and chewy toffees in the big glass jars on the shelf. Then she thought of Mr Brooks' shop in Thorne and the day her dad had bought his Woodbine cigarettes, and her favourite aniseed balls. Her mouth watered at the remembered spicy taste and she wished she had a penny to spend. On their way back to Hart Street Emmy shared her sherbet lemons with Lissie.

'Let's play hopscotch,' Emmy said when they were back in the yard. They'd just started the game when an older girl came out of the Jacksons' house. 'She's my big sister,' Emmy informed Lissie. 'She's twelve an' she's called Nora.'

Lissie thought how nice it must be to have a big sister. Nora joined in the games as did little David and the other children. They swung from the clothes post, skipped with an old length of rope and played hide and seek. And in between these delightful distractions Nelly called them into the Jacksons' cosy kitchen for drinks of fizzy pop and biscuits. Lissie began to think that living in Hart Lane might not be so bad after all, but every now and then she thought of her dad and yearned to be back home.

The clock in a distant church tower struck twelve, midday. 'Me dad'll be home soon,' Emmy said. 'He allus brings us a treat on Sat'day.'

Again, a spike of jealousy pierced Lissie's heart. She dropped the end of the rope she was winding, leaving Emmy mid-skip and Nora uselessly turning her end. Running to the steps of Jed's house, she sat down then covered her face with her hands. It just wasn't fair.

'Oi! What you doin'?' yelled Emmy, her feet tangling in the slackened rope and her attention swiftly diverted from Lissie as her dad and her big brother, Jimmy, came into the yard, home from their Saturday morning's labour in the mill.

'Dad,' Emmy cried, rushing to meet him. He held out his arms and she jumped into them. Lissie's envy deepened. Would she ever do that again with her dad?

'Whoa there, our Emmy. You'll have me off me feet,' Bill Jackson laughed as he set her down. He glanced at Lissie huddled on the step crying for all she was worth. 'What's up, Emmy? Have you fallen out wi' her?'

Emmy shook her head in denial. 'I don't know what's wrong wi' her. We were skippin' with our Nora an' she just ran off.'

'Well, we can't leave her cryin',' said Bill, going over to Lissie. 'Come on, love. Dry your eyes an' tell me what's upset you.'

Lissie raised her head. Bill looked down into a pair of moist blue eyes that looked like delphiniums after a shower of rain. He held out his big roughened hand. Tentatively, she placed her hand in his and let him pull her to her feet, surprised when he lifted her into his arms, patting her back comfortingly.

'Now, what is it?' Bill said softly into Lissie's ear.

'I want my dad,' she sobbed. 'I want my dad.'

Nelly had made him aware of the goings on, as she termed them, in Jed Fletcher's house. *Left that little girl on her own all day, they did. What sort of a mother traipses off with a no-good like him leaving a bairn of her age on her own?*

Bill Jackson had curled his lip and said he didn't know. Nelly had borne him seven children, four of whom had survived and each one as precious as the other. Now, holding Lissie, he felt her pain.

'Eeh lass, I'm sure you do, but seein' as he's not here you'll just have to mek do wi' me. So, let's have no more tears. We'll go an' see what Nelly's got for us.'

With Lissie clinging to him like a limpet to a rock, he set off down the yard. Emmy trotted beside them feeling proud of her lovely, kind dad. He always came up trumps in a crisis.

Jimmy had gone on ahead. At fifteen he had little time for crying girls. Nora had already gone into the house to warn her mother that Dad was on his way.

When Bill strode in with Lissie still in his arms and Emmy close behind, Nelly was filling dishes with scrag of mutton stew. Its smell tantalising, the Jackson children rushed to sit down at the table.

'Have we enough for one more?' Bill asked, setting Lissie on her feet.

'We've allus enough, Bill Jackson. You know that. An' when we haven't, we can allus stretch it to go that bit further,' Nelly told him as she filled an extra dish then said, 'Sit down next to our Emmy, Lissie.'

Bill pecked Nelly's cheek, and Lissie felt as though her heart might burst at the sight of all the love and affection that filled the little house. She sat down and ate hungrily. They never had meals as tasty as this in Jed's house.

'What's for Sat'day treat, Dad?' David asked after they had emptied their dishes of stew.

'What treat? I don't know what you're talkin' about.' Bill winked at Nelly. She grinned. He often played this game of keeping them in suspense.

'You do, Dad,' David insisted, his eyes pleading. 'What have you got for us?'

Bill made a game of patting his pockets and looking confused.

'I wouldn't mind an ounce o' Pontefract cakes,' Granddad said, and the others laughed. They all knew his fondness for the liquorice sweets made in a factory not many miles away from Bradford.

'Is it treacle toffee?'

'Brandy balls?'

'Mint humbugs?'

David, Emmy and Nora called out their favourites. Jimmy smirked. He knew what his father had bought.

Bill struck his forehead. 'Well, I'll be a monkey's uncle. You all guessed right.' He produced two small bags and a little slab from his pockets and handed them over. 'An' don't forget to gi' Lissie a share,' he ordered, and to Lissie, 'What's your favourite, love, so I'll know for next time.'

Lissie couldn't speak. Just to be included in this lovely family was enough. When Bill pressed her, she replied, 'Aniseed balls.'

'Hey up, what about me? Don't I get owt?' Granddad's mock plaintive wail set them off laughing again.

'Course you do, old lad.' Bill delved in his pockets again and tossed him a small bag of the flat round black cakes that were the size of a penny. Then leaving his chair, Bill presented Nelly with her own bar of Fry's chocolate cream.

'Thank you kindly, good sir,' she said in a posh, prissy voice, and they all laughed again.

'Now, don't forget,' said Bill in an important sounding voice, 'next week's Easter so there'll be no Sat'day treats.' He let the words hang in the air.

'Awww!' his children wailed, their faces crumpling, and before they could ask why, Bill cried, 'Cos I'm tekkin you all to t'fair.'

When the cheering subsided, Emmy jumped up from the table and went and sat on Bill's knee to give him a big hug.

Lissie slid off her chair and nervously asked, 'Does that mean me as well?'

'Course it does,' said Bill. 'That's if your mam lets you.'

Lissie's luminous, blue eyes met Bill's. 'I don't think she'll care,' she said.

Nelly raised her eyes to the ceiling. It pained her to think of such neglect. 'Come here, bairn,' she said reaching out and pulling Lissie onto her lap. Lissie sank into the soft warm folds of Nelly's embrace and listened to the others chatter. David said he wanted to win a goldfish, Nora wanted a turn on the waltzer and Jimmy a go on the rifle range. Lissie was just thrilled that she would be included.

When they'd talked themselves out, Nelly gave Lissie a big squeeze then said, 'Off you go the lot of you. Leave me an' your dad in peace.'

Lissie reluctantly left the haven of Nelly's plump arms and got to her feet. Emmy's granddad was dozing in his chair, a dribble of liquorice worming its way down his chin. Everybody's happy and contented in this house, thought Lissie.

Nora announced she was going to Susan's, her friend in the next street, and Jimmy went off to play football. Emmy asked Nelly if she and Lissie could go up to the bedroom and play with her paper dolls.

'Aye, but don't leave a mess when you've done.'

'Come on,' said Emmy, and as she led the way upstairs Lissie realised that she hadn't felt sad for almost an hour or so. As she and

Emmy dressed and undressed dolls and concocted stories for the dolls to enact, Lissie forgot the torment of the past few days.

'Your dad's nice and kind, isn't he?' she said, folding the tabs of a paper crinoline around the doll she had chosen to be her heroine.

'Yeh, he is, in't he?' Emmy agreed as she coloured in a paper dress that Nora had copied from one of the bought ones. 'Is your dad nice?'

'He's lovely,' said Lissie, her voice thick with emotion. 'We go for walks in the woods and fields, and he tells me stories and makes me toys and plays with me.' She paused, the ache in her chest taking her breath away. 'He's the best dad ever.'

'Then why did your mam leave him?'

Lissie froze. She couldn't tell Emmy the truth. 'I don't know,' she said, pushing the pain away and asking, 'Do you think she looks like a princess?' She held up the paper doll for Emmy's approval.

The shadows lengthened and teatime drew near.

'I'll just pop up an' see if her mam's back yet,' Nelly said to Bill midway through making fish paste sandwiches. A minute later she was back, disgust written all over her plump face. 'What does that woman think she's playin' at? She can't expect that bairn to mek a meal for herself, that's if there's owt in t'house to eat, an' I'll bet there's not.' She lifted the boiling kettle and mashed a pot of tea, and her anger as hot as the water, Nelly finished slapping fish paste between slices of bread. There were three things in life that made her blood boil: men who drank their wages and neglected their families, dishonesty of all kinds, and cruelty to children.

'Go easy with that knife, lass,' Bill jested. 'Tha looks fit to kill somebody.'

'I would if I thought I wouldn't hang for it,' Nelly retorted.

Just then Nora returned home from her friend's, and Jimmy from football.

'Go bring our David in, Jimmy, an' you, Nora, give them little lasses a shout upstairs, an' waken your granddad.'

'I'm not sleepin',' her father groused, opening his bleary eyes. 'What wi' you chuntering an' banging about it's like bedlam in here.'

When Emmy and Lissie arrived downstairs the others were sitting round the table. Emmy joined them but Lissie stood uncertainly, the happiness that she'd felt for much of the day dissipating then springing to life when Nelly said, 'Sit yourself down, lovey. Your mam's not back yet. I've just checked, an' I mended t'fire for you. You're havin' your tea with us today.' She pulled out a chair. Lissie's joy knew no bounds: things just got better and better.

'The sandwiches are lovely, thank you,' Lissie said, having tucked in along with everyone else.

'Aye, well, I don't suppose your mam'll mind you not eatin' what she left for you.'

'She said there was some bread and jam if I got hungry,' Lissie said. 'They usually bring chips or pies when they come back.'

Nelly snorted. Then, annoyed with herself for prying and not wanting to upset the child, she pulled out her hanky, pretending to sneeze. Bill understood.

'Have you been sniffin' t'pepper pot again, missis,' he said to help cover his wife's thoughtlessness which made them all laugh.

After they'd had their tea, Nora and Jimmy went out again and the others settled down for an evening round the fire, Nelly with her knitting, Bill reading the evening newspaper and Granddad puffing on his pipe. Emmy and Lissie were reading a fairy-tale book and the hands on the clock on the mantelpiece pointing to five past eight when the knock came at the door. Bill answered it.

'Is my daughter here?' Dora's face was pink with righteous indignation.

Nelly jumped up, pushing up her cardigan sleeves as if preparing for a fight.

'Aye, she is, an' it's well for her. She's had her tea so she'll not be wantin' owt. She's been here all day while you've been gaddin' about wi' yon fella.'

'I don't remember asking you to keep her,' Dora sneered. 'Who do you think you are, you an' your bloody do-gooding?'

Lissie slowly got to her feet, her cheeks red with embarrassment as she tottered to the door. Why did her mam have to be so rude? 'Thank you for a lovely tea and everything, Mrs Jackson,' she mumbled, her words almost drowned out by Dora's raucous shouting.

'When I need you to tell me what I should be doing, I'll ask,' Dora yelled, 'so mind your own business.'

'Aye, an' you mind your daughter,' Bill growled, jumping to his wife's defence.

'Night-night, Lissie. See you tomorrow,' Emmy called out.

'No, you bloody won't,' Dora spat as she dragged Lissie out into the yard and up to their own house. 'In future stay away from them, and don't be telling them things they don't need to know.' She pushed Lissie inside. 'Get upstairs and stay there.'

'Nothin' but soddin' trouble is that one,' Jed growled as Lissie dashed to safety, clattering up the stairs as though the hounds of hell were after her.

She threw herself down on the bed. At least her mam hadn't beaten her – well not yet she hadn't – thought Lissie, curling up into a ball. *And she can't stop me going to the Jacksons. If she's out all day she won't know where I am.* This satisfying thought soothed her, and reflecting on the pleasant day, she fell asleep.

* * *

'Now think on, stay in the house,' Dora said the next morning as she titivated in front of the mirror above the mantelpiece. 'I don't want to come home and find you've been bothering them people again.' She frowned, wondering what, if anything, her daughter had already told Nelly and Bill Jackson.

Lissie nodded obediently, and reassuringly said, 'I won't. I promise.'

Concluding that Lissie mustn't have divulged anything incriminating, Dora coiled her long blonde hair into a loose bun then pulled tendrils of hair loose about her face. She was wearing her new blue dress with a white lace collar.

Jed leered. 'You're a beauty all right. He'll not be able to resist once you get to work on him,' he gloated. Dora pouted prettily and winked. She was enjoying the confidence tricks she and Jed played on unsuspecting victims. He had promised her a share of their ill-gotten gains, but had yet to hand over any money. However, he had bought her the dress and a new hat trimmed with chiffon and feathers. She put it on, securing it with a long pearl-topped hatpin, another of Jed's gifts, and smiled at her reflection. The smile faded and was replaced by a look that bordered on revulsion as she turned to Lissie. 'Don't forget what I said. Stay away from the Jacksons or it'll be worse for you.'

'Get a bloody move on,' Jed barked, taking her by the elbow and at the same time glaring at Lissie as if to compound her mother's warning. His moustache twitched and the look in his coal-black eyes made her shiver.

Lissie waited impatiently until she was sure they were out of sight then she went up to Emmy's house determined to do as she pleased. Her mam did, so why shouldn't she? Her defiance burning bright and making her feel strong and brave, she spent Sunday playing with Emmy and sharing Nelly's home comforts. However, she kept a sharp eye out for her mother's return and made sure she was back in the house, sitting reading by the fire when Dora and Jed rolled in late in the evening.

* * *

On Monday morning, Lissie was smearing margarine on a crust of bread for her breakfast when Nelly and Emmy arrived at the door. Dora and Jed were still in bed having celebrated with a bottle of gin the night before.

'Get your mam. I've somethin' to put to her,' Nelly said briskly.

Puzzled and afraid, Lissie ran upstairs and shook Dora awake. 'Mam, Mrs Jackson wants to talk to you,' she urged.

'What the…' Dora lifted her frowsy head, hissing, 'Keep the noise down. Don't waken him.' She climbed out of bed cautiously.

Lissie looked with distaste at Jed's greasy hair scribbled on the pillow. His mouth hung open and his moustache looked like a fat, furry caterpillar sleeping on his top lip. He grunted and broke wind noisily. Lissie ran from the room, Dora shuffling behind in just her petticoat. Had Lissie talked too much? Was this Jackson woman here to accuse her of wounding her husband then leaving him to bleed to death? She plodded downstairs, her heart in her mouth.

'Well, what do you want?' she snarled, already on the defensive.

Nelly looked Dora up and down from the top of her tatty blonde head to her painted toenails. 'I've come to see if you want me to tek Lissie to school along with our Emmy. She'll be better off there than left here on her own all day,' she said tartly.

Dora flushed. Standing in the doorway half-dressed she felt uncomfortable in front of this plump, tidy woman in a crisp yellow blouse, grey skirt and cardigan. Her discomfort turned to indignation but before she let her temper fly, common sense kicked in: Lissie would be out of the way if she were at school. Dora forced a smile. 'That's very kind of you. I was going to take her myself,' she lied, the notion never having entered her head. She turned to Lissie who was jigging nervously from one foot to the other. 'Will she do in what she's got on?'

'I'll wait while you brush her hair an' put her in a clean smock,' Nelly said tersely. She looked pointedly at her own daughter, Emmy neat in her navy-blue pinafore and white smock.

'Please, Mam, can I go?' Dora gave a sulky nod, and Lissie's excitement mounting, she ran across the room and came back with the hairbrush. 'Find me a clean pinny,' she demanded and began brushing furiously at her long, curly locks.

Dora was suffering from a hangover, and having no inclination to prolong the situation, she shuffled upstairs for a clean smock to put over the grey dress Lissie had worn every day since they had left the cottage in Thorne. Lissie slipped it on and, beaming at Nelly and Emmy, she asked, 'Will I do?'

Nelly smiled kindly. 'You look grand, bairn.' It wasn't quite true, but eager to take herself and the girls away from this odious woman who reeked of stale drink and bodily fluids, Nelly hitched up her ample bosom and said, 'Come on, lasses, let's be off. We don't want to be late.'

'Bye, Mam,' Lissie cried exultantly as she skipped down the steps.

Dora watched her go, a cunning gleam in her eye and a crafty idea worming its way into her head.

8

'Can we go on the swing boats, Dad?' Emmy pointed to the high gantry holding the bright red and yellow curved boats, and with Lissie hot on her heels, they began pushing through the crowds. Bill and Nelly Jackson followed at a more leisurely pace with David tugging on Nelly's hand to catch up with the girls.

'Right,' said Bill as they joined the queue for the swing boats. 'When it's our turn I'll tek your mam an' our David up first then I'll tek you two.'

The Easter Fair on Low Green was a whirl of colour and noise and this being Lissie's first visit to a fairground with rides and amusements that she had never before seen, she felt hot with excitement. They had explored the gaily decorated stalls selling all manner of things, and her fingers and lips were sticky from the candy floss she had chosen – the delightful spun sugar concoction yet another new sensation. Emmy and David had preferred toffee apples that left bright yellow rings round their mouths. They had tried their luck at hooking a duck, and Bill had knocked a coconut off its post.

'Well done, Bill,' said Nelly, patting him on the back, and when

Lissie asked what she would do with it she replied, 'You can all drink the milk an' have a share of the thick white stuff inside it.'

So many first-time experiences were making Lissie's head whirl.

In fact, the past week had flown by full of new and exciting things. She liked her teacher, Miss Simms, who told her she was a very clever little girl, and Emmy's friends had become her friends; she fitted in nicely. Attending school and her friendship with Emmy and her family had left Lissie with little time to feel lost and lonely.

Now, waiting her turn, she gazed upwards at the soaring swing boats, the occupants pulling on the thick furry ropes and screaming and laughing with all their might. When it was their turn, she and Emmy tugged the rope, sending Bill careening high above their heads and as he did the same for them, Lissie felt as though she was flying.

'I'm having the best time,' she gasped, her feet once again on solid ground.

'Me too. I'm glad your mam let you come.'

'She doesn't care where I am.' Lissie's eyes darkened. For a moment she looked angry. 'She's gone to somewhere called Birmingham with Jed.'

Emmy took Lissie's hand, squeezing it comfortingly. She had reached the conclusion that Lissie's mam was the worst in the world. 'Ne'er mind your mam. Let's go on the roundabouts.'

Lissie was more than content to forget about Dora and ran with Emmy to where the carousel was spinning and the hurdy-gurdy blaring out music. Round and round and up and down it went, a celebration of sound and colour. When it stilled, she darted onto the platform, Emmy close behind.

'I'm gonna ride that one with the golden mane,' Emmy said.

'I like this one.' Lissie clambered onto the back of a dappled grey horse that reminded her of the horse in the field next to the cottage, the one she used to give carrots and apples. At first the memory made her sad but as the carousel picked up momentum, she realised that she was rarely sad these days and that during the daytime, hours went by without her thinking of her dad.

Even living with Jed was more bearable. She saw little of him or her mam, and Dora had done a bit of cleaning, more for her own sake than Lissie's, and the house was tolerable now that the smelly sheets on her bed had been changed for new ones. Of course, Lissie had more than her fair share of chores that she had never been expected to do when she'd lived with her dad. Dora had shown her how to light the fire and each day when she came home from school she cleaned the ashes out of the grate then carefully filled it with paper, sticks and coal. When it came to setting them alight, her little dirty hands trembled as she struck the match, and she sighed with relief when the flames took hold. Next, she'd wash the dishes Jed and Dora had used before they went off for the day, and once a week she washed her own underwear and smocks: a weighty enough task for a girl of seven, but Lissie was taking the line of least resistance to avoid the beatings and keep clean and tidy; her dad wouldn't want her to be smelly and dirty.

However, at night in bed she was often afraid to go to sleep in case the horror of what she now thought of as 'that nightmare' crept into her dreams. Whenever it did, all that had happened that last day in the cottage came back to torment her, and as she cried into her pillow she never gave up hope that one day her dad would come and find her.

The carousel slowed to a halt, and Lissie climbed off the horse feeling rather dizzy what with the whirling round and the thoughts that had played in her head. She swayed when her feet touched the ground. Laughing, Bill caught her up in a big hug. 'Hey up!' he cried. 'This one's as drunk as a lord.'

And in some ways, it was true. Lissie often felt drunk with happiness in the company of the lovely Jacksons and today was no exception, but she knew that lurking deep inside was an unbearable sadness that would stay with her for as long as she was separated from her father.

* * *

Spring eased its way into summer, and by then Lissie had settled into the routine of going to school, doing the chores and spending as much time as she could with the Jacksons. Dora and Jed paid her little heed as they went about their devious business, and for that Lissie was glad. During the long summer days off school, she played with Emmy in the yard or ran errands for Nelly, then in September it was back to school and before she knew it daylight hours shortened and the nights became chill.

'You've been my best friend for seven months,' Lissie said, totting on her fingers as she and Emmy walked to school one foggy morning at the beginning of December. Then sounding rather amazed, she added, 'I think that makes us nearly like sisters.'

'Aye, an' you're a better sister than our Nora 'cos she dun't play wi' me like you do,' Emmy scorned. 'Just 'cos she leaves school next year she thinks she's too big to bother wi' me, an' our David's too little. I'm glad you came to live here.'

Hand in hand the girls hurried up Crag Lane, the smoke belching from a dozen or more mill chimneys making the fog seem twice as dense. Lissie had grown used to the noise and clatter that erupted from these monstrous mills, and the greasy stink of raw wool and noxious dyes. She even knew what went on inside, Bill having told her about the rows and rows of looms that wove fine worsted cloth, and that it was his job to keep them running. He'd explained how the raw wool from a sheep's back was washed and combed then spun into a fine yarn that was threaded into a thing called a shuttle. He'd said that it was like a big needle, and when the loom was running the shuttle flew back-wards and forwards trailing the yarn that was called the weft between strong lengths of thread called warps. Then things with funny names like heddle and beater meshed the warp and the weft together and made the sort of cloth that was used to make suits and overcoats.

'Wave to me dad an' our Jimmy,' Emmy jested as they emerged from Crag Lane into High Street. Lissie giggled, and raising her free arm, she waved wildly in the direction of Lane Close Mill before continuing on past the Four Ashes pub, the bake house and the shops until they eventually arrived at the National school.

Towards the end of the afternoon, Miss Simms told the class that it was less than three weeks to Christmas. This caused a flurry of murmured wonder and expectation. 'We will of course be presenting our traditional nativity play,' she announced impor-tantly as she adjusted her spectacles further up the bridge of her thin, pointed nose. 'Parts will have to be learned, costumes made and carols practised.' Her beady eyes roved the rows of desks at which her pupils were sitting, ears alert and breath bated.

'I had a very difficult task choosing the main parts – and don't worry, you will all have a part to play,' she said coquettishly. Then pushing up her spectacles with her long, bony forefinger, she announced, 'I have decided that this year Molly Balmforth will be the Angel Gabriel.' Molly squealed with delight, her bright blonde head bobbing as she smiled beatifically round the classroom at the other girls. 'Settle down, Molly, and let me continue,' Miss Simms reprimanded.

Then her eyes came to rest on Emmy. 'Emily Jackson, you will be Joseph.' Emmy clapped her hands together and pressed them to her beaming lips. 'And Lissie Fairweather, you will be Mary.'

Lissie's mouth formed a big round O. She placed her hands on her cheeks, and her eyes widened in amazement. Then, the words rushing out on her breath, she said, 'Me? You've picked me to be Mary?'

'I have. With your lovely, long black hair and your clear diction, I think you'll make a perfect Virgin Mary.'

Miss Simms continued giving out parts, but Lissie was lost in her own thoughts. What would her dad say if he knew she had been chosen for such an important part in the nativity play? She longed to rush home and tell him. He'd be so proud, and he would make sure she learned her lines. Then she thought of what her mam might say and her joy evaporated. Miss Simms dismissed the class.

'Me an' you'll make a good Joseph an' Mary 'cos we get on with one another,' Emmy said as they crossed the schoolyard, 'an' we'll be able to practice our parts in my bedroom.'

'I hope I can be a good Mary 'cos I've never done anything like that be—'

A thump in the middle of her back prevented her from saying more. She would have gone down on her knees had Emmy not been holding on to her. She righted herself then swung round to face her aggressor.

'Who do you think you are?' Shirley Higginbottom, one of Lissie's classmates, yelled in Lissie's face. 'You shun't be Mary 'cos you've only been at our school for a bit, an' your mam's a tart what lives wi' Jed Fletcher.' She glared brazenly at Lissie. 'My mam says it's on'y mucky sluts that bother wi' him, an' you're no better than your mam.'

Stunned, Lissie heard the foul accusations and looked wildly from Shirley to Emmy then back again. She felt herself shrinking inside her coat as she stared into Shirley's pale face and squinty eyes. No one had ever spoken to her like this before and at that moment she was lost for words. But Emmy wasn't intimidated.

'You shut your mouth, Shirley Muckybottom. You're just jealous.'

'Don't you dare call me that. I'll say what I want about her.'

'No, you won't!' Lissie took a menacing step closer to Shirley. If Emmy could be brave, so could she. Shirley found herself looking into two blue eyes flashing with cold, intense fury. 'Nobody talks to me like that,' Lissie hissed.

Shirley scowled and raised her fist ready to strike again, but before she could find her mark her plaits were tugged so hard that her head was yanked downwards and she stumbled forward. Lissie gave a final tug on the plaits then shoved Shirley away. 'Don't ever call me or my mam names again.'

'Good for you, Lissie,' cried Emmy as Shirley ran off. 'I wa' going to punch her meself but I din't need to 'cos you gave her what for.' Her eyes glowing with admiration, she patted Lissie's back.

Amazed at her own courage in the face of adversity, Lissie gave a wobbly grin.

'My dad always told me to stand up to bullies and I did,' she squeaked, so overwhelmed by her actions that she could barely get the words out.

Emmy threw her arm round Lissie shoulders. 'She'll think twice afore she has a go at you again,' she said. They carried on walking, Emmy's face creasing thoughtfully as they neared Hart Lane. 'Mebbe you should try an' stand up to your mam like that,' she hazarded. Emmy knew all about the slaps and harsh words Dora regularly delivered. She'd seen the bruises on Lissie's arms and legs.

Lissie gave her a doubtful look and said, 'I don't think I'd dare.'

* * *

'Oh, Joseph, I don't want to go to Bethlehem. It is a long journey.'

Lissie placed both hands on her middle where she imagined the baby was and gazed imploringly into Emmy's eyes.

'We have to go and be counted in the census,' Emmy replied in a deep voice.

'How will we get there?'

'You will ride on the donkey and I will walk beside you all the way.'

Emmy's attempts to speak in a gravelly voice brought on a fit of coughing and the girls fell about laughing, bouncing on the big bed Emmy shared with Nora.

Outside the snow lay thick in the yard, but Lissie and Emmy were warm and cosy in the smallest bedroom in the Jacksons' house. The nativity performance in front of the school governors and parents was less than two weeks away, and Emmy and Lissie, keen to steal the show, practised their parts every day.

'It's time you were off home, lovey,' Nelly shouted from the bottom of the stairs. 'It's after six o'clock.'

Lissie's face crumpled. 'I have to go,' she said, dreading the thought of returning to Jed's house but if she was to avoid a beating, she'd better get a move on. Her mam and Jed usually arrived back at about seven, and she had to make sure that the fire was burning and the kettle boiled ready for their return.

'See you tomorrow,' Emmy said, as Lissie ran down the stairs.

'Mind how you go, bairn. It's slippy out there,' said Nelly as she gave Lissie a parting hug. Lissie trudged up the dark yard. Nelly shook her head despairingly. Several rows with Dora had let her know that keeping the child until later only made it worse for Lissie.

'Disgraceful, that's what it is,' she grumbled, slamming the door and turning to her father. 'That poor mite's on'y bit o' comfort an' happiness is when she's with us. That dirty cow treats her like a slave.'

'Don't tek on, our Nelly,' her father said, tamping his pipe with fresh tobacco. 'You do your best for the child, but she's not yours.'

'Aye, an' if she was, I'd not expect her to be lightin' fires an' washin' dishes an' doin' all the jobs that lazy trollop should be doin'.' Nelly tossed her head. 'Our Emmy told me that that poor little lass even washes her own clothes. Dora Fairweather, or whatever she calls herself, needs reportin' to t'authorities.' She banged the kettle on the gas ring then glanced at the clock on the mantelpiece. 'Our Jimmy an' Bill'll be in shortly wantin' their dinners. We'll have a cuppa to settle me nerves afore they come.'

Meanwhile, Lissie had let herself into the house, shivering at the gloomy prospect of what lay ahead. Before she had gone to the Jacksons' she'd stopped off to light the fire, heaping coal on it to ensure it stayed alight, but the dirty dishes Jed and Dora had used before they went out still had to be washed.

Moving by instinct in the almost pitch-black room, she extracted a long taper from the pot on the table then turned to face the hearth. 'Oh, no!' she cried to the empty room when she saw that the fire was almost dead. She thrust the taper into the reddest part. When it flared, she hurriedly pulled the stool up to the chimney-breast and mounting it, she turned the little brass valve on the gaslight. Gas hissed out. Hands trembling, Lissie carefully held the taper to the mantle. It popped, casting a pale, eerie light into the room and making the shadows jump.

Lissie leapt from the stool.

Down on her knees, her little heart pounding, she fed the embers with sticks, willing them to burst into flame. But the sticks were damp and the dying coals beneath them were quickly losing their redness. Wisps of grey smoke swirled lazily up the chimney. In a panic, Lissie grabbed Dora's copy of the Ladies' Home Journal that she'd left beside her chair. Ripping at the pages and making twists of paper she teased the embers. The burning paper licked the sticks. Sparks flew up the chimney and Lissie's spirits soared with them.

In her haste to make sure the fire was burning brightly before Dora and Jed walked through the door, Lissie's enthusiasm got the better of her. Instead of feeding the coal on lump by lump she lifted the half-filled coal bucket and tipped on the entire contents. She clanked the empty bucket back on the hearth, her grubby little hands flying to her mouth as she emitted a strangled cry. The deluge had smothered the burning sticks and the flames had died.

The door scraped open. Jed strode in, followed by Dora. Still on her knees, Lissie twisted round to face them. An icy trickle ran down her spine and two fat tears tracked the dust on her cheeks. She looked up at Dora, eyes wide.

'What's to do here then? No bloody fire,' barked Jed.

Dora stepped menacingly towards Lissie, but before she reached her, her eyes lit on the torn pages of the magazine. Now that Jed was giving her money, and insisting she dress up to fool their victims into thinking she was a respectable widow, she had bought the magazine to peruse the latest fashions. It was her bible. She let out a piercing scream.

Lissie was never quite sure how, in the tortuous minutes that followed, she had been removed from the hearth to halfway up the stairs, but there she was, nursing her aching head and her stinging arms and legs. Dora's final shriek had ordered her to go to her room and stay there, but she felt too hurt and exhausted to go any further. She couldn't even find the strength to cry. Seated in the cold, dark stairway with her head resting against the wall, she rubbed her hands over the soot-stained bruises that the poker had left behind on her calves and listened to her mam and Jed arguing. She breathed in the savoury aroma of hot pies and peas that they had brought back, and her empty belly rumbled.

'I've had all I can tek of her. She's nowt but trouble.'

He's talking with his mouth full again, Lissie thought distastefully. She hated the way Jed sloshed his food and talked at the same time.

'What can I do about it?' Dora sounded plaintive.

'You know what you have to do. I've told you often enough.'

'But I can't just—'

'If you want to stay wi' me you bloody well have to!' Jed's words were accompanied by a thud as he slammed his fist on the table. Lissie heard the plates rattling and the scraping of chair legs.

'Ouch!' Her mam let out a yelp. 'All right! All right! Keep your fists to yourself. You've made your point. I'll do it.'

Do what? Lissie was torn between going back downstairs and demanding to know what they were talking about and sticking her fingers in her ears to shut out the vicious argument that was still going on. Deciding that neither Jed nor her mam were likely to give her any sensible answers, she crept the rest of the way upstairs and crawled into bed.

Once there, afraid to sleep in the dark, she prayed that the unpleasant scene unfolding downstairs would not cause her to have the terrible recurring dream where her dad lay helpless on the floor, blood everywhere, and she tossed his broken head aside. Although it hadn't troubled her for several nights now, it had so often spoiled her sleep that she lived in fear of it returning.

Hopeful that this was just another of Dora and Jed's fights, the sort they had when they had drunk too much gin, and which always ended in sloppy kisses and strange noises from the bedroom, she fell into a fitful sleep.

9

Lissie was sitting in a beautiful garden, her clasped hands resting on the folds of her blue dress. Angels, their wings spread wide, hovered above her head, and the most glorious of all the angels stood before her. She gazed into the blinding light, quivering with wonder, as she waited for the angel to deliver his message.

'Get up and get dressed.' Sharp fingers bit into her arm, shaking her awake.

The dream evaporated and she found herself on the edge of the bed staring blearily at her own bare legs and wondering where her blue dress had gone. The grip on her arm tightened and she was pulled to her feet. Dora's harsh voice repeated the command.

'Why? What's happening?' Lissie stuttered, looking into her mother's frustrated face. The light from the candle Dora had brought with her flickered. Her shadow danced wildly against the wall. Brittle stars winked in the dark sky outside the window. 'What time is it?' Lissie asked, thinking that it must still be the middle of the night.

'Never you mind,' Dora snapped. 'Just get dressed and be downstairs in two minutes. Don't keep me waiting.' She turned on her heel and left the room. Lissie stood, trembling and confused. Why did her mam never take the trouble to explain what was happening?

Shivering, she pulled the chamber pot from under her bed. A cloud of steam escaped from under her bare bottom as hot pee streamed into the pot. The bedroom was freezing cold. She put on her grey pinafore and her socks and boots, and feeling thoroughly miserable and cold, she went to get a cardigan from the cupboard that held her few items of clothing.

Her eyes widened in surprise. The cupboard was empty. Yesterday it had contained two pairs of knickers, a liberty bodice, a grubby cardigan, a clean smock and her old grey frock. Perhaps her mam was intending to do a big wash, make everything nice and clean for Christmas. It was a Monday, and Nelly and the other women in the yard always washed on Mondays. She ran downstairs.

'Are you getting ready for Christmas?' Lissie asked as she entered the kitchen.

Dora pursed her pale, pinched lips and shook her head. 'Get that into you,' she said, shoving a plate with a slice of bread and butter on it across the table. She poured two cups of tea and topped them with milk. Then setting one down at Lissie's elbow, she stood by the sink to drink her own. 'Don't take all day,' she warned.

'Why have we got up so early?'

'You'll see. Now get a move on.'

Whilst Lissie ate her bread and sipped her tea, Dora stood in front of the mirror, and ignoring her collection of creams, face powder and rouge, she scraped back her hair so that it was flat to her head, all the pretty tendrils that she usually left dangling now fastened into a severe bun.

Curious, Lissie looked on. Her mam didn't look at all like she usually did when she was going out. Then she noticed that instead of wearing one of her fancy new outfits she had on the same dress that she had worn the day they had left the cottage, and her dad.

'Hurry up,' said Dora, putting on her old green coat and a battered cloche.

'Why aren't you wearing your new cape and the hat with feathers?'

Dora ignored the question and said, 'Put your coat on.'

Lissie unhooked her coat from behind the door. The sleeves were too short and it barely buttoned, the new grey pinafore dress Dora had bought her a week ago hanging well below the coat's hem. Nelly had knitted her a pink woolly bonnet and she pulled it out of her coat pocket and put it on.

'Where are we going?' Anxiety made Lissie's voice squeak. 'Are we leaving Jed?'

Dora clamped her lips together and gave an imperceptible shake of her head. Lissie thought she looked as though she might cry. Presuming that the argument they'd had the previous night had not ended in sloppy kisses and that her mam was still mad with Jed, Lissie attempted to delay their departure, not so much for her mam's sake, but her own. She needed time to think.

'I need a pee,' she said, heading for the stairs. 'I'll use the po.'

'Oh, for God's sake,' Dora moaned.

Staring out of her bedroom window at the snow-covered yard, Lissie considered what to do. If her mam was leaving Jed then it meant that she, Lissie, was leaving Emmy and the Jacksons. Emmy would be expecting her to call for her like she always did once she was up and dressed and had eaten her breakfast, but it was too early for school. Her heart lurched. Memories of leaving the cottage and her dad came surging back, the hurried bundling of clothes into bags and her mam taking the money from Dad's pockets. But this time there were no packed bags. No, they weren't leaving, she decided. Mam would never leave her new dresses and hats behind.

Then suddenly Lissie thought of another reason for making an early morning journey. She almost fell down the stairs.

'Are we going back to my dad?'

'Don't be stupid,' Dora snarled, picking up a bulging cotton bag and going to the door. 'Now come on, we've got to get moving.'

They stepped outside, Lissie thinking that the grimy yard looked pretty under the blanket of white crystals. Even the rubbish by the privy's wall had taken on a new mysterious shape. She looked up. The stars had disappeared and streaks of yellow were lighting the grey sky. Still utterly mystified as to where they were going, she trudged after her mother, treading her feet into the imprints Dora's boots made in the snow. At the neck of the passage Lissie halted.

'I don't want to go,' she said to Dora's back.

Dora swung round. 'It's not up to you.' She grabbed hold of Lissie's wrist and yanked it. 'You've got to go whether you like it or not.'

'But where?' cried Lissie. 'Tell me where we're going.' She tried to pull free but she was no match for Dora.

In silence they scurried up the passage and out into the now familiar streets. Men in flat caps and thick jackets, and women in shawls and turbans were trudging along the streets that were thick with blackened slush and horse dung.

An eerie glow from the gas lamps cast a pale, yellow light over the dirty snow that muffled their footsteps. They walked without talking, the stillness of the morning suddenly shattered as first one and then another mill hooter sounded its early morning wail. Lissie reckoned it must be six o'clock.

Dora didn't walk up Crag Lane into High Street as Lissie had expected. Instead, she led her in the opposite direction through the narrow streets into South Gate, a road unfamiliar to Lissie. Where were they going?

They came to a halt at the side of the road, Dora keeping her eyes peeled in the direction of the village. Lissie jigged up and down. Her feet were freezing.

'What are we doing?' she asked, fear and consternation making her voice wobble.

'Waiting for a lift,' Dora replied, as though it were something they did every morning.

'A lift to where?'

'You'll see.' Dora's voice sounded tight and her expression was agitated.

'I should be going to school. Emmy won't know where I am if I—'

The rumbling of an engine made Dora step off the verge, her arm outstretched as a lorry came into view. The driver slowed to a stop, the slush in the road splattering Dora's boots. 'Are you going by way of Little Horton?' she asked after he had wound down the cab window.

'Aye, are you needin' a lift?'

'Please.' She gave him her warmest smile then lifted Lissie up into the cab and climbed in after her. 'I couldn't get back last night because of the snow,' she said as the driver set the lorry into motion. 'We had to stay at my sister's but I need to get back in time for work.'

More lies, thought Lissie. How did her mam manage to think them all up?

'Where is it you work?' the driver asked as he steered the lorry carefully over patches of ice and thick slush.

'The workhouse. I do the cooking.' She giggled mischievously. 'If I don't get there in time to make their porridge there'll be ructions.'

'From what I've heard the poor buggers suffer enough wi'out havin' to go wi'out their breakfast,' the driver said. He glanced from the road to Dora then to Lissie. 'What about her? What do you wi' her when you're cookin?'

'She stays with a friend and then she goes to school.'

Lissie was amazed at how plausible her mam sounded, yet there wasn't a grain of truth in anything that came out of her mouth. She wanted to tell the lorry driver that it was all lies, but experience told her it would be foolhardy. She shrank into her coat and tried not to think about what would happen next.

Dora and the driver chatted about the awful weather as he negotiated the lorry carefully along the road, the hazardous conditions slowing the journey.

'Here we are then,' the driver said, bringing the lorry to a halt outside a pair of huge iron gates. 'Go an' feed the poor sods, an' mek that porridge a bit thicker today. Do it as a favour to me for givin' you a lift.'

'I will,' Dora chirped as she climbed down to the road. 'Come on, Lissie. Don't keep the kind man waiting.' Lissie slid reluctantly off the seat and into Dora's arms. 'Thanks again,' Dora called out as the lorry pulled away.

'Where are we? What's this place?' Lissie peered through the gaps in the gate at the large L-shaped building at the top of a long driveway.

'I've got to speak to a lady here,' Dora said, 'and whilst I'm talking to her you can sit and wait for me.' She opened the gate and set off briskly up the gravelled driveway. Lissie struggled to keep up.

'What lady?' Getting no answer, Lissie eyed the arched windows and the large front door. It was a very big house and the lady who lived here must have a lot of money and a very big family to fill it, thought Lissie. She wondered how her mam knew a lady who lived in such a grand house.

When they reached the door, Dora shifted the bulging bag from one hand to the other then pulled the chain on a shiny brass bell. It pealed musically. Lissie liked the sound of it. Stretching out her hand, she would have rung it again if Dora hadn't slapped her arm. Lissie looked at the bag and wondered what was in it. Was her mam going to sell the lady something? She and Jed were always talking about selling things.

A tall, thin girl with squinty eyes and a sore red nose opened the door. She looked unhappy. 'May I help you?' she said thickly. Green snot trickled from one nostril onto her top lip and she wiped it on the cuff of her striped grey dress. It left behind a shiny, wet smear and Lissie couldn't take her eyes off it even though it made her feel sick.

'I'd like to speak to the superintendent,' Dora said importantly. Lissie heard the new word and liked the sound of it: sooperintendant. She collected words she hadn't heard before just in case she might need to use them one day.

The girl stood back to allow them to step inside. 'Wait here,' she said, indicating two chairs in a large panelled hallway. They sat down, Dora fidgeting with her hat then brushing fluff off her coat.

'Who's she?' Lissie whispered as the girl turned a corner at the far end of the hallway from where they were sitting.

'How should I know? Don't keep asking questions.'

They waited, Dora sighing and getting more fidgety by the minute. *She's getting angry*, Lissie told herself, and thinking it wise to do as she was told, she gazed about the hallway. Large pictures of men with whiskers hung on the walls along with a brass plaque with lots of writing on it, but it was too far away for Lissie to read the words. The minutes ticked by.

Bored and confused, Lissie threw caution to the wind. 'Are we waiting for the sooperintendant?'

Dora grasped Lissie's wrist, and squeezing it until it burned, she hissed, 'Not another word, or else I'll give you the hiding of your life.' After that the silence was only broken by the tutting of Dora's tongue and her irritated sighs.

'What on earth's keeping them,' she muttered after what seemed to Lissie to be almost an hour.

The girl reappeared. 'Matron will see you now,' she said before sniffing snot noisily back up her nose.

Dora sprang to her feet. 'You wait here and keep quiet,' she snapped.

Lena Todd, born and reared in the workhouse and now skivvying for the matron looked pityingly at Lissie before disappearing round the corner with Dora hot on her heels. Lissie sat and drummed her heels against the chair legs. If her mam didn't hurry up, they'd not be back in Hart Lane in time for her to call for Emmy and go to school.

To pass the time she silently went over her lines for the nativity. Miss Simms had congratulated both her and Emmy on how well they had performed at the last rehearsal. 'You'll do the school proud,' she had said before turning to Shirley Higginbottom and reprimanding her for making nasty noises as they'd played their parts. Shirley had steered clear of Lissie after the plait tugging incident but it hadn't deterred her from showing her disapproval.

Lost in the memory of Miss Simms' praise, Lissie didn't immediately see her mother come back round the corner. When she did, she almost fell off the chair as Dora barged down the hallway and raced for the door. Running for all she was worth, she yanked the door open, slammed it behind her and was gone.

Lissie jumped to her feet. 'Mam! Mam! Wait for me.'

10

'What are we going to do with her?'

'Well, we can hardly turn the child out. She appears to have no idea where she is or why she's here.' Violet Smith, the matron of the children's wing in Little Horton Workhouse, threw up her hands in consternation. Constance Briggs, the under-matron, looked equally perplexed.

'It's most inappropriate, most inappropriate,' Victor Smith blustered, his whiskers twitching as he glared at his wife.

'Don't look at me in that accusing way,' Violet snapped. 'I followed the rules to the letter as I always do in cases like this. I listened to what the woman had to say, told her to take the child and go back home and that when we had carried out our investigation into the child's background, we would then make a decision as to whether or not to take her in.'

'Then you let her scarper, leaving the child behind,' Victor scoffed.

'How was I to know she'd just run off?' Violet's cheeks flamed. 'The scheming hussy told me she had taken the child's mother into her home as an act of charity. She said the child's mother was running away from a violent husband and had nowhere to go. It was only meant to be for a night or two but then the mother took ill and died.'

'The child told me that *that* woman was her mam,' Constance interjected.

'And the story she told you, Violet, was absolute poppycock,' Victor scorned.

'I wasn't to know that,' his wife protested. 'I did say we'd visit to verify the story before we took action.' Violet stamped her foot in righteous indignation.

'What did you say the woman called herself?' Victor barked.

Violet flushed. 'Smith,' she said. 'Florence Smith. She gave me the address of a rooming house in Manningham Lane in Bradford but said that she was being evicted at the end of the week. That she'd got herself a live-in position in Birmingham and couldn't possibly take the child with her.'

'Piffle and balderdash,' Victor snorted. 'You were had, Violet. You were had.'

To cover her embarrassment, Violet turned to Constance. 'Where is the child now, Connie?'

'Still sitting in the hall. I didn't know what to do with her till I'd spoken to you. I must say I was quite taken aback when Lena came and told me the little girl was still there when she went to answer the door to Reverend Soames.'

At the mention of one of the workhouse governors, Victor jumped. 'My good God. I'd forgotten all about him. I left him inspecting the men's workshop. I'd better get back to him.' Victor charged out of the room, quite light on his feet for a man of his age and considerable girth.

Violet wrung her hands. She detested making mistakes. *But I didn't make one,* she told herself, unwilling to admit that Dora had made her look a fool. She heaved her ample bosom up with her forearm and said, 'Bring the girl to me, Connie. I'll get her to do some straight talking.'

Connie hurried from the room, relieved that she'd got off lightly. Being caught in the crossfire that so often erupted between the matron and the master was one of the more unpleasant sides to working in the orphanage.

Lissie looked up hopefully when she heard Connie's footsteps.

Poor little mite, thought Connie as she approached her. 'You're to come with me, love.' The small, slender woman held out her hand. Her lips curved into a gentle smile. They were thin lips set in a swarthy little face, and her twinkling eyes were like currants. She made Lissie think of the little wren that lived in the garden at the cottage. Sensing kindness, Lissie took her hand.

Her chest tight, her cheeks tearstained and her feet like lead, Lissie let the small woman wearing a voluminous white apron over a black dress take her to the matron's office. She wondered if she should feel afraid, but the numbness that had set in whilst she had been sitting alone in the hall didn't allow her to feel anything other than bewilderment.

The first thing Lissie saw when she entered the matron's office was Dora's bulging canvas bag. She stared at it thinking the large lady with the fleshy face and very big titties must have bought what was in it. The lady also wore a white apron, and a funny white cap covered her streaky grey hair.

'Now child, I want you to answer me honestly,' Violet said from her chair behind a large leather-topped desk.

Lissie bit her lip and nodded. She would have liked to ask if she could go to the lavatory. She clenched her small thighs together.

'Give me your name and the place you were living before you came here.'

'Lissie Fairweather, number one Hart Lane. Emmy lives at number five.'

Violet's eyebrows shot up. 'And who pray is Emmy?'

'She's my friend, Emmy Jackson. We go to the National school together.'

'And the lady who brought you here this morning? What is her name and where does she live?'

'Dora Fairweather, and she lives in the same house as me with Jed Fletcher.'

'Is he your father?'

'No!' Lissie protested. 'My dad's Tom Fairweather – but I don't know where he is now. He got hurt and me and my mam came to Bradford.' She started to cry, fat tears rolling down her cheeks and her heart thudding. She mustn't tell the fat lady any more about her dad. She might blame her for not helping him when he was bleeding and send for the police. Her mam had said they could go to prison. Was this a prison? Had her mam escaped and left her there to take the blame? A violent shudder wobbled her so much that the birdy woman stepped close and placed her hands gently on Lissie's shoulders to steady her.

Violet gave a heavy sigh. 'Take her to the schoolroom, Connie. We'll keep her for the time being until we've investigated this whole sorry mess.'

'You'll like the other girls,' Connie said as they walked down a long dim corridor. 'Today they're doing their tasks. You can join in whilst we wait to find out if you're to stay with us.'

Lissie stopped in her tracks. Stay here in this place that smelled of old stew and a sour smell she couldn't name? 'But I've got to go back home to call for Emmy and go to school,' Lissie blurted. 'Nelly won't know where I am and her and Bill'll be worried.' Her voice had risen an octave as she delivered the garbled information. None of which made any sense to Connie, but she stored it to tell Matron.

'Not today, love. We'll keep you here till things get sorted.'

What is there to sort? Lissie thought. *All they have to do is take me back home so that I can go to school with Emmy.* Her bladder felt uncomfortably full. 'I need a pee,' she said.

Connie halted outside one of the many doors lining the corridor. 'In there,' she said, opening a brown painted door. Lissie stepped inside, her eyes boggling at the row of lavatories in little cubicles on one side of the room and a row of sinks on the other. In the nearest cubicle Lissie pulled down her knickers and sat on the pot and as she peed, she tried to think of what she should do next but nothing came to mind. She was stuck in this place and nobody but Dora knew she was here. She stayed sitting on the lavatory until her bottom felt chilly. Connie's voice asking, 'Are you all right in there?' brought her back to reality.

Out in the corridor they walked a little further then came to a stop outside another door. Connie tapped then pushed it open. 'A new pupil for you, Miss Scroggins,' she called out to the tall, heavily built woman standing behind a desk on a raised platform. Miss Scroggins looked sourly at Lissie and Lissie's heart sank.

Fifteen or so pairs of eyes of all shapes and colours stared at Lissie, and she stared back. The girls, some younger and some older than herself, were clustered round long tables all busily doing a variety of tasks. At the nearest table the girls were pinning safety pins onto small cards, their fingers still for a moment as they appraised the newcomer until Miss Scroggins' sharp reprimand had them nimbly continuing with their work.

Lissie hung her head and focussed her eyes on the floor and its herringbone pattern of shiny wood blocks. Her dad would have liked it, she thought. A yearning to be with him again brought tears to her eyes and a painful tightness in her chest.

'I'll leave you in the care of Miss Scroggins,' Connie said softly, giving Lissie's shoulder a gentle squeeze before she left the room. Lissie desperately wanted to go with her.

'Name?' Miss Scroggins' grating voice made Lissie look up into gimlet eyes of an indeterminate colour that seemed to pierce her very soul.

'Lissie Fairweather.' Her voice barely above a whisper and her heart fluttering uncomfortably, she prayed for the floor to open up and swallow her.

'Speak up, girl. Don't dither.'

Lissie repeated her name louder. A girl at the table with the pins giggled. Miss Scroggins swung round and barked, 'Mary Lumb, you're in danger of aggravating me.' Mary quickly went back to threading safety pins on a card but not before she'd given Lissie a mischievous grin. Lissie wanted to return the grin but she didn't dare.

'You can work with these girls this morning,' Miss Scroggins said, giving Lissie a shove towards the table with the pins on. Lissie tottered nervously.

'Come an' stand by me,' Mary invited, 'I'll show you what to do.'

'Why are we doing this?' Lissie asked ten minutes later as her fingers fumbled to attach safety pins of different sizes to a small, stiff card.

'To earn money for us keep,' Mary replied. 'They get tuppence a gross for 'em. Sometimes it's hooks an' eyes or buttons, but pins are the easiest.'

'Do you stay here all the time?' Lissie whispered to Mary.

'Tell you later,' Mary whispered back as Miss Scroggins bore down on them barking, 'No more gossiping. Get on with your work.'

At midday the girls trooped into a long room that smelled of stale food and disinfectant. On the walls were pictures of a man with a bushy beard and thick moustache and another of a fat lady with a lace headdress: Lissie knew they were King Edward and Queen Victoria. She sat down next to Mary at one of the long tables and an older girl clattered tin dishes in front of them whilst another girl ladled out a lumpy, greyish-looking liquid. By now Lissie was starving, and although the stew was watery and tasteless, she gobbled it down. Again, under Miss Scroggins' beady eye they were not allowed to talk. Lissie was disappointed because a thousand questions were buzzing inside her head.

It wasn't until bedtime that she got to ask them. She'd lined up with the girls, taking her turn to use the lavatory and wash at the sink and after that she had followed them upstairs into another large room where black iron bedsteads were arranged at regimented intervals along the bare floorboards, five beds in each of the three rows.

A scrawny young woman limped into the room, the heavy black boot on her left foot clumping as she made her way over to Lissie. She handed her an off-white flat, stiff piece of cloth. 'This is your nightie, an' this is your bed,' she said, indicating the bed nearest the door. Very low and narrow, and covered with a thin washed-out blanket on top of a white sheet, it didn't look very inviting.

'Ooh, goody,' cried Mary, half-in and half-out of her striped grey dress. 'You're sleeping next to me.'

Lissie managed a little smile. She'd already decided she liked Mary, but that didn't mean she wanted to sleep in the bed next to hers. She wanted to go back to Hart Lane, to Emmy and the Jacksons, or better still the cottage and her dad.

'Hurry up now before Miss Scroggins comes.' The girl with the clubfoot glanced nervously at the door.

'All right, Maude, keep your hair on,' a voice cried as a flurry of motion swept the dormitory. Nightdresses replaced grey striped dresses that were then folded and put on chairs between the beds. Boots were placed neatly at the foot of each bed.

Feeling slightly dazed, Lissie slowly followed suit. The nightdress was stiff and scratchy and far too long. As each girl finished undressing and folding her clothes she stood to attention at the side of her bed.

'Get a move on,' Mary hissed. 'You don't want old Scroggy to catch you.' She had no sooner spoken than the tartar strode into the dormitory. A sudden hush fell as all eyes were trained on Miss Scroggins – all but Lissie's. She was bent over unlacing her boots. A hard smack across her backside brought her upright.

'I see we have inherited a dawdler,' Miss Scroggins snarled, fixing her malevolent gaze on Lissie.

Lissie quailed. She was used to the pain that Dora's flailing hands regularly inflicted, but to be slapped by a stranger was beyond her experience. She fell to her knees, trembling and sobbing, 'I want to go home!'

A cold, hard hand grasped her by the back of her neck, jerking her to her feet.

Fourteen pairs of eyes, some sympathetic and others glittering spitefully, watched in anticipation for the result of what such flagrant disregard to the rules might bring.

Slap! Lissie wailed as Miss Scroggins delivered another hefty smack to her bottom. 'Stop that noise this instant and stand by your bed, you silly girl.'

Lissie scurried to the far side of her bed, tripping on the hem of her nightie. She thought she heard someone giggle. Then she stood with her head bowed as Miss Scroggins piously spouted, 'God keep us safe this night, secure from all our fears...' and as the girls joined in, Lissie closed her ears. God wasn't keeping her secure from all her fears.

The girls tumbled into their beds and Maude dowsed the lights as Miss Scroggins marched from the room. 'No talking,' Maude advised before she left.

Lissie lay between the rough sheets, her head pounding and her bottom stinging. She was wiping her tears on the edge of the sheet when she felt a warm, little body sliding into the bed. An arm was placed round her and she heard Mary whisper, 'Don't cry. Scroggy's not worth it.' Lissie's tears fell all the faster.

'You'll get used to it in time,' Mary continued, 'an' you han't to let it bother you 'cos when that rotten bitch dies, she'll burn in hell.'

Lissie gulped back her sobs and cuddled up to Mary. After a while her heartbeat slowed and she felt able to speak. 'Thanks,' she whispered. 'I'm not crying 'cos she hit me. My mam does it all the time. I'm crying 'cos I don't want to stay here.'

'But you have to when you don't have a mam or dad to take care o' you,' Mary said. 'You're too young to look after yourself.'

'I have a mam,' Lissie said. 'She's not very nice an' doesn't look after me properly, not like Nelly does. She looks after Emmy and her brothers and sister, and she looks after me.'

'Then why are you here?'

'I don't know. Why are you here?'

'I've allus been here. I wa' born here. I've never had a mam an' dad an' I've never lived anywhere else.'

Lissie's heart ached for Mary.

By now most of the girls were having whispered conversations. A voice from somewhere beyond Lissie's bed hissed, 'Hey, Lissie, are your mam an' dad dead?'

Lissie froze. Maybe her dad was dead. Perhaps that was why he hadn't come and found her.

'Lucy's talking to you,' said Mary, giving her a nudge. By now, Lucy had crept from her own bed onto Mary's empty bed, and in seconds the other girls joined her. Clustered like little white ghosts, they all wanted to find out about the new girl.

'My mam's not dead,' Lissie said. 'She brought me here then ran away.'

'Ooh, the rotten thing,' a little voice moaned.

'Where do you come from 'cos you don't talk like us?' asked

Lucy, having delegated herself as spokeswoman. Lissie reckoned Lucy was about fourteen.

'Derbyshire,' she replied. That meant nothing to the majority of the girls, many of whom had never been more than a mile from the workhouse in all their lives, Sunday church and a walk into the village now and then being the full extent of their world.

'Did you say you had a dad?' Lucy continued her interrogation. 'Where is he?'

'I think he's still in Derbyshire or...' Lissie paused, and for the first time ever she admitted her worst thought. 'He might be dead.' Having said the words out loud she began to shake and Mary put her arms round her.

'Don't let it upset you. Most of us don't have dads – or mams for that matter.'

'I have a mammy an' a daddy, but Matron says they're too drunk to look after me,' a small girl lisped.

'Ne'er mind, Jenny, you're better off in here,' said Lucy, reaching out and ruffling the little girl's blonde curls then directing her words to Lissie. 'My mam's in the looney bin an' I haven't seen her since I was six, an' the man she said was my dad got killed in the pit. He's still down there 'cos they never dug him out.'

This confidence that many of them had heard before encouraged a few of the other girls to tell their story, but most of them had nothing to tell having been left in the orphanage as babies. As Lissie listened to their tales, she began to feel almost privileged. She had spent seven wonderful years with her lovely dad, years she would never forget and when she had been taken from him, she'd had the love and friendship of Emmy and her family.

Footsteps outside the door sent the girls scurrying back to their beds. By the time Miss Scroggins peered into the room all she could hear was the slow, steady breathing of girls pretending to be asleep. Her duty was done for the day.

Lissie lay awake long after Mary had fallen asleep. She was fairly sure that her mam wouldn't come back for her, and as she resigned herself to living in the orphanage Lissie thought of Emmy and the nativity. She felt sad at not being there to play her part. Emmy's Joseph had lost his Mary, but she had found another Mary. Dwelling on that warm thought and exhausted by the unusual events of the day, Lissie fell into a deep sleep.

11

A bell was jangling and it woke Lissie with a start. Bare feet slapped the floor, calico nightdresses rustled, and lazy yawns and whispers had her wondering where on earth she was.

'Time to get up,' Mary said, giving her a gentle shake. Lissie opened her eyes to see the girls lining up at the door still wearing their nighties. Feeling utterly befuddled, she crawled out of bed, her feet tingling on the cold floor as, with Mary at her elbow, she joined the line.

'Where are we going?'

'To get washed. Cleanliness is Godliness according to Scroggy.'

Maude appeared in the open doorway looking rather dishevelled and her squinting eyes bleary. 'Walk in line, an' no talking,' she said sleepily.

The girls filed along the landing and down the stairs to the washroom, taking it in turn to use the lavatories and then the sinks. The water that splashed out of the taps was chilly and Lissie shivered as she sluiced her hands and face. Then it was back up to the dormitory to get dressed. Someone had placed a grey striped dress on her bed and she put it on. She wondered what had happened to the bulging bag Dora had left behind, for now she was sure that it had contained her clothes. That was why her cupboard in the bedroom at Hart Lane had been empty.

When the girls were all dressed, Maude marched them down to the long room where they had eaten their stew the day before. A tired-looking woman the girls called Florry slopped porridge into bowls and whilst they were eating Miss Scroggins sauntered between the tables, her gimlet eyes looking to find fault. She found it in Lissie's hair.

'Before you enter my classroom, you'd better do something with this.' She tugged on Lissie's long, black tresses. 'Fasten it back or I'll cut it off.'

Lissie almost choked on a mouthful of porridge.

'I'll plait it for you,' Lucy offered when Miss Scroggins was out of earshot. 'If I don't, she'll hack it all off. Look what she did to poor Maisie.' She nodded at a little girl whose hair was chopped to her scalp. Lissie drew a sharp breath.

Up in the dormitory Lucy bundled Lissie's hair into two thick plaits then tied them with a bit of string Mary had in her pocket, and hopeful of passing Miss Scroggins' scrutiny, Lissie trooped with the others down to the room with the herringbone floor. This morning the tables were empty.

Miss Scroggins led the proceedings with a long, tedious prayer that ended with the girls giving thanks to God and the matron and the master for the tender care provided by the workhouse to the poor orphans of the parish. Cynically, Lissie thought that 'tender care' was taking things a bit too far.

After that they had lessons in sums, reading and writing. Lissie, adept in all three subjects for her age, enjoyed the work and did her best. Ida Scroggins deliberately hid her admiration for the neat copies Lissie produced and instead found fault with her handwriting, berating her roundly in front of the class. Lissie swallowed her disappointment and choked back her tears. When the lessons ended Miss Scroggins barked, 'Bridget Flaherty, collect the books.'

A tall girl with bright ginger hair strutted round the room picking up the books, her sneering expression seeming to say she wasn't in the least intimidated by the awful teacher. When she came to Lissie's table she gave her a sympathetic smile.

'She has it in for you,' Lucy said as they went down for their midday meal.

'Yeah, an' we know why,' Mary intervened. 'It's 'cos you're really pretty. She always picks on the pretty girls. You watch. She leaves fat, ugly Molly alone, an' Vera with the harelip, an' she never has a go at them that God din't bless wi' bonny faces when he made 'em.' A low rumble of agreement came from the girls who were listening.

'But I can't help what I look like,' Lissie said. 'I've always looked like this.'

'So have I, thanks to me ma.' Bridget's green eyes flashed and her creamy complexion reddened with rage. 'Me ma wa' Irish an' had flamin' red hair, an Scroggy never misses a trick calling me carrots an' askin' me which bog I wa' born in. The on'y reason she din't pick on me this morning was because you were there.' She nudged Lissie in a friendly way. 'Thanks for gettin' her off me back.'

Lissie gave Bridget an impish grin. Like Lucy, she was one of the older girls and neither of them seemed afraid of breaking the no-talking rule as they walked to the dining room. Maude, who was in charge, let them get away with it.

'Where's your mam now?' Lissie asked Bridget, feeling that she should make some sort of response.

'Died of the drink when I wa' little so they brought me here,' Bridget said, her tone matter-of-fact as they filed into the dining room for another dish of greasy, meatless broth.

Miss Scroggins appeared and the girls ate in silence, and as Lissie emptied her dish she pondered on Lucy's and Bridget's sad lives. *I'm seven now. Will I still be here when I'm fourteen?* The broth turned sour in her mouth.

It had rained on and off for most of the morning but in the afternoon the sun shone brightly. Clustered round the worktables, the girls carried out their tasks while Miss Scroggins patrolled the room, a wooden ruler in her hand. The work the girls were doing was outsourced from garment and haberdashery factories in Bradford. Sorting and stitching sets of buttons or hooking safety pins on to cards was laborious tedious work but the girls' nimble fingers were suited to the job. This form of cheap labour was hugely beneficial for the factory owners and the money the girls earned went into the workhouse's coffers.

Lissie was dutifully pinning safety pins of different sizes through the nine holes in a little stiff card, a big one in the top hole and then down in size to the smallest in the bottom hole. She thought she was doing rather well, but sadly Miss Scroggins thought differently.

'Speed up!' She rapped the top of Lissie's head then lifted one of the completed cards for inspection. Two of the pins were in the wrong order.

Slap! The ruler in the tyrant's hand whacked the back of Lissie's right hand.

'Ouch!' Lissie pressed her stinging knuckles to her mouth.

Miss Scroggins smiled spitefully. 'That will teach you to take more care.'

'That's not fair. She's on'y new,' Bridget shouted from her place at the table where they were sewing hooks and eyes or buttons onto cards with fine white thread. Miss Scroggins swung round, brandishing the ruler. A ripple of fear mixed with anger surged through the room and might have resulted in chaos had the door not opened and Matron bustled in, stiff as starch in her voluminous white apron. Maude dithered behind her.

'Ah, Miss Scroggins, allow me to interrupt you. I see the girls are hard at work but now that the rain has washed most of the snow off the yard and the sun is shining, I've instructed Maude to take them outside.'

Ida Scroggins pasted a smile on her face and hid the ruler in the folds of her skirt. Matron did not approve of corporal punishment, but then she didn't have to deal with a bunch of unruly guttersnipes. 'Thank you, Matron. Girls, you may stand.'

The sigh of relief that had rushed through the room at Matron's timely arrival now turned to gasps of excitement – and victory. Scroggy had been stopped in her tracks.

'Right, girls, are you ready for your airin'?' This was the term Maude used for the break of fifteen minutes in the morning and again in the afternoon. She led them out into an enclosed yard, and leaving them to it, she sneaked off round the corner for a cigarette.

'Chain Tig,' Lucy announced. 'Bags I be first catcher.'

Lissie ran with the rest of the girls, hallooing like them at the top of her voice, splashing through the puddles and dodging this way and that until Lucy caught her. She joined the long chain, clasping Mary's waist as they tore round the yard, quite forgetting that her knuckles were red and swollen.

Fifteen minutes flew by all too soon and Maude, her craving for tobacco appeased, called them back into line and marched them indoors to continue their tedious tasks.

Days went by, one day very much like another: prayers, lessons, airings in the yard, and tasks. Lissie followed the routine as best she could, making light of the constant reprimands for breaking the rules; there was nothing else for it. She wasn't entirely unhappy because the friends she had made, inured by now to making the best of their situation, still managed to have fun whenever they got a chance. Even so, Lissie still missed Emmy, and the warm affection of Nelly and Bill. She didn't miss her mam and Jed one bit.

On Friday afternoon the girls were gathered in the classroom, the long tables cleared of everything but piles of brightly coloured scraps of material that the older girls had cut into short, narrow rectangles. Beside them were spools of different coloured thread, pincushions and needles.

'This is the best bit of the week,' Mary whispered.

Lissie looked at her expectantly then understood as Miss Scroggins put on her hat and bade them good day. The door opened and in came Connie Briggs. 'Good day to you, Miss Scroggins, enjoy your weekend,' she said tersely, and turning to address the girls, her face wreathed in a warm smile, she asked, 'And how are we today? All happy and waiting to hear what happens to Jo, I trust?'

The girls nodded eagerly as they chorused, 'Yes, Mrs Briggs.' Lissie wondered who Jo was. She soon found out.

Under Connie's instructions, each girl was equipped with a few rectangles of cloth and a needle and thread, and as they began to carefully stitch the pieces together Connie sat down and opened her book. Lissie soon got the hang of what to do and as she joined a red piece to a blue piece then a green one, she listened to Connie's soft, lilting voice unfold the adventures of Jo March and her sisters. The afternoon came to a close all too quickly.

'Well done, Lissie,' Connie said as she checked the results of the girls' labours.

'My dad taught me how to sew,' she replied, almost whispering the words.

Connie smiled fondly. 'He did a good job.' She turned to the class. 'You have all worked very well today. Now, let's clear things away because I have something exciting to tell you.'

When the room was tidy the girls stood waiting for what she

was about to say. They knew it would be something nice, for Mrs Briggs was always the bearer of good news. She frequently intervened if she considered the punishments doled out by Ida Scroggins too extreme, and she consistently made her time spent with the girls as pleasant as possible.

Seeing she had their full attention, she announced, 'Matron has organised a treat for us as it's Christmas next week. She has invited the guardians to attend a little celebration on Tuesday at which you will also be guests. There will be a high tea of savouries, cakes, and jellies and blancmange.' She paused, smiling at the round eyes, open mouths and glowing faces. 'Now, isn't that something to look forward to?'

The girls returned her smile and chorused, 'Ooh, yes, Mrs Briggs.'

* * *

'We allus go to church on Sunday,' Mary informed Lissie as she crawled out of bed ready to join the line at the door. She didn't feel like getting washed and wished she could have stayed under her blanket to continue the lovely dream she'd had about her dad. She'd been in the cottage with him hanging glistening baubles and shiny tinsel on the little fir tree they always decorated for Christmas.

After breakfast, Maude came into the dormitory and issued Lissie with a grey coat and beret. The coat dwarfed her and she looked in dismay at Mary who was already wearing her coat.

'I feel daft in this,' said Lissie, her bottom lip wobbling.

'Aye an' you look daft,' Bridget said, noting the dangling sleeves and the hemline that swept the top of Lissie's boots. Bridget's remark hurt Lissie. She was usually kind.

Then, Bridget's eyes ranging the line of girls assembling at the door, she pounced. 'Do a swap with Polly,' she cried, pulling a girl who was squeezed into a coat two sizes too small for her out of the line. Lissie could have hugged Bridget. She silently chided herself for thinking unkind thoughts about the beautiful girl with the flaming red hair. Polly willingly exchanged coats, and no longer feeling foolish, Lissie pulled on her beret. Maude led them down-stairs and out to the front of the building.

This was Lissie's first time leaving the workhouse from this door, and as she gazed down the driveway it brought back memo-ries of Dora hurrying her up it then abandoning her in the hallway. She wondered where Dora was now.

It was a bright, crisp December morning, the pavements rimed with thick frost and the bare branches of trees stark against a clear blue sky. Like a long grey crocodile, the girls trooped through the streets to Little Horton Lane, Mr and Mrs Smith, the superinten-dent and the matron, walking at the head of the column and Connie Briggs behind them. The superintendent raised his bowler hat whenever he saw a lady, and Matron nodded and smiled at the people they met on the way. Lissie and Mary held hands, giggling when they skidded on a patch of ice and puffing their breath so that it clouded in front of their faces. Lissie felt an air of freedom for the first time in days.

Behind the line of girls came the boys from the workhouse. Lucy and Bridget, at the rear of the line, cast frequent glances over their shoulders in the hope of catching the eye of a good-looking boy. This was the only contact they had with the opposite sex and the opportunity was too good to miss. When their master wasn't looking, a tall boy with a shock of black curly hair and a cheeky grin blew Bridget a kiss. She giggled and blew one back.

'You're going to get us into trouble,' Lucy warned, at the same time discounting her own advice as she winked back at a boy with pale, fair hair.

'Don't care if I do,' Bridget scoffed, and who could blame her? At fourteen years of age she knew how narrow her own and Lucy's lives were, and she saw no harm in experimenting before next summer when they would leave the orphanage to go into service.

All Saints Church in Little Horton, a mellow stone edifice with a tall spire and long, arched windows, took Lissie's breath away. It was much bigger than the little chapel in Thorne that she and her dad had gone to most Sundays. Her dad had said you didn't need to go every Sunday because God was everywhere, in the woods and fields and in every tree and flower, and as Lissie filed into the cloistral quiet of the church, she thought He must surely be here. Gazing up at the vaulted roof then sliding into a long, oak pew with Mary on one side and Polly on the other, she breathed in the mysterious smell of incense and burning candles. She felt at peace.

Then, her eyes roaming the splendour all around her, she saw the crib scene to one side of the altar and her heart sank. *Oh, Dad, I wish you were here to see this.* Memories flooded her mind. Each Christmas her dad had made a small stable and a manger for the little chapel in Thorne, and Lissie had helped spread the straw and put the small porcelain shepherds and kings and Joseph and Mary inside. But it had been nothing compared to what she now saw.

In a stable large enough to hold real people, several almost-life-size plaster figures worshipped round a manger, the kings resplendent in red and gold cloaks and tall glittering crowns. Lissie thought they made the shepherds and Joseph look quite drab, but Mary was beautiful in her dark blue robe and white dress. *I really wanted to be Mary in the nativity,* she thought, *and I would have been if my mam hadn't given me away.*

Lissie started to cry. Big fat tears rolled silently down her cheeks but she couldn't prevent her shoulders from heaving or suppress her sniffles.

'What's up?' Mary whispered anxiously. 'Why are you crying?'

'I don't know,' Lissie whispered back. It was easier to say that than to tell her friend that she was crying for all she had loved and lost; that no matter how kind Mary and Bridget and Lucy and the other girls were, they could never make up for the loss of her dad and Emmy and Nelly and Bill, and to be the very best Mary that Miss Simms had ever seen.

12

On Tuesday morning, the day of the special tea for the governors and the girls, Miss Scroggins handed out polishing cloths and tins of floor polish. Lissie stood in line, unsure what she would be expected to do with the yellow duster, but the girls who knew what would happen next suppressed groans, unsuccessfully. Ida Scroggins raised her hand, soon silencing those within reach with a few swift clips round the ears. With malevolent pleasure she delivered her instructions.

Tables and benches were pushed or carried to one side of the room. Then down on their knees, bony little bottoms in the air, two rows of girls faced each other to begin the strange manoeuvre of retreat and advance, the older girls applying wax to the herring-bone boards and then shuffling backwards, and the younger girls furiously rubbing the waxed areas. Back and forth they advanced, leaving a shining floor behind them.

At one point, Bridget overreached for the tin of polish. It skidded across the floor in Lissie's direction. Grinning, she whizzed it back to Bridget.

Ida Scroggins' shriek bounced off the ceiling.

'Bridget Flaherty! Who gave you permission to make a game of it?' She delivered a sharp kick to Bridget's rump. 'And you, Lissie Fairweather,' she barked, marching to where Lissie knelt, trembling. 'You had the temerity to join in.' She hauled Lissie to her feet by the back of her apron strings then shouted, 'On your feet, Flaherty. Follow me.'

Miss Scroggins trailed Lissie to the door. Bridget came upright, her stance defiant, but she held herself in check as she walked to the door for fear of what might befall Lissie who was still in the termagant's vice-like grip. Miss Scroggins flung open the door. 'Out, the pair of you.'

Heads down, the rest of the girls continued polishing but as soon as Scroggy's back was towards them, they exchanged glances, some fearful, others hostile. Low resentful muttering could be heard as their friends were chivvied out of the room, and as the door closed behind them a noisy clamour of protest arose.

Dragging Lissie with one hand and prodding Bridget's back with the other, Miss Scroggins marched them along the corridor and down a flight of narrow stairs to a small, dusty room that contained disused furniture. 'Get in there,' she commanded, tossing Lissie inside, and giving Bridget a mighty thump between her shoulders. 'Stay here till I come for you.' She slammed the door. Lissie heard the key turning in the lock. Too stunned by the events of the past few minutes to even whimper, she now began to cry.

'Oh, Lissie,' Bridget wailed, taking the sobbing little girl in her arms. 'I'm sorry I got you in trouble. It wa' all my fault.'

Lissie lifted her tearstained face and shook her head. 'It wasn't... It's hers,' she hiccuped. 'She's a horrible woman. She's to blame for everything nasty that happens to us.'

'You can say that again,' Bridget agreed, and letting go of Lissie, she flopped into a big wooden chair with a high spindle back and pulled Lissie onto her knee. 'Might as well make us selves comfy,' she said stoically. 'Now, what will we play to pass the time?'

Lissie lolled against Bridget, her tears and fears subsiding as they played a game of eye spy. If Bridget could be brave then so could she.

'I'm hungry,' Lissie complained after they had played several guessing games and rooted amongst the rubbish to see if there was anything to entertain them.

'So am I, and whilst we're locked in here the others'll be eating jelly an' blancmange an' pretendin' to be grateful to the governors for bein' so kind. I could kill Scroggy.' Bridget's tone was bitter.

The sun that had penetrated the small, dirty window in the far wall had moved round the building, and now there was barely any light in the musty room. Seated once again in the chair on Bridget's lap Lissie thought of the jelly and blancmange. Her tummy rumbled. Then she thought she'd also like to kill Scroggy – and her mam for leaving her in the orphanage.

'I hate this place,' she said, icy rage making her chest ache. She felt Bridget stiffen. 'I don't hate you or any of the others,' she gabbled, 'but I just wish I was at home with my dad.'

'We all hate this place,' Bridget said softly, 'but we've nowhere else to go. At least if you get out of here you've a dad to go to. Most of us don't even have that.'

Feeling the need to confide in this lovely girl who always came to her rescue, and the idea of killing Scroggy in the back of her mind, Lissie put into words what for some time now she reluctantly believed.

'I don't think I'll ever see my dad again. I think my mam killed him.' She shuddered as the words left her tongue.

Bridget gasped. 'Killed him? What makes you say that?'

In fits and starts, between tears of sadness and anger, Lissie told her about what had happened on the day she'd walked with her dad in the bluebell wood. 'It was so lovely,' she said brokenly. 'Then we saw my mam with a man.' As she described the scene, Bridget understood. When Lissie told her about the fight and her dad lying, bleeding, on the floor and she feeling as though she was to blame for not getting help or telling anybody, she held her all the more closely, her heart aching for the little girl.

'Do *you* think he could be dead?' Lissie whispered the words.

'He might not be.' Bridget sounded encouraging. 'If he was a strong young man like you said, he was probably just knocked out, like your mam told you. I bet he's been looking for you ever since.'

'Do you think so?' Lissie's heart swelled with hope.

'Don't be saying anything to anybody else though. You're not to blame for what your mam did, but some people might not understand an' they might make trouble for you.'

Lissie nodded solemnly.

Bridget began to sing an old Irish lullaby, her husky voice crooning the soothing words. 'Me mam wa' allus drunk when she sang it, but it's still a good song,' she said, her heart aching for herself as she too-ra-loo-lood the chorus.

* * *

Upstairs, the governors had departed and the girls were helping clear away the remains of the tea and putting the tables and chairs ready for the next day.

'Here,' Lucy whispered, shoving a fairy cake into Polly's apron pocket. 'Get some more when nobody's lookin'.' She gave similar instructions to some of the others. Then lifting a handful of paper napkins, she made a bag out of them and tipped in a large dollop of blancmange. She did the same with some jelly, secreting it in her own apron pocket where it felt damp and soggy.

'Well done, girls,' Connie Briggs praised as she bustled into the room. She had been in and out all afternoon but her task of overseeing all that the high tea entailed had left her with little time to be with the girls. In Connie's opinion this was one of the downsides of her job. Violet Smith, the matron, was pleasant to work for but she rarely became involved in the general running of the girls' unit. This meant that Connie had to manage the women who worked in the kitchen or cleaned the orphanage as well as all the other jobs the girls' unit demanded, when she really would have preferred to spend time teaching the girls useful skills and making their lives more comfortable. Most of all she would have liked to see the back of Ida Scroggins. However, Matron had a high regard for the vicious bully, and when Connie complained, she defended the harridan, saying that discipline was vital to the smooth running of the establishment.

'Did you all enjoy your tea?' she asked, smiling at the expected chorus of, 'Yes, Mrs Briggs.' She surveyed the room. 'Well, I think we're finished here so line up.'

The girls trooped to the door.

'Where's Bridget?' Connie's eyes scanned the line. 'And little Lissie?' She was secretly fond of both girls and only now did she notice their absence.

'Miss Scroggins put them out this morning for misbehaving,' Lucy volunteered, her tone ringing with disapproval, and her expression saying more.

'Whatever did they do to deserve that?'

The girls relayed the incident with the tin of wax. Connie's eyes darkened and her lips formed a thin, angry line. 'Lucy, lead the girls up to the dormitory. I'll be up shortly.'

Connie hurried down the corridor. She knew where to find Ida Scroggins. Just as she had thought, Ida was in the hallway ingratiating herself with the last of the departing governors. 'May I have word, Miss Scroggins?' Connie interrupted tersely. Ida looked displeased. The governor seemed relieved and hurried off.

'Where are Bridget Flaherty and Lissie Fairweather?' Connie demanded hotly. 'And don't tell me you have them shut up in the cellar. I specifically told you that was not allowed.'

Ida's ample bosom heaved and her gimlet eyes drilled into Connie's.

'I beg your pardon. How dare you approach me in such a manner?' she spluttered, her cheeks turning crimson. 'As for those impudent girls, I have my standards of discipline to maintain and I'll thank you not to interfere. I do not tolerate flagrant misbehaviour or rudeness from anyone.'

'And I won't tolerate downright cruelty and bullying,' Connie retorted. Swinging on her heel, she marched from the hallway then ran down to the cellar.

When Lissie heard the key turning in the lock, she looked apprehensively at Bridget. 'She's back,' she whispered, her anxiety turning to pure joy when she saw Connie. 'Mrs Briggs, Mrs Briggs,' she cried, sliding off Bridget's knee and running to the door.

Connie wrapped her arms round Lissie who buried her face in the folds of Connie's skirt, her grateful tears making a damp patch.

'Come on, Bridget,' Connie said kindly, for Bridget had yet to move. 'Let's get you out of here. I think you've both suffered enough.'

They made their way up to the dormitory, Bridget repeating the story about the tin of wax polish and bitterly complaining at the harshness of Miss Scroggins' punishment.

Connie listened, making sympathetic noises now and then but saying nothing of what she intended to do to rectify the abhorrent situation. As they entered the dormitory, the other girls cheered. Connie left them to it, and as soon as she had gone, Lucy, Polly and several of the others produced the goodies they had pilfered from the high tea.

Lissie's spirits rose as she tucked into squashed buns, jelly and blancmange. Even in the worst moments her friends always managed to bring some comfort. She looked round her at the grinning faces of the abandoned girls who had been deprived of a normal childhood. Then she looked at Bridget. She had survived ten years in the orphanage yet she still remained brave and kind. Lissie decided she too could do that. She grinned at Bridget.

Bridget grinned back. 'It in't all bad is it, kid?' she said jauntily as she helped herself to another bun.

No, it wasn't all bad, but as time went by Lissie often asked herself how much more she could take of Miss Scroggins' punishments. She did everything she could to please the vindictive termagant and was at a loss as to why this evil woman singled her out to vent her vitriolic temper.

'Lift up, let's do the other one,' Lucy said as down on her knees she buttoned Lissie's boots. It was Tuesday morning of the last week in March, almost four months after Lissie had arrived at the orphanage, and although both girls were well aware that Lissie was quite capable of buttoning her own boots, Lucy liked to mother the little ones, and Lissie enjoyed letting her do so. She lifted her left foot.

'Hurry up, she's coming,' Maude squeaked, her scrawny neck stretched as she poked her head through the open dormitory door and her squinting eyes filled with panic as she glanced back at Lissie and Lucy.

A hefty shove sent Maude staggering back into the line of girls behind her.

'Out of my way, you dunderhead,' Miss Scroggins barked, and burst into the dormitory. Her pale cold eyes raked the line of quivering girls then came to rest on Lissie and Lucy.

Lucy attempted to scrabble upright, but not quick enough to prevent Miss Scroggins from grabbing a handful of her lank brown hair and hauling her up by it. Lucy let out a shriek. 'Get in line, girl,' Scroggins roared and pushed Lucy aside. Terrified, Lissie stayed rooted to the edge of the bed on which she was perched.

'You again,' Scroggins hissed, leering down into Lissie's paling face. 'I might have known you'd be the cause of such tardiness.' She turned to Maude. 'Lead the girls down to breakfast, and no talking on the stairs.'

Lissie cowered backwards away from Scroggins' towering bulk and closed her eyes tight shut. A rough hand grabbed her, turning her over onto her tummy in one quick move. With her face pressed into the blanket, she felt the cool air as her dress was yanked up and her knickers pulled down. She knew what was coming next and she tried to squeeze herself into a ball.

Whack! The leather strap Miss Scroggins kept coiled in her apron pocket bit into Lissie's tender flesh. She howled, and continued howling as her assailant flailed the strap again and again. Finally, she was dragged to her feet.

'Tidy yourself up, girl, and get down to breakfast,' Miss Scroggins panted. She was breathing fast and her top lip was coated in spittle. She marched from the room, and when Lissie had adjusted her clothing, she followed on leaden feet.

The dining room smelled as it always did of stale wash-cloths, disinfectant and porridge. Lissie's empty stomach heaved. She felt sick, but holding her head high and trying to ignore her stinging buttocks, she walked to her place.

Gertie Cooper gave Lissie a malicious smile. In all her ten years

Gertie had never known real happiness and she took pleasure in other people's misery.

'You're in for it now,' Gertie hissed as Lissie sat gingerly down beside Mary and drew a sharp breath. 'You're gonna get it good an' proper.'

'I already did, so mind your own business!' Lissie began to eat her porridge.

'Tek no notice of her.' Mary threw Gertie a dirty look. 'Did she beat you?' she whispered, her eyes round with concern.

Lissie nodded. Her backside was on fire.

When breakfast was over, Miss Scroggins marched in and the girls bowed their heads. 'We thank thee Lord for these thy gifts...' she intoned, her sanctimonious tones making Lissie's blood boil. Were the stinging cheeks of her backside part of the Lord's gifts?

That night, her 'nightmare' rampaged into her sleep and she wakened sweating and screaming. Mary leapt from her own bed into Lissie's. She hugged her tightly, saying, 'Hush, hush, you're all right.' Lissie's trembling lessened as Mary soothed and patted and when her sobbing faded to a sniffle, Mary asked, 'Did that bad dream come again? You haven't had it in ages.'

'I... I thought it had g... gone for good,' Lissie stuttered. 'I think it's 'cos my bottom's so sore that it made it come back.'

'Scroggy's a rotten pig. We'll ask Maude to pinch a bit of lard from the kitchen to rub on it.'

With that comforting thought, Lissie snuggled up to Mary and slept.

The next morning as Lissie dressed, she noticed that her knickers were streaked with blood where the strap had broken her skin.

The girls changed their underwear every Saturday after they had their baths, and today was only Wednesday. Wrinkling her nose, she pulled on the offending garment. The blood had dried overnight and the stiff ridges scratched when she moved. Hastily, she pulled her dress over her head then rammed her feet into her boots. She had them buttoned by the time Lucy came to assist, and she brushed aside her offer to let her fix her hair. Lucy looked hurt and Lissie felt ungracious, but she couldn't afford another beating. Feeling dirty, she joined the line by the door.

The morning passed without incident. Rather than sit on the bench at the table she stood to fasten safety pins to cards. Miss Scroggins passed no remark but Lissie was sure she was smirking as she inspected the work. 'I hate you... I hate you... I hate you...' Lissie said inside her head.

After lunch, as the girls filed from the dining room and back to class, Lissie's discomfort was such that she could only totter along the corridor. Every step was agony and sitting down was even worse.

'Lissie, you're walking rather oddly,' Connie said as she came up behind her. 'Is something wrong?'

Lissie's resolve to be brave crumbled as she heard the gentle concern in Connie's voice, and when she turned to face her and saw the compassion in her warm brown eyes, she began to weep.

Alarmed, Connie took her hand. 'Carry on, girls, in you go,' she said outside the classroom door and holding Lissie back as the other girls trooped inside. 'What is it, dear child. Tell me.'

'It's my bottom,' Lissie sobbed. 'It hurts.'

Gently, Connie led her across the corridor and into the washroom. 'Can I look?' she asked and knelt down.

* * *

Violet Smith's cheeks paled and her eyebrows almost touched her hairline.

'Resign,' she echoed, absolutely flabbergasted. 'But Connie, I couldn't manage without you.'

'Nor will you have to if you get rid of that cruel bully. The girls' lives are hard enough without having to suffer the scourge of Ida Scroggins. The spiteful hag takes pleasure in punishing them at every turn and it has to stop. Now!'

She leaned forward with her hands on the desk, her faced masked in fury.

'You haven't listened to me before, Violet, but perhaps you will now. I refuse to work in an establishment where a blind eye is turned to downright cruelty.'

'Now Connie, don't get so het up. One can hardly call Ida's actions cruel. I know you objected to her shutting them in the cellar when they had misbehaved, but I look at it as a time for them to cool off and mind their manners. And the occasional slap does no harm. Spare the rod and spoil the child, Connie. That's my belief.' Violet heaved up her bosom as if to compound her words.

'An occasional slap?' Connie shrieked. 'She beat that poor child until she bled. It's up to you, Violet. Either she goes or I do.'

* * *

'You can't dismiss the woman before you've found a replacement for her,' Victor Smith blustered as he paced the floor of the matron's office. 'And anyway, I thought you approved of Scroggins. You said she was a strict disciplinarian.'

'Aye, but a mite too strict in Connie's opinion, and I'd rather lose Scroggins than Connie. You know how determined she can be when she gets a bee in her bonnet. If she leaves, I don't know how I'll manage.' Violet wrung her plump hands and gave her husband a beseeching look. It was late in the afternoon and Victor was feeling hungry and irritated by his wife's unexpected decision.

'You'll have to notify the Board of Governors that you're giving her notice. It'll be up to them to find someone to take Scroggins' place.' Victor stomped to the door. 'I'll leave it up to you, Violet. I've enough on running my side of things. There's a scabies outbreak in the mental wing and the itching's making the poor sods barmier than they already are. I've sent for Doctor Peters to bring some blue gentian to treat the affliction, for all the good it does. Some bloody Easter this is going to be.' The door slammed behind him.

* * *

On Thursday morning Ida Scroggins stood in the matron's office, a dark shade of purple suffusing her cheeks. 'You can't possibly expect me to work my notice,' she spluttered. 'I'll not hang around until you replace me.'

She glared at Violet, her eyes glittering maliciously. 'I've given you good service, kept those guttersnipes in order, and this is the thanks I get for it.' She continued to screech her own virtues at the same time letting Violet know that she thought her to be ineffective and not worthy of her position in the workhouse. 'I'll go immediately, and leave you to regret your decision.'

'I've written you a reference, Miss Scroggins.' Violet's fingers trembled as she handed it over. Having been subjected to the damning tirade she was now empathising with Connie and the girls; the woman was a termagant. She'd be glad to see the back of her.

* * *

'Happy Easter everyone.' Connie Briggs's cheerful greeting met the girls when they filed into the workroom the next day.

'Happy Easter, Mrs Briggs,' they chorused as they took their seats. Lissie breathed a sigh of relief and sat down next to Mary. She'd had a restless night. Mrs Briggs had smeared her bottom with soothing ointment but it was still painful. She had been dreading coming face to face with Miss Scroggins in case Mrs Briggs had had words with her, and now the sight of her champion was a pleasant surprise.

She was even more surprised when Connie announced that they were to forgo their usual tasks. 'Today being Good Friday you can choose something that is worthwhile and to your liking,' she said. She suggested they might read or make jigsaws, sew or draw pictures. The girls stared, wide eyed, smiles twitching the corners of their mouths as they anticipated the hours ahead.

'Now, I have things requiring my attention. Bridget, Lucy, I'll leave you in charge.' Connie smiled with satisfaction as she left behind the awestruck silence in the room, then standing outside the door, she listened to the excited hum that rose like chattering birds as the girls exclaimed over their unexpected treat.

Lissie chose to sew. She'd make Mrs Briggs a handkerchief case as a thank you present for being so kind. Selecting some scraps of blue felt she found in one of the baskets, she began to sew her neatest stitches.

'Where's Scroggy?' Lucy voiced the question on every girls' mind.

'Dead and buried, I hope,' Bridget hissed, casting a glance over her shoulder in case her nemesis suddenly appeared.

'Why isn't she here whacking our heads?'

'Shush, she might come in any minute.'

But Miss Scroggins didn't appear, and it wasn't until lunchtime that Maude told them she'd seen Scroggy leaving with a suitcase the night before. 'She's most likely gone off for the holiday.'

Lissie tucked into the lumpy mashed potato and watery mince, her appetite renewed as she thought about a few days of freedom from Ida Scroggins' wicked hands and tongue. It was going to be a happy Easter after all.

13

'Pissie Lissie, teacher's pet,' a voice hissed from behind as Lissie filed into the dormitory along with Mary. It was a Friday evening in June some seven months after Lissie had come to live in the orphanage.

Lissie swung round to face her taunter, her blue eyes flashing dangerously. If she had learned one thing during the past months, it was to stand fast in the face of adversity. 'What did you say?' she snapped.

'Pissie Lissie,' Gertie Cooper repeated. 'I saw you sucking up to Mrs Briggs like she wa' made of treacle and you wanted a lick.'

Lissie glared at the heavily built girl who at ten years old was two years her senior. Gertie scowled, ready for a fight.

'I wasn't sucking up to anybody. She was just looking at my sewing,' Lissie said heatedly. In fact, Connie had held up Lissie's neat colourful patchwork as an example in the hope that the other girls might learn from it, praising Lissie's creativity and careful stitches. The patches that the girls stitched together would eventually be united into a bedspread and then sold to raise funds towards the girls' upkeep. Connie often despaired at the quality of some of their work.

'We all know you're her favourite,' Gertie sneered, pushing her fist into Lissie's chest. Lissie couldn't deny that Mrs Briggs took a special interest in her, and being sweet tempered by nature she never provoked a fight, but she wasn't going to be bullied because of it.

'Shut your gob, Dirty Gertie, and mind your own business.' She spat out the name that Bridget had coined for the unpopular girl who bullied the younger girls and irritated the older ones by refusing to wash properly.

Gertie grabbed a handful of Lissie's long, black curls, the sour smell from her armpit wafting up Lissie's nose. She retaliated by clawing at Gertie's lank brown hair, hopeful of inflicting as much pain as she was receiving. The two girls yelped as they tussled, neither of them willing to relinquish victory, and the fight might have worsened had Bridget not waded in, breaking them apart.

'You're a jealous little bitch, Gertie Cooper. You're never happy unless you're making somebody else miserable.' Bridget gave Gertie a shove that sent her flying. 'Now stop causing trouble or Maude'll be in an' fetch Miss Perry. Then we'll all be for it.' Vera Perry had replaced Ida Scroggins.

Gertie slunk to the other end of the dormitory and threw herself down on her bed. None of the girls rushed to comfort her. They had all suffered at her hands one time or another. However, Mary put her arms round Lissie's shoulders and gave her a squeeze.

'Tek no notice of her,' Mary said as she and Lissie made their way over to their beds. 'She's a spiteful cow.'

'She is, but she doesn't frighten me.' Lissie began to undress, and as she took off her grey striped dress then put on her nightie, she wondered why it was that her pleasures were so often cruelly dashed.

She'd been thrilled when Mrs Briggs had praised her work. The kind words and warm smile of her favourite teacher had made her heart swell, and in that moment she had felt loved and wanted. Desperate to hold on to it, and silently promising to always do her best for Mrs Briggs, she had hugged the lovely feeling deep inside, until now. Gertie Cooper's spiteful words and threats had spoiled it.

Lissie climbed into bed and pulled her blanket over her head. She didn't feel like talking to Mary, and when Mary whispered across the gap between their beds, Lissie pretended to be sleeping. She was fantasising about how nice it would be to have a mam like Connie Briggs. Had she known that Connie was at that same time thinking about her she would have been amazed and delighted.

'Poor little lamb,' Connie said as she slipped a stitch onto her knitting needle.

'It doesn't do to get too fond,' Violet warned, her brow wrinkling irritably. They were spending the last hours before bedtime in the small sitting room in the matron's quarters, something they did most evenings.

'I know, I know.' Connie shook her head. 'It's just that she's such an endearing little thing, and she tries so hard to please my heart goes out to her.'

'I must say she seems to have been well reared,' Violet conceded. 'Whoever it was that cared for her in the first seven years of her life did a good job.' She sniffed. 'I can't imagine it was that slattern of a woman who left her here.'

'I think credit for that must go to her father. She often mentions him in the fondest terms. She told me he liked poetry and nature, and that he was very clever with his hands. It was he that taught her to sew. He must have been a cultured, gentle soul because Lissie's knowledge of books far exceeds that of the other girls. She's a delight to teach.' Connie spoke with such feeling that Violet frowned again, and thinking it was time to change the conversation, she asked Connie what she thought of Miss Vera Perry, Ida Scroggins' replacement. Connie didn't find her very likeable, but she was a distinct improvement on her predecessor.

'The girls seem to think she's rather dull, but at least she doesn't beat the living daylights out of them. I had hoped that when the board appointed her, she'd bring new life into the classroom. After all, she's much younger than Scroggins and should be full of new initiatives to teach the girls, but like them I find her as dull as ditchwater.' She sighed as she put her knitting to one side. 'Some of those girls have lively minds regardless of their miserable backgrounds. Take Bridget Flaherty for instance, such a spirited girl blessed with the natural qualities of leadership, yet her lack of education has fitted her for nothing but to go into service when she leaves us next month. Then there's Lissie, such an intelligent girl with a creative mind and skilful hands. Surely, she should be destined for something better than a lifetime of drudgery.' Connie's voice had risen an octave so fervent was her belief in the girls' attributes.

Violet pursed her lips. Connie's interest in the Fairweather girl was getting out of hand. 'It's a shame you never had any of your own,' she said softly, 'but what with Jim an' his tuberculosis it wasn't meant to be.' She smiled sadly at the young widow. 'And you've enough on your hands working here and devoting all your spare time to your mother, so don't go getting any notions of taking that child as your own. How is your mam by the way?'

Connie shrugged. 'Not getting any younger, and harder to manage by the day. But as long as I can keep her in her own home, I'll stick it out. I'll not see *her* ending up in the workhouse.' She finished knitting a row before adding, 'I know it would be impractical at my age to take on a child, but it won't stop me from taking a special interest in Lissie Fairweather. There's something about her that tells me she deserves a chance to make a better future for herself, and I'm going to help her on her way.'

14

LITTLE HORTON WORKHOUSE, 1910

'Come on, love, dry your eyes and get dressed.'

Lissie took the trembling little girl by the hand, helping her to remove the stiff calico nightdress that the child had been issued with the night before. It brought back memories of Lissie's own first morning in the orphanage some seven years before when she also had wakened to a whole new and confusing world.

It seemed like twice as long since her mother, Dora, had dumped her there but the memory was still sharp, as was the last time she had seen her father. Then he had been lying in a pool of blood, and although it still haunted her, she was now resigned to the fact that she might never see him again. His life might have ended on that day but she still had hers, and she had to go on.

'I know it all feels strange but you'll soon get used to it,' Lissie continued as she slipped a grey striped dress like all the orphans wore over the girl's quivering, skinny shoulders. 'I'm Lissie, by the way, and that big girl is Mary, and the other one's called Polly,' she said, pointing out her friends who were chivvying the younger girls into line by the dormitory door. 'We've been here for years and we don't seem too bad on it, do we?' She gave the tiny mite an encouraging smile. 'So, what do they call you?'

'Dolly,' the little girl lisped, wiping her tears with the back of her chubby hand.

'Right then, Dolly. Let me tie your boots and then we'll go down for breakfast.'

There had been many changes since Lissie had come to live in the orphanage. Bridget Flaherty and Lucy Boothroyd, the fourteen-year-old girls who had befriended her when she first arrived, lost and lonely and grieving for her dad, had been gone seven years now, but she would never forget their kindness. Lucy, quiet and thoughtful, and Bridget, brave and mischievous, had seen Lissie through many dark hours, and she now emulated their kindness with the younger girls. Sadly, after Bridget and Lucy had been placed in service, she had lost contact with them and missed their presence.

She didn't, on the other hand, miss Ida Scroggins one bit. Over the last seven years the wicked bully had been replaced by several different women who, whilst they were tedious and uninteresting, were more tolerant. The girls suspected that Connie Briggs had been instrumental in bringing about Scroggy's departure and their affection for her grew, none more than Lissie's. In Mrs Briggs she had found another Nelly Jackson.

Connie, who would deny she had favourites, had taken a special interest in Lissie, nurturing her in whatever way she could. Also, much to Lissie's satisfaction, her closest friend, Mary, was still with her. They were inseparable and shared hopes and dreams and many secrets but Lissie, mindful of her mother's and Bridget's warning, never divulged what had really happened to her father. She was still shrouded in guilt and her grown-up self told her it had been despicable to leave him to his fate. So, when she couldn't resist telling Mary about some of the wonderful things he had taught her, Lissie prevaricated, making up fairy tales to distract her.

Both of them now fourteen and their days in the orphanage numbered, they too would soon be going out into the world beyond these four walls. To what, neither of them knew. It was most likely into service, but Lissie dreamed of more exciting things. First, given the chance, she would find her dad. Even though the thought that he might be dead still plagued her, she had to find out what had happened to him. Wherever the orphanage placed her when the time came for her to leave, she hoped that it would be a position that allowed her freedom enough to begin her search. At night, in the dark dormitory, she whispered her hopes and dreams to Mary.

'I'd like to be placed with people who make things, you know, maybe a seamstress or a hatmaker. My dad made shoes and furniture. He was very clever with his hands,' she said wistfully. 'I don't want to end up cleaning out fireplaces and washing dishes in a big house. I had enough of that when we lived with Jed Fletcher. Housework is boring, but making something from scratch and seeing it finished gives you a thrill.'

'You'd be good at that. Your last patchwork quilt was beautiful,' Mary replied. 'I'd like to work in a shop that sells food, then I could nibble away at bits of cheese and sweets and biscuits in between serving people.'

Using one of the big words that she hoarded like a miser, Lissie laughed and said, 'You and your voracious appetite.'

'I don't know what v... varac... whatever you said means, but I know I'm always blooming starving,' Mary groaned.

'Think of it, in a few weeks' time we'll be out of here,' Lissie said, curling up under her blanket and hugging her knees with excitement, 'and if we both get good jobs, we'll be able to eat anything we like and go wherever we choose.'

On that happy note the girls fell asleep to dream some more.

* * *

Connie Briggs stood in the doorway of the draper's shop in Marine Road in the seaside town of Scarborough and hugged her widowed sister-in-law. 'Thanks for everything,' she said, sounding extremely grateful. 'I'm sure you'll like Lissie, and I know she'll like living here after all those years in drab Little Horton.'

'Who wouldn't? We have the best sea air in the whole of East Yorkshire,' Patience Foyer exclaimed, her smile slipping as she said, 'Now, I hope this girl's as good as you say she is, and that you're not bringing me a load of worry.'

'Lissie is a joy to have about the place. She's very popular with all the girls and the staff at the orphanage. And she'll be an asset to you in the shop, I can promise you that.'

'Well, think on, she's only on trial and if I don't take to her, you'll have to find another position for her. Now, off you go or you'll miss your train.'

The two women hugged again before Connie set off walking to the railway station and the train that would take her back to Bradford. It was a glorious morning in June and the sea air was bracing after the soot-laden atmosphere of Little Horton. She always enjoyed her infrequent trips to the seaside town to visit her dead brother's widow and had decided already that when she retired from work she would come to live here. She was also feeling pleased that Patience had agreed to take Lissie on trial as a live-in companion and shop assistant. Patience had no children of her own, and as she had told Connie on a previous visit, she wasn't getting any younger and her arthritis troubled her more with each passing year. She would soon need help in running the shop and overseeing the fairground amusements that her husband, Henry, had owned. Connie felt sure that Patience would find Lissie more than satisfactory.

* * *

In the week that Lissie was due to leave the orphanage, Connie could barely conceal her excitement as she told her that they were taking a trip into Great Horton to do some shopping. Lissie's mouth fell open in amazement. This had never happened before, and she breathlessly asked, 'Why?'

'You'll see,' said Connie, her eyes twinkling and her smile enigmatic. 'I'll explain why as we go.'

'Lucky you,' Mary said enviously as Lissie put on her coat that was now two sizes too small and frayed at the cuffs. 'What are you going for?'

'I've no idea. I suppose Mrs Briggs might need help running her messages. I'm just glad she's chosen me.'

Lissie and Connie took the bus into Great Horton, Lissie's head turning from left to right as she gazed out of the window at the unfamiliar landscape. Up until now, her horizon had stretched no further than the workhouse and the Sunday walk to church in Little Horton. Now, a whole new world was opening up in front of her and she was almost bouncing in her seat as the bus trundled into Great Horton and the centre of the town.

The bus was travelling slowly along a busy street and Lissie was gazing out of the window when suddenly it was as if a light had been turned on, and a vein of memory opened up. She was a child again on a grey, chilly morning walking with her friend, Emmy, down this same street that the bus was now rumbling down. They were on their way to school. She could almost feel Emmy's hand warm in hers and a pleasant shiver tickled her spine at the long-forgotten memory.

Connie had been watching Lissie out of the corner of her eye, silently leaving her to enjoy the thrill of her new surroundings but as the bus came to a halt in High Street, she sensed a change in

Lissie who was sitting quite still, the puzzled expression on her face indicating that she was deep in thought.

When they alighted in the busy main street she asked, 'Are you feeling all right, Lissie?'

'I've been here before,' Lissie whispered. 'I know I have! I saw Lane Close Mill. That's where Emmy's dad works.'

Lissie had often mentioned her friendship with someone called Emmy and Nelly and Bill Jackson, but Connie had had neither the time nor the authority to investigate their whereabouts, and had relegated them to the same part of her mind that stored the little bit of information she knew about Lissie's father: they were no more than the reminiscences of a confused child.

Now, as Connie and Lissie stood on the pavement, Lissie's eyes darted in one direction and the other and her excited cry interrupted Connie's thoughts. 'Look! That's the sweet shop where Emmy and I used to buy sherbet lemons.'

'Is this where you lived before you came to us, Lissie?'

'I'm sure it is. I'd forgotten all about it but now I remember walking up this street to school, and going to the Co-op with Emmy for Nelly's messages.' Lissie's tone of voice let Connie know she felt awed by the memory and now Connie felt rather confused. She hadn't expected this, and was it wise to pursue what might be nothing more than false memories on Lissie's part? She just didn't know.

'Let's go into that teashop across the road and over a nice cool drink you can see what else you remember.' Connie urged Lissie to the other side of the street. It had been her intention all along to treat Lissie to tea and buns whilst she told her what she had arranged for her future and now seemed as good a time as any. She hadn't wanted to tell her in the confines of the orphanage; she wanted it to be a special occasion, but now it had taken on a new dimension.

In the cosy little café, Connie ordered tea for herself and lemonade and buns for Lissie. Overwhelmed by the memories that had surged back, and now this unexpected treat, Lissie sat in a daze looking around her at the people in the teashop, a mixture of housewives and elderly men taking time out to chat and enjoy their refreshments. When the plump, cheery waitress set a glass of lemonade and two iced buns with chocolate topping in front of Lissie, she felt choked with grateful emotion.

'Thank you, Mrs Briggs,' she breathed. 'This is lovely.' She felt like crying.

'Eat up,' said Connie, 'and whilst you do, I've got something really important to tell you. The other day I went to see my sister-in-law who lives in Scarborough.'

Lissie nibbled the chocolate off the top of the bun and wondered why this news had anything to do with her.

'She's called Patience Foyer and she was married to my brother, Henry,' Connie continued. 'Sadly, he died and she's been left to run their business all on her own. She's not getting any younger and she requires some assistance.'

Lissie, still amazed at being back in Great Horton, couldn't quite grasp what Connie was telling her, but through a mouthful of iced bun she mumbled that she was sorry Mr Foyer had died. She picked up her glass and drank.

'Yes, it's sad,' Connie agreed, 'but it's a wonderful opportunity for you.'

Lissie looked at her, bemused. The fizzy lemonade swirled round her tonsils and she gulped then swallowed it. How could this man's death be an opportunity for her?

Connie realised that she hadn't had Lissie's full attention.

'Lissie! I'm telling you this because Mrs Foyer has agreed to employ you as a live-in companion and shop assistant. She owns a draper's shop and some fairground amusements. You're to go and

live with her in Scarborough when you leave the orphanage.'
Connie sat back and sipped her tea, anxious to judge Lissie's
reaction.

Lissie's thoughts were tumbling inside her head. What she
wanted to do was go and find Emmy, but conscious of the import of
what Connie had just told her she gathered her wits and focussed
on that.

'Live in Scarborough, work in a draper's shop?'

Lissie let out a whooshing breath. She didn't know where Scarborough was, but working in a drapery was far more appealing
than being put into service. And what were the fairground amusements? She pictured swing boats and roundabouts and recalled the
day Bill Jackson had taken her and his family to the fair on Low
Green. Memories flooded back, and she could no longer suppress
the urge to run and find Emmy and the Jacksons.

'Can we go and find where I used to live?' Lissie emptied her
glass then pushed back her chair.

Connie felt utterly deflated.

Lissie saw her disappointed expression and was overwhelmed
with guilt. 'Oh, Mrs Briggs. Forgive me. I'm so sorry, but this day has
been full of so many surprises that I can't think straight.' Connie
gave her a forgiving smile. 'I think the position sounds marvellous
and I'll do my best to please Mrs Foyer. I won't let you down. You
have always been so kind to me...' She was crying now and had
unconsciously reached out and grasped Connie's hand. 'And...
and... I've wished for years that you were my mother.' Lissie looked
through her tears at Connie, her expression asking if she had
spoken out of turn.

But she couldn't have said anything more pleasing, and Connie
clasped her hands round Lissie's and said, 'I wish I was, Lissie.'

They sat gazing at one another for a long moment, too over-
come with emotion to say anything more. Then, letting go of Lissie's

hand, Connie wiped away her own tears then gave her handkerchief to Lissie. Somewhat recovered, they smiled at one another, and Connie's composure regained, she pushed back her chair and got to her feet. 'Come on Lissie. We've a lot of things to do before this day is over. Then we'll go and find Emmy.'

First, they went to Dracup's ladieswear shop. Oh, the joy of trying on skirts and blouses, and eventually choosing a smart grey skirt and a blue blouse. Next, they bought soft white underwear and two pairs of grey lisle stockings. Lissie was beginning to think she was dreaming and that soon she'd wake up and find herself back in her bed in the orphanage. Finally, they chose a long grey woollen coat with a shawl collar and large shiny buttons.

'How are we going to pay for all these things?' Lissie whispered.

'All taken care of,' Connie replied briskly, her pleasure in buying clothes for the daughter she'd never had plain to see.

Lissie threw her arms round Connie and hugged her tightly. 'Thank you, thank you for everything. I feel like Cinderella in the fairy story,' she gushed.

'Now, do you think you can remember where Emmy lives?' Connie asked as she struggled to hold back her tears again.

A squeal of delight and another hug let Connie know she had asked the right question. 'Oh, I know I can,' Lissie said, her eyes dancing and her smile wide.

They set off walking down High Street, and as they progressed Lissie pointed out St John's Church with its tall spire, then the Fleece Inn where Bill Jackson went for a pint, and the Four Ashes, another pub he sometimes frequented, Lissie hastening to add that he wasn't a drinking man who neglected his family. He was quite the opposite.

'That's Old Todley,' she said as they strolled onwards, 'there's a blacksmith's forge there,' and as they went a little further, 'and that's the Wesleyan Chapel though we didn't worship there,' and a little later, her excitement mounting by the minute, 'we go down here. This is Crag Lane. Pooh, you can smell the dye works already.'

Connie equalled her enthusiasm. 'My, you do have a good memory. You must have liked living here.'

'I did eventually, but it was only because of the Jacksons. I didn't like living with my mam and that horrible man, and I missed my dad dreadfully.' Lissie stopped walking, her eyes misting and her voice seeming to come from far away as she said, 'I wonder where he is now. I never gave up hope that one day he would come and find me, but now I realise that he never will.'

Connie's heart ached for her.

A little further along Lissie said, 'This is Hart Street. We go down that ginnel.' She pointed to a narrow passage off the street and as they entered it Lissie wrinkled her nose. 'It still smells of tomcat pee.'

When they came into the yard, Lissie was surprised how little it had changed. There were still lines of washing outside Nelly's house, and she quickened her pace, her heart thudding and a choking feeling in her throat as they approached the Jacksons' house. She looked tentatively at Connie then knocked on the door.

Nelly's jaw dropped, and she stared wide eyed at the young girl and the woman standing behind her. Her lips quivered as she sought for words.

'Hello Mrs Jackson.' Lissie's voice was thick with emotion.

Nelly blinked rapidly and clutched her hands to her chest. 'Is that you, child? Are you Lissie?'

Lissie's heart soared to think that Nelly hadn't forgotten her.

'Yes, it's me, Mrs Jackson. And this is Mrs Briggs. She looks after me in the orphanage and she brought me here to see you.'

'Orphanage!' Nelly looked nonplussed. 'Oh, in heaven's name. After all these years,' she gasped. 'Is that where you went?' Then, gathering her wits, she cried, 'Come in, come in, I'm all of a piece and forgetting me manners.'

The kitchen was just as Lissie remembered it: the gleaming black-leaded range with its bright brass knobs, the table and chairs against the back wall and the gaily coloured pegged rugs and armchairs by the hearth, although Granddad wasn't sitting in his. Nelly bustled to the stove and clumsily set the kettle to boil at the same time urging Lissie and Connie to sit down.

'Can I use your lavvy, Mrs Jackson?' Two glasses of lemonade and the excitement at being back in the Jacksons' house was playing havoc with Lissie's bladder.

'Course you can, lovey. You know where it is.' Nelly waved a distracted hand then looked round her kitchen in a bemused fashion.

'I'm sorry we've taken you by surprise, Mrs Jackson,' said Connie, seeing how flustered Nelly was.

'Oh, you have, missis.' Nelly shook her head and her voice was high with curiosity as she asked, 'Did I hear rightly that Lissie was in an orphanage?'

'Yes, Mrs Jackson. The one attached to the workhouse in Little Horton. She's been with us for seven years.'

Nelly looked flabbergasted. 'Eeh, missis, I find that hard to take in. Did her mam go into the workhouse?'

'No, she just left Lissie with us. She gave us a trumped-up story and before we'd had a chance to check the detail, she took flight.'

Nelly pursed her lips and nodded to show that she understood. 'Just the sort of thing that Dora would do, the cold-hearted brazen tramp. She treated Lissie something shocking, an' her such a lovely child. I remember her going like it was yesterday,' she said wistfully. 'When she didn't call for our Emmy for school, Emmy went up for her. The house was locked an' we never saw her mam an' that chap Fletcher again. To think she was just down the road from us.'

Nelly's eyes moistened. 'If we'd a known that Dora was going to give her up, she could have had a home here. Me an' Bill loved that little girl.'

'That's easy to do, Mrs Jackson. I'm fond of her myself.' Connie and Nelly exchanged compliant smiles.

'Where's Emmy?' Lissie asked, bouncing back into the kitchen, her heart pounding at the thought of seeing her friend again.

'She's at work, love. She's a weaver in Lane Close Mill where her dad works.'

'Oh, of course. I should have realised she'd have left school,' said Lissie. 'I leave the orphanage next week. Mrs Briggs has found me a live-in position in a draper's shop in Scarborough.'

Nelly flapped her hands, distracted. 'Look, lovey, let me fill these cups and sit down 'cos I'm all of a tizz and there's so much to catch up with I...' She poured the tea with shaking hands then plumped down in a chair at the table where Lissie and Connie were already seated.

'Pardon me,' Nelly said, addressing Connie properly for the first time. 'You must think me rude for not welcoming you properly. I'm Nelly Jackson, as I'm sure Lissie's told you, and I'm so glad you've brought her here today.'

'No need to apologise, Mrs Jackson. I'd have brought her sooner had I known how close by you were. We were led to believe Lissie had lived in Bradford, in the city centre.' She chose not to mention that when Lissie had first arrived at the workhouse she had given them Nelly's address, and that Victor and Violet Smith had disregarded it as the ramblings of a confused child. Then she went on to explain how they had been on a shopping trip when Lissie had remembered living in Great Horton and that she had never forgotten Emmy and the kindness the Jackson family had shown her.

'I thought you might not recognise me after all this time,' Lissie said.

'Oh, lovey, I'd know you anywhere. How could anybody forget that lovely smile, them bright blue eyes and your lovely hair. We've often wondered where your mam and Jed had taken you when they upped and offed, but now we know where she took you, the heartless besom.' Nelly's lip curled. 'And to think you've been so near and us not knowing a thing about it.' She puffed out her cheeks in amazement. 'Our Emmy cried for days after you'd gone.'

'So did I,' said Lissie, touched to know that Emmy had missed her as much as she'd missed Emmy. 'I was downright miserable until Mrs Briggs took me under her wing.' She gave Connie a grateful smile.

Nelly also smiled her gratitude. 'I'm glad she had someone like you to look out for her. She was a lost, little soul when she came here, crying for her dad and having to live with that horrible Jed Fletcher and that mother of hers. A scheming bitch – pardon the expression – if ever there was one.'

Connie nodded her agreement.

Nelly sat back, her careworn face wreathed in smiles. 'Well, now, lovey, you're all grown up and what a grand girl you've turned out to be. But then, you always wa' a lovely bairn so it's only to be expected.'

Connie nodded again and said, 'I took to her right away.'

Lissie blushed. Then she glanced at the clock on the mantelshelf. 'What time will Emmy be home?'

Nelly turned to check the time. 'Near enough another hour, lovey. Her and Bill walk home together.'

Lissie's heart sank. Did they have to return to the orphanage before that? She looked pleadingly at Connie.

'I think we can stretch to that,' Connie said although she knew that Violet Smith would have expected them back by now. She hadn't the heart to destroy Lissie's pleasure, and was quite prepared to annoy the matron.

Nelly made a fresh pot of tea, and Lissie and Connie told her about Lissie's years in the orphanage. Nelly responded by telling them that Granddad had died two years before, and that Nora was working in the Co-op in High Street and was getting married in the autumn. 'An' our Jimmy's employed at a joinery in Bradford, and David's doing well at school,' she said with pride.

Lissie was sad to hear that Granddad was no longer with them, but she was almost bursting with excitement to think that she would soon see Emmy and the others again.

David was the first one home and Lissie was surprised by how tall he'd grown, and that his mop of blond curls was as bright as ever. He didn't immediately remember her, but then he'd only been four when they had last met. 'Our Emmy still talks about you,' he said. 'She says you were the best friend she ever had.'

When Bill and Emmy walked through the door their cries almost lifted the roof. Hugs were exchanged accompanied by Emmy's and Lissie's tears as they huddled in the corner of the room chatting nineteen to the dozen and Nelly, keeping her voice low, told Bill the story about the orphanage as she dished stew into bowls, and insisted that Lissie and Connie should stay to eat with them.

I might as well be hung for a sheep as a lamb, thought Connie as she agreed. Whilst they were eating, Lissie deliberated over whether or not to ask Nelly about Dora. She didn't truly care but curiosity getting the better of her, she said, 'Do you know where my mam went?'

Nelly put down her spoon and pulled a face. 'Can't say as I do, lovey. Her an' Jed did a moonlight flit and I've not seen hide nor hair of 'em since.'

Dora peremptorily dispensed with, they carried on eating and talking, and afterwards Lissie and Emmy went up to Emmy's bedroom and talked about her time in the orphanage.

'Aw. Lissie. I thought your mam wa' bad but that woman, Scroggins, sounds even worse,' Emmy sympathised, 'an' it must have been rotten never going anywhere but church on Sunday.'

'It wasn't all bad,' Lissie assured her. 'I had some really good friends, and Mrs Briggs is ever so kind to me. She got me the job in Scarborough. I'm going there tomorrow.'

'You don't have to go. You could come and live with us instead.' Emmy's eyes sparkled as she reached for Lissie's hand and squeezed it.

Lissie was tempted to agree, but then she thought of all that Connie had done for her, and although she loved Emmy and the Jacksons it would be foolish to turn down the position in Scarborough. If she stayed in Great Horton, she would have to look for work and she didn't want to work in the mill.

'We can write to one another and when you have your holidays you can come and stay with me by the sea.'

They parted with hugs and promises not to lose touch again, and as Lissie and Connie hurried to catch a bus back to Little Horton, Lissie declared, 'This has been the best day of my life.'

'And there are many more to come, Lissie,' said Connie.

15

Lissie felt like a great adventurer as the train chugged into Scarborough railway station at midday. What a journey it had been. It had started with a bus ride into Bradford followed by Lissie's very first time travelling by train to Leeds and then to York. Then another train to their final destination.

The journey had been mesmerising, Lissie quite alarmed by the speed of the train as it clattered and clanked over the rails, leaving behind the crowded, smoky city of Bradford, then thundering on between high bankings pink with rosebay willowherb and past rows of small houses until it had chugged into Leeds. Changing trains had been fraught with anxiety as they negotiated the crowded platforms, but she need not have worried; Connie had known exactly where to go. Onwards from York the train had whizzed through rolling countryside and fields golden with ripened wheat, and cows lazing in green meadows.

Every now and then the train stopped at pretty little stations, housewives with laden baskets alighting or boarding and men in suits going about their business. Lissie was fascinated by everything she saw, and she realised how narrow her life in the orphanage had been. Then one of the little villages they passed through reminded her of Thorne, and her enjoyment faded as she thought of her father. Where was he now? Was he lying in the cold ground? Or was he still searching for her? And why was it that she was always parted from the people she loved most?

Yesterday she had bid a tearful goodbye to Mary who was leaving the orphanage to go into service at a doctor's house in Bradford, and this morning she had hugged the younger orphans she had grown so fond of, telling them to heed their lessons and be kind to one another. Now, as she travelled from West Yorkshire to the East Riding, leaving behind her companions and all she had known for the past seven years, her new life was waiting for her.

'Welcome to Scarborough,' Connie said as they stepped down onto the platform. She shifted her overnight bag from one hand to the other. Lissie set her much larger bag down and gazed up at the station's long iron and glazed roof misted in steam that spouted from the train's mighty engine. Along the platform was the longest bench Lissie had ever seen and she pointed it out to Connie.

'They say it's the longest seat in the whole country,' Connie said and laughed when Lissie said, 'Can I sit on it for a moment?' She perched on the bench until Connie urged, 'Better make a move.'

Lissie felt awfully smart in her new skirt and blouse and her grey woollen coat slung over one arm as she walked along the platform, Connie at her side. Outside the gloomy station the sun was shining, the sky was a blue sheet, and a gentle salt-laden breeze prevented the hot day from being oppressive. Lissie looked up at the station's tall clock tower with a dome on top. Seagulls wheeled overhead or perched on the ridge of the station's roof, mewing and screeching.

'Gulls,' Connie said. 'You'll see plenty of them.'

Scarborough seemed to be a grand place. 'What's that?' Lissie enquired, pointing to a huge, impressive building with many windows behind the station.

'That's the Pavilion Hotel. There are lots of grand hotels in Scarborough. It was the first proper English holiday resort, you know,' she told Lissie as they walked away from the station. 'About four hundred years ago a lady called Mrs Farrar discovered a spring of natural mineral water in South Bay. She claimed that the water was a cure-all so people came to take the waters to improve their health. That was in the days of coach and horses so only the rich could afford to come, but now we've got trains and anyone can visit.'

'I can see why,' said Lissie as they walked past fine Georgian houses and a variety of shops. She was going to like living in the seaside town. A bright red open-top tram rattled by, people on the upper deck waving to those below on the busy pavement. Lissie's eyes followed it; she'd ride upstairs on the tram one day, she promised herself.

The pavements thronged with men in cream linen jackets and ladies in summer dresses. A cluster of children ran past wearing beach togs and carrying sand buckets and spades, their excited chatter making Lissie smile. It all seemed new and wonderful. They turned a corner into another street where a large board stood to one side of the pavement. On it was a painting of a man and woman in swimming costumes and where their faces should have been were two oval apertures. Lissie stopped and stared as a young man and his girl dodged behind the board then thrust their faces into the cut-out shapes. A man with a black cloth over his head stood behind a big black box on a tripod. 'Smile,' he shouted. The young couple obliged and the black box clicked and whirred.

'It's a camera,' Connie said. 'He'll give them a photograph of themselves later.' The young couple handed over their money and went off laughing.

'There's so much to see that I never knew about,' said Lissie as they carried on walking. She felt uplifted and at the same time undecided as to whether she was excited or afraid. The nearer they got to the sea, the stronger the unfamiliar smell of salt air. It made Lissie feel clean and alive, and she took deep breaths as they walked. Eventually they came to a long wide thoroughfare.

'This is North Marine Road,' Connie said, and a few paces later, 'This is your new home.' They had come to a halt outside a drapery, its window displaying rolls of material, sewing requisites, scarves, gloves and ladies' apparel. To the left of it was a substantial house with a shiny black door. 'And that's Patience's house. You won't have far to travel to work,' she jested, pushing open the shop door and ushering Lissie inside. The interior smelled of lavender and moth balls.

A tall, bony woman with iron grey hair drawn back in a severe bun stepped from behind the long, polished wood counter to welcome them. 'So, you've brought her,' she said, hugging Connie then appraising Lissie with sharp grey eyes. She nodded her approval. 'She's a tidy little thing.'

'Yes, this is Lissie Fairweather,' said Connie, and turning to Lissie, 'This is my sister-in-law, Mrs Patience Foyer, your new employer.'

Lissie held out her hand. Patience grasped it. Lissie thought it felt like holding a bunch of twigs. They smiled at one another.

'I'll close up and we'll go through to the house,' Patience said. They followed her to a connecting door that led into a large airy kitchen in the house next door.

Patience offered them refreshment which they were very grateful for after their long journey. Then she asked Lissie to tell her about herself, and immediately Lissie explained how much she liked sewing.

'That's good. You'll be able to help me with the alterations that sometimes need to be made to the dresses I sell.' Patience nodded at Connie as if to say she was already seeing advantages to taking Lissie in. 'Now, I have to get back to the shop, business won't wait. Connie, show Lissie her room.' With a swish of her severe black skirt, she went back into the shop.

Connie took Lissie to the upper floor. 'There are three bedrooms up here,' said Connie when they reached a long landing. Four doors led off it. 'That one is Patience's room.' She pointed to the door at the far end. 'The one next to it is the bathroom, the other one's unused, and this one will be yours.' She opened the door into a room at the rear of the house.

Lissie was overwhelmed by the size of the house and the room that was to be hers. It was pleasantly furnished with a single bed, and dark wood furniture. The window looked out on to a back yard, and in the near distance Lissie saw a large expanse of green lawns, trees and a lake.

'This is lovely,' she said, indicating the room and then the view from the window.

'That's Peasholm Park,' Connie said as she joined her at the window. 'You can walk there on your days off.' She lifted Lissie's bag onto a low stand at the foot of the bed. 'You can unpack later, but now what I fancy is a nice walk on the esplanade. It'll give me a chance to get some good fresh air before I go back to Little Horton, and you to familiarise yourself with the town.'

Lissie's heart fluttered at the thought of Connie leaving her here alone, but she pushed aside the feeling and said, 'I can't wait to see the sea. I've only ever seen pictures of it. I remember my dad telling me it goes on for ever and ever until it meets the sky.'

Connie was touched by Lissie's reference to her father. She must have loved him very much. She wondered, not for the first time, what had happened to Tom Fairweather. Initially, Lissie had told

Connie that she thought he was dead. Connie had been puzzled; surely the child would know if he had died. On another occasion she had confided that he had been hurt – she hadn't divulged how – and that if he had got better, he would come and find her. Connie had noted that although Lissie was happy to recall the things her father had said and done she had rarely spoken about her mother, only to say that she had been unkind to her. It was all very confusing, and Connie had come to accept that she might never learn the truth.

'Come on, let's go whilst the sun's still shining,' she said, and together they went downstairs and out into North Marine Road.

'This part of town is called North Bay, and over beyond the headland that's South Bay,' Connie said as they walked to the esplanade. She pointed to where the coastline jutted out into the sea. 'That's Scarborough Castle, an ancient ruin that you can see over there. The castle was built hundreds of years ago as a lookout and protection from Viking invaders,' she continued.

Lissie peered into the distance at the ruins imagining Viking long ships or pirates sailing under the headland ready to attack, their sails billowing in the wind and their banners flying.

Lissie said she'd make sure to pay it a visit as soon as she could, and when they arrived on the esplanade she cried, 'Oh, look! Look, Mrs Briggs!' Lissie spread her arms wide to take in the vista of golden sands and sparkling blue water. 'It's just like Dad said, it goes on and on and melts into the sky.' She stood gazing with delight at the rise and fall of the white crested waves and the ebb and flow of the tide lapping the beach. Lissie's childish delight at something that she herself took for granted made Connie smile.

They strolled along the esplanade into South Bay, Lissie overawed by her surroundings: the glittering sea and sandy beach on one side, and beautiful buildings on the other. Everywhere was a riot of colour and happy noise, the esplanade busy with elegantly dressed people taking advantage of the glorious sunshine. Lissie admired the ladies in their flimsy dresses and straw boaters. Some were carrying pretty lacey parasols to shade their faces from the sun, and she gave little gasps of wonder as yet again she realised how small her life had been within the confines of the orphanage walls. It made her feel rather ignorant and out of place and she said as much to Connie.

'You'll soon get used to it,' Connie replied, her heart aching for the girl whose life had been so sheltered and spartan. 'And you mustn't allow yourself to feel inferior, Lissie. You have a lively mind, you're well read, and above all you are a young woman with a very pleasing nature.' She gave a little laugh. 'And a talent for making beautiful needlework. Never underestimate what you already have. Just be determined to use your attributes to the best of your ability.'

Lissie stopped walking, the better to digest Connie's words. Then she gave a wide smile and giggled. 'I never thought of myself like that, Mrs Briggs, but you are right. I might not have seen much of the world but I've learned a lot about it from books, and I'm sure I can earn my living and make my way in life.'

Then, as they continued their walk Lissie began to see herself in a new light. None of the people strolling along the esplanade were aware of her background. They didn't know that her mother had most likely murdered her father, and that she had stood by and done nothing. Neither did they know she had been dumped in an orphanage and had spent years trying to make the best of a bad situation. A picture of the wicked Ida Scroggins reared up in her mind and immediately dissolved as she recalled Bridget and Mary's friendship and the loving care that Mrs Briggs had given her. And she was still giving it, walking along beside her helping her to fit in to her new life. Lissie's heart swelled. She glanced sideways at Connie, neat in her navy-blue cotton dress and hat with a navy and white spotted ribbon round it. Then she lowered her eyes to look at her own skirt and blouse. *We might not have parasols but we're as good as anybody, and I'm going to prove it.*

Gently she pulled Connie to a halt. The two of them were now about the same height and Lissie looked directly into Connie's warm brown eyes and smiled. 'Mrs Briggs, I want you to know that I will always be grateful for all you've done for me. Thank you for bringing me here, and finding me a place to live and work, and thank you most of all for giving me this wonderful opportunity. I promise not to disappoint either of us.' She blew out her cheeks and grinned.

Connie struggled to hold back her tears. 'I have every faith in you, Lissie.' Her voice rang with sincerity. 'That was quite a little speech,' she giggled to hide her emotions, 'now let's finish our walk before we go back for tea.'

They continued walking, mingling with the crowd outside a beautiful circular yellow sandstone building which Connie told Lissie was called the Spa. Lissie clapped her hands to her cheeks in delight as the orchestra on the bandstand in front of the Spa struck up a lively tune. Fascinated, she watched the conductor waving his baton as violinists and cellists flexed their bows, and brass and woodwind instruments blared. Lissie clasped Connie round her waist and laughing merrily, they danced to the strains of a Viennese waltz.

By the time they arrived back in North Marine Road Patience had closed the shop and Lissie and Connie found a tea of ham and tomatoes waiting for them. Over the meal and later as they sat in the parlour, Connie and Patience did most of the talking and Lissie sat quietly listening to them as they reminisced about people and places she knew nothing about. Patience appeared to be paying her scant attention, and even when Connie brought her into the conversation Patience briefly acknowledged her contribution then just as quickly reverted to gossiping with Connie. Lissie was rather surprised by this. She had imagined that Patience would have conducted some sort of interview to get to know her. She had mentally prepared what she would say if the opportunity arose. As the evening drew to a close, she asked to be excused, saying she was tired after all the excitement.

'Sleep well,' said Connie, giving her a hug.

'There's a box of matches on the dresser to light the gas mantle,' Patience informed her. 'Breakfast at seven-thirty.'

Lissie had had no time to take stock of the room that was now hers and as she stood in the middle of the floor her gaze roamed from the bed covered with a blue and white quilt to the little pegged rug beside it and then to the chest with four deep drawers and a tall wardrobe with a mirror in one of its doors. On the chest was a pair of pewter candlesticks and a bowl and pitcher decorated with roses. She had never known such luxury.

She stowed her new underwear and stockings in the top drawer of the chest and a few other bits and pieces of clothing in the drawers below. Then slowly undressing, she hung her coat and her skirt and blouse in the wardrobe. She slipped into the nightdress she had brought from the orphanage then crossed to the window and drew back the curtains. The night sky was bright with stars. She traced the constellations as her dad had taught her to do, silently naming each one. The Pole star winked. Softly, Lissie intoned the childish verse. '*Star light, star bright, grant the wish I make tonight.*' Then she closed the curtains, dowsed the light and climbed into bed.

She felt strange and lonely, and could barely remember a night when she hadn't been surrounded by whispering, snuffling girls in beds alongside her own. She wondered if Mary was liking her new position in the doctor's house. Connie had given her Mary's address in Bradford. Tossing and turning, she told herself she'd write a letter to Mary describing how marvellous Scarborough was.

The silence was oppressive, and she prayed that she wouldn't have *the* nightmare. It was a long time since she'd last wakened to the terrors of seeing her dad lying on the floor, because the company of the other girls had kept it at bay. Now, as she lay in the darkness waiting for sleep to take her, she not only felt lonely; she felt afraid.

16

The next morning Lissie wakened still feeling sad and lonely, and after breakfast she felt even sadder as she bade Connie a tearful goodbye.

'Don't look so miserable,' Connie said. 'I'll be back in a month or so to see how well you're getting on, and in the meantime, you can write to me.'

Lissie stood outside the house watching Connie's departing back, waving when Connie looked over her shoulder before she turned the corner.

'Don't stand there all day,' she heard Patience cry, 'there's no time for idling. The shop opens at nine.'

Lissie hurried back into the kitchen. It was a bright, airy room with windows looking out into an enclosed yard, and in the centre of the floor a large deal table and chairs. Copper pans hung from a brass rail above the gas stove, and a white pot sink and draining board with counter tops either side filled the space under the window. Neat and tidy, rather like Patience, who was clearing away the breakfast dishes, her movements rather clumsy and laboured.

'You can wash up and wipe the table,' she said. 'Plates and bowls go in this cupboard.' She tapped a door. 'And cups in this one.' She tapped again, and Lissie noticed for the first time that the joints of her fingers were swollen and knobbly.

That must be the arthritis that Connie had mentioned.

Lissie ran water into the sink and began to wash the dishes. She didn't in the least object to performing this task; after all, she was here to assist, but Patience's terse orders made her feel uncomfortable. A bit of light-hearted chat would have made her feel more at home.

Patience disappeared into the parlour, and when Lissie had done all that she had been asked to do she stood for a moment gazing out of the window. The house seemed too quiet after the bustle and noise in the orphanage. There was nobody to engage in conversation, nobody to laugh and giggle with. The company of the other girls had always made the day go quicker.

The silence grew, and along with it came an intense feeling of loneliness. An anxious knot formed in her stomach. Was this what it was going to be like every day? She turned from the window and adjusted the six chairs round the table, moving them so that they sat at equal distances from the table and each other. Then she wiped the deal table again, aware that she could hear the ticking of the longcase clock on the wall beside the door. It showed quarter past eight.

Patience entered, her stiff black skirt making a sound like autumn leaves rustling in the breeze. Her long-sleeved shirtwaist had a pintucked bodice and in the centre of the high collar she wore a cream cameo brooch that did little to soften the severity of her appearance. Her cold grey eyes raked the kitchen and she nodded her satisfaction.

'It's time to open the shop,' she said, making for the connecting door. 'Now remember, you are only here on trial. If I'm not pleased, I won't hesitate to send you packing.' She opened the door and Lissie followed, her heart in her boots. She had reached the conclusion that Patience Foyer was hard to please.

The connecting door opened directly on to the space behind the long highly polished counter. Against the wall glass-fronted cabinets displayed neat piles of garments and beneath the cabinets were serried rows of narrow drawers. The interior of the shop was in darkness and Lissie kept close behind Patience, unsure of her footing in the gloom as they walked into the body of the shop and over to a raised platform that housed the window display.

'This will be your first task each day,' Patience said, demonstrating how to open the window blinds. Lissie watched carefully as Patience pulled the cords and secured them on cleats attached to the walls on either side of the platform. Light flooded in, but even so the shop was still dimly lit. 'I don't light the mantles until late afternoon at this time of year.'

Next, they went back behind the counter, Patience pointing to the garments in the cabinets: shirts, vests, liberty bodices, blouses, and many more. Lissie's head began to spin. Then drawers were pulled open to reveal a wide variety of sewing requisites and sundry items.

'You'll have to remember where everything is,' Patience said, sliding a drawer shut then hobbling over to the side wall that was lined with shelves stacked with more goods. 'Bolts of material, sheets, blankets...' Patience fluttered her knobbly fingers impatiently. 'It's simply common sense You can see for yourself what there is, and you mustn't keep the customers waiting so take a good look and retain it in that pretty little head of yours.'

There were hats on stands and rails from which every item of clothing that anyone might ever need was hung, and before long

Lissie lost track of what she was seeing. Panic played in her chest and head.

'Now, I'll show you how to measure lengths of fabric although you're to leave any big orders to me.' Patience went back behind the counter. Lissie noticed, not for the first time, that she walked stiffly and was in the habit of running her hands over her hips and thighs. Her poor legs must be aching, she thought.

'You do know your feet and inches, don't you?' Patience was now standing in front of the brass measuring rule that was inserted into the edge of the counter.

'Oh, yes, Mrs Foyer, I'm good at measuring,' Lissie said, pleased that at last she had something to say. 'I have to measure accurately when I'm making my quilts.'

Patience raised her eyebrows. 'Quilts?'

'Yes, I made them at the orphanage. They sell them to raise funds.'

'Do they indeed.'

Had Lissie imagined it? Was there a hint of warmth and interest in Patience's remark? Her spirits were further raised when Patience handed her a bolt of blue cotton cloth and she accurately measured out the lengths that Patience dictated.

'You can measure,' Patience praised, 'but can you make change?' She opened the money drawer and said, 'I've spent one shilling and eleven pence and given you a half-crown.'

Lissie quickly handed over a penny and a sixpenny piece. A few more calculations correctly made and Patience was satisfied.

The clock on the wall chimed nine times.

'Go and open the door.' Patience handed Lissie a large bunch of keys, holding them by the one that would unlock the door.

Lissie felt quite important as she turned the key. Maybe Mrs Foyer was beginning to like her.

'Remember now, be polite and pleasant and make sure to make a sale.'

* * *

The days blurred into one as Lissie did her best to please. From early morning until seven o'clock each evening, she performed the household chores, washing and ironing, sweeping and polishing, and in between, whenever Patience required her, she worked in the shop.

The best part of any day was serving the customers, helping them choose a new hat, a pair of gloves or underwear. She especially liked handling the colourful fabrics and measuring out the required lengths, all the while aware that Patience's eyes were watching, and quick to find fault. She never corrected Lissie in front of a customer but afterwards there often followed a sharp reprimand.

Lissie had plenty to occupy her during the day, and time passed quickly enough, but after that the hours dragged. Sometimes she ventured out for a short walk on the esplanade, the summer evenings still warm and light, but she had yet to go as far as Peasholm Park or the castle on the headland. She felt places like that should be visited in the company of a friend, but Lissie knew no one other than Patience.

After the shop closed and they had eaten their evening meal, usually in silence, Patience went into the parlour to sit at a little escritoire and count the day's taking and attend to her ledgers. There was also a well-stocked bookshelf and Lissie asked if she could borrow the books and magazines from it.

'Help yourself,' Patience had said without raising her head. 'Most of them were Henry's books. He was a great reader. I prefer the magazines.'

So, Lissie had grown into the habit of taking a book and going up to her room to read. By the end of the third week in Scarborough she had perused Annie S Swan's magazines and been enthralled by *Weldon's Quilting,* travelled with Jack London into the wild with *White Fang,* devoured Forster's *Howard's End,* and empathised with Hope's *Prisoner of Zenda.* She had also written to Mary and Connie, but whilst Mrs Briggs replied almost immediately she had yet to hear from Mary. And with each passing night, she missed the camaraderie of the girls in the orphanage even more.

Three times since taking up her duties Patience had asked her to make the necessary alterations to dresses customers had purchased. Lissie had turned up the hem on a gown, adjusted the darts of the bodice of another and shortened the sleeves on a blouse with cuffs. It was tricky enough work, and she had taken great care to make her stitching as fine as she could. She had felt proud of her achievements and the owners of the garments had been delighted, but Patience had been sparing with her praise. She'd scrutinised each garment then grunted, 'Not bad,' and, 'That'll do.' Lissie had felt like screaming.

On the Monday morning at the beginning of her final week on trial Patience called for her to go into the shop. Lissie smoothed her white apron and patted her hair then hurried through the connecting door, eager to assist. Patience was serving a gentleman who wanted to buy a pair of leather gloves, and two ladies were waiting their turn.

The first woman simply wanted a spool of black thread so Lissie speedily dispatched her then gave her attention to the other customer.

'How may I help you?' she asked politely of a stout woman with ruddy cheeks. The woman leaned over the counter and whispered, 'Bloomers, large, in pink.'

Remembering that Patience had told her that ladies' personal apparel was not to be flaunted but served discreetly, particularly if a gentleman happened to be in the shop, Lissie bent to the drawer under the counter where these items were kept and slipped out two different types. Then motioning for the woman to move further down the counter away from the man procrastinating over black or brown gloves, and using her body as a shield, she slid the bloomers onto the polished top, all the while trying not to giggle. With embarrassed whispers and explanations, the woman selected the pair with a double gusset and Lissie popped them in a bag. 'Thank you for your custom,' she said, taking the florin the woman proffered, then handing her a penny change. Lissie found this subterfuge highly amusing but she couldn't share this with Patience. In fact, she shared virtually nothing with her other than following her orders and doing her best to please whilst yearning for a bit of silly chat about the foibles of the customers, or anything else for that matter.

But Patience was deliberately playing her cards close to her chest. She liked the girl; she was pleasant and willing and an extremely capable needlewoman but it wouldn't do to get too attached. Even though Connie had vouched for the girl's exemplary character she had only had dealings with her in the workhouse. Goodness only knew what she might get up to now she was free of its confines. She might turn out to be a thief or a wanton seeking out the company of men on her days off. Only time would tell.

And that time was running out, Lissie was reminded as she dressed the next morning. In two days, at the end of July, Patience would make her decision, and Lissie would either stay or be left with no option but to find another position and another place to live.

She had just finished the ironing when Patience asked for her assistance.

The shop was busy and Lissie worked as efficiently as she could. Patience might not be friendly but now understanding the wisdom of *better the devil you know,* Lissie had reached the conclusion that she'd be disappointed if she was dismissed. Not only would she have let herself down but she would be letting Mrs Briggs down. That would be hard to bear.

'You used too large a sheet of paper to wrap those,' Patience said after a young mother had purchased three small vests for her fractious children who were tearing round the shop like demons. 'And keep your eye on small children; they cause damage.'

Lissie sometimes wondered how many pairs of eyes and hands Patience thought she had.

Later that day, an elderly dowager and her daughter dithered for ages over the choice of a tablecloth and napkins. Lissie patiently showed them what was in stock but failed to make a sale.

'What's wrong with you, girl? Can't you spot a time waster? Don't pander to them. Make their minds up for them,' Patience snapped.

Something in Lissie also snapped.

'I understood that it was my duty to give the customers the best possible service. At least, that's what you told me.' Her blue eyes flashed. 'Now you're telling me I'm wrong for doing right.'

Patience blinked. 'Oh, showing a bit of spirit, are you?'

Lissie looked down at the floor. She was for it now. To her surprise she thought she heard Patience chuckle but when she raised her gaze, she saw not a glimmer of humour as Patience indicated the pile of tablecloths and napkins scattered on the counter. 'Put them back on the shelves,' she ordered.

Breath whooshed from Lissie's lungs. She hadn't been aware that she was holding it but Patience heard it and hid a smile.

Late in the afternoon of the last day of the month, as Lissie was putting an unsold scarf back in the window display, she saw a large sleek car draw up outside the shop door. A uniformed chauffeur hurried to open the car's rear door for his mistress and a woman of middle years stepped out, the silver buckles on her shoes glinting in the late afternoon sunshine as her feet touched the pavement. In her voluminous maroon velvet coat and large feathered hat, she cut a striking figure. Adjusting a fox fur tippet over her ample bosom then brandishing her silver-topped cane, she strutted imperiously into the shop.

'Leave the important customers to me,' Patience had told Lissie, but Patience was already attending an equally grand mother and daughter who were buying linens for the younger woman's trousseau.

'Good day to you Mrs Foyer,' the grandly dressed woman barked.

'Good day, Lady Saville.' Patience looked rather flustered, her glance flitting from the women she was serving back to Lady Saville and then to Lissie. 'With your permission, Lady Saville, Lissie will attend to you until I'm free.' She shot Lissie a warning glare.

Lady Saville didn't seem best pleased. She looked Lissie up and down then gave a brief nod. Lissie drew herself up to her full height and said, 'How may I be of service, Lady Saville?'

'Material for curtains, six yards,' came the brusque reply. Lissie led the way over to the rack that held the rolls of material.

Lady Saville poked her stick at one roll of fabric after another, sniffing and tutting and muttering comments such as, 'Too thin, too plain, decidedly drab,' and, 'I really shouldn't have to worry my head with such menial tasks,' as Lissie unrolled them for inspection.

Lissie, afraid of losing a sale, decided to take control.

'What room in the house are the curtains for, and what colour are the walls and the carpet? You need to consider those before choosing your fabric.'

Lady Saville's expression made Lissie wonder if she had been impertinent, but then her fleshy face broke into a wide smile. 'Of course, how clever you are. It's a bedroom for my niece, she's coming to stay and it requires freshening but not refurbishing. Now, let me think. The walls are cream and the carpet's red.'

'Then might I suggest this, Lady Saville?' Lissie took a roll of expensive cloth from the rack and draped a length of it over her arm. 'The cream background will tone nicely with the walls and the red peonies will pick up the colour of the carpet.'

'Excellent,' Lady Saville cried, fingering the quality of the fabric and nodding her satisfaction. 'You've a good head on you, girl.'

Lissie was measuring the cloth against the brass rule on the counter top as Patience's customers departed. She was cutting the required six yards when Patience hurried over. Lissie's hand trembled but she continued slicing precisely.

'I see you found something to your liking, Lady Saville,' Patience gushed.

'Credit must go to your clever assistant, Mrs Foyer. She knew exactly what I needed. She's an asset to your establishment.'

Lissie wrapped the large parcel and delivered it into the chauffer's hands. 'I'll call again, Mrs Foyer.' Lady Saville swept out to the waiting car.

In the silence that followed, Lissie put the shears back on the hook.

'Well done, Lissie. You handled that sale beautifully.' Patience's voice rang with sincerity. She smiled wickedly. 'She's an awkward besom at the best of times. Folk like her can ruin a shop's reputation if they go away unsatisfied. She usually comes in and has me tearing the shop apart until she finds something to her liking, but it's important to keep customers like her happy. And you did.'

Lissie could hardly believe what she was hearing. Not only was

Patience praising her, she was talking to her like a friend. Basking in a warm glow, she began tidying the rolls of material on the rack.

'I didn't want her to leave without making a purchase, and neither did I want her to buy something that she found unsuitable once she arrived home with it.'

Patience laughed. 'Like Lady Saville said, you've a good head on you. We can look forward to you making lots of successful sales in the future. I have a notion you and I will make a good team.'

17

The ice had been broken. Lissie began to enjoy working with Patience, and Patience appeared to appreciate her company. They no longer ate their meals in silence and in the evenings they sat in the parlour, Patience working at her ledgers and Lissie making alterations to the dresses they had sold. More often than not the conversation revolved around the day's business, and Lissie discovered that her employer had a wry sense of humour.

'Did you see that overfed daughter of Mrs Nelson's squeezing herself into the grey chiffon dress she fancied, and giving me a look that could kill when I suggested she try the larger size,' Patience chortled. 'I was waiting for the seams to split wide open and the buttons to fly off and pepper me like gunshot. She'll not be able to take any deep breaths when she's out and about. Those garments are not as robust as tailor-made.' Patience was referring to the ready-to-wear skirts, blouses and day dresses that she kept in stock for her clientele, most of whom were middle-class and couldn't afford their own dressmakers.

Lissie laughed. 'The chiffon made her look like a wrinkled sausage, and talking of holding your breath – who's that smelly old man who buys a white handkerchief every other day? Whenever he comes in, I want to hold my nose in my fingers.'

'That's Captain Buckle. A retired seaman. I've told him time and again that the handkerchiefs can be washed but he just throws them away. Mind you, after he's filled them with snot, they're most likely fit for nothing else. He takes snuff, you see. That's why his moustache is yellow.'

'Not as yellow as the hair of that chatty young woman who came in this afternoon. I think she must have dyed it that colour. You know the one I mean?'

'Oh, that little trollop. What did she buy?'

'A tablecloth. The expensive lacy one with the scalloped edges. She told me she'd just got married.'

'Oh, she got married all right, the scheming young hussy. It's not six months since she came to work for Brigadier Spencer, you know, the dapper old chap with the handlebar moustache who lives in that big house at the end of Cliffe Road. Now she's the lady of the house with a husband old enough to be her grandfather. They say she leads him a right merry dance. She'll run through his money in no time. Mind you, he'll probably not last long – but then that's why she married him.' Patience gave a wicked little laugh. 'It'll take more than a fancy tablecloth to keep her happy.'

'Oh, Mrs Foyer, you say the funniest things,' said Lissie, laughing at Patience's summation of the Brigadier's new wife. She always found Patience's character assassinations of their customers amusing, and as she threaded her needle ready to sew the hem of a dress that required shortening, she thought how nice it was that they now spent their evenings in each other's company rather than in separate rooms.

'By the way, Mrs Foyer, you'll need to re-order that line of tableware because the Brigadier's wife bought the last of it. We're running low on elastic and there's less than two yards of butter muslin on the roll.'

Patience smiled gratefully and jotted down the items in her order book.

'I have to admit that your sharp eye and sensible head make my life a lot easier, Lissie.'

Lissie flushed with pleasure.

Indeed, life was pleasant now that Patience had accepted her, and when Mrs Briggs wrote to say she was coming for the weekend, Lissie was thrilled. In order to let her see that she was happily settled in her new home, she decided to venture further afield and finally pay a visit to the castle on the headland. She had promised Connie that she would. She let Patience know of her intentions.

'Then finish early at lunchtime tomorrow. You've earned a day off.'

* * *

On Friday afternoon Lissie made her way to the headland and the ancient castle. Part way up the ascent she paused to watch the sun glimmering on the waves in South Bay. Then, musing on which foreign shores the endless sea had touched, she continued walking until, just below the castle, she came to a small stone church with a square tower that was surrounded by a graveyard. Pushing open the gate she went in.

Strolling between the graves, and stopping every now and then to read the inscriptions, she came across a headstone bearing the name Anne Brontë. Mrs Briggs had told the girls in the orphanage about the three Brontë sisters from Haworth who had all written books and since then Lissie had read Charlotte's *Jane Eyre* and Emily's *Wuthering Heights*.

Intrigued, Lissie knelt down. She saw that Anne had died on 28

May 1849. She wondered why she was buried in Scarborough. She would ask Mrs Briggs. After reading a few more headstones, she left the graveyard and climbed the track leading to the castle. Up here the breeze was much stronger than on the lower slopes and Lissie imagined what it would be like to stand on the windswept headland in a gale, watching a storm-tossed sea crashing onto the beach below. It made her feel exhilarated and she quickened her pace, her long black hair streaming like a banner as she ran to the ruins.

All that remained of the ancient fortress were crumbling towers linked to walls with long narrow windows yet it still stood tall, a bastion against invaders. Seagulls like sentinels perched on the ramparts, their sharp eyes keeping lookout. Feeling like an explorer, Lissie darted round the corner of the tower nearest the sea and almost collided with a girl about her own age. Startled, they both gasped.

'Aw, sorry pet,' the girl said, 'ah didne see you cumin.'

'Me neither,' said Lissie, curious about the girl's strange accent. 'I wasn't expecting to meet anybody up here.'

'Aye, me an' all. Ah cum here on me day off for a bit o' piece an' quiet.'

'That's just what I'm doing,' Lissie replied. 'I've not been here before and I wanted to see what the castle looked like close up.'

'Are you on your holidays?'

'No, I work here in the drapery on North Marine Road for Mrs Foyer.'

'Ahm at the Grand meself.' The girl pointed to the large hotel in the near distance. 'Ahm a chambermaid there.' The girl flicked strands of long fair hair from her cheeks. 'Wind's gettin' up. Go back round the other side in t'shelter.'

Lissie retraced her steps and the girl followed. In the lee of the tower, they rested against its walls. 'Ahm Meggie Burnap from

Newcastle on Tyne,' the girl said. 'What's your name, an' where are you from?'

'Lissie Fairweather, and I'm from...' She hesitated. Where did she come from?

'From Thorne in Derbyshire,' she said. There was no need to mention the orphanage to a total stranger.

'Ahm glad I met you, Lissie. Mebbe we can meet again. Ah don't know anybody in Scarborough except for them ah work with an' they're not right pally. Ahm always at a bit of a loose end on me day off. It 'ud be nice to have a friend.'

Lissie's heart soared. 'I'd like that. I've missed my friends in the... in Thorne.'

They walked together down the hill and onto the esplanade, Meggie telling Lissie what a chambermaid's job entailed and Lissie telling Meggie about her work in the drapery. By now the sun was low in the sky and as Lissie looked out to where the sea met the sky it seemed as though the water was ablaze.

'Isn't that just beautiful,' she breathed.

'Aye, it's a bonny sight all right,' Meggie agreed. 'What do you say to goin' to the Pavilion for a cup of tea or an ice cream?'

Lissie knew that Patience would be expecting her back for tea, but she was loath to refuse. She'd found a friend in Meggie and she was intent on keeping her.

* * *

Connie was delighted to find that Lissie and Patience were happy living and working together. She had feared that her sister-in-law would be too difficult for Lissie to accept, and she had worried that her favourite charge might run away.

'It was hard at first,' Lissie told her when they went for a walk later that day. 'We didn't seem to know how to behave towards one another. All I did was carry out Mrs Foyer's orders, and I never seemed to please her. But now we get on like a house on fire.' She giggled. 'We laugh at the funny things that happen in the shop, and we spend lovely evenings sitting together doing the alterations.'

'I'm so pleased it's worked out for you, Lissie. You're almost like one of the family now and it will make my visits to Patience all the pleasanter.' She clasped Lissie's hand. 'Shall we walk to the Pavilion for a glass of lemonade?'

Then Lissie told Connie about her new friend, Meggie Burnap. 'She's from Newcastle and she's a chambermaid at the Grand Hotel. Her regular afternoon off is Friday and Mrs Foyer's agreed to letting me have Friday afternoons off as well so we can meet up.'

'That's lovely. You need friends of your own age,' Connie agreed, her lips curving into a proud smile as she said, 'You have made yourself at home here in Scarborough, haven't you?'

'To begin with I didn't think I would. It all seemed strange and lonely after being in the orphanage, but I'm gradually finding my feet,' Lissie said cheerily.

Over an ice cream and lemonade Lissie described her visit to the graveyard. 'Why is Anne Brontë buried here when her father had a parsonage in Haworth? I remember you telling us that so I thought she'd have been laid to rest there.'

'It's a sad story, Lissie,' Connie replied, warmed to know that her former pupil had held on to the things she had taught her. 'Anne was very ill, you see. She had tuberculosis, and her sister, Charlotte, thought the sea air might improve her health. Their sister, Emily, and their brother, Branwell, had both died only a few months before and not many days after Charlotte and Anne arrived in Scarborough, Anne also passed away. This was her favourite place so Charlotte had her buried here.'

Lissie looked as though she might cry. 'Imagine that,' she said on her breath. 'Poor Charlotte, standing in that graveyard all alone as they put her sister in the ground. I bet it was raining and the wind blowing cold off the sea, and her heart breaking 'cos she was the only one left.'

'Yes, it must have been dreadful. However, I'm not sure Charlotte would have been there alone. I'm sure their father would have travelled from Haworth,' Connie said, touched by Lissie's compassion and impressed by her beautiful imagination.

Later that evening when Lissie had gone to bed Connie told Patience what Lissie had said. 'She's as happy as a sand boy now but she did say that at first you hadn't known how to behave towards one another.'

Patience nodded in agreement.

'I'd got that set in my ways with only myself for company that I didn't know what to do with her. I'm not used to dealing with children never having had any of my own.' Patience shook her head regretfully and gave Connie a sympathetic smile. 'Me and you are a pair, aren't we? No chick nor child between us.' Connie nodded and returned the sad smile. 'I liked her from the start,' Patience continued, 'but I didn't want to get too attached to her in case she turned out to be a wrong 'un, or just upped and left... and now,' she gave a satisfied sigh, 'I'm glad you brought her, Connie. She's put new life in me.'

* * *

On Monday morning after Lissie and Patience had bidden Connie farewell they went into the shop. It was still early, and more than half an hour before opening time. Lissie's confidence high, she mooted a plan that she had contemplated ever since she had arrived in the drapery.

'Mrs Foyer, I have an idea. I've been giving it some thought for a while now. Can I tell you about it?'

Patience was rattling the day's float into the money drawer. 'Aye, go on,' she said, frowning and sounding rather wary.

'It's the window display.' She gestured at the low platform on which gloves, scarves and tableware were haphazardly scattered amongst a couple of hats on metal stands and a cardigan fastened round a headless mannequin.

'What about it?'

'It doesn't look very attractive,' Lissie said tentatively.

'Is... that... so?' Patience's sardonic expression and long-drawn-out words let Lissie know that she felt she was being criticised.

Lissie dropped her gaze. Silently, she chastised herself. *Oh dear, me and my bright ideas. Please don't let me have spoiled our friendship.* She struggled to redeem the unintended slight.

'It doesn't do justice to the lovely things we sell. You have such a good eye for buying the right things from the wholesalers but if the customers don't see them at their best, they won't ask for them, Mrs Foyer,' she gabbled, hopeful that Patience would hear the truth in what she was saying.

'In other words, you think you'd make a much better job of it. Is that what you're trying to say?' Patience's wry smile reassured Lissie.

'I could try,' she said, her blue eyes sparkling with anticipation.

'Well, get started then. It won't be busy this morning, it never is on Mondays so you'll have plenty time to show me what you can do.'

'Oh, thank you, Mrs Foyer,' said Lissie, hurrying to the window to begin clearing it ready for the new display she envisaged.

'Can I hunt in the store for things?' Lissie was referring to the cluttered little room behind the shop.

'Help yourself, there might be something you can use.'

Back and forth Lissie went, finding the things she needed. Patience served a few customers, deliberately keeping her nose out of what was happening at the window. *Give the girl her opportunity, see what she comes up with,* she told herself, raising her eyebrows as Lissie crossed the shop with a pile of empty boxes.

'Can I borrow a clean white sheet from upstairs?' Lissie asked.

'You know where they are,' Patience replied, her curiosity mounting as Lissie skipped up to the airing cupboard.

Up and down from the platform, and occasionally stepping outside to check her handiwork from the street, Lissie happily toiled to achieve the desired result. Two hours later, she and her employer stood out on the pavement gazing at the finished window display.

'My, Lissie, you've done us proud,' Patience exclaimed.

Lissie felt as though her heart might burst. Not just at the sight of what she had achieved, but that Patience had said 'us'.

'That dress looks twice the price the way you've showed it off,' said Patience, pointing to the full-size mannequin now wearing a blue cotton dress with a flared skirt and a white sailor collar braided with blue. Lissie had found the mannequin in bits in the store, and after re-assembling and dressing it, she had put a straw boater with a blue and white striped ribbon at a jaunty angle on its head. At the mannequin's feet she had artfully draped a blue wool jacket along with a pair of white stockings and gloves in a darker blue.

'If they buy the dress, they might also buy the hat, the gloves and the jacket because they can see it makes a complete outfit,' Lissie said.

Patience nodded her agreement, her gaze fixed on the display.

The mannequin stood to one side of the window and in the centre a pyramid of boxes draped with the white sheet had different designs of napery in blue and white on each level. At the other side of the window was a gentleman's dark blue cardigan, a white cotton shirt, a pair of blue and white striped braces and a navy and white braided yachting cap.

'Oh, Lissie, that maritime theme is just perfect for a shop by the sea. We'll give Marshall & Snelgrove a run for their money with a display like this.' Patience was referring to one of the town's most prestigious department stores. 'All those different shades of blue catch the eyes rightly. I'll say this for you, Lissie, you have a good eye for colour.'

'Mrs Briggs used to say that when I used to make the quilts in the orphanage,' said Lissie, feeling overwhelmed by Patience's praise.

'Aye, talking of quilts. Why don't you take the ends of some of the rolls in the shop and make a quilt or two. We could sell them.'

Lissie's heart leapt. 'Oh, could I, Mrs Foyer? I'd love to make quilts out of such lovely material. I've only ever made them out of cheap cotton scraps before.'

'Well, now's your chance to make us some really fine quilts,' Patience said, smiling at her assistant's enthusiasm.

Thrilled with the success of her morning's work, Lissie viewed her future in Foyer's Drapery with fresh eyes.

18

'Mrs Foyer was ever so pleased with me,' Lissie told Meggie as they stood outside the shop on Friday afternoon looking at the window display. 'I didn't think she'd agree to me doing it but she didn't interfere one bit.'

'Ah'd love to wear that,' Meggie said, pointing to the dress with the sailor collar, 'but on my wages ah'd never afford it, an' sailor collars are all the rage.'

'I could make you a collar and you could attach it to that dress you're wearing,' Lissie said, indicating Meggie's round-necked navy cotton frock and thinking of the material Patience had said she could use.

'Eeh, could you, Lissie?' Meggie's eyes lit up. She was a buxom girl, shorter in height than Lissie, and her pretty plump face and cloud of fine fair hair reminded Lissie of the cherubs she had seen in religious pictures.

Meggie had called at the shop for Lissie so that they could spend their free afternoon together. Patience had greeted her pleasantly, asked her about her job at the Grand, and told her she was pleased that Lissie had found a friend. Now, as they walked down North Marine Road she said, 'She's nice, is Mrs Foyer.'

'She is, although I didn't much like her to begin with. I thought I might not be able to stick her, but now we've got to know one another I'm glad I didn't give up on her.'

'Aah hated Mrs Hopper, the housekeeper, from the moment aah first met her an' I haven't changed me mind,' Meggie moaned. 'Aah work as fast as aah can an' she still shouts at me. Aahm sick o' mekkin beds an' pickin' up after people.'

'Maybe she'll soften with time. Mrs Foyer did.'

'Aah wouldn't bet on it,' Meggie scoffed.

'Let's do something really nice,' Lissie said, wanting to cheer Meggie up. 'What do you say to going to The People's Palace? I've not been there and Mrs Foyer says there's all sorts to see.'

'Aye, there is, but the tickets cost an arm an' a leg,' said Meggie, and then not wanting to be a kill-joy, 'Johnny the doorman at the Grand told me they've got real live monkeys. Aah've only ever seen pictures of 'em.'

'Me an' all,' said Lissie, thinking that there was a lot of things she'd never seen in real life, and as they walked towards Valley Bridge she decided to confide in Meggie. If they were to be friends, they should be honest with one another.

'I've not seen much of anywhere or anything,' Lissie said. 'I lived in an orphanage for the last seven years before coming here.'

'Eeh! You never did. You poor thing,' Meggie exclaimed. 'Warrit awful?'

As they strolled along Lissie told her what it had been like, the good and the bad, and how Mrs Briggs had come to her rescue.

'Eeh, aah don't know what I would have done wi'out me mam an' dad,' Meggie said. 'It near broke me heart comin' here but there's no work in Newcastle for lasses like me, so I had to, me bein' the eldest. Me dad canna work any more since he wa' hurt in the shipyard an' me mam needs the bit I earn to help feed the young'uns. I send half me wages home.'

Lissie felt sorry for her. The wages Patience insisted on paying her went mostly unspent and she was gathering a nice little nest egg. 'I'll pay for us to get into The People's Palace,' she said, and not wanting Meggie to feel like this was charity she added, 'You can buy us a cup of tea afterwards.'

'Aw, that's real nice of you, pet.'

By now they had arrived at the grand entrance that led into the underground aquarium and zoo. The Palace was a vast complex built under the Valley Bridge. It had a concert hall, a dining room, a fernery and huge tanks of water for sea creatures as well as cages for animals. Lissie paid and they entered the foyer, stopping to look at the boards that explained what was on offer.

'Let's gan to the aquarium,' said Meggie, her excitement mounting.

Inside the massive tunnel they stared in awe at the huge water-filled tanks.

'Look! They're seals.' Lissie pointed to the large grey slippery creatures that were basking on rocks or swimming lazily in the dark waters surrounded by cascading waterfalls and rocky gardens. They stood for a while, spellbound, before moving along with the crowd.

'What's them?' Meggie asked, looking distastefully at the long greenish-brown animals that lay supine in beds of reeds. 'Look at the size of its jaws. It 'ud swallow you whole if you fell in.' The alligator slowly opened and closed its huge mouth.

'Look at all them teeth.' Lissie shuddered at the thought of being clamped between the rows of razor-sharp needles.

In the aviary, Lissie fell in love with the birds of paradise. 'They're so graceful and colourful,' she said. And when they went into the zoo, Meggie cried, 'Eeh, look at them little fellas. If aah had one as a pet aah'd train it to pinch Mrs Hopper's white cap an' swing on her hair.' Meggie's eyes gleamed with vengeance as she laughed at the monkeys' antics.

'I'd have a bird 'cos Mrs Foyer would say the monkeys were rude the way they stick their bums in the air.' That set them off laughing, and thrilled by all that they had seen, they left The People's Palace and went out into the late afternoon sunshine.

'Thanks for payin' for me, Lissie. Aah couldn't have afforded it, but I will buy us a cup of tea.'

In a small tea room, Meggie paid for the teas and Lissie bought two ham and tomato sandwiches. 'I don't have to go back for my tea. I told Mrs Foyer I'd eat out and I'd like you to join me,' she said, handing Meggie a sandwich. They had so much to talk about that by the time they left the café and were strolling on the esplanade the sun was a fiery glow on the horizon.

They hadn't gone far when they drew level with two boys who were lolling against the sea wall. One of them looked about the same age as the girls and the other one maybe a year or two older. The younger lad called out to the girls and they giggled and carried on walking.

'Have you ever had a boyfriend?' Meggie asked as they pretended not to notice that the boys were dogging their footsteps.

'No, I don't know a thing about boys. The only boys we ever saw were when we walked to church on Sunday.' Lissie explained what she meant by that and went on to say, 'There was one I used to look out for but I never spoke to him 'cos we weren't allowed so he winked at me and I smiled back.'

'Aah had a lad in Newcastle. He wa' nice an' he kissed me goodbye when I came here but I don't suppose aah'll ever see him again.' By now the boys were right on the girls' heels and Meggie turned and said cheekily, 'Are you lads follerin' us?'

'If you'll let us,' said the lad with a shock of fair hair. 'I'm Jimmy and me mate here is Flynn.' The older boy flicked a lock of hair, black as a raven's wing, from his brow then nodded and smiled, his laughing blue eyes meeting Lissie's.

'Aahm Meggie and she's Lissie, an' aah fancy an' ice cream so are you lads gonna buy us one?'

Shocked by her friend's boldness, Lissie blushed. But Jimmy laughed and said, 'Aye, if that's what you want.'

They found a stall and sat on the promenade wall licking ice cream cones sprinkled with hundreds and thousands, and Lissie, feeling carefree and daring, readily joined in the banter with Meggie and the boys.

'Do you ladies fancy a whirl on the carousel?' Flynn flashed Lissie a tempting smile. She wasn't sure she did after eating the ice cream, but Meggie had jumped to her feet and was raring to go. The boys led the way and they all trotted to Peasholm Park.

On the way there they established that fifteen-year-old Jimmy worked for his father in the family butcher's and that Flynn, who was nearly seventeen, worked at the amusements ground they were walking towards.

'What about you, Lissie? Where do you work?' Flynn asked.

'Foyer's Drapery on North Marine Road,' she replied.

When Flynn chose not to mention that Patience Foyer was also his employer, Jimmy gave him a curious look and was about to open his mouth but Flynn gave an imperceptible shake of his head. He didn't want this lovely girl to report back to their boss that he was giving free rides on the carousel. Jimmy understood, winked, and kept quiet.

Round and round and up and down they went, music blaring and the hot, sweet smell of candy floss wafting on the air as Lissie, her heart thudding and her palms moistening, gripped the pole that suspended the horse on which she and Flynn were sitting, his thighs pressed against hers and his arms round her waist. Reminded of the fair in Great Horton that Bill Jackson had taken her to along with Emmy and his family, she felt a lump in her throat. She'd written twice to Emmy and received a letter back telling her how lucky she was to have a lovely job and be living in a marvellous place like Scarborough.

She did feel lucky. The new and wonderful things she was experiencing seemed never ending. And there was more to come.

Breathless with excitement, and her feet back on the ground, Lissie ran with the others to the roll a penny stall, then the hook-a-duck and the coconut shy. They were having so much fun that it wasn't until she stopped to admire the strings of coloured lights that were now ablaze that Lissie realised dusk had fallen. Meggie, also aware of how late it was, looked anxiously at Lissie.

'Aahd best get a move on. Aah've to be back for nine,' she said, her face creasing with disappointment.

She had no sooner spoken than a gnarled old man wearing a chip hat and a leather jerkin approached them and, clapping his hand on Flynn's shoulder, he said, 'I'm off now.' He hobbled away on bandy legs.

'Sorry, girls. I've got to leave you. It's my turn to run the carousel.'

'You work here?' Lissie asked, amazed.

'Yes. I was just taking an hour off but now I have to get back to it.'

'An' I'll have to leg it back to the Grand else Mrs Hopper'll be hoppin' mad an' have me guts for garters,' Meggie cried.

'I'll walk with you,' Jimmy quickly offered, his gallantry fading as he mumbled, 'I've to go that road anyway.' He turned to Lissie. 'Are you coming?'

'No, I'll just nip through the park to North Marine Road. It's closer and I'm already later than I should be.' She smiled at Jimmy then hugged Meggie. 'I'll see you next Friday.' Meggie and Jimmy hurried off.

'I'd better get to work,' Flynn said. 'Will you be all right on your own?'

Lissie gave him a bright smile. 'Course I will. And thanks for all the fun.'

'We'll do it again,' Flynn said, anxious to be off. 'See you around.'

Lissie hurried along the path feeling as light as a feather. It had been a splendid afternoon filled with pleasures. She'd seen and done things she had only ever imagined in her wildest dreams, and furthermore she had made two new friends in Jimmy and Flynn. Life had never felt better.

Near the end of the path, she walked past a seedy-looking man. He was standing almost hidden in the shrubbery, his cigarette glowing in the half-dark. Lissie, still bouncing with euphoria, paid him no heed. A few paces more and she was conscious that he was walking closely behind her. She quickened her step. The path ahead of her was empty as was the vast expanse of grass on her left, and to her right were shrubs and trees. Sweat moistened her armpits and the thudding of her heart was so loud that she thought he must be able to hear it.

Too late, she broke into a run, only to find herself in an iron grip as he threw her against the hedge. She screamed and kicked to no avail, winded when he pushed her down on the ground, her head in the shrubbery and her feet sticking out on the path. Then he was on top of her, yanking at her skirt, his rough hands mauling her thighs as he tore at her knickers. When she screamed again, he clamped a dirty hand over her mouth, his other hand probing her most private places. Bile rose in her throat and she felt as though she might choke on it.

Pressed to the ground under his weight, Lissie struggled and squirmed but her movements seemed to excite him all the more and now he was grabbing at his baggy trousers with his free hand.

Lissie had listened to girls in the orphanage gossiping about the awful men that their feckless mothers had brought home, heard tales of how they had interfered with them in the dead of night. The stories they had told were sickening, and she knew in that instance that she was about to be subjected to the disgusting things that had happened to them. Her head spun, then her mind went blank as she suddenly drifted into semi-consciousness, aware only of a hard, wet thing being pushed between the tops of her legs.

Constable Sam Hardcastle doing his rounds on night duty gasped and leapt into action when he saw a pair of women's shoes and pretty ankles sticking out from the hedge underneath a pair of shabby brown boots. 'Oi! What's going on here?' he yelled, grabbing the tail of the man's coat and dragging him upright. The miscreant lashed out and with his loosened trousers in danger of tripping him, he broke free and ran.

Sam let him go. He knew who he was and would arrest him later. Now it was imperative to assist the young girl who, still flat on her back, was gazing blearily up at him through terrified eyes. 'Come on, love,' he said gently, pulling Lissie to her feet. She fell against him sobbing and shuddering.

'I don't think he...' Sam waggled his fingers, lost for words as he told Patience what he had come across. 'She said it had most likely been only minutes afore I came along, although I'm sure it felt like a lifetime to her, poor lass.'

'She's such an innocent little thing,' Patience said, handing Sam a cup of tea then standing wringing her hands in consternation and biting her bottom lip. 'But I think she has some understanding of that sort of thing. When I asked had he pushed himself into her down below she said he hadn't. Mind you, she's terribly distressed. I gave her a bath and checked her over and she doesn't appear to be harmed, well, at least not her body. It's up here, I fear for.' She tapped her head.

'Aye, that sort of thing can linger in the mind for long enough,' Sam agreed. He drained his cup, ready to leave. 'Have no fear, Mrs Foyer, we'll nab him again afore the night's over, but what use it does I'm not sure. He's not long out of gaol from the last time we caught him. He can't keep his hands off young women.'

'He should be locked up for good,' Patience snapped.

'You try telling that to t'magistrates,' said Sam. He put on his helmet. 'I'll call again in a day or two and see how she is. You take care of her, Mrs Foyer.'

'I will, Sam, and thanks for coming along when you did.'

After Sam had gone, Patience hurried back upstairs to Lissie's bedroom where Lissie was propped up against her pillows staring blankly at the wall.

'How are you feeling now, love?'

'I don't know.' Lissie's reply sounded as though it came from a long way off.

'Try not to dwell on it,' Patience said, fully aware that it was easier said than done as she sat down on the edge of the bed and took Lissie's hands in her own. What had happened couldn't be undone and Lissie had her whole life in front of her. Patience felt shrouded in guilt.

Has Connie told this poor young lass anything of the dangers that lurk in the world outside the orphanage? I know I haven't, and I should have done after she's led such a sheltered life in the company of just girls and women. A good mother would have warned her daughter when she got to a certain age, not left her to get a rude awakening. Had I taken the trouble to educate her in such matters she'd not have been walking on her own in the park at that time of night.

Patience squeezed Lissie's hands. Lissie heaved a great sigh then, as though wakening from a trance, she began to sob. 'I... I'd had such... a lovely day,' she hiccupped, tears streaming down her cheeks. 'He... he just crept up on me... I did fight him, Mrs Foyer,' she sobbed, her hysteria mounting in her desperation to let her employer know that she hadn't given her attacker any encouragement.

'Oh, you poor child.' Patience folded Lissie in a warm embrace and rocked her back and forth as though she was a babe in her arms. 'There, there, let it all out,' she crooned, thinking that if Lissie tried to bury her ordeal it would torment her all the longer.

But Lissie shrank from her, mumbling, 'I can't. I don't even want to think about it.' She slid under the covers. 'I'm tired, Mrs Foyer.'

'Course you are,' Patience said, dropping a kiss on her brow and quietly leaving the room.

It was all right to say she didn't want to think about but it wouldn't go away and during the night Lissie tossed and turned, one ugly dream after another invading her sleep. Confused scenes of her dad lying on the cottage floor, his blood flowing, became entangled with the dirty man pressing her into the earth. She woke bathed in sweat, her heart pumping and the rank smell of him thick in her nose. Towards dawn, she got up and sat by the window, gazing out into the darkness. Everything looked black and she thought she would never feel clean again. Only hours before, she had been glad to be alive. Now she felt anything but.

19

In the days that followed, Lissie kept to her bedroom. 'I can't face anybody yet,' she solemnly told Patience. 'I'm sorry to be a nuisance, but I just can't.'

Patience accepted this without complaint. 'When you're ready,' she said, going downstairs to run the shop on her own, do the household chores and in between nurse Lissie like one would a sick child. She tempted her with tasty meals, but Lissie had no appetite. 'Thank you, Mrs Foyer. I'm sorry I didn't eat it,' she said, sounding utterly contrite.

Day after day, up in her room lost in her misery, Lissie tried to read in an attempt to block out the horrors of her ordeal but nothing captured her imagination or distracted her from her dark thoughts. What if the policeman hadn't found her? What if that awful man had finished what he'd started? She'd heard of girls of her age who had given birth to babies foisted on them by hideous men just seeking their own pleasure. One of the girls in the orphanage had told them her sister had had a baby at thirteen by the man who was living with her mother. They'd carted her off to an asylum, she'd said.

Up and down stairs Patience ministered to her, always kind and gentle and never giving up hope. When Meggie called for Lissie the next Friday Patience told her. 'She's not in any fit state to see anybody today. Come again next week. She should be better by then.' She made no mention of the attack. If Lissie wanted to confide in her friend, she'd leave it up to her.

A week later, in which Lissie had ventured out of her room for an hour or two to do the household chores but still begged not to attend Patience in the shop, Meggie called again. This time Patience said. 'Go up and have a word with her. I think she'll be glad to see you.'

Meggie mounted the stairs and Patience went back into the shop holding her breath and praying she had done the right thing.

Lissie looked up from the book she was reading as Meggie entered the room, surprised to see her friend. 'Oh, I thought it was Mrs Foyer,' she said, a flutter of uncertainty catching in her throat. She felt embarrassed.

'Mrs Foyer told me you haven't been well but I've missed you so I had to come again. Are you feeling better?' Meggie spoke with such sincerity that tears sprang to Lissie's eyes. Before she could prevent herself, she told Meggie everything, and as her friend hugged her and whispered soothing words Lissie felt as though she had put down a heavy burden that she had been carrying for too long.

Later that night, she sat by the window watching the darkening sky and stars pricking the sky. Out of nowhere she recalled something her father had told her back in the cottage in Thorne.

The cat had given birth to five kittens, one of them with a head too large for its body. The mother cat kicked it out of the basket, and no matter how many times Lissie returned it she would find it crawling around, blind and helpless, on the cold floor of the shed.

Lissie had felt an empathy with the tiny creature and was determined to save it.

Then one day, after her mother had given her a beating, she had sought refuge in the shed to wait for her father to return from the village. In her haste she had raced inside and trod on something soft. It was the kitten.

'It was an accident, you didn't mean to kill it,' her dad had said as she'd sobbed in his arms, but Lissie's grief had bordered on hysteria. Taking her on his knee in the dark, musty shed he'd told her that sometimes terrible things happened but that she mustn't let them take control. *If you fall, you pick yourself up and carry on. Nothing is impossible if you believe in yourself and moving on is the best way to get on in life*, he had said. As she remembered his words, she wondered what he would think of her now, hiding away and dwelling on her misfortune. He wouldn't approve. And even though he was no longer part of her life she wanted him to be proud of her, praise her for her fortitude and courage, and be pleased with how she was facing the future.

That night, she slept soundly. No nightmares invaded her dreams and she wakened feeling renewed. She had done nothing wrong. She was still the decent ambitious girl she had been before the attack, she told herself as she dressed to go downstairs: that filthy miscreant had not stolen her life.

Patience passed no remark on Lissie's recovery but her smiles and the pleasure she took from her assistant's company told a different story. On the next Monday, late in the afternoon after the shop had closed, a knock on the house door had Lissie hurrying to answer it. She stared, surprised to see Flynn standing on the step with a leather bag in his hand. She blanched, the colour leeching from her cheeks as she wondered what Mrs Foyer would say to a young lad calling for her.

'You look like you've seen a ghost,' he said, his blue eyes dancing and his grin wide. He gestured with the bag. 'I've come to see Mrs Foyer,' he continued, 'so are you going to let me in?'

What did he want with Patience? Lissie felt a flutter of panic in her chest. 'Why?' she asked nervously.

'I work for her. It's her carousel you were riding on the last time we met.' He spoke carelessly as though Lissie should have known.

Lissie's jaw dropped. 'Oh, you never said,' she replied, her tone accusing.

'You never asked,' Flynn scoffed. 'Now, are you going to keep me standing here all day?'

Lissie stood back and Flynn walked directly to the kitchen. He had clearly been here before.

'Ah, Flynn,' Patience cried, her smile welcoming. 'What brings you here? Where's Harry?'

'He's laid up, Mrs Foyer. His legs are giving him bother and his chest's bad.' He handed her the leather bag.

'Oh dear, that doesn't sound good. Still, I'm sure you can run the rides as well as Harry, if not better.' Patience pursed her lips, deep in thought. 'Will you sit and take a cup of tea, Flynn? We need to talk.'

'That I will, Mrs Foyer. I've left Pete and his lad minding the rides.' Flynn sat down at the table and Patience put the kettle on and set cups, milk and biscuits in front of him.

As they talked, Lissie stood silently in the doorway feeling uncomfortable in Flynn's presence and trying to make sense of things. Flynn was also in Mrs Foyer's employ, and Harry must be the elderly man who had spoken to Flynn that night at the fairground, the man who regularly called on Saturday evening when Patience would take him into the kitchen out of Lissie's hearing. She was so deep in thought that she jumped when Patience said, 'Will you join us, Lissie?'

Lissie sat down, her discomfort increasing when Patience introduced her.

'Flynn Corrigan, this is my companion and assistant, Miss Lissie Fairweather.'

'Pleased to meet you, Miss Fairweather.' Flynn's eyes twinkled mischievously.

'And you, Mr Corrigan.' At Lissie's prim reply, Flynn's lips twitched. She could tell he was trying not to laugh out loud. They sipped their tea.

Patience lifted the leather bag off the table. 'I'll put this away,' she said and went into the parlour. Lissie and Flynn exchanged amused looks.

'Why didn't you say we'd already met?' she hissed.

'I was leaving it up to you, and when you pretended not to know me, I thought it was because you didn't want Mrs Foyer to think you were gadabout girl,' he said, deliberately keeping his voice low.

Lissie giggled at the description. 'We'd best keep pretending for now or she'll think we have something to hide,' she whispered as they heard the parlour door close and Patience's footsteps in the hall.

'So, as I was saying, Miss Fairweather, the carousel and the children's rides are all powered by a huge engine,' Flynn expounded as Patience came back into the kitchen, 'and it's my job to keep it running.'

'That's very interesting, Mr Corrigan,' Lissie piped, her ribs aching with suppressed laughter.

'And keep it running, he does,' said Patience, sitting back down at the table. 'He's a good reliable lad and I have every faith in him. Now, down to business. Maybe you'd leave us to it, Lissie.'

Lissie stood. 'Good evening, Mr Corrigan. It was nice meeting you.'

'And you, Miss Fairweather. Perhaps we'll meet again.'

Lissie took the stairs two at a time and, bursting into her bedroom, she flung herself on the bed and smothered her laughter in the pillow. Oh, but Flynn Corrigan was funny, and she sincerely hoped they would meet again.

In the months that followed that evening, summer days faded into a glorious autumn then into a harsh winter. Lissie and Flynn and Meggie and Jimmy became the best of friends; nothing romantic, just good pals who enjoyed talking and laughing together on their days off work.

'What'll it be today, ladies?' Flynn asked as they met outside The People's Palace on a cold November afternoon, the sea rumbling in the distance and rainclouds gathering overhead.

'Somewhere warm and dry,' Lissie said, pulling her woollen hat closer over her ears and shivering even though she was wearing a new thick winter coat that Patience had bought for her from a travelling salesman who called at the shop once a month. It was navy blue with a high collar and deep pockets. Lissie felt rather glamorous and grown-up whenever she wore it.

'We could go in here,' said Meggie, gesturing at the entrance to The Palace. In they went, enjoying the exhibits twice as much in the company of the boys.

'Look out, Meggie! That alligator's coming to get you,' Jimmy shouted as the creature pushed its knobby snout against the glass wall. Meggie screamed and jumped a foot in the air, then fell against Lissie laughing when Jimmy knocked on the glass and the alligator turned tail and glided into the reeds. They rounded off their visit in the monkey house, the boys pulling funny faces at the monkeys and imitating their movements. It was all so much fun, and Lissie had never felt happier.

The holiday season was long over so visitors to the resort were few and far between. They almost had The Palace to themselves and when they were back on the esplanade the jolly crowds that had thronged the town were noticeable by their absence. The outdoor amusements had been dismantled or covered over with huge tarpaulins, and the ice cream and candy floss vendors had disappeared. Even so, Lissie still thought that Scarborough was a magical place and that there was nowhere else she'd rather be.

'What will you do now the rides are closed?' she asked Flynn when they were seated in a small café enjoying hot drinks and buttered crumpets.

'I paint the carousel and the merry-go-rounds. Get 'em all spruced up ready for next year,' he said, after wiping a dribble of butter off his chin. 'It's slow work 'cos you have to follow the patterns carefully and get the colours just right.'

Lissie pictured the doe-eyed horses, their long lashes and smiling mouths, and their brightly coloured harness. 'Do you think I could help,' she asked, thinking how wonderful it would be to paint the ornate patterns that decorated the rides. Her eagerness made Flynn smile.

'If Mrs Foyer says it's okay, it's all right by me. I need all the help I can get, but we don't want to get on the wrong side of the boss so ask her first.' He paused then said, 'Can you paint?'

'I can give it a try,' Lissie said, her eyes sparkling.

Later that same evening, as Lissie sat at the sewing machine in the room next to the parlour putting the finishing touches to the quilt she was making, Patience came in to see how she was progressing. Lissie eased her foot off the treadle and the whizzing needle stilled. Lissie sat back and looked expectantly at Patience.

'It's beautiful,' she said, her knobbly arthritic fingers stroking the quilt's red and white triangles and its centrepiece of red and gold hexagons. She had told Lissie that if there was less than a yard of fabric on a roll, she could use it to make the quilt and Lissie, thrilled to be working with such fine material, had carefully planned the intricate design of white and red cotton lawn and gold brocade.

'Do you think anybody will buy it?'

'I'm sure they will. It's a work of art.'

Glowing under the praise, Lissie thought this was as good a time as any to ask Patience if she could help Flynn paint the merry-go-rounds. She had already confessed to having met Flynn before that evening when he'd called to tell Patience that Harry was unwell. She had thought it unfair to lie.

Instead of being annoyed, Patience had laughed at their subterfuge mimicking Lissie's: 'And you, Mr Corrigan,' then adding, 'You sly little puss.'

'I thought you might be cross,' Lissie had said then. Now, when she broached the matter of helping Flynn paint the merry-go-round, Patience raised no objections and told her she held Flynn in high regard.

'And if you paint as cleverly as you quilt, you'll be helping him, so go on Monday. The shop's always quiet then.'

'Thanks, Mrs Foyer.' Lissie's eyes gleamed with anticipation and later when she was in bed thinking about the next day, she recalled the times she had helped paint the toys her father had made for her and her heart ached for him.

'You're a natural,' Flynn said as he studied the carousel horse Lissie was working on. 'You've picked out the colours in his harness a real treat, Lissie, and made his eyes look as though he'd give you the ride of your life.'

She had flecked the horse's large dark brown eyes with gold to make them look alive, and painted the ornate harness in swirls of blue, red and gold.

'Can I do another one then?'

'I should say so. With your help we'll have the carousel finished before Christmas, then we can start on the merry-go-rounds in the new year, get them spanking new, ready for Easter.'

At the mention of Christmas Lissie's eyes lit up. It would be her first proper Christmas since she had been forced to leave the cottage in Thorne. She didn't count the ones in the orphanage as a true celebration of the season. Memories flooded back to the time she had gone with her father into the woods to gather holly and ivy, and deck a small fir tree with glistening baubles and candles. He was never far from her mind but as the years had gone by, she rarely indulged in remembering the things she and her dad had done together; some recollections were too painful.

Now, paintbrush in hand, she pictured his strong hands and heard his voice saying, 'Clever girl, Lissie.' Tears sprang to her eyes.

'Hey, what are the tears for?' Flynn sounded alarmed.

'I was remembering my dad,' Lissie whispered.

Flynn knew nothing of Lissie's background. There had never been a reason for her to tell him. He'd simply accepted that she lived with and worked for Mrs Foyer and had seen no reason to enquire further.

'Did he die?' he asked gently, touched by her sudden sadness.

'I don't know. He might have. We didn't stay to find out,' she sobbed.

And before she could prevent herself, she confided in Flynn all that she had kept secret. He listened without interruption, horrified and angered as she described how her mother had attacked her father then dragged her away from her home before abandoning her in the orphanage. 'So, you see, I don't know whether he's dead or if he's still alive and wondering what became of me.'

'You poor kid.' Flynn patted her shoulder. 'Dry your eyes, and stop worrying. Just keep hoping he is alive. As for feeling guilty, you were an innocent child then. It's your ma who's to blame and she's long gone,' he said, his eyes flashing with anger, 'and good riddance. It sounds like you're better off without her.' He gave Lissie an encouraging smile that slipped into a thoughtful frown. 'After all this time there's no point in telling anybody else about it so we'll just keep it between you and me.' He tapped the tip of Lissie's nose. 'And just remember, you're not guilty of anything.'

Lissie felt a loosening in her chest as though Flynn had pulled a string deep inside and that the knot of guilt that entangled her heart had unravelled. She wiped her fingers across her eyes then gave him a wan smile. Flynn didn't think she was to blame for not helping her dad, and she trusted him.

* * *

Over the next two weeks Lissie and Flynn met on Mondays and Tuesdays to paint the carousel horses. Although they had plenty to talk about, Flynn didn't raise the subject of Lissie's father and what she had told him about her mother. Neither did Lissie. Instead, she talked about what she would like to do for Christmas.

'I'm going to ask Mrs Foyer if we can get a small tree,' she said as she painted a silver star on a saddle. 'What will you do on Christmas Day?'

Flynn put down his brush and flicked his thick dark hair back from his forehead. 'Harry's missis will cook a dinner and I'll share it with them. It'll be quiet enough, but then everybody keeps to their own families on Christmas Day.' He sounded decidedly unenthusiastic.

Flynn rented a room in Harry's house, and Lissie pictured him sitting with the old couple, Harry grumpy now that he was unable to walk. It wouldn't be much fun.

'Why don't you go and stay with your own family then?'

'They're travelling with a circus and I wouldn't know where to find them.'

Lissie felt sad. Not knowing where your parents were seemed almost as bad as for Flynn as it did for her not knowing what had happened to her father. Suddenly, she had an idea but she didn't mention it to Flynn.

When it was time for her to return home she walked along the sea front, mulling over how she might persuade Patience to make the notion a reality. The esplanade was windswept and chilly, only a few people braving the elements and it seemed rather sad when she compared it to the bustling crowds in summer. The dark grey sea ebbed and swelled, and apart from an almost inaudible clacking of pebbles where the water lapped the shore, everything was silent.

After tea she sat at the sewing machine. Patience had insisted on bringing it into the parlour now that the nights were so cold and as Lissie treadled or cut out patterns, Patience attended to her ledgers. The red, white and gold quilt had sold within an hour of going on display in the shop window, and Lissie had orders for two more: one in blue and white and the other in a multitude of colours. She was working on the blue and white one, a Christmas gift for the daughter of one of their best customers.

'I've just to put the border on this and then it's finished,' she said, running a long seam down the quilt's edge.

'Good girl,' said Patience, closing her ledger and leaving her chair at the bureau for an armchair by the fire. 'Mrs Nelson will be pleased. And there's no hurry for the other one. Mrs Garrett said it 'ud do after Christmas.'

'I'm glad about that. I've cut out the hexagons but they're the devil to sew together. I'll run up some more of those nightdress and handkerchief cases. They only take minutes to do.'

'Aye, they're selling well. We're getting quite a name for ourselves what with our bespoke designs.' Patience sounded awfully pleased and proud. Lissie decided that the time was right to mention the idea that she had cogitated on as she'd walked on the esplanade.

'It's a shame Mrs Briggs can't be with us on Christmas Day,' she said.

'It's a downright pity, but I suppose she has to put her duties first. They work her like a donkey in that place.' Patience shook her head, exasperated, then her face broke into a big smile as her gaze met Lissie's. 'But if she didn't work in the that orphanage, I wouldn't have you now, would I?'

Lissie took a deep breath. 'I... I've been thinking... that if there's to be just the two of us, we... we might invite some guests.' Her hesitation turned to a gabble as she assured Patience, 'I'd do all the preparation and the washing up. All you would have to do is oversee the cooking.'

Patience looked at Lissie as if she had suggested they fly to the moon.

'Guests? Who would we invite?' Then her amazed expression softened to one of wry humour. She thought she already knew who one of them could be. 'Did you have anyone particular in mind?' she asked lightly.

'I thought it might be nice to ask Harry and his wife... and Flynn.'

A flicker of a triumphant smile twitched Patience's lip. She'd guessed right.

She looked into Lissie's sweet, open face and saw the pleading in her eyes. Clearly, it meant a lot to the girl, and Patience suddenly realised that she held much of Lissie's happiness in her hands. In turn, Lissie had made her happier than she had been for many years.

Patience smiled fondly, her mind dwelling on Lissie's willingness to keep the drapery thriving, and the fairground in good shape.

She pictured the lovely window display Lissie had created. It was beautifully Christmassy, the delightful array of red hats, scarves, gloves and a long woollen cape against a snowy white background decorated with sprigs of holly and trailing ivy over hung with silver stars. The display had not only received fulsome comments from her customers, it had increased trade. The girl deserved a reward.

Then, thinking it unwise to give Lissie the idea that she could wind her round her little finger, Patience said, 'I suppose it 'ud save poor Joan from having to go to the bother. She's not in much better shape than Harry – and it would be unchristian of me to refuse seeing how hard you've worked so yes, go ahead and invite them.'

Lissie tossed aside the quilt and ran across the room to deliver a grateful hug.

'Oh, Mrs Foyer. I could kiss you. It's going to be the best Christmas ever.'

20

'That wa' the best goose I've ever tasted, and them sprouts were a treat although I'll be full of wind for t'next day or two,' said Harry, patting his belly then belching.

'Manners, Harry,' Joan chastised him. 'We don't need to know.' She beamed from Patience to Lissie, her fleshy cheeks pink. 'Like he says, the dinner wa' grand, and all the better for not having to make it meself.'

'Thank you very much, Mrs Foyer, and you too, Lissie. It was splendid.' Flynn bestowed a warm smile on his employer then gave his friend a broad grin.

Patience and Lissie accepted the compliments modestly.

It was almost four in the afternoon, and they were seated round the circular table in the dining room, Harry on Patience's left, Joan on her right, and Flynn next to Lissie, all wearing paper hats that Lissie had fashioned out of the coloured tissue paper they used in the shop to wrap small items. She had dressed the table with a large white cloth and the pair of tall brass candlesticks that she'd taken from the mantelpiece in the parlour were festooned with sprigs of holly and trailers of ivy.

Lissie got to her feet and began clearing the empty plates. 'Now, who's for pudding?' she asked cheerily although she felt full and slightly exhausted. She had been up since seven peeling potatoes and sprouts and basting the goose under Patience's watchful eye then setting the table before, at the very last minute, rushing up to her room to change into her best blue woollen dress.

'Here, I'll give you a hand.' Flynn pushed back his chair and she gave him a grateful smile. He looked particularly handsome in a white shirt and a dark grey waistcoat, his thick black hair curling round his ears and in the nape of his neck. Once they had collected the plates, they went into the kitchen and piled them into the sink. 'What now?' he asked.

'Help me lift the pudding out of the pot.' Lissie gingerly lifted the lid from the simmering pot. Between them they took the earthenware bowl from the water, and careful not to scald their fingers, they upended it onto a plate. The pudding slid out with a loud sucking plop.

'Yippee!' Flynn eyed the glistening fruity mound. 'Did you make this?'

'Mrs Foyer did. We agreed that if she dressed the goose and made the pudding that I'd do the rest.' Lissie blew through her lips, wafting the damp tendrils of hair sticking to her brow.

Flynn laughed. 'You look as hot as the pudding.'

'Cheeky beggar!'

They grinned at each other.

'Now for the custard.' Lissie poured the thick yellow liquid from the pan into a jug. Then they went back into the dining room, Lissie carrying the jug and Flynn proudly bearing the pudding aloft. He set it in front of Patience.

'Get that bottle off the sideboard, Flynn, and do the honours.'

Flynn fetched the brandy and Patience poured some over the pudding. Harry provided the match and as the liquor's blue and yellow flames flared, they all clapped their hands and cheered. Lissie, quite overwhelmed, had to struggle to eat her pudding. This was what Christmas and life was all about. Good food with good friends, a warm safe place to live and a creative, rewarding job. She had never felt more content.

When the pudding dishes were cleared away and sweet sherry poured for Patience and Joan and bottles of beer for Harry and Flynn, they played charades. Lissie was first to take the floor and with gestures and wondrous smiles she enacted a child's delight on opening her presents on Christmas morning.

'I know it,' Patience crowed, 'you're opening Christmas gifts.'

Lissie sat down and sipped her lemonade, almost choking on it with laughter as Flynn mimed looking out to sea, one hand over his brow and the other flinging an imaginary harpoon. Then he tussled with the invisible whale until he was exhausted. 'It's *Moby Dick*, and I'm Captain Ahab,' he cried when the others failed to guess. Lissie was surprised. She hadn't known he was a reader. Something else she didn't know about him, she mused.

Harry gave his version of *Humpty Dumpty*, and Joan mimed a comical interpretation of baking and burning cakes that had them roaring with laughter.

Harry suggested a game of cards, and when Lissie fetched the pack Flynn said, 'Now you three sit where you are, and no cheating. Lissie and I are going to finish the washing up.'

Lissie felt like jumping for joy at his thoughtfulness as she followed him into the kitchen. She washed and he dried and when the dishes were stacked, she said, 'Thank you, Flynn. You're the best friend I ever had.'

He tossed the drying cloth to one side, and taking both her hands in his he leaned forward and kissed her cheek. 'Merry Christmas, Lissie.'

* * *

The new year and 1911 was turning out to be everything Lissie could
have hoped for. She had a comfortable home with a woman she
had grown to love and respect and a job she adored, and she had
the wonderful friendships of Flynn, Meggie and Jimmy. Even so,
she still thought about her dad and her longing to find out what
had become of him. In bed, wide awake, she envisaged going to
look for him. After all, when she was younger, she had made a
promise to do just that and the opportunity came when it was least
expected.

She was in the shop tidying the glove drawer when the bell
jangled and in came Ernest Hargreaves, a traveller in sewing requisites, and a long-time friend and supplier of goods to Foyer's Drapery. 'Good day to you, Mrs Foyer,' he said.

'Good day to you, Ernest. We were expecting you. We're running
low on spools and needles and...' she turned to address Lissie,
'check how much white lace ribbon we have left and if we need any
more elastic.'

Lissie did as she was asked, and Ernest and Patience chatted as
he took spools of thread from his large suitcase. Patience selected
different colours of thread and packets of needles.

'We have two full cards of white lace,' Lissie informed them,
'but we're almost out of elastic in all widths.' The transaction
completed, Ernest closed his suitcase.

'Where are you for next then?' Patience asked him.

'Castleton tomorrow. I've some business down that way and
seeing as how the wife's sister lives in Sparrowpit I'm taking her for
a visit and killing two birds with one stone.'

'That's no way to talk about your wife and her sister,' Patience
quipped.

Ernest roared with laughter and Lissie giggled. Up until then she hadn't paid attention to their conversation but when Patience remarked, 'It's a grand place to go for a day out is Castleton,' Lissie's ears pricked and suddenly her heart began to thud. She clutched the edge of the drawer that held the elastic, her knuckles whitening as memories assailed her.

A picture of her dad lying bleeding on the floor flashed before her eyes and she thought she felt Dora's clawing fingers as she dragged her out of the cottage. Castleton! That was where they had run to on that terrible day. It was near to Thorne, the village where she had once lived. Her thoughts tumbling, she let go of the drawer and tottered to the counter.

'Can I go with you?' she heard herself say then blushed at her impertinence. Patience and Ernest, surprised by the urgent request, looked at her curiously.

'I mean... I... Oh, Mrs Foyer, I want to go to Castleton and find out about my dad. Please,' she looked at Ernest, 'if Mrs Foyer gives her permission will you take me with you?'

Bemused, Ernest looked from Lissie to Patience.

'Go and put the kettle on, make Ernest a cup of tea,' Patience said.

On pins, Lissie made the tea, and when Ernest came through to the kitchen he was smiling. 'It looks like you've got yourself a lift to Derbyshire,' he said.

Lissie felt like whooping for joy. Instead, she said, 'Thank you. I won't be any trouble to you and Mrs Hargreaves.'

Arrangements were made that Ernest would collect her at seven the next morning and that they would stay overnight with Mrs Hargreaves' sister and return the following day. 'Is that all right?' she tentatively asked Patience.

'Course it is, lass. Go and put your mind at rest. You'll never settle till you know.' Patience looked at Ernest. 'You'll be in safe hands, Lissie.'

'Don't you worry, Mrs Foyer, we'll take good care of her,' Ernest replied.

'You'd better.'

Lissie's heart glowed at Patience's retort. She felt loved and grateful.

That night Lissie barely slept. Tomorrow she'd find a way to get from Castleton to Thorne and go to the cottage, and maybe...

* * *

Riding in the back seat of a car and stopping off at an inn for refreshments was a new experience for Lissie, and she enjoyed every mile of the journey. As they drove into Castleton almost three hours later, her excitement mounted. Sarah Hargreaves was jolly company and while Ernest carried out his business at the drapery shops, she and Lissie wandered the town.

'My dad once said he'd bring me here and we'd go down the Blue John Mines and see the crystal caves,' she said before wistfully adding, 'He promised to buy me a purple and yellow crystal.'

'Well, you can buy yourself one now, there's plenty here to choose from,' Sarah replied as they came abreast of a shop window full of the Blue John.

Lissie gazed at the crystals and brooches and other trinkets. She had money that she had saved from her wages. She deliberated for a second. 'No, it wouldn't be the same,' she said, hopeful that she'd find her dad and that he could make the purchase. Her heart quickened at the thought.

Sarah shrugged. Patience had told Ernest about Lissie's background and he had told Sarah enough to make her aware that this journey was important to Lissie so she decided not to interfere. 'Let's get a cup of tea, I'm fair parched.'

They had arranged to meet Ernest outside The Bull's Head inn and as they waited for him something stirred in Lissie's memory. This was the pub Dora had brought her to the night following the attack on her dad. She gave an involuntary shudder. Ernest appeared and they were back on the road again. By now it was just after midday. 'We come to Thorne before we get to Sparrowpit, so here's what we'll do. I'll drop you off there and come back for you in an hour or so. How does that sound?'

'That will be grand,' Lissie said, pleased that she would make this part of the journey alone. Had she been able to see into Ernest's mind she would have known that he too thought it best to let her make her search on her own. As they drove into Thorne, Lissie glanced from left to right on the lookout for something familiar. Then she saw Mr Brooks' tobacconists and sweet shop. 'Put me down here,' she said. 'I know where I am.'

Ernest brought the car to a halt and repeated that he'd be back within the hour and would meet her on that spot. Lissie climbed down and he and Mrs Hargreaves drove off to her sister's. Lissie stood gazing up and down Church Street. It wasn't much changed since she'd last walked along it with her dad, and the church and the school brought memories flooding back. The houses to which they had delivered mended boots and shoes still had doors painted in the same colours.

On hot feet she hurried out of the village and up the lane to the cottage.

Her breath caught in her throat as she entered the yard, not so much because of the speed she had been walking but at the sight of the little house where she had spent seven happy years with her father. She stood, breathing heavily, taking in the cottage's low white walls and small windows. She knew exactly what lay beyond the open door. Unbidden, a picture of her dad lying on the floor in a pool of blood flitted through her mind then mingled with happier scenes; sitting on his knee listening to his wonderful stories, helping him carry out his tasks, and feeling loved. Mesmerised, she gazed with fear and longing.

'Can I help you?' The voice broke into Lissie's reminiscences. She jumped. She'd been so intent on looking at her old home that she hadn't noticed the young woman and a small child in the far corner of the yard by the privy. The woman had a mop and bucket in her hand.

'I'm Lissie Fairweather. I used to live here,' she said, almost apologetically. 'I wondered if you know the whereabouts of my father, Tom Fairweather.'

The woman frowned. 'Can't say as I do. We came here about two years ago, an' the people who lived here before us were called Burton – a couple with two children.'

Lissie's heart sank. 'Sorry to have troubled you,' she said to the woman.

'Sorry I couldn't help,' the woman replied as Lissie turned and walked away.

She went back to village by way of the wood. It was too early in the year for bluebells, but she recalled the carpet of blue flowers and her dad pretending that they were sailing the ocean. Sadly, the memory was swiftly followed by the image of her mother up against a tree moaning and crying out as the man she was with pleasured her. It made her feel sick, and she almost ran from the wood back into the village to Mr Brooks' shop.

The smell of cough drops and tobacco was still as strong as she remembered it, and Mr Brooks was there behind the counter looking very old and rather frail.

'Hello, Mr Brooks. Do you remember me? I'm Lissie Fairweather, Tom the cobbler's daughter.'

Mr Brooks peered at her over the top of his spectacles, his rheumy eyes crinkling at the corners. 'Ah, yes, Tom Fairweather. And little Lissie,' he said.

'That's right. Do you know where my dad is? I've come looking for him,' she said, dreading that he would tell her Tom was in the graveyard by the church.

'Looking for him?' he asked, scratching his head in bemusement.

'Yes. We got separated a long time ago. I haven't seen him for years and I don't know what happened to him. Please, can you help me?'

Lissie's impassioned cry startled Mr Brooks. He blinked and shook his head. Then, his brow knotted and his lips pursed, he stared into her face for a long moment. 'Ah, yes, I remember. And you're Lissie. It's coming back to me now.' His bleary eyes brightened as though he had just fully comprehended the situation. 'And you don't know where your father is,' he continued, his voice querulous and high with surprise.

Lissie's breath caught in her throat. What was he about to tell her? She shook her head, her eyes begging him to go on.

The old man gave her a puzzled look. 'Well, Lissie, it was a strange to-do altogether as I recall. Tom had some sort of an accident.' He paused, searching his mind, then his troubled expression cleared as he said, 'Had the man who kept the horse in the field by the cottage not found him in time he would have died.'

Lissie's breath whooshed out of her. She gripped the edge of the counter feeling for a moment as though she might faint. Then her heart beginning to race, she cried, 'Then he's alive!'

'Oh, yes. He came to say goodbye before he went away.'

'Do you know where he is, Mr Brooks?'

The old man shook his head. 'Tom left the village years ago. I thought he'd taken you and your mother with him.'

'No, it was my mother who took me away from him,' Lissie said bitterly. 'I thought I might still find him here, but the woman living in our cottage had never heard of him.'

'No, I suppose not,' said Mr Brooks, looking quite exhausted, 'and I'm sorry I haven't been any help either. I do hope you find him, my dear. He was very fond of you, and well respected in the village.'

Lissie thanked him, and leaving a rather dazed looking Mr Brooks staring after her, she went back into the street to wait for Ernest, her veins tingling with excitement and her heart and mind filled with hope. Her mam hadn't killed her dad after all, and for the first time in eight worrisome years, Lissie felt free of the terrible feeling that she was guilty of having left him to die. He was alive, and now she could live in hope that one day she would find him.

21

SUMMER 1912

Lissie found it hard to believe that she had been living in Scarborough for more than two years. They were the happiest years she had ever known – although not quite – as she sometimes reflected whenever a memory of her dad and the cottage in Thorne came to mind. But the memories were now vague like something she had dreamed and try as she might, she could never recapture them with any clarity.

She never failed to marvel at how much her horizons had broadened since leaving the confines of the orphanage, and now she was sixteen she considered herself to be wiser and very nicely placed in the world. For this she readily gave credit to Connie Briggs and Patience. She had a comfortable home, she was well fed, and she lived and worked with a woman she had grown to love and respect.

'I couldn't be happier living and working with Mrs Foyer. I've so much to be thankful for and it's all due to you, Mrs Briggs,' she told Connie on one of her regular visits.

Connie gave a modest little smile. 'The pleasure's all mine,

Lissie,' she said, thrilled that her protégé had lived up to expectations, 'and Patience tells me she couldn't manage without you.'

Patience's arthritis had become more problematic in the last year and her hands were now so clawed that she could no longer cut lengths of fabric or wrap parcels, and her hips and knees were so painful that standing behind the counter for long hours was impractical. These days she usually perched on a high stool by the money drawer and simply supervised the running of her business.

'I'll admit I was wary of taking you on, but you were a blessing in disguise,' Patience confided one day in July after wishing a customer good day then depositing the coins Lissie handed her from the recent sale.

'That's very kind of you to say, Mrs Foyer,' Lissie said as she tidied the counter. She didn't in the least object to taking on the responsibility of running the shop. It presented new challenges. Now, she not only served customers and dressed the window, she also dealt with the wholesalers, selecting goods.

'I'd never have bought those Chinese tunics but we've already sold three of 'em, and as for those skirts with the narrow hems, I don't know how women can walk in 'em,' Patience commented.

Lissie giggled. 'They're called hobble skirts, Mrs Foyer, 'cos you can only hobble when you're wearing one. It's what the Gibson Girls wear,' she said, referring to the designs of the illustrator, Charles Gibson. 'I saw them in the *Ladies' Home Journal* and thought that our summer visitors might like them.'

'Gibson Girls! Never heard of 'em,' Patience harrumphed, but when Lissie went and fetched the magazine she said, 'Hmm. I see what you mean. It takes a young head and an eye to spot the latest fashions. Like I said, I'm lucky to have you.'

'And I'm lucky to have you, Mrs Foyer.' Lissie voice was warm with sincerity.

Lissie had just finished serving another customer when Dick, the gawky young postman, arrived with the afternoon delivery. He handed the letters to Patience then gave Lissie a cheeky wink.

'Is she behaving herself today?' he quipped.

'To whom do you refer?' Patience's tart response made his pock-marked cheeks turn beetroot. 'And in answer to your question, young man, we both are so get along with you.' Dick rolled his eyes at Lissie and scarpered.

'He has a fancy for you, but he's not much of a catch,' Patience remarked, flipping through the letters. 'Oh, there's one for you, Lissie. It looks like it's from that friend of yours in Bradford.' Emmy had written a few scrappy replies to Lissie's long newsy letters over the past two years. Sadly, her dear friend, Mary, from the orphanage who had gone to work in Bradford had never written back even though Lissie had sent a letter and two postcards of the lovely beaches in Scarborough.

Lissie tore open the envelope then scanned the single page. 'Emmy says she can come the last week in July. The mill closes for them to overhaul the looms and she wants to stay from the Saturday to the Thursday.' Suppressing her excitement, she looked enquiringly at Patience. Last summer Patience had agreed that Emmy could stay with them rather than in a boarding house and Lissie had been disappointed when Emmy wrote to say she couldn't afford to come to even if she was getting free board and lodgings.

'Is it still all right for her to stay here?' she now asked.

'Aye, of course it is.'

'Then I'll write back this evening.'

'Talking of this evening, if you're seeing Flynn tell him the electrician's coming to fix the lights on that merry-go-round tomorrow morning.'

'I will,' said Lissie, turning her attention to two young women who were looking to buy one of the new Chinese tunics.

When she wasn't working, Lissie spent her time with Flynn and

Meggie and Jimmy, and although she and Meggie were close, it was Flynn's company she most enjoyed. She was looking forward to meeting him that evening when the shop closed.

* * *

Gulls wheeled and cawed overhead and the setting sun's reflection on the glassy blue sea looked as though gold coins had been scattered on it. The streets were busy with holidaymakers, and sunburned children toting buckets and spades and their weary mothers, burdened with bags of wet towels, were making their way back to their lodgings. Well-dressed ladies and gentlemen strolled arm in arm, no doubt making their way to the esplanade in South Bay to listen to the outdoor bands and sip cocktails in the Spa or dine in one of the big hotels.

Now, as Lissie mingled with the happy crowds on her way to Peasholm Park and the amusements, she felt the familiar thrill that she always experienced ever since taking that first walk with Connie. And the prospect of showing it off to Emmy in just over a week's time pleased her even more.

Flynn's eyes lit up as she joined him by one of the merry-go-rounds. 'My friend, Emmy's coming to stay next Saturday,' she told him. 'You'll like her, she's great fun.'

'I'll be the judge of that.' He gave her a half-smile and flicked his hair back from his forehead. Lissie grinned. Flynn had firm beliefs in what he liked and didn't like and was very much his own man. Lissie admired that. Not for a moment did she think that Flynn's lack of enthusiasm was because he didn't want to share her with Emmy. Pushing the envious feeling to the back of his mind, he turned and beckoned to one of the lads that helped run the rides.

'Keep an eye on things for an hour. I'm off for a walk.'

The lad's eyes slid to Lissie and he gave Flynn a sly grin. 'Okay by me,' he said.

They walked into the park past the open-air theatre and round by the lake, easy in each other's company. Tonight, they were on their own as Jimmy was at a scouts' meeting and Meggie working. She had recently left the Grand and was now working in the Royal Hotel where she was much happier.

'Did you finish reading *King Solomon's Mines*?' Lissie asked.

'I did, and I've started into *The Invisible Man*.'

'Don't tell me about it. I haven't read it yet,' she said.

Their shared interest in books was always a great source of conversation, and with Patience's permission they were steadily working their way through Henry Foyer's large collection of novels.

'There's an invisible man in the troupe my mam and dad travel with,' Flynn said. He had lots of interesting stories about the years he had spent with his parents and the travelling fair that had been his way of life until he had decided to settle in Scarborough. She loved listening to them and hearing about the different places he had been.

'A real invisible man?' she exclaimed. 'I don't believe you.'

'And you do right not to,' Flynn laughed. 'He's a big hairy chap who sits in a tent all day wrapped up in bandages and tells the crowds he has to wear them because otherwise they wouldn't be able to see him. He dares them to come up and take off the bandages to prove it, but nobody ever does 'cos he tells them that if they do, they'll become invisible as well.'

'That's just plain daft. I can't believe that people would pay to see him.'

'You'd be surprised what people will pay to see and hear, Lissie. You see, they want to believe in the mystery. That's why they let my mother tell their fortunes with the cards and the crystal ball.'

'And can she really see into the future?'

Flynn hooted with laughter. 'Not at all. She just makes it up and tells them what they want to hear.'

Talking and laughing, they walked on, Lissie musing on why it was that whenever she was with Flynn she felt as if she was where she was meant to be.

The shadows had lengthened, the trees and shrubs casting dark patches on the path, and as Lissie and Flynn strolled through the park, they passed by several couples taking advantage of the fading light to kiss and cuddle. Unexpectedly, Flynn put his arm round Lissie's waist and pulled her close. He'd never done that before but she leaned into him feeling the warmth and strength of his muscular frame. Her heartbeat quickened. She wondered what it would be like to kiss Flynn. They continued walking in this way out of the park and into the streets until they came near the drapery shop.

'I have to get back. You'll be safe from here,' Flynn said but he didn't remove his arm. Instead, he put his other arm round her and turning her to face him, he looked deep into her eyes. She gazed back at him, sure he must hear the thud of her heart. Very gently, his lips brushed hers. 'Sweet dreams, Lissie.'

She watched as he walked away, his broad back and his long loping stride tempting her to run after him. *I'm in love, I love Flynn,* a little voice inside her head sang over and again. Amazed, she ran the tip of her tongue over her lips, tasting the sweetness of his kiss then, on feet that felt as though she was walking on clouds, she ran to the house door and let herself in.

Flynn Corrigan's lips twitched in a satisfied smile. He had waited a long time to do that. He would have preferred to kiss Lissie with the passion he felt, but she was so innocent he was afraid of frightening her and ruining a beautiful friendship. He couldn't bear it if he lost that. He'd just have to bide his time. He would wait forever if he had to, and when he was sure that his feelings were reciprocated, he'd make his move. Furthermore, he had other things to occupy his thoughts. His expanding business required much of his attention. With the money he earned working for Patience he had, one by one, purchased two sideshows and three stalls on the fairground, his little empire growing at a steady rate. In the winter months he not only refurbished Patience's roundabouts but hired himself out to others to do the same for them, his talent for keeping the rides in good working order in high demand. He shared his ambition to become a major player in Scarborough's amusement business with nobody other than Patience Foyer. He trusted her wise advice and Patience, having spotted his potential for success, spurred him on to greater things. But before he approached Lissie with a view to them becoming a couple who would spend the rest of their lives together, he had to establish his own. And in the meantime, as Lissie negotiated her own future, he would be there ready and waiting for her to declare her feelings for him.

* * *

'Oh, it's so good to see you again,' Lissie cried as Emmy stepped down from the train. The platform thronged with weekend visitors. It was Saturday, just after midday, and with the shop closed for lunch, Lissie had nipped out to meet her. Emmy put down her small shabby suitcase and they hugged.

'It's good to see you an' all. I never thought I'd get here what with having to change trains an' all that. I've never been so far from home before.' Emmy sounded rather put out.

'That's how I felt the day Mrs Briggs brought me here, but you've arrived safe and sound and we're going to have a marvellous time now you're here.'

'I should bloomin' hope so after all the money I've spent.'

This wasn't quite what Lissie had expected. Fleetingly, her spirits drooped then rose as she silently excused Emmy's disgruntlement. It was a long journey.

On their way to the house, Lissie pointed out the sights in much the same manner as Connie had done when Lissie had first arrived in Scarborough. Emmy seemed to cheer up when she saw what the town had to offer but when she remarked, 'You're livin' on a pig's back,' she sounded bitter and envious. Lissie's spirits sank a second time. When had Emmy become so hard and dissatisfied?

Lissie couldn't help noticing that for all they were the same age, Emmy seemed so much older. Her dark brown hair was cut in a sleek bob, her cheeks rouged and her lips a vivid scarlet. The dress and jacket she had on were a gaudy mish-mash of pink and green and made her look blowsy and rather cheap, and the heels of her strap-over shoes were so high that she clopped rather than walked. Lissie felt childish in her flat black shoes, grey skirt and white pin-tucked shirtwaist, her long black curls held back with a white ribbon. She wondered what Patience would make of Emmy. It made her feel nervous.

When Lissie introduced Emmy, Patience's expression said it all. Her gimlet eyes raked Emmy up and down then slid to meet Lissie's. *What have we here*, they seemed to say. They sat down to tea and sandwiches that Lissie had prepared earlier, a crisp white cloth on the dining-room table and Patience's best cups and saucers and an ornate cake stand holding iced buns and biscuits. Emmy ate greedily.

'So how is everybody at home, Emmy? Are they all well?' Lissie asked brightly.

Emmy shrugged, and through a mouthful of bread and cheese, she mumbled, 'Same as usual.'

Patience sniffed, and Lissie flushed, embarrassed by her friend's bad manners. An awkward silence filled the room. Patience asked to be excused.

'She's a cold fish,' Emmy hissed as soon as Patience was out of earshot. 'I'm surprised you've stuck her for this long.'

'She's nothing of the sort.' Lissie kept her voice low but her hurt and annoyance was high. 'She's goodness itself to me.'

'Oh, I can see that, what with your big fancy house and your la-di-dah tea sets,' Emmy scoffed. She grabbed for the last iced bun and stuffed it in her mouth.

Lissie was close to tears. 'Why are you being like this, Emmy?'

'Like what?' Emmy pushed back her chair. 'Where's your lavvy? I need a pee.'

Lissie led the way upstairs, her heart in her boots.

'This is the bathroom and this is your room,' she said curtly, opening first one door then the other. Emmy ducked into the bathroom and Lissie stood fuming on the landing. It was all going terribly wrong. She was dreading the next five days.

Emmy came out of the bathroom. 'Very posh,' she sneered and when she saw her bedroom she said, 'Very nice,' in the same ungracious tone.

Lissie placed Emmy's suitcase on a stand at the foot of the bed. 'I have to work this afternoon. Saturdays are always busy and Mrs Foyer can't manage on her own. When you've unpacked you could take a walk on the esplanade, get some sea air, and then tonight I'll take you to meet my friends.' Even to her own ears her cheeriness sounded forced. She gave Emmy directions to the esplanade.

'I suppose I'll find it.' Emmy didn't seem too enthusiastic and Lissie felt guilty.

'I'm sorry I have to work today but we'll have the next four together. Mrs Briggs is coming tomorrow and Mrs Foyer's closing the shop until Thursday. We'll all have a proper holiday.'

'Good! That's what I came for.' Emmy gave a jaunty smile. Lissie almost gasped with relief. Of course, Emmy must be feeling out of her depth and that's why she was being so surly. After all, Scarborough was a far cry from Great Horton, and the house in North Marine Road was nothing like the shabby little house in the yard behind Hart Lane.

Somewhat cheered, she left Emmy to unpack and went down to the shop. A short while later she heard the house door bang. Emmy had taken her advice. Lissie smiled. Once her friend stopped feeling out of place things would be fine.

22

Emmy was in a much pleasanter mood when she returned from her walk, and after a tea of ham and salad, as she and Lissie got ready to go out and meet Meggie, Jimmy and Flynn, they chatted like the old friends they had once been. 'Our Nora's married now, you know, and expectin' a babby afore Christmas,' Emmy said as she took off the gaudy dress. 'Our Jimmy workin' for a joiner, and our David got a job in the mill office. Me mam's ever so proud of him.'

Lissie was delighted to hear they were all doing well, and that Emmy seemed more like her old self. Leaving Emmy to finish getting changed, Lissie went to her own room, and taking off her work clothes she dressed for the evening and went back into Emmy's room.

'Ooh! Look at you.' Emmy's tone was a mixture of envy and sarcasm as she took in Lissie's embroidered Chinese tunic and grey hobble skirt. The tunic had had a loose seam and frayed embroidery – something Lissie hadn't spotted when the wholesaler had delivered it – and after she had repaired it Patience had said she might as well keep it. She had been saving the outfit for a special occasion such as tonight. Now, as she saw Emmy's lip curl, she wished she had chosen to wear something plainer.

'It was damaged so I got it cheap,' Lissie gabbled while wondering why she should have to excuse her appearance.

'It's well for some,' Emmy growled, pulling at the low square neckline of her dress which was a violent shade of purple and made from flimsy material trimmed with rather bedraggled lace. In Lissie's opinion it was even more unsuitable than the one she'd been wearing earlier. Her make-up was heavy and garish and Lissie thought sadly that she looked like a tart.

Out loud, and desperate to appease the situation she said, 'That's a pretty dress, Emmy. That strong colour suits you.'

'It'll have to since I've not got much choice.' Even so, she managed a smile and said, 'Your tunic's very fashionable.'

The awkward moment over, the two girls set out for the esplanade where they had arranged to meet Lissie's friends. Outside the Pavilion introductions were made, Emmy almost ignoring Meggie and Jimmy and giving all her attention to Flynn. She fluttered her eyelashes and held his hand too long for Lissie's liking and when they went inside for refreshments Emmy hooked her hand through Flynn's arm. He glanced at Lissie and rolled his eyes.

Later, they strolled on the esplanade then on to the fairground, Emmy flirting madly with Flynn. He was giving her no encouragement, but Lissie was seething, nonetheless. At the fairground, Flynn left them to attend to a problem with one of the roundabouts. The others were walking towards the carousel, Jimmy a few paces in front of the girls, when Emmy said, 'That Jimmy's a bit gormless but Flynn's a real looker. I could go for somebody like him.'

Stung, Meggie flared up. She adored Jimmy and had once told Lissie that whilst he wasn't much to look at, he was the kindest, most decent lad she had ever known; not like them mucky porters and kitchen hands in the hotel who were just after one thing.

Meggie stopped in her tracks and turned to face Emmy.

'Excuse me,' she said through gritted teeth, 'nubbdy asked for your rotten opinion so shut your mouth. Jimmy might not be like the fellas you keep company with, an' if they're owt like you ah'll bet they're a right shitty lot 'cos only fellas like that 'ud mess wi' a trollop like you.'

Emmy's jaw dropped. She hadn't expected to be challenged. She stared at Meggie, pretty and prim in her blue calico dress with a sailor collar, and her fair hair tied in bunches with matching ribbons.

Jimmy had wheeled round when he heard Meggie's raised voice, his pale moon face a picture of concern.

'Oi! Who are you calling a trollop?' Emmy lunged at Meggie and grabbed a handful of her hair. Meggie yelped. Lissie tried to push between them but it was Jimmy who dragged Emmy off, pinioning her hands behind her. Meggie reeled back, clutching her sore scalp. Spitting and cursing, Emmy struggled to free herself from Jimmy's grip.

'What the hell's going on?' he bawled.

'She... she wa' sayin' awful things about...' To spare his feelings, Meggie stopped short. Then seeing Lissie's stricken face, and feeling pity for her – she knew Lissie had set great store by their making her friend welcome – she made a desperate attempt to recover the situation.

'Aw, it's oreight, Jimmy, man. Tek no notice of me. Emmy din't mean to upset me, did you? Aah took offence, but it wa' over summat an' nowt.' She turned to Emmy. 'Sorry for losin' me temper, pet.'

Emmy, caught by surprise for a second time, mumbled, 'Sorry for pulling your hair, Meggie.'

Lissie's heart went out to poor Meggie. She knew that she was making the peace for her sake. 'That's very kind of you, Meggie.' She could think of nothing to say to Emmy. Her disappointment was too deep.

They stood watching the carousel's merry whirl, the lights twinkling and the music blaring, but the joy had gone out of the evening. When Flynn came to find them, he immediately sensed the strained atmosphere, and Lissie's glum face saddened him. He put his arm round her shoulders and pulled her close. She leaned willingly against his broad chest, taking comfort from his nearness. He dropped a kiss on her hair and she felt her troubles melting. When she turned to look round, Emmy was no longer there.

'Where did she go?' Lissie asked Meggie.

'Who cares? She's bloomin' horrible.'

Jimmy told Flynn what had happened and Lissie's insides curdled with shame. 'I knew she'd be trouble from the start,' Flynn growled.

'I'm sorry for bringing her. She never used to be like that but still, I'd better go and find her.'

Lissie dejectedly set off walking and the others followed her.

They wandered between the sideshows and the roundabouts but Emmy was nowhere to be found. It was getting late, the crowds dwindling and the rides shutting down. Lissie was panicking. Where could Emmy be? Had she made her own way back to the house?

They were making a second circuit of the fairground when from a dark alley between the candy floss stall and the hoopla, yawps of laughter attracted their attention. Three lads lolled against the side of the stall passing a bottle between them, and in amongst them was Emmy.

At Lissie's anxious cry Emmy flung out her arm and shouted,

'Hey, Lissie, come and join us.' One of the lads shoved the bottle in her hand and Emmy took a swig.

Flynn dived into the alley and the lads took to their heels.

'Aw, what did you do that for?' Emmy swayed up to Flynn and threw her arms round him but he shrugged her off.

Lissie ran and grabbed her friend. Emmy fell against her, laughing. Her breath smelled of strong spirits. 'We were on'y havin' a bit o' fun, and he spoiled it,' she slurred, shaking her fist at Flynn.

'Jimmy, you and Meggie begin walking Lissie and her back home,' Flynn said, too disgusted to call Emmy by name. 'I'll just check that the rides are all closed down then I'll catch you up.' He strode off, his rigid back letting Lissie know he was furious. She had never been more mortified.

Emmy stumbled along between Jimmy and Lissie, and when Flynn caught up with them Meggie and Jimmy hurried off. Flynn didn't speak until they reached the house in North Marine Road. Emmy tried to kiss him goodnight but he dodged aside and taking Lissie in his arms, he hugged her, whispering, 'Try to get her inside without Mrs Foyer seeing her.' Emmy was slumped on the step.

Lissie nodded, her eyes brimming with tears. Gently, Flynn wiped them away with his thumbs. 'You weren't to know,' he said, cupping her cheeks in both hands then kissing her. It was a proper kiss, warm and tender, and Lissie feared her heart was about to break for love of him. He stood until Lissie opened the door and pulled Emmy in after her.

Patience, always a night bird, hobbled into the hall when she heard them.

'Good evening Mishish Foyer,' Emmy said then hiccupped.

'I see somebody had a good night.' Patience's biting remark made Lissie flush to the roots of her hair.

'I'm sorry, Mrs Foyer. She wandered off and got into bad company. I didn't think...' Lissie's tears flowed.

'What you crying for, Lissie?' Emmy tried to hug her.

'Get her up to bed,' Patience said. 'I'll have words tomorrow.'

* * *

'Oh dear, I don't know what to say.' Connie Briggs shook her head and gave Lissie a sympathetic look. She had arrived shortly before midday and Lissie had wept as she told her the sorry tale. Emmy was still in bed, and when Lissie had gone to ask if she was ready for breakfast Emmy had snarled, 'Go away and let me sleep. I'm on me holidays.'

'She's here until Thursday and I don't know what to do with her,' Lissie said.

'What had you planned to do?'

'I'd arranged for a picnic up at the castle this afternoon, but I doubt Meggie will turn up, and if she won't come neither will Jimmy. Flynn might.' Lissie looked hopeful, and Connie pitied her.

'Well, that's what we'll do then. Go and make the sandwiches.'

* * *

The picnic was a desultory affair for all the sun was shining and the sea as flat as a duck pond. Lissie gazed out over the shimmering water, not daring to look back down the headland to see if her friends were approaching. Emmy sat sullenly picking at the food. In truth she was ashamed of her behaviour the previous night but she couldn't bring herself to make reparation. Patience and Connie attempted to draw her into conversation without much success. And when it was obvious that Meggie, Jimmy and Flynn would not be coming they packed up the baskets and went back to the house.

On Monday, Lissie and Emmy went shopping. Lissie bought gifts for Emmy to take back with her to Great Horton: an ashtray with a picture of the castle on it for Bill, and a milk jug decorated with scenes of Scarborough for Nelly.

'I'll come and visit you in autumn,' Lissie said, 'I'd love to see Nelly and Bill.'

'I'm going home tomorrow,' Emmy said by way of reply.

'But you're meant to be here till Thursday.' A gamut of emotions swept through Lissie: disappointment at the spoiled holiday, relief at Emmy's impending departure, and a crushing sadness that she and Emmy would never again be the friends they had once been.

Later, in the evening, Emmy packed her suitcase ready to leave the next day while Lissie watched miserably. She couldn't help feeling that she had somehow failed her friend even though common sense told her it was the other way round.

'I'm sorry you didn't get to enjoy your holiday,' she said.

Emmy snapped the clasps on the suitcase. 'It's not your fault, Lissie. It's mine.' She flopped down on the bed. 'I came expecting to have a good time but when I saw you in your grand clothes, and the lovely house you live in I was mad with jealousy.' Her face crumpled and her voice impassioned, she croaked, 'You have everything, and I have nowt, Lissie... I live in a mucky yard where the sun never shines... I hate working in the mill but there's nowt else for me so I do daft things to make my rotten life a bit more exciting. It's me who should be sorry.'

'Oh, Emmy.' Lissie shifted up the bed to embrace Emmy's quivering frame. Holding her like a mother soothing an unhappy child, she rocked her gently, saying, 'I'd no idea how miserable you felt.'

'Well, now you know,' Emmy sniffled. 'Like I say, Lissie, you've got everything and I've got nowt.'

'You've got a mam and dad who love you.' Which is more than I have, Lissie thought, wondering if she would ever see either of them again.

'Yeah, you're right, but they're not too happy with the way I'm carrying on.'

'Then make them – and yourself – happy. Stop feeling sorry for yourself.'

Lissie pecked Emmy's cheek and wishing her sweet dreams, she went to her own room. The next morning on the station platform she repeated what she'd said and waved Emmy off, her heart heavy for the loss of her friend.

Having nothing else to do she went in search of Flynn. She found him in the little booth he called his office. 'Emmy's gone back to Great Horton,' she said.

Flynn grimaced. 'Perhaps as well,' he muttered, then seeing Lissie's glum expression, he pulled her onto his knee and put his arms round her. She nestled her head on his shoulder, comforted by his warmth and told him what Emmy had told her the previous night and how she, Lissie, felt she'd let her down.

'How could I have got it so wrong?' she asked him.

'She was only a little girl when you knew her. Time and circumstances change people, Lissie. You told me Emmy was a kind girl, full of fun, and that her parents were generous-hearted, loving people. They most likely still are, but their way of life is different to yours and that affects how they behave. Emmy works in a mill doing a job that you say she hates, and that she lives in a house in a poor area. It's no wonder she was envious when she saw Mrs Foyer's grand house, and saw how successful you are at doing a job you love.'

He shifted her on his knee so that he could see her face.

'I must admit I found her cheap and tawdry but maybe she acts like that as a defence. She's compensating for the lack of glamour and excitement in her humdrum life. If you spend your time with a certain type of people, you become like them. That's why I parted from my parents as soon as I was able to fend for myself. I didn't want to be like them, moving from place to place and being looked down on as an itinerant lazy good-for-nothing by ordinary decent people. And I was right to do so. By staying here and working hard I've earned people like Mrs Foyer's respect and my business interests are flourishing. I'm not boasting, but I am proud of the way I've turned out. Just like you should be, Lissie. You didn't have the best life in the orphanage but you behaved in a way that made Mrs Briggs take an interest in you. She spotted your worth, and you haven't let her down. Poor Emmy doesn't seem to have had a chance to improve herself yet but you never know, things might turn out right for her in the end. So don't go blaming yourself for the upset she's caused. Just put it down to experience.'

'You're so wise and sensible,' said Lissie.

'I should hope so. I'm nearly twenty years old.'

'And I'm almost seventeen but I feel like a child, compared to you. You always know what to do and say.'

'Not always, Lissie.'

'But you do.' Lissie clutched the lapels of his jacket. 'I won't ever lose you, will I, Flynn? Please say we'll be friends forever.'

For a second, he was perfectly still. Then he tightened his arms round her, almost knocking the breath out of her. She felt the thud of his heart against her own, and when she looked into his face, she was overwhelmed by the emotion she saw there.

'I love you, Flynn,' she whispered.

'And I love you, Lissie Fairweather, but I was afraid to tell you – in case you didn't feel the same.' He gave her a lopsided smile. 'For ages now I've wanted to tell you that you are more precious to me than any other person on this earth, that you make me feel complete.'

'I know just what you mean,' Lissie said. 'I've known for a long time that we belong together. Like a piece of a jigsaw you fit into my life and make me feel as if I've come home.'

She began to cry happy tears. When Flynn's lips found hers, she wanted to stay in the moment forever.

23

NORTH YORKSHIRE, SPRING 1914

Tom Fairweather sat back on his heels and set aside the chisel he'd been using to craft the large piece of wood he was working on. It was shaped like a giant teacup with a curving handle, and it and the others he had already made had been ordered by the pleasant young man from Scarborough who ran a fairground there. Six equally large saucers were leaning against the wall of his workshop waiting to be attached to the teacups.

For almost two years now Tom had been living and working in Pickering. It was the longest he'd been settled in any one place in almost ten years. He had travelled the length and breadth of Derbyshire and Yorkshire and further afield in search of Lissie and Dora, without success. In that time, he had grown weary of moving from place to place, the certainty of finding his beloved daughter fading with each passing year.

When he'd first arrived in Pickering, he'd taken lodgings with a widow who had lost her husband two years before. He had been a carpenter, and attached to her premises was a workshop filled with tools and machinery. When Tom had shown an interest in renting

the workshop and the room above, Amelia Harrison had been glad
of the extra income. Tom Fairweather seemed like a decent soul,
mild-mannered and fond of his own company. His business had
started in a small way but as his reputation for quality craftsman-
ship spread beyond Pickering he was never without work.

In those two years, Tom had grown fond of Amelia and she of
him although neither of them made their feelings known. Tom was
the lodger and Amelia his landlady. He had told her about his
search for Lissie but he had not divulged the real reason for them
being parted. He'd simply said his wife had left him and taken the
child with her. Amelia had supported him by asking folks about a
girl called Lissie Fairweather but to no avail. Her compassion for his
loss comforted Tom, and although he was resigned to never finding
Lissie, there wasn't a night that he didn't think about his little girl.

He stood, brushing sawdust from his knees and prepared to join
Amelia for the evening meal that they usually shared. Tomorrow
Flynn Corrigan was coming to check on the progress of the roundabout. He had requested that it be completed in time for Easter
when, once again, the holidaymakers would flock to Scarborough
to enjoy all the fun of the fair.

* * *

Less than twenty miles east in North Marine Road, Lissie pulled
down the blind and closed the shop. Custom had been brisk and
her feet ached. She really should consider taking on an assistant
now that Patience could no longer share the work. With Easter only
three weeks away customers were looking to buy new outfits or
ribbons and bows to trim last year's bonnets and dresses. And in
summer when the resort thronged with Wakes Week trippers and
the better-off filled the large hotels, trade should be even busier.

Lissie had already placed orders for a variety of souvenir linens such as tea towels and handkerchiefs, the sort that holidaymakers could buy to give as gifts to those back home, with an eye to capturing that corner of the market.

Turning out the lights, she went through into the house and straight to the dining room where Patience spent much of her day. With Flynn's help, Lissie had converted the dining room into a bedroom for her and installed a commode behind a screen now that she was no longer able to climb the stairs with ease. She'd also hired a daily woman to see to her needs. Lucy Trimble lived close by and popped in and out several times a day. On good days Patience still managed, with the aid of her walking sticks, to hobble between the house and the shop so that she could keep in touch with her customers.

'I'm not done for yet,' she told Lissie.

Now, as Lissie entered the dining room, she smiled broadly. 'Busy day, eh?'

'It certainly was. I must have measured out a mile of ribbon, and I sold two of those new dresses with the dropped waistlines.'

'Well, Mrs Trimble's left a fish pie for tea and lovely egg custard for afters.' Patience smacked her wizened lips. 'I've had mine, so off you go and get yours. Is Flynn calling round this evening?' she asked as Lissie headed for the kitchen.

'He'll be here about half past seven.' By now everyone who knew them accepted that Lissie and Flynn were a couple with plans for a future together.

* * *

Lissie ate the fish pie then took her dish of egg custard into the dining room. She was keenly aware that Patience missed the gossip and friendly exchanges she had had with her customers so Lissie went out of her way to keep her informed.

'Mrs Hutton bought sheets and pillowcases for her daughter's hope chest today. I asked when the wedding was and she said that Agatha hasn't yet got a beau but she hopes she will by the end of the summer.'

Patience guffawed. 'He'll have to be blind as a bat and two sandwiches short of a picnic if he's to wed Aggie Hutton.' She continued chuckling throatily at her own wit then said, 'Talking of marriage. Is Meggie still set on marrying Jimmy Stockdale in the autumn?'

'She is. She's taking him to Newcastle to meet her mam and dad on her next weekend off, and tomorrow Flynn's going to Pickering to check on his new merry-go-round.'

'He's a good lad, full of new ideas, and a canny businessman at that. I recognised that in him soon after I'd met him. He's as kind and decent as the day is long and I'm proud to think I've helped him on his way.' Smiling fondly, Patience leaned back against the cushions in her chair.

'You talk about him like he's your son,' Lissie said, agreeing with every word.

'I wish he was,' said Patience, her lips trembling and her eyes losing their sharpness. Lissie felt her pain. 'Well, he's as good as,' she responded.

'Aye, he is that, and I'd have liked you as a daughter,' Patience continued, her mood still sombre.

Lissie's heart swelled. 'Oh, Mrs Foyer, that's the nicest thing you've ever said.'

Patience shook her head as if to dispel her sorrow then cackled, 'But it's as well you're both not mine otherwise there'd be no grand romance. You two are made for each other.'

Lissie laughed, and hearing the front door, she ran to welcome

Flynn. He took her in his arms and kissed her. 'You smell delicious,' he said, rubbing his cheek against her hair before kissing her again.

'Hey, stop your canoodling and get in here!'

Laughing at Patience's orders, they went hand in hand into the dining room.

'Good evening, Mrs Foyer. Good to hear you haven't lost the use of your voice.' Flynn went and sat at the little table beside Patience's chair and picked up the pack of playing cards. 'What's it to be tonight then? Gin Rummy or 500?'

The next morning Flynn took the train to Pickering then made his way to the house in Hatcase Lane. Tom Fairweather greeted him cheerfully, and Amelia Harrison offered him a welcome cup of tea before the men crossed the yard to the workshop. Inside, Flynn was delighted with what he saw.

'They're just how I imagined them,' he said, running his hands over the smooth wood of one of the giant teacups. 'And the paint-work's brilliant.' He stepped back to admire the different cups, some painted bright yellow with large black dots and others decorated with butterflies and flowers. 'Perfect,' he said.

Tom smiled with relief. It was the biggest job he'd undertaken since arriving in Pickering. 'I'm pleased that I've interpreted your idea to your satisfaction, Mr Corrigan. I enjoyed making them.'

Flynn clapped Tom's shoulder. He liked this soft-spoken, diffident man. 'Time to settle the bill then.' He peeled notes from the bundle he'd taken from his pocket, then spat in the palm of his hand before shaking Tom's hand.

'Thank you kindly,' Tom said. 'Will we celebrate with a bottle of beer?'

Tom went to fetch the bottles from the other end of the room and Flynn roamed the sparsely furnished, tidy room, his eyes alighting on a well-stocked bookshelf. Tom Fairweather was clearly a man who valued culture above comfort, he thought as he surveyed the book titles.

'I see you're a reading man like meself,' Flynn remarked as Tom came back with the beer. 'Tell me, what did you think to *Moby Dick*?'

'Melville's a great writer,' said Tom, handing Flynn a bottle, 'but I prefer Kipling. In my opinion he captures the emotions and a feel for the place better than any other writer.'

Flynn agreed. 'Aye, *Plain Tales from the Hills* is my favourite.'

'Mine would be *The Man Who Would Be King*.'

They drank their beers and talked about books and the new roundabout Tom was working on.

'I'll take delivery next week then,' Flynn said eventually. 'Can you organise a cart to the railway station from this end, and I'll organise one at the other end?'

Tom said he could and they parted on the best of terms.

'Spread the word if you will, that Tom Fairweather will do a good job at a fair price,' Tom said as they shook hands again.

'I will,' Flynn promised.

Not until he was on the train back to Scarborough did Flynn make the sudden, amazing connection. He smote his forehead. How could he have been so stupid. Initially, he'd paid no heed to the woodcarver's name, so pleased was he to have found someone who could meet his demands for the new merry-go-round.

Fairweather, Fairweather, Fairweather; the name drummed in his head in tandem with the rhythm of the train's wheels.

* * *

Flynn arrived back at the fairground, his thoughts in turmoil. The three young lads he employed were busy oiling and assembling the rides ready for Easter. He worked alongside them for the rest of the afternoon, his mind rehearsing what he might say to Lissie. It would be cruel to raise her hopes if the woodcarver was not her father. Maybe he should sound Tom out before mentioning any of his suspicions to Lissie. He tried to picture Tom's face to see if there was any resemblance to Lissie's. Their mouths and noses were similar, he thought, but so what? Lots of people had fine, straight noses and well-shaped mouths. Finally, he reached the conclusion that it would be wiser to approach Tom first.

Even so, that evening Flynn couldn't resist telling Lissie about the teacups and the man who had made them. They were sitting in the dining room, Patience snoring gently in her bed, Flynn having lifted her into it after a rumbustious game of Gin Rummy in which he had jokingly accused her of cheating and Patience had retorted, 'Winning's what life's all about, young man. Mark my words.'

'He's a real craftsman, Lissie,' Flynn said as he described the teacups, 'and he's an interesting chap all told. He prefers Kipling to Melville, and he must like poetry. He has a great collection on his bookshelf.'

'He sounds like my dad.'

Flynn's heart missed a beat.

'My dad was good with his hands, and he loved Kipling. He often read to me from the *Just So* stories and he knew lots of poems by heart.' Lissie bit her lip, the memory causing a sharp pain in her chest. 'I still miss him, Flynn.'

Flynn folded her in his arms. Should he speak out, or was it too soon? He imagined her joy if he reunited her with her father, then shuddered as he thought of the crushing disappointment she would feel if he was wrong.

'You're trembling,' she said, pulling away and looking closely at him.

He shrugged. 'Someone must have walked over my grave,' he jested, and jiggled her on his knee to make her laugh. Lissie was in such a good place at the moment that it would be foolish to destroy her happiness for what might be a only a mere notion on his part. He would bide his time.

24

The resort was crowded with people making the most of the Easter weekend. Day trippers arrived by the hour in charabancs or on the train, eager to enjoy what Scarborough had to offer to blow away the tedium of toiling in the mills and factories. The weather in March had been atrocious with storms, floods and even snow in some parts of the East Riding but April had arrived in all her glory with dry, warm sunny days to bless the holiday.

The new ride at the fairground was a great attraction as little children piled into the giant teacups and whirled round and round, but every time Flynn looked at it, he thought about the man who had made it. He looked at his pocket watch: any time now Lissie would be coming to meet him.

She was strolling along past the beach still crowded with frolicking children paddling in the shallows under the careful eyes of their parents. The sea was a greenish-blue, the tide on the turn, and seahorses cresting their way to the shore to demolish lovingly built sand castles and drive the holidaymakers to other pursuits. Some would hurry to catch the last train back to the smoky towns from which they had escaped for the day, others to the boarding houses for supper.

On reaching the fairground, Lissie pushed her way through the crowds to find Flynn. He was standing watching his latest acquisition, a satisfied smile on his handsome face that was tanned by years of exposure to the sun and the sea air. He looked very much the successful proprietor in his crisp white shirt and new leather jerkin, a jaunty red neckerchief at his throat and his glossy black hair curling about his ears and in the nape of his neck. Lissie fell in love with him all over again.

'It's marvellous,' she exclaimed on reaching his side. 'The man who made it certainly has a gift.'

Flynn wondered if the roundabout's creator was the gift that Lissie had been hoping for these past eleven years, but he didn't voice his thoughts. Instead, he called to one of his lads to keep an eye on things, and took Lissie for a drink on the terrace of the Grand Hotel. There they sat and watched the setting sun turn the sea a rosy red as they talked about their respective businesses and other shared interests. At that moment life seemed perfect, and Flynn was going to do nothing to spoil it.

The next few weeks passed by in a blur of activity, Lissie fully occupied with running the shop and entertaining Patience. Although Mrs Trimble saw to Patience's daily needs, Lissie, painfully aware that she spent her days cooped up in one room, felt it was her duty to give her some quality of life. To that end, she had hired an assistant. She could hardly believe her luck when the advertisement she had placed in the Gazette brought Elspeth Lowry to her door. A woman in her thirties, Elspeth had been employed in the drapery department at Marshall & Snelgrove – one of the North of England's most prestigious stores – before she married and had her children. The youngest had recently started school and she was once again available for work.

Lissie took to the well-spoken, attractive woman immediately and within days was impressed by her efficiency: she knew the drapery business inside out. Confident that she was leaving the shop in Elspeth's capable hands, Lissie purchased a bathchair and for an hour or so on most afternoons she walked Patience along the esplanade or round the town, Patience in her element as they stopped to pass the time of day with acquaintances and take tea at the Spa.

Flynn was busy too, his expanding business of rides and sideshows taking much of his time. Although he revelled in his work there were moments when his conscience plagued him. And so, on a day in early June he took the early morning train to Pickering and called at the house in Hatclose Lane.

'Tom's working in St Peter's Church. They've ordered some new pews,' Amelia told him then gave him directions to Hall Garth, the hill on which the church sat. Flynn walked briskly up the slope and into the ancient building. Adjusting his eyes to the gloom after the bright sunlight, he saw Tom further down the aisle, a measuring tape in his hand. Flynn paused to take in the magnificent medieval wall paintings, then with his footsteps ringing on the flagstones in the hallowed silence, he approached Tom.

Tom looked up, surprised.

'Hello, what brings you here?' he asked, slipping the measuring tape into his pocket and holding out his hand. 'Have you another order for me?'

Flynn grasped the outstretched hand and in a tight voice he said, 'I need to talk with you. I need answers to some questions.'

Tom looked even more bemused. He gestured for Flynn to sit. He perched on the end of a pew and Tom sat across the aisle facing him. 'What is this about?' he asked. 'Nothing wrong with the teacups, I hope.'

'No, nothing like that. They're a great success, the kids love 'em.' Distracted, he tossed out the remark, and in an attempt to settle his nerves he sucked in his breath as he searched for the right words to broach the subject. He had to tread carefully. Meddling in another man's affairs could cause offence, and Flynn liked Tom too much to want to annoy him.

Tom patiently waited for an explanation, his eyes alight with curiosity.

Eventually, Flynn leaned forward in his seat, his arms resting on his knees and his hand clasped tightly as he looked directly at Tom. 'It's a strange business,' he began, 'and one you might not wish to discuss but I need you to be honest with me. Do you have a daughter?'

Now it was Tom's turn to draw a deep breath. He paled, his face crumpling and his lips pressed together as though he had been struck. He stayed like that for a long moment, and in the cloistral silence Flynn could hear the thud of his own heart. Had he been right all along?

'Why do you ask?' Tom's voice wavered.

'It's the name you see – Fairweather. Not common in these parts and I happen to be in love with a young lady called Lissie Fair-weather who comes from Derbyshire, and I wondered—' He got no further.

Tom sprang to his feet. 'My Lissie! Have you found my Lissie? Is she here with you?' He barged down the aisle towards the door.

'No, I came alone,' Flynn called after him and got to his feet.

Tom stopped in his tracks and whirled round. 'Where is she?' he cried, his voice cracking under the strain.

'I'll tell you when I'm certain that you're the man I'm looking for, so calm down and tell me about *your* daughter. I have to be sure we're talking about the same Lissie, and not just a coincidence of names.'

Flynn's tone authoritative, Tom did as he asked and they sat down again.

'I did have a daughter,' Tom said, his voice barely above a whisper. 'I called her Lissie, and she was seven years old when she was taken from me.' He shook his head despairingly and closed his eyes. When he opened them, Flynn nodded for him to continue. Tom told much the same story that Lissie had told Flynn, and then about the years he had spent searching for her. When he finally stumbled to a halt, Flynn reached across the aisle and took his hand, squeezing it reassuringly.

'Tom Fairweather, you've found your daughter.'

* * *

Lissie was serving a customer with a pair of bloomers when Flynn entered the shop shortly after midday. She raised her eyebrows, surprised to see him at that time of day. He gave her an enigmatic smile in return then, when she had completed the sale, he told her to go through to the house and into the hall. He'd meet her there. Bursting with curiosity, she left Elspeth to mind the shop.

'What's brought you here?' she asked as she met Flynn in the hall.

'I've someone I want you to meet.' He sounded awfully mysterious.

'Who?' Lissie frowned. Who amongst Flynn's acquaintances was important enough for him to interrupt her at work?

'Wait here. I'll go and get him.' He went to the front door and opened it wide, beckoning with his hand to someone outside.

Tom Fairweather stepped inside nervously, twisting his soft felt hat in his hands. A tentative smile twitched at his lips and his eyes misted with tears as he gazed at Lissie. He opened his mouth as if to speak but no sound came out. He broke out in a sweat, the fear of rejection making his heart thunder.

Lissie stared at the tall, handsome man. His curly black hair was greying at the temples and fine creases etched his mouth and round his eyes. Lissie swallowed the lump that filled her throat. She knew that face, it was the face that appeared in her dreams, a face that she had thought she would never see again in her waking hours. She began to tremble. Tears sprang to her eyes and she felt as though she might faint as she gazed in wonder at the man standing nervously in the doorway, his eyes pleading for recognition.

'Dad,' she whispered. 'Dad, is it really you?'

'Oh, Lissie. My little Lissie.' Tom stumbled forward, arms outstretched and Lissie fell into them weeping openly and clinging to him for dear life. Flynn stood by, tears welling.

'I'll leave you two to talk,' he said gruffly then quietly let himself out.

* * *

Oh, what pure joy the reunion brought, so much to tell and so many painful moments to recall yet in the telling of them a wonderful unburdening of the soul. For the next two days Lissie left the shop in Elspeth's capable hands whilst she and Tom spent the daylight hours on the esplanade and beaches walking and talking, and in the evenings with Patience and Flynn to talk some more. Every precious moment brought them closer as they renewed old bonds and vowed never to be separated again.

Tom told how he had lain bleeding only to be found by the man who kept the horse in the field by the cottage when he had called to collect his repaired boots, and how after a short spell in the infirmary in Thorne he had closed the cottage and gone in search of

Lissie. He had travelled far and wide, staying in one place long enough to earn a little money before moving on, never losing hope that he would find her.

'I never forgot you for a moment, Lissie,' he told her the first day they walked on the esplanade. 'I kept you in my heart. With time I no longer felt your touch or smelled your hair sweet as meadow flowers, but as those senses faded another heightened. Memory. Memory became my friend. So, I read to you, I held you and whenever I came to some beautiful, peaceful place I even danced with you.'

Lissie's tears had been so hot then that she thought their tracks might mark her cheeks for ever. Her dad said the most evocative things, and she loved him all the more. Of her mother they spoke very little other than to tell the outrageous detail of how she had abandoned Lissie. Tom had wept when he heard this.

'I can't honestly say I've ever missed her,' Lissie told Tom.

Flynn was overjoyed for Lissie, as was Patience, and the next two days passed all too swiftly. But finally the time came when Tom had to return to Pickering, his workshop and Amelia. 'I have a decent livelihood there, and I've grown fond of Amelia,' he explained. 'I wouldn't want to just walk away but we can see each other as often as we please. You have your place here with Patience, and in Flynn you have a wonderful man to care for you.'

Lissie was saddened to see her dad go, but she saw the reason for it. She had Patience and Flynn, and now her father. What more could she want?

25

There was much to-ing and fro-ing in the month of June, which included Lissie and Flynn going to Pickering where Lissie enjoyed meeting Amelia, and Tom bringing Amelia to Scarborough for the day.

On Sunday, 28 June 1914, the shop and the fairground were closed and after dinner, with Flynn pushing Patience in her bathchair and Tom linking arms with Lissie and Amelia, they walked along the crowded esplanade. There had been a thunderstorm the night before, and now Scarborough was basking in a heatwave, the beach just the place to be for many of the day trippers.

'A good day for business,' said Flynn, regretting that the law forbade the opening of the fairground. 'Still, the ice cream is in great demand.' He nodded at the long queue outside one of his stalls and grinned.

'It's almost too hot to be pleasant,' Patience complained, fanning her face with her handkerchief then catching sight of one of her customers. 'Good day to you, Mr Hanson, are you well?'

'Good afternoon, Mrs Foyer. I am indeed well and in far better shape than the Archduke Franz Ferdinand.'

Patience frowned. 'What ever do you mean?'

'I just heard it on the wireless. He and his poor wife have been assassinated.'

'My goodness me! Whatever is the world coming to?' Patience exclaimed.

'Yes, shocking indeed,' Mr Hanson agreed then went on his way.

'Very hot-headed, those foreigners,' Patience remarked, but the news had caught all their attention, and they talked of little else as they made their way back to North Marine Road.

The next morning, as Lissie took her mid-morning cup of tea, she read the details of the dreadful event in the *Gazette*. The Archduke Franz Ferdinand, heir to the Austrian throne, had been shot and killed by a Serbian nationalist. Although she felt sad for the foreign prince and his wife, she wasn't unduly disturbed, but in the days that followed political temperature was steadily rising, enough to rival the heatwave in Scarborough.

In the shop, customers talked about what they were hearing on the wireless. Germany and Austria-Hungary were going to make the Serbs pay for the Archduke's death. There was going to be a war. When Lissie talked it over with Flynn, to her consternation, he too seemed alarmed.

'Kaiser Wilhelm says the German Empire should wage war on Serbia as soon as possible,' he said grimly. 'If they do, the Russians will fight back, and I have an uneasy feeling that if that happens, we'll be dragged into it.'

'But why? England's miles away from those countries.' Lissie felt bemused and anxious.

'Distance has nothing to do with it. It's all to with the treaties we have with other countries. Britain has promised to defend them if they are threatened.'

And as each passing day in July brought with it a further threat of war, Lissie began to understand what Flynn had told her.

'I'd enlist to fight the buggers if I wa' younger,' an elderly man buying a vest told her with patriotic fervour. 'I wa' in't Boer War, you know.'

'Do you really think our men will have to fight?' Lissie shuddered.

'Course they will, lass. T'Russian's are fightin' t'Germans an' t'Germans are threatening to invade France an' Belgium so it's our job to stop 'em. You don't want to wake up one morning an' find a German on your doorstep that's sailed across t'Channel or worse still moored his bloody battleship in our harbour.' He marched out of the shop as if he was going into battle.

Lissie leaned with her elbows on the counter, her head in her hands. What if Britain joined the war? Would Flynn go and fight? And what about her dad? She began to tremble. She had only just found him. He couldn't leave her again, and life without Flynn would be unbearable.

The bell above the shop door tinkled and she jumped to attention, but when the customer asked for two yards of white muslin Lissie's hands were shaking so badly, she could barely hold the scissors as she cut the material.

* * *

Later that same evening, she shared her worries with Meggie as they sat in the parlour choosing a pattern for Meggie's wedding dress.

'Aah know what you mean,' said Meggie, 'I asked Jimmy if he'd have to join the army afore we got wed an' he said it'll be ages afore it has owt to do wi' us, if ever.' She pointed to a picture of a dress in the *Woman's Journal* on the table in front of them. 'Aah like the shape of that neckline an' them long sleeves.' The wedding was set to take place at the end of September, and like any girl about to be married, Meggie thought of little else.

'I can easily make you something like that,' Lissie said as she perused the illustration. 'It's nice and simple and it 'ud look lovely made in white voile.' But unlike Meggie, the thoughts of impending war wouldn't leave her mind and she asked, 'Do you think Jimmy will want to go and fight?'

'Oh, aye. He said seein' as he's a leader in the boy scouts it 'ud be expected. An' seein' as how we'll be livin' with his mam and dad, an' me working in the butcher's shop when I leave the Royal at the end of the month, he'd not worry about me if he had to go away.'

Lissie admired Meggie's equanimity and wished that she could shake off the feeling that their lives were about to change forever.

* * *

When Flynn called that evening, she bombarded him with questions. 'I don't think we'll have a choice,' he said, pulling a copy of the *Gazette* from his pocket. 'Britain's given Germany an ultimatum.' He pointed to the article on the front page. 'They've got until midnight tonight to declare peace.'

'And what if they don't?'

'Then we'll be at war.'

* * *

A few days later, as Lissie walked into the town centre, she was struck by the change in the people she met. The declaration of war had them talking of little else, and already on the walls of some of the buildings and in the shop windows there were posters of the King and Queen and others declaring 'War against the Huns' and 'Keep Calm and Carry On'. And as summer drifted into autumn and the holiday season drew to a close, she saw queues of excited young men outside the hastily established recruiting office in Market Street waiting to take the King's shilling and fight for their country.

'Will you enlist?' she asked Flynn and her father, terrified that they would.

'It 'ud be cowardice not to, if things get worse,' Flynn said, 'but they're saying it'll all be over by Christmas so I'll let the hare sit for a while.'

'I'm not a fighting man,' Tom said, 'but if things escalate, I'd volunteer to be a stretcher-bearer or something similar.'

Lissie couldn't disagree with either of them, but she prayed it would be over by Christmas before either of the loves of her life did anything drastic.

* * *

In a letter to Connie Briggs, Lissie told her that she was reunited with her father. Connie replied that she was delighted for her, and hoped to meet him one day but sadly her visits to Scarborough would be curtailed for the time being. Her mother was very sick and Connie had to spend all her free time caring for her. Lissie wrote back saying she would miss her visits and that she hoped her mother would make a speedy recovery, at the same time knowing it was highly unlikely; Connie's mother was very frail.

A weekend trip to Newcastle on the last Friday in September did much to lighten Lissie's mood. The train journey was exciting, and with Flynn by her side she had no fear of going to a strange city to be bridesmaid for Meggie. They were made royally welcome by

Meggie's family, and the following day Lissie walked down the aisle of St Thomas's church behind Meggie dreaming of her own wedding day.

Meggie looked a picture in the white voile dress that Lissie had copied from the one they had seen in the *Woman's Journal*, and Lissie was just as pretty in pale blue, her striking black hair laced with fresh flowers. Jimmy waited at the altar for his bride with his best man, Flynn, by his side, both of them handsome in dark grey suits. In a beautifully simple ceremony, Meggie and Jimmy exchanged their vows.

Afterwards in the church hall, Lissie was dancing with Flynn to the tune of 'Moonlight Bay' when he said. 'You know you've stolen my heart, Lissie, so will you promise to marry me come next spring?'

Lissie had dreamed of this moment and now she felt as though she was floating. 'Oh, yes, Flynn. I'd like nothing better than to be your wife.'

His lips found hers, and lost in the music and their love for one another they danced on.

When they and the newly-weds returned to Scarborough on Sunday evening they were in great spirits.

Patience wasn't living up to her name; she grew tetchier by the week. 'What's happening?' she asked several times a day.

'Quite a lot,' Lissie told her. 'The town's full of young men wearing uniforms and going off to training camps. Mrs Hanson's son went off this morning, and the British Expeditionary Forces are already in Mons in France. Old Mr Scott says it's the first shots fired since the Battle of Waterloo.'

But as the days grew shorter and winter winds lashed the sea on to the esplanade, there was an air of keep calm and carry on in Scarborough, and Lissie's anxiety lessened. Perhaps it would all blow over after all.

Flynn dismantled the carousel and the roundabouts and put them in storage ready to be refurbished for next spring, and Lissie created a Christmassy display in the shop window. Most of the inhabitants in the little town of Scarborough went about their business, and apart from those who were missing sons, husbands and fathers, the men who had answered the early call to defend their country, they were not unduly affected by a war that for many seemed to be far away from their peaceful shores.

On Tuesday night, December 15th, Lissie and Flynn kissed goodnight on the steps of the house in North Marine Road, Lissie shivering in the cold blast blowing off the North Sea. A handful of brittle stars were scattered across the dark sky.

'See you tomorrow,' said Flynn, hugging her closer and giving her a final kiss.

Back inside, Lissie checked that Patience was sleeping then went upstairs. In bed, she lay musing on the plans she had for Christmas, the first with her beloved dad for more than eleven years. She'd make it extra special, she told herself as she fell into a deep, dreamless sleep.

She wakened the next morning at seven o'clock and looking out of the window, she saw that the town was shrouded in a thick mist. It swirled over the roof tops and along the coastline masking everything in a dank grey blanket. What else could anyone expect at this time of year, Lissie told herself as she put on the black skirt and white blouse she wore in the shop.

Down in the kitchen she made breakfast, ate her own, then went to see if Patience was awake. She was, so Lissie went back to the kitchen, returning to the parlour with a dish of porridge and tea and toast.

'The mist's as thick as pea soup,' she said as she propped Patience up on her pillows. 'I don't think we'll see too many customers today if it doesn't lift.'

'Then I'll stay here, cosy and warm and forgo my early morning sprint on the sands and my cold dip in the sea,' Patience said, her sarcastic jest making Lissie laugh. Patience's body might have played her foul but her mind was still razor sharp and her witticism always lightened what was now a tedious life. Still chuckling, Lissie went back to the kitchen, and about to clear the ashes from the grate and light the fire, she glanced at the clock on the mantelshelf. Its hand showing a quarter to eight, she had more than an hour to do her household chores before she needed to open the shop.

Up on the rocky headland overlooking the town, a police constable and two coastguards were on duty at the coastal station close by the ancient castle. 'Can't see a damned thing out there the mist's that thick,' said Jack Carr as he ducked back in from the station's doorway to where his colleague and the policeman sat huddled round the stove drinking tea.

Fred Lightowler put down his mug and got to his feet. 'There's allus summat to make this job hard to do,' he said, pulling on his oilskins ready to go on patrol.

'Aye, you can say that again,' PC Hunter agreed as he drained his mug and prepared to accompany the coastguards out into the murk.

Aboard the fishing trawler, *St Cloud*, its skipper was cautiously making his way into the harbour. Since the war began the light-house no longer sent out its warning beam and visibility was poor, the heavy mist and thick fog hampering his view of the bay. The fishing had been plentiful and he was looking forward to landing his catch of cod and whiting.

'We'll land this lot sharpish an' get home for breakfast an' a nice warm fire,' he shouted through the open wheelhouse window to his crew who were piling boxes of fish on the deck in preparation for them to be winched ashore.

'An' not a minute too soon in this bloody weather,' a deckhand yelled back.

Peering through the wheelhouse window into the haze, the skipper slowly manoeuvred *St Cloud* and as he rounded Castle Hill he saw three huge warships. At first, he thought they were British until he spotted the German war flags. 'Bloody hell!' he yelled to his crew, 'them's the enemy. Bloody Germans.'

The horrified crewmen stared in amazement then flung themselves to the deck as with a mighty roar, a missile skimmed over the trawler's bow. Revving his engine, and heedless of colliding with the trawlers already at anchor, the skipper zoomed into port as another blast from one of the warships demolished the coastguards' lookout shelter on Castle Hill.

'Jesus Christ,' the policeman gasped then thanked God that he and the coastguards had left the lookout only minutes before to obtain a better view of the territory they were guarding. They ran for cover beside an old water tank as shells whistled overhead.

'They must be aiming for the naval wireless station,' one of the coastguards surmised as another shell hit the castle's great tower. Next to take a direct hit was the south-facing wall, the ancient stones crumbling into heaps of rubble. The coastguards and the policeman stared in utter shock and amazement at the destruction then sought cover under the water cistern, feeling helpless in the face of the bombardment as more missiles whistled overhead.

Lissie heard the bangs and thuds, and dropping her duster, she ran into the dining room. Patience was sitting up in bed, her eyes wide as she and Lissie looked at one another fearfully. The noise continued and Lissie ran to the front door to peer out, her heart in her mouth.

'It's the Germans! They're bombarding the town,' yelled a man in an ARP uniform as he dashed past. Hot on his heels, another man shouted, 'Three German warships in the bay, better take cover, lass.' The men pounded out of sight and in the distance Lissie could see smoke and flames and clouds of dust. She darted back inside.

'It's started, the Germans are here. They're bombing the town,' she cried as she rushed to Patience's bedside. 'Let me get you up. We'll shelter under the stairs.' She helped Patience out of bed, her hands trembling under the feel of the old woman's limbs that were crabbed and knotted with arthritis.

'The blackhearted buggers. Why can't they leave us in peace?' Patience groaned, as with Lissie supporting her, they made their way into the hall and into the sloping roofed space under the stairs. It had been Flynn's suggestion that they should shelter there if the worst came, and Lissie had put a chair and some cushions and blankets in place, along with magazines and books. She made Patience comfortable in the chair and then sat on the floor at the old woman's feet, listening to the bombardment that was now continuous.

'I never thought I'd live to see such a thing,' Patience muttered then flinched violently as a particularly loud explosion made the house walls shake. Lissie's heart raced. Should they stay here? Were they safe? Where should they go?

Another massive explosion broke her panicked thoughts. Flakes of plaster fell from the ceiling in the hallway and an acrid smell seeped into the house. Lissie took Patience's hands in her own, squeezing them reassuringly, and at the same time wondering what Flynn was doing. Was he in danger? Had he tried to come to help them and been killed in the street? Her imagination running riot, she crept from under the stairs, and in the kitchen she made a pot of tea, the panacea for all ills.

Flynn, shocked by the devastation that the German gunboats had already inflicted on the town, was dashing to North Marine

Road and Lissie and Patience, frantic to check that they hadn't suffered any harm.

Out in the streets, streams of men, women and children, some still in their nightclothes and in stockinged feet, struggled along the road to nearby Scalby to escape from the shells that were raining down on the town. Fire engines roared through the streets, bells clanging, and ARP men who had never expected to put the brief training they had received into action raced to bring order to the ensuing chaos.

Flynn hadn't gone far when he was forced to halt as a German shell made a direct hit on a house in Castle Street. Windows shattered, the front wall caved in, and amid the screams and shouts from the occupants within, he joined in the rescue of a woman and three small children.

'My husband,' the woman shrieked, pulling herself from Flynn's arms and trying to get back into the blazing house. 'Sammy! Sammy! Where are you, love?'

Flynn caught her in his strong grasp, and his heart went out to her as members of the rescue team brought out the broken body of her husband.

Desperate now to get to Lissie and Patience, he left the woman in the care of her neighbours, and cursing the Germans for all he was worth, he ran like the wind to the drapery.

'Lissie! Mrs Foyer! Are you all right?' Flynn yelled as he burst through the door. Lissie threw herself into his arms. 'Oh, Flynn! Flynn! Thank God,' she cried.

A short while later the bombardment ceased, and reassured that those he loved were safe, Flynn went out into the street where he learned that the German battleships had sailed north leaving Scarborough in ruins.

In the afternoon, placing Patience in Mrs Trimble's care, Lissie and Flynn walked the town, horrified by the destruction. Shops, houses, hotels, churches, hospitals and schools had all suffered. The Grand Hotel lay in ruins, and Lissie thanked God that Meggie no longer worked there. As they met people they knew, they learned that a postman had been killed, and a young boy scout had met his death on the way to buy a newspaper in the hope of finding his picture in it. Lord Baden-Powell had recently paid a visit to the local scout troop and the boy had been presented to him.

'Oh, the poor little soul, and his poor parents.' Tears sprang to Lissie's eyes and she struggled to hold them back as they walked past houses with their fronts torn away and fragments of furniture and children's toys lying in the rubble. 'Where will the survivors live now?' she asked, her heart aching for the families who were now homeless.

In the days that followed they learned that seventeen people had been killed and more than eighty injured in Scarborough, and that on the same day the German High Seas Fleet commanded by Admiral Franz von Hipper had also decimated the ports of Whitby and Hartlepool. In total, 137 people were killed in the three towns.

'This is Not Warfare this is Murder.' Patience read the headlines in the *Daily Post* out loud. 'Damned right it is,' she growled, outraged by the cruel damage the Germans had inflicted on her town. 'It says here that Winston Churchill is calling the Germans the baby killers of Scarborough, but where was he, and what was he doing to protect us when it happened?'

'Don't upset yourself, Mrs Foyer. We're alive and unlike poor Mrs Hanson three doors down, we didn't sustain any damage,' Lissie soothed as she got ready to open the shop. Funerals were taking place all over the town, and black crepe armbands, veils and hats were in demand. Marshall & Snelgrove's department store had been badly damaged and she was reaping the benefit of its customers. It was bittersweet to think that her takings were being enhanced by such a dreadful event.

In her struggle to accept what had happened to the peaceful seaside resort, Lissie waited, her breath sometimes catching in her throat and her chest tightening whenever she thought about Flynn's and her father's reaction to the war that had now wreaked havoc on their doorstep.

26

'Oi! Get down out of there, you'll get hurt,' Flynn shouted to the three young lads clambering over the rubble of a house in Raleigh Street in the half-light of early evening. Hunting for fragments of shells had become the latest rage, young lads searching for souvenirs of the German attack, some to keep and some to sell to the day trippers attracted to the town to see the damage for themselves.

The lads glanced at the muscular man with the angry face and scarpered. It annoyed Flynn to think that people took a voyeuristic pleasure in other people's misfortune. He was also irritated by his own mixed feelings. Earlier in the day he had walked through the town where colourful posters urged its inhabitants to:

UP AND AT 'EM! AVENGE SCARBOROUGH

Outside the recruitment office the lengthening queue of young men tempted him to join them. But first he must discuss it with Lissie. He hated the thought of leaving her and his thriving business, but turning a blind eye was not in his nature, and as he arrived at the house in North Marine Road he had more or less made up his mind. He rapped on the door then let himself in, his heart heavy as he entered the parlour to be met by a weary-faced Patience, a stolid, embarrassed Jimmy, and Lissie holding a weeping Meggie in her arms. All eyes turned to Flynn.

'Jimmy enlisted today,' Lissie said hollowly by way of explanation.

Flynn looked at Jimmy, his expression a mixture of surprise and admiration.

'That's right, I did,' Jimmy blustered. 'We can't just stand by an' let 'em win.'

Meggie lifted her head and blinked back tears. 'Aah don't know whether aah should feel proud or blazin' bloody mad,' she hiccupped, freeing herself from Lissie's arms. 'We've on'y been married three months an' now he's going off to fight an' he might...' She gave Jimmy a beseeching look.

'Be proud,' said Flynn, going over to Lissie and taking her hands in his. 'Just as proud as I hope you'll be, Lissie. We have to go if we're to defend those we love.'

'You're going too?' she gasped, a little voice inside her head telling her that she had always known he would.

Flynn nodded. This wasn't the way he had intended to tell her but now it was inevitable. He pulled her to her feet and embraced her. 'We'll do our best to stay safe, won't we, Jimmy? The Hun won't know what's hit 'em once we get over there,' he said, his attempt at jocularity failing to raise a smile.

'When Henry Foyer went off to the Boer War, I thought I'd never see him again,' Patience said, her sharp grey eyes softening. 'He'd been courting me but a few months and I wasn't sure about him. He was a bit flighty, you know. When he came back, he was wiser and made all the better for the experience so I married him and I've never regretted the day even though we never had any children.'

She smiled fondly at Lissie then Flynn. 'Sometimes we have to be brave to get the best out of life and you, Lissie and Flynn and Meggie and Jimmy, have got to face up to that. Love will carry you through.'

Lissie's tears welled in her eyes and when she looked at Flynn, she saw that Patience's little speech had affected him in the same way. They both knew that she looked on them as the children she had never had.

'Now, put me into my bed, Flynn, then the four of you go into the kitchen and Lissie, make a pot of tea. I'm parched,' Patience ordered.

In the kitchen, Lissie and Meggie made tea. Lissie filled the spouted cup that Patience used and took it into the parlour, returning just in time to hear Flynn ask, 'What regiment did you enlist in, Jimmy?' Her heart sank. He was definitely going to enlist.

'Tenth Battalion East Yorks. Will you join me? I'd like to think we can do this together.' Jimmy's bottom lip trembled as he made his request.

'Course we will, an' while we're away you two girls look after one another and Mrs Foyer.' Flynn gave Lissie and Meggie an encouraging smile.

'We will,' they choroused, the smiles they gave in return rather forced.

* * *

'I don't know how long I'll be away,' Flynn told Lissie as they cuddled in an armchair in the kitchen on the night before he had to report to a training camp in Ripon, 'but if I'm not back before the season starts will you keep an eye on the rides and the stalls? I've talked it over with Billy and he's going to run them for me and mind the rides Mrs Foyer owns, but I want you to see to the money – you know – collect the takings, pay the wages and that sort of thing.'

'I'll do my best,' she said, feeling rather overwhelmed by the responsibility this would entail, but understanding that they couldn't just let the businesses fold. 'Now that I've got Elspeth in the shop, and Mrs Trimble seeing to Mrs Foyer, I'll have time to do that.' She frowned. 'Will Billy have enough young lads to help him run the rides? The town seems empty of young men these days.'

She knew that Billy wouldn't be enlisting. His humped back wasn't wanted by the army, but he couldn't work single-handed.

'He's got three or four lads lined up for Easter. They're all too young to join up, although if they lie about their age as some are doing, he could find himself short-handed. If that happens, he'll just have to close the rides. The stalls are taken care of. Molly says she can do the ice cream with her daughter now that Jack's away, and the others are all run by women so there's no problem there.'

Lissie realised that Flynn's intention to enlist had not been a spur of the moment thing; he'd been planning this for some time. She felt hurt that he hadn't shared this with her but when he kissed her she silently excused him. It was so like him to have made sure everything was in place before he made his final decision.

'I'll miss you dreadfully,' she said in between passionate kisses.

'Not as much as I'll miss you,' he replied, his voice thick with emotion.

* * *

It was pouring with rain the next morning as Lissie and Flynn and Jimmy and Meggie made their way to the railway station. Even the sky's crying, Lissie thought, as clinging to Flynn's arm, they walked through the streets past the damaged houses and hotels that were testament to the reason for their journey.

The station platform was crowded with men, some in uniform, and their girlfriends or wives and children hugging them for what might be the last time, Lissie thought glumly. *Please God send him back to me*, she prayed, placing her hands behind Flynn's neck and twining her fingers in his long dark hair as she stamped the feel and smell of him in her memory.

Jimmy and Meggie stood a few paces away, doing much the same.

A train snaked alongside the platform, clanking and grinding to a halt. Steam hissed up to the glass roof, doors flew open, whistles blew, and with one last urgent kiss Lissie let go of Flynn and stepped back, smiling bravely. 'I'll write every day,' she said. 'Take great care.'

Lissie and Meggie stood, arms round each other, as they watched Flynn and Jimmy board the train, their hearts trapped in their throats. A whistle blew, the train puffed steam and trundled down the line as the girls waved and cried.

'Aah don't know what I'll do wi'out him,' Meggie sobbed.

'We'll look after one another.' Lissie sounded braver than she felt.

* * *

Weeks, then months, blurred one into the other, daylight hours lengthening and chill winter days warming into spring. As Easter drew near, Lissie met regularly with Billy to check that the rides were ready to open for the Easter holiday.

'Have no fear, Miss Fairweather, I'll not let Mr Corrigan down,' he assured her. Although Billy was of a similar age to Flynn his hunched back and grizzled features made him appear much older, and Lissie found him to be a good manager and a faithful employee. 'There wa' a time when I wa' down an' out wi' not a penny to bless me name,' he continued, 'but Flynn Corrigan saw me right. There's nowt I wouldn't do for him.'

Such devotion made Lissie's task easier, and when she called on the women who ran the stalls they were just as loyal and amenable. In her letters to Flynn, along with the loving sentiments, she was able to let him know his businesses were in safe hands. Ripon, where he was training, was less than seventy miles away but it might as well have been a million in Lissie's opinion. During the day she was so busy caring for Patience, serving in the shop, and overseeing Flynn's businesses that she didn't have too much time to dwell on missing him. At night she fell into bed exhausted, but she didn't sleep. She was filled with longing for him and was keenly aware of how much she had relied on and confided in him. Whenever his letters arrived, the sight of Flynn's sloping, untidy writing sent an agonising pang of loneliness through her, and she'd struggle to hold back her tears. But life had to go on. She couldn't afford to let her emotions get the better of her.

* * *

'You look pleased with yourself.' Lissie couldn't help but notice Meggie's impish smiles and gleaming eyes when they met outside the booth that was Flynn's office at the fairground.

'Aah'll tell you why when you've done the business,' said Meggie, sounding positively enigmatic. It was the final night of the Easter holidays, and although they were in the habit of spending two or three evenings a week together now that their men were in Ripon, they hadn't seen one another for over a week, both girls far too weary after toiling all day, Lissie in the drapery and Meggie in the butcher's shop. Trade was always busier at holiday times, and people had flocked to the resort even though there was a war on.

When Billy saw the girls, he leapt off the whirling carousel and shambled to meet them. He unlocked the booth and they went in. 'Trade's not what it was but it's been better than I thought it would be,' he said as Lissie sorted out the wages and bagged the profits. 'Let Flynn know we're managing rightly.'

'I will, Billy, and thanks for doing a good job.' Lissie gave him a warm smile.

'Now, what is it you've got to tell me?' she asked Meggie once they were walking away from the rides and the blare of the music.

Meggie stopped in her tracks. 'Aam havin' a bairn,' she crowed, clasping Lissie's hands and jigging her round and round. 'My Jimmy's gan to be a daddy.'

'Oh, Meggie, how wonderful.' Lissie suppressed a twinge of envy as she hugged her friend. 'Does Jimmy know?'

'He will when he gets my letter.' Meggie grinned. 'Aa've known for a while but aah didn't say owt 'cos me mam says it's bad luck to tell anybody afore you're twelve weeks gone.'

Lissie felt suddenly protective of her friend. 'Do you think they'll soon get leave?' she asked, thinking how sad it was that Jimmy wasn't at home to share Meggie's delight. 'Flynn says they will when they've finished their training.'

'Aah bloomin' hope so. Aah canny wait to see the look on Jimmy's face,' Meggie chortled, her smile slipping into a scowl as she snarled, 'This blasted war has a lot to answer for, keepin' a man from his family for months on end.'

'The army's bound to give them leave soon. Flynn says they've nearly finished their training.' They walked on, each thinking of the man they loved until Lissie broke the silence and attempted to raise their spirits. 'I'll begin making baby clothes so that little Master – or little Miss Stockdale – is the best dressed baby in Scarborough.'

'Oh, that'll be grand, Lissie.'

'I'll bet Jimmy's mam and dad are thrilled.'

'They are. Mr and Mrs Stockdale are ever so good to me, even though they have me up to me armpits in sausage meat an' making pork pies all day. Still, it's better than skivvying in the hotel.'

'We're both lucky to live with such kind people. Mrs Foyer's a dear and I couldn't ask for better although I do wish my dad lived in Scarborough,' Lissie sighed. 'But he's settled in Pickering, and he has his woodworking business and Amelia. I can't expect him to give them up just to be close to me.'

'Are they coming this Sunday?'

Tom and Amelia visited every other Sunday as Lissie couldn't leave Patience to fend for herself for a whole day. She was growing more fragile with each passing month.

'They are,' Lissie replied. 'And I'd better get back. Mrs Trimble will have gone home by now and I don't like leaving Mrs Foyer on her own for too long.'

* * *

On Sunday, Tom and Amelia arrived shortly after midday, and almost immediately Lissie sensed the tension between them. After the welcoming hugs and kisses, Lissie left them with Patience in the parlour and went into the kitchen to tend to the dinner she had prepared. It was getting harder with each passing week to put tasty meals on the table. Food prices were shooting up and there wasn't as much choice in the shops. The price of sugar had doubled and flour was scarce. Even so, she had managed to make a mince stew with the meat Meggie had brought the night before, and used the last of her flour to make Yorkshire puddings.

Tom helped Patience to the kitchen table and when they were

all seated, he said, 'I've volunteered as a stretcher-bearer. I leave for Salisbury next week.'

Lissie almost choked on a mouthful of pudding. Amelia looked pained and shook her head. *Ah, that's why they're out of sorts with one another*, Lissie realised. *She doesn't want him to go, and neither do I.*

'It's a non-combatant role,' Tom continued. 'I made it clear I wasn't a fighting man.' He looked from Lissie to Amelia as if begging their permission.

'You'll still be in danger,' Lissie cried, 'you can't not be if you're lifting men from the battlefield. I don't want you to go.'

'Neither do I,' Amelia said resignedly, 'but he's determined to play his part.'

'I think it's very noble of you, Tom.'

'Thank you, Patience. What with the worsening situation in France, I don't see how I can sit back and let others fight for me – and you.' Tom looked from Patience to Amelia then Lissie.

'That's right,' said Patience. 'The end of this war's nowhere in sight, and even though we've had a few victories we're by no means winning. Like Kitchener says, your country needs you.' She sighed heavily. 'I never thought I'd live to see the day that Mons, Ypres and the Marne were names as familiar to me as Leeds and Bradford.' Foreign names were now on everyone's tongues.

They ate in silence for the rest of the meal. Lissie had lost her appetite, and Amelia had barely touched her food. Tom took Patience back into the parlour and, leaving her with Amelia, he went back to the kitchen where Lissie was washing up. He stood behind her, close enough for her to breathe in the scent of freshly carved wood and the sweet musky smell that was his alone. It brought back memories of her childhood. She turned to face him.

'Do you really have to go?' she asked brokenly.

'I do. I wouldn't be the man I think I am if I didn't.' He pulled her to his chest, his chin resting on her hair. She didn't know whether she felt terribly sad or just downright angry.

'But there are plenty of others who want to fight. Why you?' she asked, her anger winning through.

'That's precisely why I'm going. It's to help those like Flynn have a better chance of survival. He went because he knew it was the right thing to do. Everybody has a part to play, and yours is to keep the home fires burning.' He gave her a quirky smile, and Lissie's lips twitched in response to his use of the well-known slogan.

'Oh, Dad, you always do and say the right things.'

'I try, and so must you.' He dropped a kiss on her cheek and in that moment she felt brave enough to face anything.

When the time came for Tom and Amelia to return to Pickering, Lissie hugged her father and said, 'I'll come to see you off.' Then she turned to Amelia. 'Do still come and visit us. You're part of our family now.'

Amelia's smile was grateful. 'I will, Lissie. We'll miss him together.'

'Aren't I the lucky man,' Tom jested. 'Two beautiful women who love me.'

* * *

During the next week, Lissie was already feeling the pain of losing another man that she loved as she waited for the day her father went to Salisbury to take up his duties. On Sunday morning, Meggie arrived to look after Patience and Lissie got ready to go to Pickering to spend time with Tom.

'Aah'm beginning to show,' Meggie said proudly, patting her stomach as Lissie packed her overnight bag. 'Afore long aah'll be askin' you to let me skirts out.'

Lissie noted her friend's little bump and her shining hair and glowing skin.

'You're positively blooming. You look the picture of health. Talking of which, I've given Patience her pills. She gets the next dose at lunchtime then about an hour before she goes to bed to help her sleep. Thanks for doing this, Meggie.'

'It's a small price to pay for the lovely nightgowns and matinée coats you've made for this one.' Meggie patted her bump again. 'An' don't you worry, me an' Mrs Foyer'll get on fine. I know she can't hold the needles any more but she can tell me how to turn the heel,' she said, pulling a pair of knitting needles and an unfinished baby bootee from her bag.

Assured that Patience was in good hands, Lissie went to hug her goodbye.

'I'll be back on Monday morning. Elspeth will open the shop,' she said.

'Away and stop fussing over me. Give my regards to your dad and wish him well for me.' Patience gave her a gentle push. 'Now, off you go. Meggie and I have that knitting to put right if it's to grace the feet of the next generation.'

* * *

In Pickering, Lissie was careful to include Amelia in the conversations and the walk they took. After all, she loved Tom too and he loved her. But late in the evening Amelia left them alone, Lissie thankful for her thoughtfulness, as was Tom.

'You will keep an eye on her, won't you?'

Lissie assured him she would. 'We've a lot in common. We've both had to live without you in our lives, and now that we've got you, you're about to leave us so we'll have to take care of one another.'

'That's my girl. You've grown into a beautiful, intelligent, caring young woman, Lissie. But then, I always knew you would.'

'I must take after you,' she replied, cuddling closer to him where they sat on the couch. 'You will be careful, won't you? I couldn't bear to lose you again.'

Lissie looked deep into his eyes.

'You won't, Lissie. I'll always be with you, and you with me even when we're apart.' Tom smiled a wistful smile. 'I used to picture you and I'd weep tears of sadness, the kind that settle on your skin then seep into your heart. I saw you in my eyes and heard your voice even when you were out of reach. The sun was your smile, the moon your eyes, and you were the poems I read. You were always in my mind, and that's how it will be when I'm away. If you let it be like that for you, we'll always be together.'

Lissie listened to his words and heard the truth in them. That was how she had felt about him, and how she felt about Flynn. A love so powerful that it encompassed every fibre of your being, every thought, every action. Whilst she held that love she knew she would never be alone.

'I love you,' she said. 'You make me a better person, and I'm proud of you.'

'And I of you.'

* * *

The following morning, yet again Lissie stood on the station platform feeling that her heart was about to break. Sadly, she watched Tom take his leave of Amelia. Then it was her turn. She clung to her father. 'Stay safe,' she whispered. 'Come back to us.'

As the train trundled out of sight, she took Amelia's arm and they walked out into the street, grieving for the man they loved.

When she arrived home later that day, the first thing she heard was Meggie shouting from the parlour. 'Is that you, Lissie? There's a letter for you, an' I think I know who it's from.'

Lissie ran down the hallway to find Meggie and Patience sitting with broad smiles, and Meggie waving an envelope. Lissie grabbed for it. It had been more than two weeks since she'd received Flynn's last letter. She scanned the single page.

'They're coming home on leave, Meggie,' she whooped. 'They'll arrive the day after tomorrow.'

Patience chuckled with delight as the two girls jigged excitedly round the parlour. 'That's put a smile on your faces. I'm jealous. I wish I had a young man to come and sweep me off me feet.'

'Oh, but you do, Mrs Foyer. Flynn will be just as pleased to see you.'

Patience's eyes moistened. 'And me him,' she said fondly.

Is this to be the pattern of my life? Lissie wondered as once again she stood on the station platform with Meggie at her side. The girls had dressed for the occasion, Lissie in a smart dark blue jacket over a pale blue woollen dress and Meggie in a dark green coat with a matching hat, the colours of their outfits reminding Lissie of the bluebells in the wood in Derbyshire. But the memory didn't make her sad. Today was a day for rejoicing. Flynn was coming home.

After what seemed an age the train from Leeds wheezed alongside the platform. Doors flew open and passengers, many of them in uniform, alighted straight into the arms of their waiting loved ones. The crowd dwindled, leaving the platform almost empty. Lissie gave Meggie a look of intense disappointment mixed with fear and Meggie returned the look, her body sagging.

It was Jimmy's idea to wait until the platform was clear, and Flynn had laughingly agreed. Finally they stepped from the train.

'Aw, would you look at the pair of 'em,' Meggie cried as arms swinging, they marched in step, smart in their khaki uniforms and their caps set at a jaunty angle. 'Jimmy! Jimmy!' She ran to meet him. He looked broader, more of a man than before, the sort that would be a good father, she thought as he clasped his arms round her.

Lissie was filled with such overwhelming love that she could only stand and stare as Flynn approached. His eyes were fixed on her, and she imagined she could feel the heat of his desire. She lurched forward into his arms and was smothered in kisses. Suddenly, all her worries and misgivings took flight. Flynn was back where he belonged.

The sky was studded with stars, the August night air still warm from the heat of the day. The waves breaking on the shore made a sound no louder than the intake of breath followed by a long withdrawing sigh as they scraped the shingle. Lissie and Flynn walked hand in hand until they found a smooth dry patch of sand between the rocks. They sat on a large flat rock, his arms wrapped round her as they drank in the peaceful silence of their last night together.

It had been a glorious seven days. Whenever there had been just the two of them, Flynn and Lissie had filled the hours with love and kisses and deep conversations about their future together. Patience's joy at having Flynn back, even for a short spell, was palpable and he, aware of her decline and out of love and respect for her, had made sure to pay her plenty of attention. On some of the days they had met up with Meggie and Jimmy walking the esplanade and the fairground, Flynn filled with admiration for the way Lissie and Billy had kept his businesses afloat even in the depleted circumstances the war had brought to the resort, and

Jimmy as proud as a peacock at the prospect of becoming a father. They walked the streets of the town, pleased to see the rebuilding of the damaged houses and hotels, and drank in the Pavilion, tea for the girls and beer for the men, Meggie and Lissie laughing at the way they quaffed their pints: yet another sign of the manliness that soldiering had taught them.

Now, it was almost time to let them go again, and Lissie's heart ached as she gazed out to sea. 'You'll be so much further away,' she said, as Flynn's regiment was moving to Salisbury Plain when they returned to Ripon.

'Distance is nothing,' he said against her hair. 'Wherever I am I'll carry you in my heart. I love you more than life itself, and to know that you are waiting for me here will see me through whatever comes my way.'

27

The war in Europe dragged on with no end in sight and Lissie felt as though her life was on hold. Each hour seemed the same as the one before with nothing for her mind to catch on to. Without Flynn the days slipped by, indistinguishable from one another, fast merging into weeks and months with only letters and memories to keep their love alive.

Flynn's letters couldn't tell her exactly where he was, the censors forbade it, but he cleverly made reference to pyramids and having more sand than Scarborough so Lissie guessed that he was in Egypt. She was glad he wasn't on the Western Front in France. According to the newspapers terrible things were happening there.

In October, Meggie gave birth to a beautiful baby boy, Edward James. 'Do you think he looks like his dad?' she asked Lissie as they sat in the room above the butcher's shop.

Lissie gazed into the baby's moon face and pale blue eyes and was reminded of the young Jimmy when they first met. 'He does, and Jimmy will be so proud.' The baby gazed solemnly back at her and she suddenly had an idea. 'I'll buy one of those Kodak box cameras and we can send photographs with our letters. They sell them in Boyes,' she said, referring to one of the town's biggest department stores.

'Aw, Lissie, that's a grand idea. Aah want Jimmy to know what Eddie looks like. His mam says he's the image of Jimmy when he was a bairn.' Her happiness faded. 'God knows how old he'll be afore his dad comes home to hold him.'

It did seem as though the war could go on forever and that it worsened day by day. The obituary columns in the *Gazette* and the *Daily Post* made miserable reading as one family after another lost a father, a husband or a son, and Lissie spent much of her day in the shop commiserating with bereaved customers and hoping against hope that they would never have to reciprocate should anything happen to Flynn or her father.

One humdrum week followed another, broken by visits from Amelia and Connie, but Christmas was a meagre affair as food shortages began to really bite. 'I had to queue for almost an hour in the grocery and when I got to the counter they had no cheese,' Lissie complained when the women gathered on Christmas Day, 'and we wouldn't have any meat if Meggie's in-laws hadn't sent us a rabbit.'

'Even so, we're better off than many others,' Amelia remarked. 'It's the women left alone with little children I feel sorry for. They expect so much from Santa Claus and are disappointed when Mam hasn't been able to buy a bike or a doll's house.'

'I'm glad that Matron and I knitted soft toys for the little ones and hats or scarves for the older girls because usually the Board of Governors give them an orange and a few walnuts and this year there aren't any,' Connie told them.

'Yes, but whilst we don't have much to celebrate, I'm sure our Christmas will be far cheerier than the poor men fighting this awful war,' Lissie said.

The others nodded as their thoughts strayed to Flynn, Tom and

Jimmy. 'Top up the glasses, Lissie, and we'll drink to our brave boys,' said Patience, tapping the bottle of sherry with her spoon. Their glasses refilled, they raised them and as one they chorused, 'To Flynn, Tom and Jimmy.'

'Bring them home safe, and soon,' Lissie concluded tearfully.

* * *

On the bright side, little Eddie thrived and the weather in January 1916 was exceptionally mild. It eased Patience's aches and pains but there was no denying that she was deteriorating rapidly.

Heavy mists hung over the town, as depressing as Lissie's thoughts, and the tedium of performing the same chores gave nothing to lighten her days. In some strange compensatory trick, as she tried to sleep, the nights were vivid, filled with startling dreams of Flynn running for his life under a hail of bullets, or trudging through endless sand dunes searching for water. Then, she would wake sweating and exhausted, her pillow damp with tears.

And so, in this way Lissie lived from one day to the other, caring for Patience and attending to her own and Flynn's businesses, winter fading into a fitful spring.

* * *

In the late afternoon of a windy day in March, Flynn and Jimmy stepped down from the train that had brought them back to Scarborough for ten days' leave. They had both agreed to keep their homecoming a secret in order to surprise Lissie and Meggie, but this time as they left the station their steps were not jaunty for they were both battle-weary. In the town centre they parted, Jimmy to the butcher's shop and Flynn to the drapery, their spirits rising as they anticipated the welcome they would receive.

Lissie was alone in the shop, Elspeth having gone home early, when Flynn walked in. For one moment she thought that she was dreaming – he was never far from her thoughts – then she let out a cry and rushed from behind the counter into his arms. Breathing in the smell of sweat and cordite, she returned his kisses, and when the rapturous reunion ended they went into the house to Patience's room.

'Oh, my! What a sight for sore eyes,' she croaked as Flynn stepped in. She held out her arms, and hiding his dismay at how frail she now was, he stooped to kiss her cheek. Lissie fondly looked on, and when Flynn sat beside the bed she noted the pallor of his cheeks and the weariness in his eyes. This terrible war was taking its toll on him and she determined to take special care of him during the next ten days.

Flynn's presence filled the house with joy, Lissie in her element as she cooked meals for him from their limited rations that he said were so much tastier than army fare, and Patience forgetting her aches and pains whenever he was near.

In the flat above the butcher's shop Jimmy had fallen in love again, this time with his baby son, Eddie. At almost six months old, Eddie was a chubby little lad with a gummy smile for everyone and Jimmy, loath to put him down, proudly took him everywhere. On the day they visited Lissie and Flynn he marched into the house carrying his son as though he was holding the crown jewels. Meggie beamed her delight; her little family was complete for the moment.

But ten days seemed like ten minutes and before they knew it they were once again saying goodbye. When Flynn bade farewell to Patience he silently acknowledged that he might not see her again, and her sad expression let him know that she was thinking the same. As Lissie and Flynn left the house to go to the station, she felt as though a door was closing on her life and she wondered how long it would be before it opened up again.

At the station Jimmy clung to Meggie and Eddie and cried openly with them.

Flynn held Lissie close and kissed her with passion. 'Stay safe, darling,' he said.

'And you, my love,' she replied, her heart breaking into a million pieces.

* * *

In early April Flynn wrote: *My regiment has said goodbye to sand and sunshine and hello to rain, mud and trenches. I've yet to see the Eiffel Tower* (the name of the landmark had been blacked out) *but they say it's even grander than Blackpool Tower.* The clue let Lissie know he was somewhere in France. Her anxiety increased, the reports in the newspapers making dreadful reading. Just how terrible things were came to light in the first week in July.

'But the newspapers said it had been a victory,' Meggie cried as she and Lissie were walking down Queen Street, Meggie carrying the bag of wool she had just bought in Boyes department store to knit Eddie a cardigan, and the news boys on the street corner waving their papers and bawling, 'Absolute carnage! British troops decimated! Local men declared dead!'

Lissie froze, then gathering her wits, she ran across the street and bought two newspapers. Returning to Meggie, she shoved one in her hand and they hurried to perch on a window sill outside a shop to read about the terrible things the news boys were still loudly proclaiming.

Every day in the previous week the newspapers had been reporting that the combined British and French forces were to mount a campaign against the Germans at a place called the

Somme. The customers in the shop had talked of little else because the British High Command had stated that it would end the war. When the campaign started on the first day in July the newspapers had trumpeted that it had been a success. Now, on the third, they were telling a different story.

'Catastrophic losses. Sixty thousand casualties,' Lissie read out loud, her voice coming out on her breath. Was Flynn one of them? Or her dad? She just didn't know. She had no idea where exactly in France their regiments were.

'The men were ordered to walk across No Man's Land to the German lines and they were mown down in their thousands,' Meggie squealed, her disgust apparent. 'Bloody walk when they should have been runnin' for their lives.'

With trembling hands Lissie turned the page, her voice hollow as she read, 'British troops brutally repulsed.' The words sounded ugly. 'Oh, God, listen to this, Meggie,' she cried. 'Hundreds of dead were strung out on barbed wire like last week's washing and bodies laid in mud like wreckage washed up at a high water-mark.'

By now both girls were weeping and they saw that they were not the only ones. People in the street who had also heard or read the same news huddled in groups to share their horror and disgust whilst others walked along in stunned silence, tears wetting their cheeks, many of them fearing that their lives were about to be changed forever should their loved ones be amongst the twenty thousand dead.

Meggie crushed the newspaper into a ball and stuffed it into the bag of wool, choking on the words, 'What if my Jimmy an' your dad an' Flynn were there?'

'We just have to pray that they weren't,' Lissie said.

* * *

'No news is good news,' Lissie reassured Meggie when almost two weeks later they stood outside the town hall reading the latest posting naming the local men who had fallen in action. Unlike many of their neighbours the telegram boy hadn't paid them a visit and Lissie was sure that they would have heard by now if Flynn, Jimmy or Tom had been taken from them. Three days later when a letter arrived from Flynn, she ran through the town to the butcher's shop to let Meggie know that Flynn was alive and well and that as far as he knew Jimmy was too. As for Tom, he couldn't say, but when Amelia paid her Sunday visit, she too had received a letter from Tom. He had been granted leave.

On Sunday afternoon Lissie, Meggie and Amelia sat at Patience's bedside sharing their fears of the past two weeks and rejoicing in the fact that their menfolk had, for now, escaped the horrors of this terrible war. 'I feel as though I can breathe again and maybe get a good night's sleep,' said Lissie, but her thoughts were never far away from what was happening in France. The Battle of the Somme raged on as did battles elsewhere so a letter from Flynn telling her his regiment '*had moved on and were away from the worst of it*' gave her some consolation.

When Tom arrived Lissie was shocked to see how pale and drawn he looked. By now she was almost getting used to celebrating a few brief days with the men she loved, and making sure they were filled with love and care. Before he returned to his regiment Tom told her he was going to ask Amelia to marry him. He was going to ask the army chaplain how to obtain a divorce from the wife he hadn't seen since that fateful day in Thorne when Lissie was a little girl.

'It should be quite easy,' Lissie told him. 'After all, you can prove you've been separated for years but...' She frowned. 'You might have to find her first.'

Even so, she went back to Scarborough delighted that her father had found love with Amelia, but as summer waned into autumn and another half-hearted Christmas was celebrated, all that Lissie wanted was for the world to right itself and the war to be over.

* * *

'Aw, look at the way he can go.' Meggie's voice was filled with pride as little Eddie scampered over the sand, stopping every now and then to inspect a dead crab or pick up a seashell. 'It's a cryin' shame his dad's not here to see.'

'It's downright wicked,' Lissie agreed, tucking back strands of hair that the mad March breeze had blown across her cheeks. 'This rotten war's deprived hundreds of children of their dads – some forever.' She clapped her hand over her mouth. 'Oh. Meggie, I'm sorry. I didn't mean that...'

'Aah know you didn't, pet.' Meggie patted Lissie's arm. 'But it's true, i'nt it?'

Lissie nodded. 'I never thought it 'ud last this long. If anybody had told me in the summer of 1914 that we'd still be at war in spring 1917, I wouldn't have believed them.' She sighed bitterly. 'It makes them that said it would be over by Christmas look like fools.'

'They're all fools as far as—' Meggie broke off to shout, 'Hey, Eddie. Don't get your feet wet.'

Their moans about the war forgotten, they ran and rescued Eddie just in time to prevent the next wave from soaking him, then they made their way back to North Marine Road where they had left Connie and Amelia – both paying a weekend visit – caring for Patience.

'I'm worried about Patience,' said Lissie as they neared the drapery. 'She's so frail, and that chest infection's not clearing up.'

'Aye, she's gone downhill this last week. Aah don't like the look of her meself,' Meggie agreed, lifting Eddie up in her arms to carry him into the house.

Lissie's heart lurched. There was no denying that Patience's health was failing but to hear someone confirm it was frightening, and later that evening her fears were compounded when Connie also expressed her concern. 'I think we'll have to prepare ourselves for losing her – and soon.'

It came sooner than they had expected. The following weekend, the doctor having warned Lissie that pneumonia was hard to beat in someone as frail as Patience, she sat by Patience's bed waiting for Connie and Amelia to answer her urgent summons. Holding her benefactor's knobbly hands in her own, she prayed that they would arrive in time to say goodbye.

Silence hung heavy in the room, broken only by Patience's laboured breathing as she drifted in and out of consciousness. Lissie gazed into the wrinkled face that she had grown to love. Patience's eyes were closed and her mouth set in the firm line that Lissie knew so well. She recalled how her heart had sunk when she first saw Patience's stern glare on the day that Connie had brought her to Scarborough. Then she had feared her employer, but now she loved her with every fibre of her being. Gently, she traced Patience's cheek with her forefinger and Patience's eyelids flickered then opened, her gaze sharp and lucid. She drew in a wheezing breath and forced a smile. 'Lissie,' she croaked, 'dear Lissie.'

'I'm here, Mrs Foyer.'

'I know you are. I might be short of breath but I'm not blind,' Patience said, making Lissie smile. 'And I'm glad that you are, and,' a wicked twinkle lit up her eyes, 'and I can meet my maker knowing that I'm leaving my business in good hands.' She squeezed Lissie's hand. 'You've brought me... more joy than... I ever hoped for,' she continued, her words coming in fits and starts and interrupted by the ominous gurgling in her lungs. 'I bless the day... Connie brought you to me... and that we gave each other happiness that would have been denied us had she not.'

'Oh, Mrs Foyer, you gave me so much more than that,' Lissie gushed, choking back tears. 'You gave me a home and taught me how to earn my living, but more than that you gave me your love and affection. You're the mother I never really had and...' Her heart was so full of love for this frail old woman that she couldn't put it into words and wrapping her arms round Patience, she raised her up and held her close. They stayed like this for a long moment before Lissie eased Patience back onto her pillows.

Patience lay back, a smile wreathing her face. 'Thank you,' she wheezed. 'Now remember... to take good care... of my boy, Flynn and marry him... as soon as this war... is over.' Before Lissie had time to tell her that she would, the sound of the front door opening made Patience raise her bristly grey eyebrows. Her eyes gleamed mischievously. 'It must be time for me to make my goodbyes.'

Connie and Amelia, having met at the station, came quietly into the room. For the rest of the day they sat with Lissie and Patience, mostly in silence, and every now and then responded to Patience's ramblings. It was Connie who answered when she talked about Henry, memories only they could share, and when Patience asked for Flynn, Lissie told her he loved her. As the sun went down Patience breathed her last, the rather wry satisfied smile on her lips making it all the easier for Lissie to let her go.

* * *

As Lissie was preparing to face life without Patience, Emmy Jackson was pulling pints in the Four Ashes public house in Great Horton. She was bored and feeling a bit squiffy having consumed three gin and limes, but it passed the time.

'Hey, don't I know you?' A rough voice made her turn to look at the tawdry woman with ratty blonde hair and her face caked in make-up waiting to be served. Emmy stared at her through bleary eyes. She looked familiar. Before she could think why, the woman said, 'You're the Jacksons' kid from Hart Lane, aren't you? The one that played with our Lissie.'

Then Emmy remembered. It was Dora Fairweather, Lissie's mam.

'Yeah, that's me,' Emmy slurred, thinking that the years hadn't been kind to Dora. The bags beneath her eyes were like plums and deep creases etched her cheeks and round her mouth. 'What are you doing back in Bradford?'

'Oh, I've been back a while – doing this and that,' Dora said carelessly. 'What are you doing working here? I thought you'd have worked in the mill.'

'I do, but I'm engaged to the landlord's son so I'm helping out here.'

'Ooh, you've done all right for yourself.' Dora sounded envious.

'Yeah, I suppose so,' Emmy said but not really believing it, 'and your Lissie's done even better for herself since she left that orphanage that you dumped her in.' Emmy's spiteful accusation was lost on Dora.

'Oh, you're still in touch with her then?'

'Yeah, we get the odd letter now an' then.'

'Done well, you say.' An avaricious gleam lit Dora's eyes. 'What's she up to these days?'

'Living in Scarborough. Runs a drapery for an old woman who'll most likely leave her everything when she pops her clogs,' said Emmy bitterly, the disparity between her own impoverished status and the comfortable living Lissie had acquired still stinging. 'You should see the big house she lives in and the lovely clothes she wears. I once went there for me holidays.' She slurped her gin and lime, depressed by the memory of the last time she had seen Lissie.

'Ooh, tell me more,' Dora begged, her cunning mind working overtime. 'Where's this shop and what's it called? Is it a big business?'

'Can't remember the name. It's on a road near the sea.' Tired of Dora's probing and the smell of her cheap perfume making Emmy feel nauseous, she moved down the bar to serve another customer.

Scarborough – running a shop – maybe owning it outright one day, Dora mused as she sipped her beer. There was money to be had there. But first she'd need the price of the train fare to the seaside. Her eyes ranged the taproom looking for a potential customer. Downing the last of her beer, she sashayed across the room to where a man sitting on his own was staring miserably into his pint glass. 'Looking for company for the night, love?' she asked coquettishly, pushing out her bosom and flicking her straggly blonde locks.

* * *

Lissie sat in the dining room with Connie on her right and Patience's solicitor at the head of the table. They had arrived back from the well-attended funeral less than an hour ago, George Snowball insisting he accompany them back to the house to read the will. 'It was Mrs Foyer's wish that I do it immediately after the interment,' he'd said.

This had irritated Lissie. She had wanted to be alone with Connie, or better still alone with her thoughts. Now, her mind was spinning and her throat had suddenly gone dry as her thoughts clattered inside her head.

George Snowball shuffled the papers in front of him then beamed at Lissie, exposing the thick pink gums of his false teeth.

'Well, say something, Miss Fairweather. You seem rather shocked.'

Lissie blinked. It was too hard to take in. What was she going to do now? She swallowed noisily and looked from the solicitor to Connie, tears wetting her lashes. Connie smiled back and patted the back of her hand.

'She left the shop and the house to me?' Lissie's voice was barely above a whisper.

'Indeed, she did, Miss Fairweather,' the solicitor boomed. 'Apart from the fairground rides that she bequeathed to Mr Corrigan and a few other small bequests that is,' he added, nodding at Connie. 'You are a most fortunate young woman, and I hope that Birdsall and Snowball can be of future service.' He stowed the documents in his briefcase and stood. 'Congratulations, my dear.'

Connie showed him out. Lissie, too shocked to move and unsure that her legs would support her, stayed seated. She owned all this, a house and a thriving drapery business, but she knew in her heart she would give it all up just to have Patience back.

'Will you come and live here?' she asked Connie as they sat drinking a cup of cocoa before bed.

Connie shook her head. 'No, Lissie. I'm not yet ready to leave the orphanage. There are too many little lost souls like you once were who still need me, and...' She paused, her head on one side and a little smile quirking her lips. 'I've met someone. I never imagined that I'd marry again but Peter is a lovely man and I've been on my own for too long. He's asked me to marry him and I've accepted.'

'Oh, Mrs Briggs. I had no idea. I'm so pleased for you.' Lissie jumped up to hug Connie. When they retired for the night, Lissie tossed and turned until the first grey light of dawn seeped through the gap in her bedroom curtains.

The next morning, her mind still in a whirl, she stood with Connie on the station platform promising to attend the wedding when a date was fixed.

'I'm glad I brought you to Patience,' Connie said. 'You made her happier than she'd been for years. She was so proud of you. She loved you, Lissie.'

'And I loved her,' Lissie said brokenly. 'I don't know what I'll do now that she's no longer here.'

'You'll be fine, Lissie. You're already a good business woman, and once this damned war's over, you'll have Flynn by your side. Look to the future, love.'

'I will, Mrs Briggs, and thank you for being such a wonderful friend.'

Connie laughed. 'Don't you think it's about time you called me Connie? We'll always be the best of friends so it's first names from now on.'

She boarded the train, Lissie waving and calling, 'Goodbye, Connie. I love you.' Connie blew her a parting kiss.

Lissie walked back to the drapery feeling very alone. In the last twenty-four hours her life had changed and she knew it would never be the same again.

28

Lissie read Flynn's letter, tears choking her throat at the sadness he expressed on learning of Patience's death. She had written to him immediately after Patience had died, and then again two nights after Patience's funeral. He must have received both letters because when she got to the end of his reply it made her giggle.

So now you're a business woman in your own right. Congratulations. I hope you won't think yourself too grand now for a poor soldier like me.

How like Flynn to say something silly to make her smile, she thought. He was so brave and optimistic, never complaining, and yet she knew from what she read in the newspapers that the war on the Western Front was brutal, that the troops were bogged down in mud and that every success was followed by tragedy, many of them very close to home. Lissie lived in fear of the lad on his bike, his leather pouch containing the piece of yellow paper that she dreaded might be for her, and only this morning as she had opened the shop the telegram boy had called at the house two doors further down North Marine Road to let Mrs Woodhouse know that her husband had been killed. Lissie had heard her screams. She had hurried to comfort her then, leaving her with another neighbour, she had returned to the shop wondering if they would in turn have to comfort her one day soon. Her gloomy thoughts had stayed with her until the postman arrived with Flynn's letter. She tucked it into her pocket.

'Good news?' Elspeth asked, seeing Lissie's smile.

'Flynn. He's alive and well, and wants to know if I'll be too grand for him now the shop's mine.'

Elspeth chuckled. 'It won't change you one bit. You're still the lovely girl he fell in love with, and knowing you, you'll stay that way. You're not one for airs and graces. I've never worked for a kinder, more thoughtful person than you.'

Warmed by Elspeth's words, Lissie set about changing the window display.

It had taken Dora somewhat longer than she had intended to raise the price of a train ticket to Scarborough. These days she struggled to make the rent on a shabby room and put food in her mouth. Her looks had faded, and the men in her life were now few and fleeting. She made a rather sorry spectacle as she stepped down onto the platform in her worn, ill-fitting coat and bedraggled felt hat.

'Can you direct me to a drapery shop near the sea?' she asked the ticket collector on the gate. He noted her rouged cheeks and garish blue eyelids; a trollop if ever there was one, he thought, as he told her there were several draperies in the town. Annoyed by his unhelpfulness, Dora tossed her head and marched out into the street. Time to begin her search. She'd have to make it quick. She couldn't afford a bed in a guest house, and she didn't want to sleep on the street tonight. Still, it wouldn't be the first time she'd had to do that.

Dora plodded up and down the unfamiliar streets on the lookout for a drapery. Finding one, she went in but no one called Lissie worked there. She tried two more, and in the second one the woman said, 'You could try Foyer's on North Marine Road.' She gave Dora directions. By now, it was dusk and she was cursing herself for not having caught an earlier train.

Outside Foyer's she peered through the window then hissed, 'Got her.'

She stood for a moment watching her daughter serve an elderly woman. My, but she'd grown into a beauty. Dora might not have seen her for almost fifteen years but she recognised that mane of black hair and the fine features so like Tom Fairweather's. Dora waited until the customer came into the street then straightening her battered hat, she sallied into the shop. Lissie was putting money in the till and looked up with a smile.

'Hello, lovey, it's nice to see you.' The throaty voice turned Lissie's blood to ice. She stared at the dishevelled woman and time stood still. She knew it was Dora without a doubt. A gamut of emotions stormed through her brain: the horror of Dora's brutal attack on her dad, the sudden departure from the cottage and the miserable childhood that had ensued. The memories all fought with one another inside her head and rendered her speechless.

Dora came nearer the counter, an uncertain smile curving her red lips and her voice smarmy as she said, 'I ran into Emmy Jackson and she told me where to find you so I thought I'd look you up, see how you're doing, love.' She glanced round the shop. 'You seem to have done all right for yourself.'

'No thanks to you,' Lissie retorted, a burning hatred fizzing in her chest. She thrust back her shoulders. 'What do you want?' Her stern tone made Dora blink.

'Like I said, love. I wanted to see you,' Dora wheedled. 'I've missed you.'

Lissie gave a harsh laugh. 'Missed me? You couldn't wait to get rid of me.' She darted from behind the counter and locked the shop door, desperate for there to be no witnesses to this scene.

'Aw, don't be like that, Lissie. I was having a hard time after your dad threw us out. Being on your own with a kiddy and nowhere to go's not easy but—'

'Threw us out,' Lissie screeched. 'You almost killed my dad! You left him to die! Then you ran away to save your own skin. You made me believe I was as guilty as you are. You abandoned me without a second thought to satisfy your own needs. You're a vicious, evil woman with no sense of moral decency.'

Dora flinched at the fire in Lissie's flashing blue eyes. So... she did remember. Dora had been hoping that Lissie had been too young to remember the details of why they'd left Thorne. But although Dora felt panicked by the tirade, she had heard the word 'almost'. She swallowed noisily, and in a voice thick as treacle she asked, 'Do you see owt of your dad these days?'

Something, despite her confusion, warned Lissie not to divulge that she and Tom were reunited. She couldn't allow Dora to spoil the happiness he had found with Amelia, even if at this moment they were miles apart.

Lissie gathered her wits and shrugged carelessly. 'How could I? You dragged me away when I wanted to help him, then dumped me in the workhouse. I was a prisoner for seven years. He could be dead for all I know.' The word 'dead' made her shiver. He was in the midst of the fighting in France. *Don't let my lies visit any harm on him*, she silently prayed.

Dora wasn't about to give up. She scrabbled for something positive to say. 'Aw, he'll not be dead, love. We'd have heard if he was.'

Lissie looked at her as if she was stupid. 'How? How could we have heard? You talk like a fool.' Lissie went back behind the counter. 'Now, I'm asking you to go. I've nothing more to say to you, Mother.' Her final word sounded like an insult.

'Go where?' Dora struggled to reverse the situation. 'I don't have anywhere to go – and I've no money to pay for a bed. You can't turn me out, love. Give me a chance to make things up to you.'

Appalled by Dora's grovelling and her audacity, Lissie curled her lip. 'Do you really expect me to take you in after what you've done?'

'I'm your mother,' Dora cried, squeezing fat tears down her raddled cheeks.

She is my mother. The realisation of the fact was suddenly quite shocking. She saw nothing of herself in Dora – didn't want to – yet, this downtrodden woman had given birth to her, had nursed her, and, she thought rather sadly, you only have one mother. *If I turn her out into the streets I'll be just as bad as she is. I could give her some money. That'll get rid of her, but then she'll only come back for more. If only Patience was here to advise me. She'd know what to do.* With a sinking heart, Lissie made a decision.

'You can stay for tonight.' She began emptying the money from the till into a canvas bag. Dora's eyes were hawk-like. 'Come through this way,' Lissie said, slamming the drawer shut.

In the kitchen, Dora hovering at Lissie's elbow and offering to help make the evening meal, Lissie became aware of how unpleasant her mother smelled. 'You're filthy. You need a bath,' she said curtly. 'I'll show you to the bathroom and the spare bedroom.' She led the way upstairs and Dora smirked inwardly. She'd won this round. Nice big house and a bed for the night.

'Me underwear could do with changing. I was in that much of a rush to come and see you I forgot to pack some.' In truth, she was wearing the only underwear she possessed, but there was a shop full of the stuff downstairs. No harm in taking advantage. It wasn't as if Lissie couldn't spare it.

'I'll leave some out on your bed,' Lissie said, opening first one door then another and pointing, 'Bathroom, bedroom.'

She went back into the shop and got a cheap cotton vest, a pair of knickers and a petticoat. As an afterthought, she went to the dress rail and took down a grey cotton house frock that Patience had bought from a wholesaler several years before. It was drab and shapeless and had failed to attract a buyer, but it would do for Dora. At least she'd smell fresher and look less disreputable. Lissie left them on the bed.

When Dora came back into the kitchen Lissie served up two plates of a shepherd's pie she had made earlier. She had made her mind up that she would feed and clothe and provide shelter for her mother, but she wouldn't talk to her.

'Haven't you owt else a bit more stylish and colourful?' Dora flicked the skirt of the grey dress disparagingly.

Lissie saw red. Her rule of silence was instantly broken. She slammed her cutlery on the table, her cheeks blazing. 'You are the most ungrateful person I've ever met. It's no wonder Dad used to beg you to alter your ways. You wanted for nothing with him yet you were never satisfied.'

'Satisfied,' Dora drawled. She leaned with her elbows on the table, sneering into Lissie's face. 'You've a lot to learn, my girl. You see, that wa' the problem. Tom Fairweather couldn't satisfy me even when he tried. Him and his boring poetry and country walks. He was as dull as bloody ditchwater wa' your dad.'

Hurt beyond words to hear her dad described in that way, Lissie fought back. 'Then why did you marry him?'

Dora sniggered. 'That wa' just another of my many mistakes. I thought I wa' pregnant – not by him, mind – but the other fella had beggared off so I got daft Tom drunk and made him make love to me.' She gave a nasty laugh. 'When I told him I was in the family way he couldn't wait to do the right thing an' marry me, the silly bugger.'

Lissie paled. 'Am I that baby...? Is Tom... not... not my dad?' She felt sick.

'Aye, course he is. I'd just panicked an' made a mistake. T'other one came to nowt. There wa' no baby, but by then it wa' too late. I wa' hooked up wi' saintly Tom, an' a year later you came along.' Dora looked at Lissie with contempt. 'You're his all right. You an' your hoity-toity ways.' She flicked her tatty hair disdainfully. 'Let me tell you this, girl, you wouldn't have had all this if I'd stayed with Tom Fairweather, and don't you forget it.' She forked a mouthful of pie between her lips, noisily sloshing the food.

Lissie, her appetite destroyed, got to her feet. 'I don't want to hear another word from you. I'm going to my room, and I want you gone first thing tomorrow.'

She lifted the canvas money bag that she'd left on the table before making dinner and making sure the adjoining door into the shop was locked, she stamped out of the kitchen. She usually put the money in the bureau in the parlour, but this time she took it upstairs to her room. She didn't trust Dora.

That night, Lissie hardly slept a wink. Her thoughts were in turmoil and every sound in the house had her on edge. What was she going to do about her mother?

* * *

It was after eleven the next morning when Dora appeared in the kitchen. Lissie was taking her tea break while Elspeth minded the shop. Dora was wearing the grey dress and she had deliberately left her face unpainted and coiled her hair in a matronly style. She almost looked respectable.

'I'm sorry about last night, love,' she mumbled, looking and sounding utterly contrite. 'I shouldn't have said what I did. Let's not fall out over things we can't undo. I want us to be friends – please.' Two fat tears rolled down her cheeks.

To her surprise, Lissie found herself feeling sorry for the downtrodden woman who seemed to have no sense of right and wrong. What Dora had said the previous night was true. She wouldn't be in this house and be a successful business woman, or have found her father and met Flynn had things been different. Maybe she should give her a chance to redeem herself.

'There's tea in the pot and bread in the crock,' she said getting to her feet. 'I have to go back in the shop.'

'I'll wash up and tidy round for you, make meself useful.' Dora said eagerly. Lissie was tempted to tell her she couldn't remember her ever being useful, but instead she nodded and left her.

In the next uneasy few days Lissie lived on her nerves and Dora moped about the house pretending to be motherly, but actually she was bored to death. 'I can fetch the messages if you give me some money, love,' she said on the third morning of her stay. 'It'll save you time.'

Lissie gave her a grocery list and the money. Have faith, she told herself. Perhaps she is trying to make a fresh start. As she served customers Lissie pondered on the matter of her father and Amelia. Should she try to persuade Dora to divorce him? She'd willingly pay her to do so. She still hadn't reached a decision when much later in the day, a policeman brought a very inebriated Dora back to the house. 'There was an altercation in The Britannia pub and seeing as how this lady said she was staying with you I thought it best to see her home,' he explained. Lissie groaned, her cheeks beetroot as she thanked the constable.

After that she refused to give Dora money no matter how often she begged. Dora sulked and cursed, and Lissie tried her best to forge a friendship, but it was hopeless. They had nothing in common, and nothing to say to one another. Lissie wrote to Flynn and told him about Dora but she didn't mention her in a letter to Tom. Just when Lissie thought she couldn't take much more, she awoke one morning to find Dora gone. Gone also were the silver sugar tongs, the gilt mantelpiece clock, two brass candlesticks and the photograph of Henry Foyer in a heavy silver frame. The little brass keyhole on the bureau had been prised out but the bureau remained locked. Lissie didn't know whether to laugh or cry.

'Has your mother gone back home?' Elspeth said when it became obvious that Dora wasn't in the house. Lissie had done her best to keep them apart.

'Yes, she went yesterday,' Lissie replied and hoped it was the truth.

* * *

Spring turned to summer and still the war raged on. As Lissie made her way to and from the fairground on her weekly visits to Billy, or went into the town to buy goods, she dreaded bumping into Dora, but as the months rolled on, she began to relax. By the end of August, she was certain she'd seen the last of her.

On Saturday morning, Amelia arrived at the drapery tight-faced and nervy. 'Tom's coming home,' she blurted as soon as she saw Lissie. 'He's sustained an injury and been declared unfit for duty.'

Lissie paled and cupped her cheeks in her hands. 'Unfit for duty,' she echoed, at the same time wondering how badly injured he was.

'It was just one of those cards where they tick the boxes,' Amelia continued. 'I don't know how badly he's hurt but it says that he'll be transported back home on Monday the twenty-seventh.' Amelia bit her lip to stem her tears.

Lissie's heart had missed a beat. Transport him home. Were they about to get Tom back broken beyond repair? She'd seen some of her neighbours' sons and husbands with missing limbs or shell-shocked out of their senses, and her heart crumbled. She enfolded Amelia in her arms, trying to find words to comfort her and reassure herself that Tom wouldn't be one of those men.

On Sunday evening she went with Amelia to catch the train to Pickering. The walk to the station did nothing to ease their anxiety. The drained and weary faces of passers-by, the stark remains of dwellings that had been bombed three years before, and the increasingly long lists outside the recruitment office of men who were dead or missing all bore testament to the ravages of war. Lissie and Amelia were dreading what Tom's arrival would bring.

The next morning, after a sleepless night in the little house in Hatcase Lane, Lissie helped Amelia prepare for Tom's homecoming. Amelia lit a roaring fire even though the September day was quite warm, and together they made soup and a meat and potato pie, their unspoken hopes and fears rattling in their minds for neither of them knew what to expect. Then they sat and waited, Amelia or Lissie dashing to the window each time they heard the sound of a vehicle on the road.

'He isn't coming,' Amelia said forlornly as the afternoon shadows lengthened.

'We'll have another cup of tea. They did say today,' said Lissie, getting to her feet, unwilling to give in. She trudged towards the kitchen thinking she might drown in tea they'd drunk so much of it, when the rattle of an engine made her whirl back to the window. A canvas covered lorry had pulled up outside.

'He's here,' she cried, racing for the door, Amelia at her side. They ran down the garden path into the street, dread in every step.

Lissie, her heart in her mouth, watched the driver jump from the cab. He saluted and grinned as he made his way to the back of the lorry. 'There's a welcome home party for you, Tom,' he said as he lifted the flap. Lissie looked at Amelia, and Amelia looked back, their expressions asking a thousand questions.

The end of a wooden crutch appeared followed by another then with the driver's assistance Tom swung himself down to the ground. His left leg was encased in plaster but otherwise he was whole. Amelia made a sound halfway between a sob and a giggle. Lissie felt as though she might explode with relief.

* * *

'He broke his leg falling into a shell-hole,' Lissie told Meggie when she arrived back in Scarborough. 'It was pitch dark and they were collecting the wounded from the battlefield to take them to a field hospital behind the lines.'

'Aw, the poor man. Still, it could have been worse. Did he say if he'd ever come across Jimmy and Flynn out there?' Like many other civilians, Meggie had no comprehension of the massive area being fought over. France was France.

'I did ask him but his battalion isn't theirs, and when I asked what it was like over there he was very tight-lipped about it. He said he'd rather I didn't know. That it didn't bear talking about.' She gave a deep sigh. 'He might only have a broken leg but he's haggard and his skin is grey. He tries to be hearty, but in his quiet moments he has a look in his eyes that wasn't there before. It's as though he's in pain, although he says his leg doesn't trouble him. I think he's seen things that he'll never be able to talk about.'

Meggie began to cry. 'An' my poor Jimmy an' your Flynn are out there seein' it day after day. Aw, Lissie what are we going to do if...'

Lissie, aware that she'd been thinking out loud, felt suddenly guilty.

'Oh, Meggie, I'm sorry.' She jumped up and cradled her friend in her arms. 'I didn't mean to upset you. It was thoughtless of me. Jimmy and Flynn will be all right. They'll look out for one another. They'll come home. I can feel it in here.' She thumped her chest. 'I don't know how I know it, I just do,' she cried.

29

On the Ypres Salient in the shelter of a wall that was all that remained of what had once been a prosperous Belgian farm in Hooge, Sergeant Flynn Corrigan and his company – or what was left of them, for casualties had been numerous that day – were waiting for the rations to be brought up the line. They had been on the move for twenty hours or more now, slipping and slithering along duckboards or trudging through mud knee deep, salvo upon salvo of Jerry whizz-bangs flying over their heads and thudding into the earth too close for comfort. Their water bottles and their bellies were empty but their ears were ringing with the noise.

The torrential rain that had pelted from the heavens for the past four days showed no signs of abating and as they sat with their backs against the wall, the downpour spattered and bounced off their mud-caked uniforms and trickled down the backs of their necks. Not that it mattered. They were already soaked to the skin. Groaning and muttering – trying to light a fag – nigh on impossible for all but the most desperate – they sprawled in the mud, their bellies rumbling. Apart from the biscuits that broke your teeth and the last scrapings from a large tin of jam, these hardy lads hadn't eaten since dawn and it was now pitch black.

The Salient straggled inland from the coastal town of Nieuport and bulged out in a rough semi-circle to the east of the Ypres district. It then snaked along high ground to merge with the plain at Armentières and Arras and on to the Belgian border. It had been formed by accident in 1914, forged by retreat and held by the iron determination of the Allies. Ypres was the key to the channel ports and the Germans knew it, so it was the Allies' job to drive back the Germans. Heavy shelling had hammered the surrounding villages into dust and debris, and in heavy rain the flat land, torn up by shells, rapidly became a quagmire. A man had as much chance of being drowned in mud as he had of being shot.

Unfortunately for the Allies, the Germans occupied the high ground. The troops called them hills although they were really just folds in the ground sloping gently up from the flat plains of Flanders. The Germans also had concrete bunkers and pillboxes whilst the Allies had to make do with dug-outs burrowed in the ramparts of their shallow trenches. They threw up breastworks of mud and barbed wire and crouched in stinking ditches, or like tonight, they took shelter wherever they could.

'Where's that bloody ration party? Me belly thinks me throat's cut,' a voice cried out. 'Hey, Sarge, what time is it?'

Flynn took his watch from his breast pocket, handling it carefully in his mud-caked fingers. 'Quarter to ten. They should be here anytime soon,' he called back with a lot more confidence than he felt. They were already behind schedule. This wasn't unusual. The transport officer and his team of men were just as likely to come under enemy fire or get bogged down in the mud.

Earlier that evening a runner had informed Flynn's battalion that orders were to stand down until dawn when they would join with the troops whose job it had been to take nearby Sanctuary

Wood. If that venture had been successful, they would join them at first light as back-up on the Menin Road. As they had made their way to the ruined farm, German Very lights had lit up the sky and a barrage of shells had hurtled down on them, taking out some of their pals. They had left their scattered limbs and mangled bodies where they were, just four more husbands, fathers, brothers or sons to claim a muddy grave in Flanders.

Three years ago, Flynn would have abhorred doing such a thing. Now he thought little of it. He'd seen too much, and as he waited to be fed, his mind was not on them but on his aching guts and what tomorrow might bring. By now a peaceful lull hung over the farm, no Very lights flared in the purple sky and the rattle of artillery had subsided. The near silence was strange and unnerving.

'Fritz must be taking an hour off and having his dinner,' Private Jim Jones remarked sourly. A lad of no more than seventeen, his spotty face was as gaunt as that of a man three times his age.

'Aye, he'll be tucking into them big fat sausages they have and washing 'em down with Bosche beer,' Flynn growled.

'I wonder if the fifty-third has had any success at Sanctuary Wood.' The grizzled older man who had been a school teacher was referring to the brigade who had led the attack, and his despondency was such that Flynn could tell he doubted it. He smiled wryly at the hypocrisy of the name; Sanctuary Wood was no safe haven and even the names Zonnebeke and Zillebeke sounded evil to him.

'We'll know by tomorrow,' he replied grimly.

Only this time last week Flynn had been behind the lines, on leave in Poperinghe or 'Pop' as the troops called it, taking a bath – the first in three months – in the huge vats installed in a brewery near the field station. It had felt like heaven as he'd peeled off his stinking singlet and long johns before jumping into the first vat filled with steaming hot, soapy water already scummed over by filth and lice from the men who had gone before him. Then he'd swung on the ropes suspended above the vats into the second one, slightly cleaner, and finally into the tepid fairly clean water of the third. After he'd dried off, he'd been issued with clean underwear far too small so he'd had to do a swap with a skinny little chap whose singlet had come down to his knees. His uniform had been fumigated to get rid of the ever-invasive lice and, clean and presentable, he'd spent the afternoon sitting in the peace and quiet of Skindles Hotel writing a letter to Lissie. He'd bought a delicately embroidered lacy postcard and written on it: 'I'll pop a ring on your finger when I come home,' and underlined the words 'pop a ring' to give Lissie a clue as to where he was. He had also bought a cheap metal brooch engraved with the name Ypres – another subtle way of cheating the censor. By evening he'd been drinking coffee and wine in an estaminet, enjoying a sing-song and playing cards before heading for Talbot House and a proper bed for the night. Now, as he shifted uneasily in his sopping wet clothes and scratched his chest – the lice never stayed away for long – he yearned to be anywhere other than the Ypres Salient and most particularly with Lissie in his arms.

The rattle of limbers, as the transport that conveyed the rations were called, broke Flynn's reverie. He jumped to his feet shaking rivulets of rain from his tunic. The others began to stir, some merely lifting their heads with hopeful looks on their dirty faces while others struggled upright.

'Sorry we're late,' Quarter Master Jimmy Stockdale called out as the first mule-drawn wagon hove into view. 'Gerry decided to have a pop at us on the way up and we lost one of the wagons,' he explained as he and his team began doling out bacon and bread, beans and biscuits, good hot strong tea, and rations of cigarettes and tobacco. Water bottles were refilled from two-gallon petrol tins and the rum ration given into Flynn's care. Some for now and the rest before they went into battle.

Flynn ate ravenously and in between mouthfuls he asked Jimmy for news. 'Not good,' he said. 'There's word that the fifty-third got lost on the way to Sanctuary Wood and suffered lots of casualties. We passed some stretcher-bearers on the way up. They can't keep on top of the job.'

'Why doesn't that surprise me?' Flynn's face twisted with anger. 'What was it you said when we arrived here? "They must know I'm a butcher because this bloody place is a slaughterhouse."' Flynn had laughed then, but he wasn't laughing now.

'Aye, and I wa' bloody right.' Jimmy said, hiding his misery by checking that the limbers were all unloaded. 'I'd best be getting back. We'd a hell of a job getting these bloody wagons up and it'll be just as bad getting 'em back down. The more the mules struggle the deeper they sink, but you can't tell 'em that.'

'The lads are just as bad.' Flynn clapped an arm across Jimmy's shoulders. 'Watch out for Fritz. Stay safe,' he said, his voice thick with emotion.

'You an' all, mate.' Jimmy's voice wobbled and he swallowed noisily before turning and barking orders to pack up. The ration party headed off into the night, the Very lights silhouetting them as they trundled away.

The pelting rain had eased off to a steady drizzle and, fed and watered, Flynn's company were in a better mood. Some of them cleaned their rifles or read over letters that they knew by heart, and others took it in turn to hold up a ground sheet at the four corners to make a shelter as out came the cards. For an hour or more the soldiers seemed to forget their troubles, cheering if they won and groaning when they lost, with the flimsy cards disintegrating bit by bit in their rough hands. Flynn sat thinking of Lissie's sweet smell and the feel of her. Then to the boomph of guns somewhere in the east he went and lifted one of the jars of rum. They were stamped with the initials of the Special Ration Department, the soldiers joking that the SRD stood for 'seldom reaches destination', but tonight it had and Flynn poured a small measure of rum into each man's tin cup with the words, 'Might help you get some sleep. We've a big day tomorrow.'

'They're all bloody big days in this hell-hole,' Gunner Robinson remarked.

'I don't suppose there's any chance of a refill?' Corporal Charlie Watson asked cheekily, holding out his cup. Charlie was a fearless Geordie who reminded Flynn of Meggie. He had a silver tenor voice and sang almost non-stop on route marches. One time Gunner Robinson had told him to 'shut the fuck up', Charlie had grinned. 'I canna, man, it's the only thing that keeps me going,' and he'd carried on singing. Now, he waved his cup under Flynn's nose but Flynn shook his head. Separated as they were from their lieutenants, and their captain dead, he was now the senior in rank of the motley crew and it was his responsibility to get them to the Menin Road the next day.

'Okay lads. We'll save the rest for the morning,' he said, stowing the empty jar beside the full one, his mind on the hazardous journey they would have to make in a few hours' time. He didn't add that they might need it.

30

In Scarborough on a day in early September the sun was shining and the resort was still busy with late holidaymakers taking advantage of the fine weather. The postman had just been and brightened Lissie's mood with a letter and a small parcel from Flynn. Before she had time to open them, the bell above the shop door jangled. A policeman and man wearing a long raincoat and a trilby hat came in. Lissie tucked the letter and the little parcel in her smock pocket.

'Miss Fairweather?' the policeman asked.

'That's right,' Lissie replied. 'How may I help you?'

'It's with regards to a Dora Fairweather, Miss.' The policeman coughed then glanced at the man in the hat.

'Why? What has she done now?' Irritation swept through Lissie's veins.

'Is it convenient to have a word, Miss Fairweather?' the man in the trilby asked. 'I'm Detective Sergeant Frank Shaw and this is Constable Lumb.'

It was close to midday and Elspeth was away for her lunch, so Lissie went and locked the shop door then invited the two men to follow her through the adjoining door into the house. In the kitchen she gestured for them to sit at the table. 'What is it you want to talk about? I haven't seen my mother for several months. We're not close.'

The constable and the detective exchanged quizzical glances. Lissie felt her palms grow clammy.

'Let me begin by establishing some facts, Miss,' DS Shaw said, somewhat lugubriously. 'Are you Dora Fairweather's daughter?'

'I am,' said Lissie, by now thinking that things were serious.

'Then it is my sad duty to inform you that Police Constable Lumb found your mother dead in an alley in Bradford on the night of the fifteenth of August. We have reason to believe foul play was the cause of death.'

Lissie gasped. 'Dead! Murdered,' she cried as his words sank in. She plumped down in the nearest chair, her cheeks ashen.

'Unfortunately, yes. She was strangled with her own scarf.' Shaw paused in an attempt to muster some sympathy for Lissie, but he had dealt with so many similar cases his compassion was in short supply. 'We thought you might have information that would lead us to the culprit.'

Lissie shook her head. 'I can't help you. I barely knew my mother.' She then went on to tell him how Dora had left her in the orphanage and how she had turned up in Scarborough only to disappear days later. She didn't divulge that Dora had robbed her. Instead, she asked, 'How did you find me?'

'Our enquiries led us to an associate of your late mother who told us your mother had a daughter in Scarborough who owned a drapery business.'

'An associate,' Lissie echoed.

'Yes, a woman who, like your mother, earned her living as a prostitute. We're here to check if what she said was true.' He sneered. 'You can't believe a word them prossies say.'

A prostitute! The colour came back to Lissie's cheeks. How

awful to hear her mother described in such bald terms. She struggled to gather her wits.

'And you don't know who did it?' Lissie felt as though she was in the middle of a nightmare. She pictured Dora lying in a dark alley, her eyes wide with fear.

'As yet we've made no arrest but we have our suspicions. Your mother kept company with some very unwholesome characters.' Shaw clearly had no sympathy for Dora.

Strangely enough, Lissie found that she did. Dora might have been a selfish, unscrupulous woman but she didn't deserve to be murdered.

'I'll have to let my father know,' she said, wondering how Tom would feel.

Shaw perked up. 'Your father? Where is he?' Suspicion glinted in his eyes.

'He lives in Pickering. He returned from France five days ago. He was a stretcher-bearer on the Western Front until he was injured.'

Shaw's shoulders slumped as he calculated the dates. 'We can rule him out then,' he said to the constable.

'Of course you can,' Lissie said heatedly. 'My father would never do such a thing. He hasn't seen my mother for fifteen years. She almost killed him.' The moment the words left her lips she wanted to bite them back.

'Is that right?' Shaw drawled. 'And when was this?'

Her heart pounding, Lissie told him what had taken place in the cottage in Thorne when she was seven.

'And you're sure he wasn't in the country on the fifteenth of August?'

Lissie had heard enough. She leapt to her feet. 'Check with the East Yorkshire Regiment. I'm sure they'll confirm exactly where he was,' she spat, her cheeks blazing. 'Now tell me exactly what we do about my mother.'

'You can claim the body for burial. Our investigation's finished here for the time being.' Shaw pushed back his chair and the policeman stood. He gave Lissie the name of the hospital morgue and Lissie showed them out. As soon as Elspeth returned from her lunch break, Lissie caught the next train to Pickering.

'Why didn't you tell me Dora had visited you?' Tom's face puckered with concern and he plucked distractedly at the cuff of his jumper, the wool fraying in his fingers. He'd somewhat recovered from his initial shock but the news of his ex-wife's murder had affected him badly. Amelia had made a pot of strong sweet tea then left them alone. They needed time to absorb this dreadful event and deal with a part of their lives in which she had played no part.

'Why didn't you think you could tell me?' Tom repeated.

'I didn't want her to hurt you again. She hadn't changed. She was still the same selfish, ungrateful person who wanted everything but never gave anything in return. I even contemplated asking her to divorce you so that you can marry Amelia,' Lissie said, going on to give a dismal account of Dora's behaviour and the theft. 'She didn't know how to be decent.'

'Sad, but true,' Tom agreed, his voice cracking. 'Still, she didn't deserve such a terrible death, and she was my wife and your mother. It's only right that we give her a Christian burial.'

On the gruesome trip to Bradford, Tom hobbling on his crutches from the house to the station and onto the train, Lissie asked him the same question she had asked Dora. 'Why did you marry her?'

Tom grimaced as he told much the same story as Dora's. 'I was young and foolish, trying to be a big man. I got drunk – the one and only time in my life – and I made love to Dora. When she told me she was pregnant, I did my duty. There was no baby, not then, but by that time I'd married her. You didn't come along until a year later.' His crumpled face broke into an unexpected smile. 'I'm grateful for that. You were the only good thing to come out of the marriage.'

'I'm grateful too.' Lissie squeezed Tom's hand. 'I wouldn't have had you for a dad if things had been different. She did something right after all.'

The hastily arranged funeral and interment were as grim as to be expected and they returned to Pickering two days later, relieved to have it over and done with. 'I know I should be grieving, and in a way, I am,' Lissie said on the homeward journey, 'but I can't cry for her.'

'I feel the same,' Tom said, 'but don't shed tears; she caused you enough pain when she was alive and it would be wrong to let her death spoil your future. We have a lot to live for, Lissie, and a lot of happiness to seek. Happiness doesn't come looking for you, you have to make your own and that's what we must do. You with Flynn and me with you and Amelia.'

'How is it you always say the right things?' she said, smiling at the oft repeated phrase whenever her dad put her mind at rest.

* * *

The beautifully embroidered sweetheart postcard stood on Lissie's dressing table along with the other cards Flynn had sent. The 'Ypres' brooch was pinned to whatever blouse or dress she happened to be wearing, and with each passing day she missed him all the more.

Meggie was a great consolation. She was in the same boat. And little Eddie's antics provided them both with pleasurable distraction. He seemed to learn something new every day, and as Lissie told his mother about Dora's gruesome death, Eddie was building towers of coloured wooden blocks then demolishing them with gusto.

'Eeh, that's terrible,' Meggie consoled, 'but you weren't close in life so don't let her death mek you miserable for the rest of your own.'

Lissie agreed, and told Meggie her dad had said much the same thing. She showed Meggie the postcard from Flynn.

'Ooh, that's lovely. I'll ask Jimmy to send me one. And that brooch is nice,' she said, pointing to Lissie's lapel.

'They must be somewhere near Ypres,' Lissie said, fetching the atlas from the bookshelf and setting it on the table in front of them. She turned the pages to the map of Belgium. Each time Flynn had given her a clue as to his whereabouts, she and Meggie tracked their progress. Interpreting the clues made them giggle. *We've dropped anchor in a rotten place and the lice are eating us alive,* with 'anchor' underlined, had told the girls he and Jimmy were in Ancre, and *'Don't harass me,' our officer says, and being a good Yorkshire lad like all of us, he drops his aitches,* let them know they were in Arass. The funniest had been the one that told them he and Jimmy were in Messines: *The food's that bad we mess in us pants.* Once they had guessed the clues, they scanned the newspapers for information about what was happening in these foreign places. It made them feel closer to the men they loved, as though they were helping them stay alive and fight the war. However, it didn't take away the fear and they often shed tears of loneliness and despair.

* * *

Despair was something with which Flynn was now very familiar. He'd led his small company to the Menin Road and in the next few days they had been constantly on the move, not travelling far but nearer and nearer to the front line. An hour before dawn on a day in September – he wasn't sure which day – he gazed at the bleak rain-swept expanse of mud over which they would travel to their next rendezvous point, then fell into line and shuffled forward under the weight of his rifle, bandolier and knapsack filled with Mills bombs. Behind him Private Jim Jones was laden with his rifle and bandolier and a spade and a length of thick rope. 'I could hang meself wi' this if there were any bloody trees left standing to tie it to,' he jested as they moved out.

Knee deep in slush, they trudged over the uneven ground. Flynn thought back to the time when the tunnellers, like moles, had dug miles underground to lay mines or listen in the galleries to the Germans who were doing exactly the same thing. Then, when the mines were detonated, Hill 60 had erupted, changing the landscape forever. It had been a triumph for the Allies, but now he wondered how many undetonated mines were still there under the ground he was walking on. One false slip into a hole could blow them all to kingdom come. He felt the suction of the mud pulling his feet from under him and heard the loud plop as he dragged them free and was glad when they arrived at a section of duckboards. As he stepped on, he glanced down and saw something round like a football. He nudged it with his boot. It was a man's head, its mouth wide open and filled with mud. At the same time, Gunner Morris stepped on the man's body, releasing a stink so vile and putrid that Flynn and Morris threw up their breakfasts. But still they trudged on, each step taking them closer to the front line.

By now the sun was up, its sickly yellow rays slanting through the clouds and casting a ghoulish light on the bleak terrain and the lines of men in khaki. Like giant mud beetles, they slipped and slithered along the duckboards, dreading the thought of falling off into the morass of liquid mud that could smother them in an instant. They avoided looking down in case they glimpsed an arm or a leg or an entire body lying face down in the mud. The expressions of those that were lying face up showed the effort they had made to try and save themselves.

Sometimes the ground oozed blood. It was like a living nightmare.

They hadn't gone far when they were caught by an enfilade of German machine guns firing from the ridge above them. The watchword: 'Keep your heads down' rang out as under a hail of bullets, they dived for cover, taking shelter wherever they could. Flynn lunged into a shallow shell-hole with Jones and Charlie, burrowing as deep as they could. Jonesy began digging, throwing up mud to form a bastion of protection. They stayed there for almost an hour, the stagnant, stinking water in the shell-hole seeping into their uniforms as bullets whizzed over their heads. Charlie began to hum 'It's a Long Way to Tipperary'.

Orders came to move out. By late afternoon they had made better progress. Now they were within the range of German shells, flying shrapnel and fountains of mud thrown up by explosions splattering them as they pressed on.

Charlie began to sing one of his made-up lyrics to the tune of 'Mademoiselle from Armentières'.

'They took his arm, they took his leg, an' sent him out to thieve and an' beg,' he warbled and the others joined in on the 'parley-voo'. Charlie was still singing when a bullet pierced the right side of his neck and exited on the left. Sick at heart, Flynn cradled him in his arms until the stretcher-bearers took him away. 'You're going home to sing in heaven, lad,' he whispered in Charlie's ear after the bearers had lifted him onto the stretcher. Now, the mood was blacker than ever. Nerves were taut, tempers frayed. Angry remarks such as, 'Watch where you're putting your bloody feet', met with sharp retorts of, 'Fuck off', and, 'Keep that up and I'll shoot you me bloody self'. The unlucky few were hit and slipped into a muddy grave, but sodden, filthy and weary, Flynn and his pals struggled on.

At times bedlam broke loose as teams of half-crazed men and horses and infantrymen sought cover. In every direction Flynn saw nothing but smoke and flames thick in the air from exploding shells. At dusk orders came to dig in. Flynn and Jones and the others were glad to hear it for they were worn out and thirsty. With Polygon Wood at their rear and a formidable line of German pill-boxes to the fore, they scrabbled to mount the Lewis guns on the unstable ground. They kept sinking.

'Empty the ammo boxes and make a base, put the guns on top,' Flynn said. That worked, and he set about giving more orders that were carefully listened to. 'You lot, over there,' he continued, pointing to a ridge of mud then telling Jones and Robinson to come with him to a forward position. 'I'd follow him to hell an' back,' Jones declared as they dug in to face the enemy. It was something he'd said more than once, with good reason. The lads had great faith in their sergeant and some had Flynn to thank for saving them in more ways than one.

On that grisly strip of land that separated the British line from the German front they returned shot and shell. Heart-stopping Very lights lit up the sky picking out the gun emplacements and a barrage of shells hurtled down on them, pieces of steel slicing into the unfortunate. When the bombardment abated, the wounded started to appear white, haggard and half-crazy with fright. The dead stayed where they were. Stretcher-bearers dodged here and there, lifting those that could be saved.

Then came a sudden strange lull; Fritz was withholding fire. Flynn looked up into the star-studded sky. In the eerie almost silence, he was dragging on a cigarette, enjoying the bitter taste of it when Private Harris, a nervous, bookish lad from Whitby who some of the others made fun of for his prim and proper manner, leapt to his feet and ran screaming towards the enemy lines. 'Mother, mother,' he screeched at the top of his lungs. 'I want me mother.'

Like lightning, Flynn raced after him, lunging and bringing Harris to his knees close to the remains of a German dug-out. They rolled in a flurry of arms and legs then crashed into the trench. A thick yellow-green cloud enveloped them, the acrid stink of the fumes of chlorine gas they had released from a hidden stash stinging their eyes and choking their throats.

The smell of chlorine wafted to where Private Jones was crouched, and realising what it was, he pulled on his gas mask and rushed to their aid, dragging Flynn then Harris out of the trench. In a fog of chlorine, they rolled away from the trench then lay panting and heaving. Flynn staggered to his feet, his eyes streaming. 'I can't see,' he cried. 'I can't bloody see!'

'I've got you, Sarge, I've got you,' Jones yelled as a hail of gunfire sent mud spurting up round their feet. Harris was crawling towards them when a huge lump of shrapnel sliced off the top of his head. He was gone and there was nothing they could do but save themselves. Half-carrying Flynn, Jones led him back to the dug-out. Gunner Robinson, seeing a party of stretcher-bearers nearby, signalled for them to come over to the dug-out.

In the ensuing panic Flynn found himself being pushed into a line of walking wounded. 'Keep your hand on the shoulder of the man in front,' someone ordered. Behind him, someone clapped his left hand on Flynn's right shoulder. 'I'm right behind you, Sarge,' he said, his right hand holding a field first-aid pad to a huge gash in his own head. Over his shoulder Flynn growled, 'That's good to know. I can't see a bloody thing.'

Blindly he shuffled forward, contemplating on what the rest of his life would be like if all he could see was a blur of shadows. Flynn pictured Lissie's lovely face and her beautiful smile then he summoned up colourful images of his carousel and roundabouts. Would they now be something he had to commit to memory because he would never see them again? That thought filled him with horror and tears sprang to his useless eyes.

31

The letter arrived on the last day of September. Letters from Flynn were Lissie's life-line and she was feeling anxious because she hadn't had one for almost three weeks. Each passing day her fears had mounted.

'Aw, don't worry, letters get lost, pet,' Meggie had sympathised when Lissie had expressed her dismay. 'The last time Jimmy saw him he said Flynn was fine.' Then, undoing the consolation she had just supplied she thoughtlessly added, 'Mind you, his last letter did say he hadn't seen him for some time.' It hadn't eased Lissie's mind one bit.

Tom had said much the same thing. 'It's nothing short of a miracle that letters get through as regularly as they do in all the chaos over there,' he told her.

Now, Lissie held the letter in her trembling hand and stood rigidly, staring at the unfamiliar writing on the military envelope, afraid to open it.

'Oh no! No!' Her strangled cry attracted Elspeth's attention.

'What is it, Lissie?' Elspeth abandoned the customer she was serving and hurried over to Lissie. When she saw the envelope, her heart went out to her employer: she knew the heartache of receiving a such a letter. 'Go into the house,' she said, pushing Lissie towards the adjoining door. 'I'll be with you in a minute.' Elspeth went to attend to her customer and Lissie, her feet and her heart feeling like lead, walked into the kitchen. She slumped into a chair at the table and placed the envelope squarely in front of her. A feeling of numbness crept up from her toes to the top of her head. *Flynn, oh Flynn*, she silently cried.

A couple of minutes later, Elspeth came in. 'I've locked the shop door. We won't be disturbed,' she said, sitting across the table from Lissie. 'Open it,' she urged. 'That way you'll know. It might not be as bad as you think.'

Lissie's fingers felt as though they didn't belong to her as she tore at the flap on the envelope. Removing the single sheet of paper, she forced herself to read the words on it. Elspeth held her breath.

'It's from a nurse in a hospital in London.' Lissie's voice sounded hollow. 'Flynn's lost his sight. He asked her to write to me. She says he'll be transferred to Weston House on the third of October and...' Words failed her, and crushing the letter in her hands, she rested her head on the table and wept.

Elspeth reached across the table and gently stroked Lissie's hair. 'It does say suffering from what may be temporary blindness, Lissie. He's in the right place and he's receiving treatment. My neighbour, Willie Cummings, was blinded by gas in 1916 but he can see again,' she comforted, desperately and deliberately withholding the fact that his lungs were so tattered he could barely draw breath or walk two yards.

Lissie lifted her head, her eyes expressing all the sorrows of the world.

'It's early days, love,' Elspeth gabbled, 'and Weston House is only down the road. You'll be able to visit him every day.'

Lissie nodded dumbly. She was picturing Flynn's beautiful dark eyes that shone with a lust for life or gazed tenderly into her own, their warmth letting her know that she was loved. Would they now be blank? Would the lights of joy, excitement and mischief that so often danced in them be no more than a dull grey uncomprehending stare? She took a deep breath and got to her feet. She had to stay strong for Flynn, and if the worst happened and there was no cure, she would be his eyes.

* * *

In the early October morning a mizzling rain engulfed the town, as grey and unwelcoming as Lissie's thoughts. She had barely eaten or slept since receiving the letter and her head ached from morning till night. The letter hadn't given the time of Flynn's arrival at Weston House but she presumed it would be later in the day. Even so, she wasted no time as she made a cup of tea and forced down a slice of toast before taking a bath in sweet-smelling oil. She washed her hair then after drying herself she put on her best blue dress and brushed her mane of black curls until they gleamed. She'd go to the convalescent home as soon as Elspeth arrived to look after the shop, and if she had to sit waiting for Flynn to be delivered, she was prepared to wait all day.

At 9.30 a.m. she left the shop and walked down North Marine Road, her mind tumbling with thoughts of what to expect and her chest tight with anxiety. Weston House was a grand Victorian residence on the esplanade in South Bay and was less than a fifteen-minute walk away. When the sea came into view, Lissie paused to gaze out over the rolling grey waters. The beach was empty, the rippled sand patterns undulating and untrodden. Cockle shells like little white caps and pebbles of varying shapes and hues mingled with trailing seaweed, nature's handiwork creating patterns that spoke of eternity. *They will be there long after we are all gone*, thought

Lissie, as she recalled sunny summer days, children building sand castles, flying kites and the esplanade alive with happy holiday-makers in colourful clothes. This was where she had first met Flynn.

She closed her eyes, imagining the swarthy handsome boy with dark eyes that danced with excitement, and his gangly moon-faced friend with the cheeky smile were walking towards her. Her heart began to flutter just as it had on that day, and when she opened her eyes and carried on walking, she thought how that chance meeting had changed both hers and Meggie's lives. In the early days they'd had fun on this esplanade, got to know each other, and fallen in love. Oh, what happiness there had been then.

Now, the esplanade held none of those delights, and although the mizzling rain had ceased, Lissie found nothing to lift her spirits. Yes, she longed to be reunited with Flynn, to feel his touch, hear his voice and see his dear face. But he wouldn't see hers, and that thought weighed heavily. She had heard people say that men who came back from the war were changed, and not the same people their wives or mothers remembered. Only the other day in the shop Mrs Caldwell had been telling them that whilst she was thrilled to have her son back home where he belonged, she didn't understand him any more.

'He's moody,' she said. 'One minute he's sitting quietly and the next he's bawling his head off. I've never seen such a temper. Our Johnny wa' always pleasant and kind. Now everything irritates him, an' he jumps out of his skin at the slightest noise. When our little Frankie slammed the door, I thought our Johnny wa' going to kill him he carried on that badly.'

Lissie had sympathised with Mrs Caldwell, and as she approached Weston House, she realised that she was now the one to whom people would offer sympathy and she didn't want that. She wanted Flynn and everything else to be like it had been before

this rotten war. His blindness wouldn't stop her from loving him –
she couldn't; she'd love him all the more – but things were bound to
be different, she couldn't deny that.

Outside Weston House she stopped and gazed at the imposing
architecture of the splendid building. Then pushing back her
shoulders, she mounted the steps and went into the dark interior,
the incongruous hospital smell of disinfectant mixed with furniture
polish making her nose twitch. In the large hallway, nurses, doctors
and orderlies bustled in and out of adjoining doors or wheeled
chairs or trolleys up and down its length, but even with all this
movement the atmosphere was hushed.

'Can I help you?' A young nurse in a bright red cape smiled at
Lissie.

'I've come to see Sergeant Flynn Corrigan. I got a letter
informing me he was being brought here today.'

'That'll be the transfers from St Thomas's. They haven't arrived
yet,' the nurse said cheerfully, and seeing Lissie's distress she took
her by the elbow. 'We don't know how long it'll be before they do so
why don't you wait in here till he comes.' She led Lissie into what
might have once been a sitting room judging by the grand furniture. Its windows overlooked the sea. 'Make yourself comfortable,
you could be here for some time.' She gave a little laugh. 'We never
know what to expect in this place. I'm off duty now so I'll leave you
to it.'

The nurse hurried off and Lissie went and sat on a chair by the
window. At first, she just sat staring into space, numb with worry,
then seeing some magazines on a side table she lifted one and list-
lessly thumbed through it. An elderly couple shuffled into the room
and sat on a couch near the door. The woman was sobbing pitifully
and the stooped man did his best to comfort her. Then a doctor in a
white coat came in, his haggard face apologetic as he talked quietly
to them. They nodded their heads, and the woman cried all the

harder as they followed him out of the room. Other people came and went. None of them looked happy. If they were by themselves, they didn't meet the eyes of the other visitors, and if they were accompanied most of them held whispered, tearful conversations.

Lissie's eyes drooped. She hadn't slept much the night before and although she tried to prevent it, she dozed off. She was wakened with a jolt, startled by a commotion outside. Two military ambulances were parked at the doors. Men on stretchers were being carried into the building, the orderlies shouting directions to the bearers. She leapt to her feet and rushed into the hallway, almost colliding with an orderly carrying a pile of towels.

'Steady on there, lass. What's the rush?'

'Are those the men who've come from London?' she gabbled.

'They are. That's the last of 'em,' he said as the stretcher-bearers disappeared down the corridor.

'Were there others besides them?' Lissie urged.

'Oh aye, a dozen or so of 'em. They allus take the walking wounded in first.'

Lissie felt annoyed and guilty. She'd been sleeping when Flynn arrived. That was if he had. 'Do you know if Sergeant Flynn Corrigan was among them?'

'I can find out for you. Wait here.' The orderly wandered off. Lissie's heart drummed a tattoo and her palms moistened. Any minute now...

'He's been taken to ward seven,' the orderly said on his return. 'I'll take you down there but you'll have to get a doctor's permission to see him.'

Lissie felt as though she was walking on egg shells as she followed the orderly out of the hallway and to somewhere at the rear of the house. A tired-looking young doctor was just exiting a room and the orderly stopped. 'With your permission, Doctor Glenn, this young lady's here to see Sergeant Flynn Corrigan.'

'Thank you, Watkins. Leave her with me.' The doctor gave Lissie a sad smile. Her stomach lurched. He gestured to a window seat overlooking the gardens.

'We'll sit here while I explain the nature of Sergeant Corrigan's injuries,' he said.

Lissie didn't like the sound of that. She sat down with a bump.

'He was the victim of a chlorine gas attack and when that happens the corneas of the eyes are damaged. We know how to treat this, and sometimes the loss of sight is only temporary – on the other hand it may be that Sergeant Corrigan will be partially or completely blind for the rest of his life.'

Lissie heard the compassion in his voice and she choked back a sob.

'He received immediate treatment in France and further work was carried out in London but...' He gave a small shrug. 'We will continue to treat him here, and who knows, he may yet be lucky. He's strong and healthy otherwise.' Doctor Glenn stood. 'Go in and cheer him up.'

Lissie's legs felt like twigs as she followed the doctor into a large, long room that might have once been a ballroom. She was unprepared for what she saw and drew in a sharp breath. It was crammed on either side with rows of black iron bedsteads and in those beds were men, or what could be seen of them for they were swathed in bandages and dressings. Some of them were moaning and tossing restlessly while others lay perfectly still and silent. One of them gave an anguished, almost inhuman, cry. Lissie broke out in a sweat and averted her eyes. The cry slurred into an ugly gurgle and she began to feel sick.

On trembling legs, she tottered after the doctor to the end of the room where there was an arrangement of chairs and small tables in a large bay window. The doctor went and stood in front of one of the large wing chairs. 'You have a visitor, Sergeant Corrigan.' He beckoned for Lissie to come forward.

Slowly, she stepped round the chair to face Flynn, her heart in her mouth.

Flynn sat rigidly in the chair, his hands resting on his knees in the way that Lissie remembered so well. His eyes were closed, his long dark lashes feathering his high cheekbones. His face was thinner than she remembered and bitter lines edged the corners of his mouth. She leaned forward and took his hands in hers. His eyelids fluttered and he took a deep breath. Then his eyes flew open.

'Lissie,' he said. 'Lissie, is that you?'

'Yes, it's me, Flynn,' she said, stooping further until her cheek pressed against his. He pulled his hands free and clasped her to his chest. She felt the thud of his heart against her own like a captive bird trying to break free from its cage. They stayed like this for some time, her tears dampening his shirt front and his tears wetting her hair. 'You smell delicious,' he whispered into her hair.

When she eventually eased away from Flynn, she saw that the doctor had gone. She glanced from left to right. Save for three men sitting in chairs close by, their eyes covered with bandages, she and Flynn were alone. Then she did what she had been too embarrassed to do in the doctor's presence. She placed her lips on Flynn's and kissed him soundly. He groaned with pleasure and was returning the kiss with passion when suddenly he tore his lips from hers and pushed her away.

Shocked, Lissie reeled on her heels. 'What... Flynn... what...?'

'Don't, Lissie, don't do that.' His face twisted in anguish. 'You do know that I can't see you, Lissie, that I'm blind and I...' His voice broke, and she tried to hush him to stop talking but he waved his hands to silence her. 'I don't want you to tie yourself to me. You mustn't feel obliged to.'

'But I want to, I love you, and we'll get by. You're here, and alive and well, and that's all that matters now,' Lissie gabbled.

Silently, he digested her words, his cold expression brooking no opposition.

When he broke the ominous silence he said, 'You say that now, but you'll get tired of me bumbling around unable to do much for myself.' Flynn spoke without a hint of self-pity, and Lissie knew he was only thinking of her. *How brave he is*, she thought, swallowing the lump in her throat.

'Never!' she cried, so adamantly that it made the man in the chair furthest away jump. 'From now on I'll be the eyes for both of us.'

Flynn gave a grim chuckle. 'But I don't want you to be,' he said, his voice low and grating. 'I think it will be best if you don't come here again.' He averted his head so that his sightless eyes were turned away from her, his lips clamped and his face closed. She reached for his hands again, clasping them and feeling the calloused knots hard against her own soft flesh. Hands that had gripped a rifle and scrabbled through rough terrain in pursuit of killing his fellow man. She shuddered and did not resist when Flynn shook himself free, but she wasn't beaten, yet. She leaned forward, looking into his face, searching for the mind within the body of the good, proud man that he was, her face so close to his that she knew he could feel her breath on his lips.

'But... but I love you, Flynn. I want to help...'

'Go away, Lissie. I don't need or want you,' he barked.

Lissie couldn't believe what she was hearing, but the hurtful words had hit their mark and she fled from the ward, tears streaming down her cheeks.

'He doesn't want to see me again,' she sobbed when Meggie called that evening.

'Aw, love, don't take on so. He's hurt and confused. He doesn't know what he's saying.' She paused to pour tea into two cups. 'Don't give up on him. If you think there's still a chance for you an' him then keep on going to see him and, who knows, mebbe he'll see sense – an' mebbe he'll get his sight back.' Meggie sounded far more convincing than she really felt. 'Now drink your tea.'

'I love him so much I can't imagine living without him.' Lissie sniffed and sipped. 'It makes no difference to me that he can't see.'

'Aye, but it does to him. Like I said, don't give up yet,' Meggie replied.

After that, Lissie went every day to the convalescent home for an hour in the morning and then again in the afternoon. Flynn sat silently, his hands gripping the chair arms as he stared straight ahead, refusing to engage in conversation or even acknowledge that he heard Lissie's impassioned pleas to allow her back into his life.

She was there when the nurse made her frequent daily rounds and bathed his damaged eyes with a colourless solution. 'We wash them with alkaline to irrigate them,' Nurse Mulligan explained. 'It's marvellous stuff an' more often than not it cleans the corneas and the sight is restored in a week or two,' she continued, her Irish accent thick.

Lissie's spirits rose. 'Does that mean he might see properly again?'

'It can and it can't,' Nurse Mulligan replied, her contrary answer quenching Lissie's raised hopes. 'This lad's nearly at the end of his treatment and he's not showin' much improvement.' She placed the used swabs in a kidney dish. 'Stubborn sort o' fella, isn't he?' She gave Lissie a knowing look and Lissie knew she was referring to Flynn's recalcitrant attitude towards her.

'Don't talk about me as if I wasn't here,' Flynn snapped. 'It's my eyes that don't work, not my ears.' He swivelled his head. 'You'd better leave, Lissie.'

Lissie blinked back tears. 'See you tomorrow, Flynn,' she said, making for the door, her feet as heavy as her heart.

'Have faith in the Good Lord,' Nurse Mulligan whispered, the kidney dishes on her trolley rattling as she walked alongside Lissie and on to the next patient. The rounds were constant, and during the following days Lissie saw nurses carefully removing blistered skin from burned faces, arms and legs or dressing the stumps of missing limbs. They were sights she would never forget, the real horror of war there before her eyes. And still Flynn wouldn't speak or listen to her.

Each day he sat in sullen silence, hating not being able to see things clearly yet seeing blurred images and hearing muffled sounds he would rather forget. He heard Charlie singing and saw the blood spurting from his neck as he fell, and he felt his feet sinking into the bodies of men who had fallen as he ploughed on into the German line. He prayed that the nightmare would end and he tried his utmost to banish it from his memory, but try as he might, he still saw bloodied bodies trapped by the wire as they were blown apart in a hail of German bullets when all he wanted to see was Lissie's beautiful face.

It was a shame for Lissie to have to see him like this. He was still so handsome on the outside yet inside he seemed tormented with an ugliness she couldn't penetrate.

One day when he was in a particularly black mood, he turned on her angrily. 'Look, Lissie, I'm going to spend the rest of my days seeing nothing but blurred shadows, and I don't want your pity. I'll get through this on my own.' Lissie felt his pain, but she clung to the hope that Nurse Mulligan had given her; it might only be temporary, and each night Lissie prayed that she was right.

On another day as they sat silently side by side in a seat by the window, Flynn quite unexpectedly turned to face her and ran his fingertips gently over her face. 'You're just as beautiful as I remember,' he said before withdrawing his hand and snapping, 'Go away and don't come back.'

In despair, Lissie did as he asked, the thought that he might never again see her or any of the lovely things that had given him so much pleasure tugging at her heart. She had never felt more helpless.

After she had gone, Flynn cursed his moment of weakness. He loved her but to his way of thinking it was unfair to tie her to a blind man. Her loyalty made it all the more difficult for him to pretend he didn't want her, but overwhelmed by what the future had in store for him, he thought he was doing the right thing.

'Sergeant Corrigan will be discharged from here the day after tomorrow,' the doctor told Lissie when he met her in the corridor at the end of Flynn's third week in Weston House.

'Where to?'

'His home address here in the town. He's refusing to go to the rehabilitation workshop in Sheffield and there is nothing more we can do for him here.' The doctor shook his head in exasperation. 'He's given up on himself. As far as I can tell, the damage to his eyes has healed, the corneas clean and in working order. It's almost as if the chap doesn't want to see again.' His white coat flapping, he strode off in a flurry of annoyance, leaving Lissie equally irritated. She went in search of Flynn and found him sitting, as usual, in one of the chairs in the ward's bay window. She pulled up another chair and sat facing him. He stared stonily into the distance above her head, and when she took his hands in hers, he pulled them away and folded his arms across his chest. She told him about her conversation with the doctor.

'You must come and live with me, Flynn,' she said.

Flynn stiffened and tossed his head dismissively.

'What? And ruin your reputation?' he sneered. 'Think of the gossip, Lissie. It's not as if we were married.'

'No, but we soon can be, and in the meantime I'll—'

'No, Lissie! We can't, and let that be an end to it.'

He stood abruptly, and with his white stick he began tapping his way between the chairs and down the ward past the beds before disappearing into what Lissie had learned was a bathroom. She waited for some time but he didn't come back. Feeling utterly disillusioned and rather foolish, she left.

Out on the esplanade, a cold wind blew in from the sea and the grey clouds overhead were as leaden as her footsteps. How would he manage alone in his lodgings on St Mary's Walk, she wondered, and why was he putting them both in this predicament when there was a solution to the problem? She found it hard to believe that he had fallen out of love with her.

'Why is he behaving in this way?' she asked her father and Amelia when they called the next day. They had paid Flynn a brief visit and had been shocked by his cold, aloof attitude towards them. Tom knew first-hand the strange effects that years spent fighting on the battlefield had on many of the men he had come across in his time as a stretcher-bearer, men who had lost limbs or, like Flynn, their sight, and then there were those who had no obvious injuries but had lost their minds. He feared that Flynn fell into the latter categories – sightless and senseless – and the words of comfort he now offered to Lissie sounded hollow.

'Give it time,' he said, 'it's a great healer. Look after him as much as he allows you to. Be the friend he needs.'

32

On the day Flynn was discharged from Weston House, Lissie pleaded with him to go to her house in North Marine Road. 'Please, Flynn, listen to what I'm saying. It makes sense to have someone help you get used to your new circumstances,' she reasoned, kneading his hands in hers.

'Why will you not understand? I don't need your help, Lissie.' He pulled his hands free, dismissing her with an angry glare. 'And don't feel obliged to come calling on me. I have to learn to manage on my own.' Flynn shook himself free of her supporting hand, and tapping with his stick, he made his unsteady way down the steps outside the front door and onto the pavement. She continued to beg until the orderly came to help him into the ambulance. Again, he refused and she watched sadly as the ambulance drove away to St Mary's Walk. It was just after ten o'clock, and in the cold, pale light of the November morning, the sea beyond the esplanade was a sheet of gun-metal grey. It looked hard and forbidding and as bleak as Lissie felt as she walked back to the drapery.

She waited on tenterhooks for the hours to pass, her mind not on her job, and when it came to three o'clock she said, 'I'm going round to Flynn's. I'll buy some groceries on my way.'

Elspeth smiled sympathetically. 'Yes, do that. It'll put your mind at rest.'

* * *

The house door in St Mary's Walk was unlatched and Lissie knocked then walked in. Flynn was sitting in the bosun's swivel chair that he had bought when the contents of an old cargo boat had been sold off. Hearing her approach, he spun the chair round to face the door. 'Who is it?' he growled.

'It's me, Lissie. I've brought bread and ham and a few other things you'll need,' she said brightly. Flynn groaned out loud.

'The people at Weston House have already fixed me up with the necessaries.' His curt response tore at Lissie's heart.

Undeterred, she crossed to the table to unload her shopping. A knocked-over mug had spilled milk over the oilcloth cover and it was now soaking into the remains of a half-made sandwich. She thought that her heart would break.

The room was bitterly cold, the fire that someone – no doubt from Weston House – had lit for Flynn's return was now just smouldering embers and the coal scuttle empty. Hurrying out to the yard, Lissie replenished the scuttle then revived the fire. That was when she noticed the smashed teapot lying in a puddle close by the hearth. He had tried to make himself a meal and ended up in this sorry mess. Tears sprang to her eyes.

'Oh, Flynn,' she cried, turning to face him, 'please let me help you.'

He leaned forward, his hands gripped tightly round the chair's arms and a wild look in his eyes. 'How many times do I have to tell you, Lissie? I don't need your help. I don't need anyone's help so leave me alone.' He slumped back in the chair, his next words jarring as though he was tearing them from deep within his soul. 'We've been apart for too long. I've changed. You've changed. You're a successful woman with her own business whereas I have nothing to offer you.'

'Don't say that! It's you I want, not some grand millionaire – and as for you saying you have nothing – you still have the rides and the stalls that you own. You are—'

'A man who can't see to run his own business?' Flynn snarled. 'Do you think I want to sit here waiting for Billy to drop by with the takings? Where's the pride in that? I'm done for, Lissie. Done for.'

'No, you're not! We love one another and we'll—'

Again, Flynn interrupted her. 'You're wrong there, Lissie, very wrong. I don't love you any more.'

Lissie saw and heard the pain it caused him to say those words, and suddenly her blood boiled. She took two quick paces and towered over him, seething with rage.

'You might not love me, but I love you and I'm not going to let you destroy what we have,' she yelled as the flat of her hand swiped his face.

Flynn gasped, shocked by the stinging blow, and his jaw dropped open in amazement. A bright red patch stained his cheek, and Lissie instantly regretted her actions.

'I... I'm s... sorry,' she stuttered, 'I shouldn't have done that but I'm at my wits' end to make you see sense.' Cloaked in shame, she crossed the room, and lifting a brush and shovel, she began sweeping up the broken teapot, the shards of pottery scraping against the flagged floor, ominously loud in the ensuing silence.

Flynn sat without speaking, a gamut of emotions flashing across his gaunt face. He was a fool, he silently told himself, a stubborn idiot who had thought that denying his love for Lissie was the noble and right thing to do. His cheek still stinging, he rubbed his hand over it, the corners of his mouth twitching into a wry smile. Lissie Fairweather was a woman to be reckoned with.

He could hear her moving about the room, surprised that she hadn't marched out in temper, and he turned his head this way and that as he tried to locate her position. The thick grey mist through which he peered began to dissolve and things started to take shape. He blinked rapidly. Blink, blink, blink. Then he closed his eyes tight and kept them shut, not daring to believe what was happening. When he opened them, his breath caught in his throat and he stared at the indistinct outline of a figure and a patch of colour.

Lissie was down on her knees, her pert behind stretching the fabric of her dress as she mopped up the puddle of tea.

'Leave that, Lissie. Don't spoil your dress. It's one of my favourites. I always liked seeing you in it,' Flynn said.

Lissie looked over her shoulder at him, her eyes wide and wonder colouring her words as she asked, 'How do you know what I'm wearing?'

Flynn didn't immediately answer, and when he replied his tone echoed hers. 'It's the blue one. The one that matches the colour of your eyes.'

Lissie leapt to her feet. It was happening. His sight was returning. She ran to him, and Flynn opened his arms wide to receive her.

* * *

Amazement followed by a deep sense of relief and then pure joy filled each day as Flynn's sight slowly improved. Little by little things he thought he would never again see clearly began to take on a sharper form and he was able to dispense with his white stick. On a return visit to Weston House to see the doctor he was advised to frequently rest his eyes and Lissie made sure that he spent a part of each morning and afternoon lying down, his face covered with a piece of black linen. Sometimes Flynn would make the cloth rise and fall with his breath as he made ghostly noises and she would laugh. Flynn's spirits had been restored and whilst he accepted – not readily – that his sight might always be impaired, he no longer saw himself as a burden on Lissie.

This gave a new and vivid meaning to his life as he and Lissie strolled along the esplanade, the rolling sea bluer than he remembered and Castle Hill greener, although in fact the sea was wintry grey and the hill shrouded in mist. He rejoiced in the love that he had thought would be denied him for the rest of his life. It made his heart sing. And Lissie's heart sang all the louder. She had her Flynn back where he belonged. Tom's leg was healed, and he and Amelia were now man and wife. God had been kind to them. Now they could look to the future with renewed hope.

By the beginning of November there was a lightening in the atmosphere in the town although most days it was shrouded in icy mists and the sea a squall of momentous grey waves. The war had turned, the Germans were on the run and Allied victories began following one on the other.

'Thank God General Pershing's American troops and the Canadians are fighting alongside the Allies,' Tom remarked as he sat in Lissie's cosy kitchen with Amelia and Flynn on the first Sunday in November.

'Aye, Ludendorff's been forced to withdraw the Germans back to the Hindenburg Line and rumour has it that they're running out of munitions and food,' said Flynn, his blue eyes flashing with zeal at the enemy's retreat. He knew all too well what it was like to be in the muddy wastes of France facing a foe that had seemed impregnable and could have taken his life.

'The victory at Mons means a lot. It's starting to look like it's the beginning of the end,' said Tom, his fervour matching that of Flynn's.

'Do you really think so?' Lissie's voice was high with hope. 'Will it be over by this Christmas – four Christmases since it all started – and they promised it would be over by the first one?'

'We can only pray that it will,' Amelia said, and they all nodded agreement as they exchanged sad smiles and reflected on the British men who had given their lives for the cause, eighty thousand in August alone, most of them eighteen and nineteen-year-old untested recruits sent into battle by Lloyd George to defend the nation. Would they ever forget the last four awful years of conflict even if the war was to end at that minute? How many years would it take before they could put such horrors behind them? In those early days of November, it seemed to Lissie as though time was hanging by a thread.

On the evening of the tenth day, Flynn was on his way back to the house in North Marine Road from the workshop where his fairground rides were stored. He had been supervising the lads who were repairing and painting the rides ready for the next season, hopeful that despite the country being at war the resort would still attract the holidaymakers. He had missed running the rides and attending to his ice cream stalls and as he walked along under a purple sky studded with stars, he recalled a time not that long ago, when he had thought he might never see them or anything or anyone ever again. He gave a huge contented sigh. When he heard a newsboy on the corner of Hoxton Road yelling out the headlines his heart lurched with hopeful anticipation of even better things yet to come, and he stopped to buy the latest edition of the *Scarborough Mercury*. Then, quickening his pace, he ran the rest of the way to Lissie's house. She was in the kitchen.

'Kaiser Wilhelm's abdicated,' he announced excitedly, slapping the newspaper onto the table where she had set two places ready for their evening meal of shepherd's pie. Lissie looked up from the pan of potatoes she was mashing ready to put over the cooked mince.

'And so he should. He's to blame for this awful war,' she replied tartly, reaching for the cheese grater before turning to Flynn. 'Do you really think it will make a difference, or will the Germans find somebody just as wicked to take his place?' she asked, her abhorrence of the Kaiser as sharp as the teeth on the grater but her longing for the war to end jaded. Sprinkling cheese on top of the potato, she then put the dish into the oven and said, 'It'll be browned in a minute or two.'

'His abdication could make a great deal of difference, Lissie,' said Flynn as he pushed past her to wash his hands in the sink. 'He knows his army is defeated.'

'Aye, well let's hope it is. Now sit down and eat, and stop talking about war,' she said vehemently as she lifted the pie from the oven and slammed it onto the table with a determined thud.

On the 11th of November, Flynn arrived early at Lissie's door to put up some shelves in the shop. She had decided to rearrange the interior in readiness for her Christmas display, and now that his sight was fully restored, he wanted to make himself useful.

'Will we set a date for the wedding?' Lissie asked as she shifted boxes of shirts to make space for the new shelves. 'We could go and see the vicar to get the banns read, if you like. A Christmas wedding would be nice.'

Flynn was measuring a length of wood. 'I'd like that,' he said, his eyes lighting with enthusiasm and his words warm and eager. Then putting down his tape and picking up his saw, he frowned and wistfully added, 'But I had hoped to have Jimmy as my best man and there's no word of him coming home yet.'

'Then we'll wait,' said Lissie with a slight hint of disappointment. 'It wouldn't be the same without him, and seeing as Meggie's
going to be my matron of honour it only seems right.'

'It's not that I don't want to marry you,' Flynn hastened to say on
hearing her dismay, and his cheeks reddening as he recalled the
cruel words he had said to her when he had thought that he would
be blind for the rest of his life. 'I'd marry you this minute, right now
if the vicar was handy, but I'd—'

Lissie prevented him from saying more. She didn't doubt him
for a second.

'I know you would,' she chortled. 'I just wasn't thinking clearly
but I want to be your wife more than anything in the world.' She
proved it by throwing her arms round him and planting a smacking
kiss on his open mouth. 'We'll wait just as long as we have to,' she
said.

At the same time as Flynn fixed the shelves and Lissie served
her customers, the wires in the newspaper offices of the *Scarborough
Mercury* and the *Gazette* hummed, bringing the news that the
country had been waiting for. Then the wireless operators, eyes
wide and faces creased in smiles, shouted out what they were hearing. Editors, typesetters and clerks scurried into action whilst
others rushed to the doors out into the street to spread the news by
word of mouth. Peace had finally been declared.

* * *

In the drapery shop, Lissie and Flynn were unaware of the joy
flooding the town until the shop door was suddenly flung open and
an excited voice yelled, 'The war's over!'

The bearer of the unexpected news disappeared just as
suddenly as he had arrived and Flynn dropped his screwdriver and
leapt to his feet.

Lissie clapped her hands to her cheeks, then they both dashed to the door. Up and down the street windows and doors were being opened, curious faces looking from one to the other as they digested the cries of those bringing the wonderful news.

'Is it really over?' Lissie caught hold of the sleeve of a young man she recognised as one of the *Mercury*'s reporters.

'Aye, they're calling it an Armistice,' the man said, airing his knowledge rather pompously. 'They met in a railway carriage in Compiègne where Marshal Foch for the French and Admiral Wemyss for the British demanded the fighting be stopped and—'

'If that's all it took, why didn't they do that four years ago?' Lissie interrupted, her cheeks blazing with rage.

The reporter shrugged. He didn't have an answer to that and hurried on his way. Lissie turned to Flynn, confusion and anger masking her features. He put his arms round her. 'No matter, Lissie. If what he says is true then let's accept it for the marvellous news that it is,' he said, his eyes ablaze and his smile wide.

'Everyone else seems to think it's true, but I find it hard to believe,' she said doubtfully. 'He told us they just sat down and decided to stop fighting,' she cried, her voice bitter. 'It's a bit late for that, isn't it?'

Her tears spilled over and Flynn pulled her into his arms. 'You want to believe it, don't you?' he said, feeling her pain and his own at their forced time apart and the terrible loss of the lives of good men. They stood lost in their own thoughts as the people in the street shouted and cheered, and as midday approached, even Lissie was daring to believe that the war was over.

She closed the drapery and as she walked through the streets with Flynn, church bells were pealing triumphantly and the town blossomed with flags flying from windows and roof tops. Lorries and carts trundled by with cheering people on board, and the older generation of men who had kept the town's band alive marched up and down outside the town hall playing regimental tunes and popular songs. As they made their way into the centre of the town, Lissie and Flynn celebrated with passers-by, hugging and singing and dancing for joy. Then they dashed to the butcher's shop to share the good news with Meggie. She met them at the door with Eddie in her arms, laughing and crying at the same time.

'Aah still haven't got my Jimmy back,' Meggie said with tears in her eyes as she and Lissie held one another close.

'He'll be home soon enough,' Lissie comforted then took Eddie in her arms and whirled him round. 'Your daddy's coming home, Eddie, the war's over, my love,' she cried, hopeful that it wouldn't be long before Jimmy was back in the bosom of his little family. They stayed with Meggie and Eddie for the rest of the day, Lissie coaxing an envious but somewhat appeased Meggie to go out into the streets to join in the celebrations that were increasing in momentum, the noise rising and the townsfolk's long pent-up nerves bursting forth in high spirits.

'It's all right for you to be glad, Lissie, you've got your man back,' Meggie said as they stood listening to the band blaring out 'Pack Up Your Troubles in Your Old Kit-Bag' and watching people of all ages jigging along to the melody.

'I have and I'm grateful for that, but it took him to be nearly blinded for life to bring him home early,' Lissie said with feeling, 'and while my Flynn can see again there's hundreds of women at this very minute sitting behind closed doors crying their hearts out because they know their husbands and sons will never come home again. This rotten war has a lot to answer for, Meggie.' This sad reminder took some of the pleasure out of the day. Lissie wondered if there were wives and mothers and girlfriends in Germany too rejoicing now that the fighting was over. Were they waiting for their men to come home to pick up the pieces of the lives they had left behind and live in a country at peace with the rest of the world?

Such a terrible waste, and one that she hoped would never happen again.

Bonfires lit up the overcast sky as Lissie and Flynn made their way back to North Marine Road and as she watched the flickering beacons, she felt a renewed hope tingling in her veins. 'We've a lot to be thankful for and more to look forward to,' she said, thinking of Flynn's recovered sight and the wedding that she wanted to take place as soon as Jimmy returned home.

Flynn stopped walking and pulled her into his arms. 'We have, Lissie,' he said, his voice eager with conviction as they resumed walking. 'Now we're no longer at war people will be looking to make the most of their freedom. You just watch. Come Easter, Scarborough will be packed with holidaymakers and that will be good for business. I'm getting the rides and stalls painted and your dad has a few ideas for two new kiddy rides. He's working on them now.'

At the mention of her dad, Lissie smiled, glad that her father and Flynn were such good friends. 'He's full of grand ideas,' she said, her face alight with pride.

'He is, and with his help I want to expand my business and turn the fairground into the best in England.' Flynn's enthusiasm was contagious and Lissie let her imagination fly.

'And I'm going to revamp Foyer's Drapery. I'll sell off the out-of-date stock we've had for years at cheap prices, and cut down on the amount of fabrics and sewing requisites we keep. Then with the money, I'll buy the latest fashions in ladies' wear to attract a whole new clientele, young women with an eye for style.'

'That's the spirit, Lissie. Between us we'll build an empire.'

33

The first weeks of 1919 were disappointing and frustrating, Meggie waiting for Jimmy to return from duty, and Lissie itching to set a date for her wedding. Christmas had come and gone, and whilst they had done their utmost to make it a merry occasion, food was still scarce and the queues for meat, bread and other staples just as long as they had been during the war. In fact, nothing much seemed to have changed other than the influx of young men in the streets, so long absent that it took Lissie a moment to think where they had all suddenly appeared from whenever she walked into town. It was Sunday and the drapery closed so she was going to call on Meggie and ask for her help in sorting through the stock she intended to sell off cheaply so that she could bring Foyer's into the new year with a bang.

Meggie was more than eager to do something that would take her mind off waiting for Jimmy to come home, and leaving Eddie with his grandparents, she readily accompanied Lissie back to the shop.

'Aah thought he'd be home for this Christmas, an' now here we are in February an' they still haven't given his unit their marching orders,' Meggie moaned as they walked along the esplanade.

'It does seem a terrible shame, especially when you see all these other fellows home already,' Lissie commiserated as a gang of young men, some still wearing their army greatcoats, came towards them.

'Afternoon ladies, are you looking for company?' one of the lads asked cheekily when they came abreast.

'Not yours,' Meggie snapped, 'so gan on your way.'

The lad raised his eyebrows then grimaced at his mates who were laughing at his failed attempt. 'Ungrateful buggers. They mustn't know we fought a bloody war for 'em,' another of the lads sneered.

'Aye, you did, an' my man's still fighting it,' Meggie shouted as Lissie hooked her arm and hurried her away.

'Don't get upset. They don't mean any harm,' she said.

However, once they were in the shop and started sorting through the things for the sale, Meggie soon forgot her misery. 'What about these?' she asked, dangling a voluminous pair of pink cotton bloomers from her waist and kicking up her legs like a chorus girl.

'Sale,' said Lissie, laughing and indicating to one of the piles of garments on the floor in front of the counter, 'we've dozens of 'em. Patience, bless her, was always inclined to order the same things every time the traveller called, and she never sold anything off cheap. Some of this stuff dates back to before the turn of the century.' She opened a drawer under the counter. 'And whilst you're at it, missis, you can try these on for size.' She tossed a pair of heavy-duty corsets at Meggie. 'They'll keep you in check.'

Giggling, Meggie wrapped herself in the stiff pink fabric criss-crossed with laces and studded with hooks and eyes. 'It's like armour plating. They should have given our lads these to ward off the bullets,' she crowed, her smile slipping as she remembered the men who hadn't dodged the German bullets. Tearing off the corset, she chucked it onto a pile. Lissie knew what she was thinking.

'I've ordered lots of newer shorter knickers in white cotton in all sizes and a whole new range of brassieres, but I'll keep a few of everything that the older customers like,' she said in a businesslike attempt to divert Meggie's sudden despondence, 'so if you fill this drawer with two dozen of those bloomers and the one next to it with a dozen pairs of corsets the rest can go in the sale.'

By the end of the afternoon, they had filled boxes with the over-stocked unwanted items and now Lissie was neatly writing the reduced prices on stiff white card for Meggie to attach to each box. Later Lissie would dress the window with the things in the sale, hopeful of attracting bargain hunters and getting rid of the surplus stock.

'What next?' Meggie asked as she tidied the shelves and rails.

'Put the sewing stuff on that table by the door,' Lissie told her, breaking off from crayoning in the huge letters that formed the words GRAND SALE on a large piece of card.

'Will that do?' Meggie asked as she finished setting out spools of thread, ribbons and lace and other sewing requisites. She stepped back to admire her handiwork.

'That's grand,' Lissie praised, going to the shop door to attach the large sale sign to the glass. 'Let's hope when I open up tomorrow that the customers flock in and that by the end of the week most of this stuff is gone to make room for my new lines.'

Meggie nodded enthusiastically. 'How's your wedding dress coming along? You haven't shown me lately. Is it nearly finished?'

Lissie surveyed the shop thoughtfully at the same time wondering how long it would be before she would get to wear her wedding dress. 'It's almost finished, just the pearl buttons to sew down the back,' she replied, and not wanting to dwell on the subject, she said, 'Come on, leave that for now, we've earned a cup of tea. Thanks, Meggie. You've been a great help.'

'That's what friends are for,' Meggie chirped as she followed Lissie into the kitchen. Over a welcome cuppa she said, 'Aah know you're disappointed 'cos Flynn wants to wait till Jimmy comes home but mebbe it's not so bad him being late. A spring wedding's much nicer than one in the depths of winter.'

'It is,' Lissie agreed, although secretly she thought it didn't matter what the season was. She burned to be Flynn's wife.

On the dock at Cherbourg on the first day of March, Jimmy Stockdale breathed in the salt-laden air and felt the sea spray moistening his cheeks. It was just like being on the esplanade in Scarborough, he thought, the longing to see his wife and son making him dizzy with excitement. He was on the last leg home, the clearing up he and his unit had been doing in France, finished. It had been his job to feed the troops and these last few weeks had been extremely trying, supplies irregular and his days spent struggling to acquire tins of corned beef and Maconochie stew, tea and biscuits. But not any more. He'd done his duty and soon he would be back with his lovely Meggie and little Eddie – although Eddie wouldn't be that small now, he thought sadly. He was, according to Meggie's letters, a walking talking lively boy and Jimmy hadn't been there to see him grow. Blast the bloody war.

All around him war-weary men were on the move, shuffling into orderly lines to board the ship that would take them back to Blighty, and Jimmy picked up his kitbag, buttoned his greatcoat then squared his cap on his head. He wasn't particularly looking forward to the crossing, the grey waters of the English Channel heaving in the brisk March wind but damn it! He'd put up with a few painful hours of sea sickness as long as he had to because when the journey was over, he'd feel the soil of England and not the mud of France under his feet.

'We're the lucky ones,' the chap walking beside him soberly muttered.

'We bloody are,' Jimmy replied, thinking of the men in his regiment that he'd seen blown to bits by a German shell or lying in mud dying slowly from a Hun's bullet. 'And by God, when I get home, I'm going make the most of being alive.'

Two days later, after a nightmare sea journey and a tedious trek by train, he planted his feet on the platform at Scarborough station then marched out into Londesborough Road. It was the middle of the afternoon, the sun shining and the smell of the sea wafting inland driven by a stiff breeze. Jimmy stopped and let his gaze roam over the familiar buildings. My, but they looked grand. Everywhere he looked was just as he remembered it. It felt bloody marvellous.

Out of the blue, he thought of Flynn and felt sorry for him. When he'd been brought back to Scarborough he hadn't had this pleasure. Thanking God that his friend's sight had been restored, Jimmy set off at a run down the street, eager to reach the butcher's shop and home. He hadn't notified anyone of his arrival. He wanted to surprise them.

Meggie was in the little garden at the rear of the butcher's shop playing ball with Eddie. He was a sturdy little chap, and his moon face and reddish-brown hair were so like his father's that whenever Meggie looked at him her heart ached for her husband. Now, as she watched Eddie chase the ball to the bottom of the garden then stand tall ready to throw it back to her, she was filled with pride. She'd done a grand job rearing him on her own – his dad would be proud of him – but how long would it be before he was here to play ball with him?

'Come on, Eddie. Throw it back,' she urged, confused as to why her son was standing stock still, the ball clutched against his chest and his eyes as big as saucers as he fixed them on the door behind her.

She turned round, the ground shifting under her and legs feeling like jelly when she saw Jimmy leaning in the doorway, his cap pushed to the back of his head and his smiling face at odds with the tears that were wetting his cheeks.

'Aw, Jimmy man,' she cried, tottering towards him, then flinging herself into his open arms and smothering his face with kisses. Jimmy found her lips and covered them hungrily but his eyes were looking beyond her to where Eddie was still standing, transfixed.

Meggie, sensing her husband's distraction, pulled away from him crying, 'Aah canna believe it. You're back.' She let out a whoop and turning to Eddie, she shouted, 'Your daddy's here, Eddie. This is your daddy.' Eddie dropped the ball.

Blinded by tears, Jimmy ran and scooped Eddie up in his arms, holding him so tight that it knocked the breath out of the boy.

'Gerroff! Put me down,' Eddie protested as the stranger attempted to kiss his cheek.

Jimmy burst out laughing. 'He's mine all right,' he said, but inside he felt hurt that his son didn't know who he was. But then why would he?

'It's your daddy, the man in the picture on the sideboard,' Meggie explained as she wrapped her arms round them both. 'He's the man I tell you about every night before you go to sleep.'

Eddie's forehead wrinkled as he looked solemnly at Jimmy then to Meggie and back again. 'Why is he crying?' he asked.

'Oh, son. I'm crying 'cos I'm so happy to see you,' Jimmy blubbered. 'You're so big and strong and beautiful and...'

'I *am* strong,' said Eddie, struggling to be put down but pleased by the compliments. Jimmy set him on his feet and Eddie looked up at him thoughtfully. 'I like you,' he said, 'an' if you want to be my daddy then it's okay by me.' He looked to Meggie for approval.

His parents were clinging to each other laughing and crying at the same time. Thinking that grown-ups acted very strangely at times, Eddie asked, 'Can we play ball now?'

'We can. We can play whatever you want whenever you want,' Jimmy whooped, tossing his greatcoat on the grass and lunging for the ball. Eddie chased after him, and Meggie watched her husband and son tussling for the ball. It was the most beautiful thing she'd ever seen. Her man was home safe and sound and she wanted for nothing more.

* * *

Lissie's delight equalled that of Meggie's and Flynn's when the Stockdales arrived at the drapery that evening. After much hugging and catching up, Lissie and Meggie left Jimmy and Flynn in the kitchen with a bottle of rum and taking Eddie with them, they went through into the shop. Lissie switched on the new lights that had been installed earlier in the week.

'Ta-da!' she announced, spreading her arms wide under the blaze of lights from three elegant chandeliers that had replaced five gas brackets on the walls.

Meggie gasped. 'Aw, Lissie, it's like a palace,' she squealed, lifting Eddie up to take a closer look. 'See, Eddie. Auntie Lissie's fancy new lights.' Eddie stretched his arms, reaching for the sparkling pendants. 'Oh, no you don't, me laddo,' Meggie reprimanded, hastily lowering him back to the floor then turning to her friend.

'They're fantastic,' she crowed, her cheeks pink with pleasure.

'Aren't they just? I hated the gas mantles. I was always afraid of them setting fire to the stock but now with a flick of a switch we have light.' Lissie threw her hands in the air and did a little twirl.

'What do you think Patience 'ud say?' she asked, her eyes glinting mischievously.

'Aah think she'd screw up her face an' pull on her chin then tek it on board just like she did with all your other good ideas to make Foyer's the best drapery in Scarborough,' Meggie said sagely. 'You'll give Marshall & Snelgrove a run for their money afore you're done.'

Lissie laughed then said, 'I think that's going a bit far but what with the sale being a great success and my new lines bringing in younger customers I'm getting there, Meggie.'

Just then, a rather tipsy Jimmy and Flynn blundered into the shop. 'What's wi' all the squealing?' Jimmy slurred before staring up in amazement at the twinkling chandeliers. 'By bloody hell, Lissie. It's like a fairground.'

'Aye, there's no stopping her these days. She's a right Bobby Dazzler is my Lissie.' Flynn trotted somewhat unsteadily to her side and threw his arm across her shoulders. 'And now you're back at last to be my best man, Jimmy, I can make her my wife.' Lissie turned in his arms and gave him a smacking kiss. Meggie and Jimmy cheered, and little Eddie, not to be out done, shouted, 'Love you, Auntie Lissie an' I like your pretty lights.'

Later that night, after the Stockdales had left, and Flynn was getting ready to go back to St Mary's Walk Lissie stood in the hallway kissing him goodnight.

'Not long now before I don't have to do this,' he said against her hair. 'Tomorrow we'll go and see the vicar and get the banns called.'

Lissie felt as though her heart would overflow with love for him and for her friends. She lingered on the doorstep watching him walk away until he disappeared from view then she raised her eyes to the starlit sky. Brittle stars winked back at her and she thought of the many times she had wished on them.

* * *

Tom stood in the hallway of the house in North Marine Road nervously twitching the cuffs of his smart grey jacket and his eyes fixed on the stairs down which his daughter would come at any moment.

When Lissie appeared he drew a deep breath of admiration and wonder.

'Oh, Lissie, my darling girl, you look beautiful,' he said, drinking in the vision of loveliness before him. Her slender figure was sheathed in a dress of the softest white silk and the fine lace veil covering her lustrous black hair fell round about her shoulders into a flowing train.

Slowly, she descended the stairs, smiling into her father's eyes. When she was by his side she slipped her hand into the crook of his arm. 'Well, are you ready to give me away?' she asked, her blue eyes sparkling.

'Only because I'm giving you to one of the finest men I've ever known,' Tom said. His gentle grey eyes moistened. 'It seems like only yesterday that you were my little girl, and now here you are on your wedding day, and I thank God that we found each other in time for me to have this honour. Shall we go?'

The sun was high in the sky, and the pealing of the church bells competed with the mewing of the seagulls as Tom and Lissie stood in the doorway of St Mary's Church. The bells fell silent and when the organ rang out the time-honoured march, Lissie and Tom approached the altar.

'Who gives this woman to this man today?' the vicar intoned.

'I do,' Tom said solemnly then smiled warmly as he placed Lissie's hand in Flynn's. Flynn returned the smile.

And as Lissie stood between the two men whom she loved with all her heart, she knew that all her wishes and dreams had come true.

ABOUT THE AUTHOR

Chrissie Walsh was born and raised in West Yorkshire and is a retired schoolteacher with a passion for history. She has written several successful sagas documenting feisty women in challenging times.

Sign up to Chrissie Walsh's mailing list here for news, competitions and updates on future books.

Follow Chrissie on social media:

x.com/walshchrissie

facebook.com/100063501278251

ALSO BY CHRISSIE WALSH

Sixpence Stories

Introducing Sixpence Stories!

Discover page-turning
historical novels from your
favourite authors, meet new
friends and be transported
back in time.

Join our book club
Facebook group

https://bit.ly/SixpenceGroup

Sign up to our
newsletter

https://bit.ly/SixpenceNews

Boldwod

Boldwood Books is an award-winning fiction publishing company seeking out the best stories from around the world.

Find out more at www.boldwoodbooks.com

Join our reader community for brilliant books, competitions and offers!

Follow us
@BoldwoodBooks
@TheBoldBookClub

Sign up to our weekly deals newsletter

https://bit.ly/BoldwoodBNewsletter

Printed in Great Britain
by Amazon